PRAISE FOR *ANDRONE*

"Taut intrigue reels readers into a thrilling yet thoughtful narrative about the futility of war and the cost of doing the right thing, and a clever, quantum twist will please sci-fi fans. Worrell should make a splash with this."

—*Publishers Weekly*

"Dwain Worrell's *Androne* straps you into the cockpit at page one and doesn't let go; it's a truly cinematic, character-centered Möbius strip of war, loyalty, and love, with action so good you might forget how to breathe."

—Karen Osborne, author of *Architects of Memory*

"A crazy-cool ride into the unknown. Paxton is a multilayered, futuristic hero, and [*Androne*] reads like a high-end video game on steroids with a destiny of Shakespearean magnitude."

—Niels Arden Oplev, director of *The Girl with the Dragon Tattoo*

ALLIANCE

ALSO BY DWAIN WORRELL

Androne

ALLIANCE

DWAIN WORRELL

Published by 47North, Seattle

www.apub.com

Amazon, the Amazon logo, and 47North are trademarks of Amazon.com, Inc., or its affiliates.

ISBN-13: 9781662511981 (paperback)
ISBN-13: 9781662511998 (digital)

Cover illustration by Danny Schlitz

Printed in the United States of America

To Mier

PROLOGUE

I watch her then, as she twists her own hair into braids, as her smile lights up like twelve little white bulbs shining out from her dry lips. I watch as she turns her head to graying mountaintops, pointing, her smile louder—laughter. I watch, maybe too long, maybe too hard through the strain of my myopic eyes, because now she returns the gaze, appearing to investigate my look. And my look, in that moment, is a capsized expression, eyes and lips all twisted up into the other. I must be impossible to read, leering at the girl, puzzling over her. Regret and rage and so much sympathy in one look, as I struggle to think up the kindest possible way for her to die.

Harmony kept spinning her hair down into wiry, black plaits, but roughly designed, thorny, and uneven, and that was wind, flitting her hair flirtatiously and spinning her braids and fingers out of sync.

She'll bite her fingernails before long. It's her frustration. It builds like that. And I know. I know her. She'll huff next, not sigh, *no*, she huffs. She will dig into the pockets of her eyes to hide her face; these are her quiet insecurities. I know this because I've studied Harmony. I've studied her like a book, like a science, like she's my fucking religion—and she is, literally, factually. Harmony is an integral part of the Chronic religion. And I know every equation of her, every algorithm and chemical bond to who she is.

The wind leans into us now. It peels back the hood from over Harmony's braids, spitting the earth up in brown particles, and the ground overflows her. I call for Harmony. We all call, the others too overprotective. They outshout me, and she scurries into the shelter—*shelter*, metal poles and animal skin, framed into a triangular tent. Our little sheepskin pyramid is already too small for the six of us, but Harmony balls in on herself, knees to chest in the smallest corner of the space.

The sun sets sideways, and the light leans and the hills roll blankets of shadow, and then the sandstorm does the rest. Light caves in. The night collapses in on us. The gale stirs the sand in circles, even inside the tent. We cover our mouths and squint our eyes shut. The conversation goes cold, not that it was feverish before, but now we go hours without a word, and that gives me the space to think. I think about drugs, killing her in an overdose, and maybe the beautiful child—so kind and so clever—will float off peacefully to some other heaven, and none of the prophecies of the girl deity will come to pass. She will fade gently, peacefully, like some stillborn demigod.

I think too much. I think until my eyes close in around my subconscious, and I nearly drift off—*nearly* fall asleep. But then I feel this weight on top of me, this bubbling heaviness pressing against my back. That, I think, is the weight of eyesight. Her eyes and her sight, pressing down on top of me.

Harmony sits on the edge of my peripherals, her head aimed in my direction, and now she observes me, thinking some thought in her little head.

I don't think she knows what I plan to do—*no*, but she knows something. It's there in her look. It's been there for weeks now, months maybe, this question marooned on the island of her eyes. And what she knew she wouldn't tell me. *I know her.* Her emotions implode in on her, every sadness or rage shrinking violently inward. She covers her feelings with sarcasm. I couldn't cut the words out of her with my knife. But wait, *no*, now she is sliding toward me. And that is unlike her. It is alien to Harmony. Her arms climb across the stubborn dirt. Moving to my left, *no*, my right? Strange. She's different somehow. I haven't seen this before. She leans into me, nestling her lips near my ear.

"I know," Harmony whispers. "I know what's happening to you. I know you're sick."

That's what she knows, this ailment that strikes from my insides out. This sickness that corsets itself around my guts until I vomit the morning's rations. The spots on my skin I hide under long sleeves. The hairline receding away under this headscarf. She has seen all my hidden parts.

"I know a healer at Port Pepsi who manages these ailments," she says, nodding, as if to sway me into subliminal agreement. "It's on our path, or at least partway there."

"I do not need your healer," I say, and that's true. If I overcame the Nikon virus, then I'll recover from this in a week's time. "I am not sick," I tell her. "You know little of nothing."

"I know you went on the pilgrimage," she says, her features hard now. "I know you were gone for a long time. And you saw something, right? You saw something that changed you, because you came back different. Not just sick. You came back . . . unlike yourself. Like you are not you."

Oh. She knows a lot. She knows me. And maybe she knows me better than I know her. It won't be long until she puts it all together. Harmony is a smart woman, and I have been putting it off for far too long. Putting it off because I love her. And that's why I push her away, that's why I keep my distance. Even now, as she sits lonely in this crowded tent, all I feel is my affection. But my will cannot bend for love. I have to do it now. I need to find a necromancer, one who lives in September or August near the Day of Descent. My love for you, beautiful, *beautiful* you, will not influence my resolve. You have to die, Harmony, my love, my Peacemaker, my destroyer of worlds.

3

the final weapon
is a mind
—John Steinbeck

PART I

Peacemaker

1

The church's suite was immense, a room with many doors leading to many corridors. It was furnished with two beds, Knole sofas, desks and cabinets, and even a bath, the water still dripping from its spigot. Floor-to-ceiling windows opened the space to the outside without the filter of glass, and the room breathed the evening sunlight, and it never exhaled. Outside, the ancient skyscrapers stood with their ancient propaganda: the holy Golden Arches, the bitten Apple of divinity, and the grand Red Bull of the warrior nations. The tribes of her time revered one insignia or the other, and they fought under these banners. Worshipping, tattooing, and waving war flags of these ancient logos. *Half-wits.* But with the church's insignia carved into the walls and ceiling, wasn't she guilty too? Everything that her eyes could see belonged to the church, including Harmony herself.

She stood beside the bathtub naked, a puddle underneath her, her arms hugging her chest, one leg wrapped around the other, because she felt like the church was watching. Their techno-witches with their binocular eyes, they saw everything. All that light stretched the puddles into a mirror. Harmony hated being naked, all her little scars adding up to a gash so wide that she could fit ten knives inside. And still she stood there, staring at the clothes they had prepared for her. The symbol for the church was stitched into them. If she wore them, then it meant that Harmony, the great rebel, was now a part of the fucking Church of Time.

How? How did she get here? Was it that day thirty years ago? That day the Androne protected her. That day she lost someone that she couldn't remember. On that day, thirty years past, Harmony was orphaned and Aurora became her caretaker; her mother or something like it? But Harmony tried not to think about that part. Aurora, her mother, was long dead now, and somehow thoughts of her felt prickly in Harmony's head, the good and bad so sharply contrasting that it was . . . *yes*, it was a prickly thing for her.

Harmony had rebuilt broken machines in her childhood, a little girl with hands barely big enough to hold their parts, but she remade them, aerial drones or quadrupedals, and soon that became too easy. Soon she learned to hack satellites from necromancers, and within a year she was teaching those same necromancers new tricks. People traveled from miles away to learn from her, and many stayed, and many more followed her, and all of this by the age of twelve. Barely two years after, young Harmony performed a miracle. She found a way not only to hack into ancient satellites but to send signals backward in time. She could hack into the machines from the past, drones from hundreds of years ago that she could control. She could fight back.

Maiden Messiah, some would say, but even as an immature sixteen-year-old, Harmony had dispelled any notions of prophethood. She hated the church, a church that collaborated with the invaders from the past, the occupiers of her time. The past controlled the present with their machines, and the church conspired with those men from history for so long. So why now? Why so suddenly did they want to conspire with her? The church wanted to work with Harmony and her followers now. The church wanted a coup against the past. And Harmony had painfully, reluctantly agreed. These were the compromises of progress, she hoped. This was the path that she had chosen, the winding road that had brought her into the Church of Time's bathroom suite.

"Harmony?" a voice called from the other end of the room.

Fuck.

Harmony spun, twisting her back quickly toward the voice. She snatched up the church's clothes off the bed and started to climb into the synthetic rubber two-piece. She glanced back, scowling, and recognized the face behind her.

"Gemini!" Harmony snapped, wrestling her arms into sleeves and her neck into the tight, rubbery top.

"I'm sorry," Gemini said. "The choir is—"

"How long were you standing there?" Harmony interrupted.

"Not long," she said, calmly, in her nonchalant Gemini way. "The choir is at readiness. They are requesting you to input your code."

Gemini was Harmony's most trusted ally. Maybe not the most trusted; no, Harmony probably trusted Emit more. But Gemini had something that Emit didn't. She was the only person Harmony knew who hated the church more than her, and she trusted that. Gemini was reliably cold and calculated, not under the influence of torrid emotions—Gemini rarely showed any of that. She was a creature of pure logic, and Harmony trusted these traits. But even Gemini, trust or not, shouldn't have been staring at Harmony completely naked.

Harmony pulled the skintight suit up her legs. She pedaled her feet into the pants, hopping from left to right, kicking desperately to get into her clothes—the church's clothes. And all the while Gemini approached.

"Can you . . ." Harmony held her hand out, gesturing for Gemini to stop where she was. And Harmony wobbled, off balance by the extended limb. "Shit. Just wait there, Gemini."

Gemini stopped and turned to her side, offering Harmony faux privacy and at the same time revealing something in her hand. A small silver suitcase. Light shattered against the metal. Shards of brightness cut at Harmony's eyes.

"What's in the case?" Harmony asked, finally climbing into her pants. Both the top and bottom fit her perfectly, like a second skin. "Whoa," she said then, interrupting herself. "The fit is . . . it's like they had measurements."

"Are you speaking to me?" Gemini asked.

"No, I was saying, *uh . . .*"

What was she saying? *Shit.* Her thoughts jumbled in her head now, like she was juggling everything. Her mother. The satellite. Then church and their clothes. That suitcase. "That case." She remembered, pointing at it now. "From the church?"

"From your mother," Gemini said, stepping closer. "A postmortem."

Harmony would rather it be from the church. On a day as important as today, with all the hacking and coding she would have to do, she couldn't afford to be distracted in memory. *Fuck that.* Whatever gift or inheritance her mother wanted her to have today, she wasn't taking it.

"No." Harmony shook her head, retreating from the bathtub and falling onto the Knole sofa. The seat creaked as she landed on it, like it was a thousand years old. *It probably was.* "You can give it to me after."

"There won't be time after," Gemini said, following her to the sofa, like a persistent little sister.

Gemini had been her mother's apprentice years after Harmony left home. And while Harmony was raised by Aurora as a child, Gemini was raised by her as a young adult. Her apprenticeship included translation, sign language, and the study of religious presaging. All the shit Harmony didn't want to learn. They were raised separately, but by the same woman, and there was a sisterhood of sorts between them. They resembled each other, but not at all in the physical architecture, their features and skin tones polar opposites, day to night. The resemblance was in their habits. Strangers up until a few years ago, the two women, at times, related as if they had known each other for a lifetime.

"They're calling for me, right?" Harmony asked, pointing in the direction Gemini came from. "The impatient little techno-witches?"

"Yes. The choir is set. The drone pilots are stationed at their cockpits. They're all ready to begin."

Gemini's hand recoiled from the locks to the case. But all wasn't well with Gemini. Her head rested unstably on her shoulders like it might fall off. Something else was rattling around her brain.

"Let's just get it over with," Harmony said. "Try this collaboration thing." She shrugged then, because she still worried about allying with the church, but it was too late to turn back now. "I know you don't want to do it, but let's just—"

"Get it over with," Gemini agreed.

Harmony moved toward the largest of the many exits leading into the hall. Gemini followed slowly, dragging her feet and nearly dragging the suitcase, which appeared to weigh her arm down. She even started to open the case again, insistent as she was, as insistent as their mother. But Gemini paused, and Harmony turned back to her.

"You knew my mother," Harmony said. "In the end, I mean."

"I studied under her."

"Apprenticeship. Yes." Harmony picked at a knot of hair slung over her brow, a bid to buy herself more time. She didn't quite know the right question to ask.

"Harmony—"

"Did she talk about me?" Harmony interrupted. "She wasn't much of a talker I know but . . ." She chuckled awkwardly and should have stopped there, but she bumbled onward. "I left Port Siren, and I started coding and hacking, and then Aurora took you on and taught you things she never taught me. I mean, I'm not jealous. That's not what I'm saying. What I'm saying is that I'm glad she had somebody, you know. You were there. Am I making sense?"

The conversation stumbled into an ugly pause. Gemini stared at Harmony like she saw something for the first time—like she saw everything. Harmony had tried covering up the meaning with all those wandering words, but it was see-through, and Gemini kept staring at all of that naked emotion.

"You're not," Gemini said, taking her fingers off the suitcase's locks. "I don't know what you're saying."

But she did, because Gemini peeled her fingers away from the locks, giving Harmony what she was asking for. Just a little time. *Just let me get through this day.* Gemini lowered the suitcase and would save that postmortem gift or inheritance or whatever it was until another time. *Thank you*, Harmony thought.

"We should go. I have a lot of hacking to do."

"Yes."

They stepped into the corridors together, as close to hand in hand as they could be. And Harmony needed her there as the church's floodgates opened. The saintly children greeted them in the hall, a hundred whistling preadolescent voices. Techno-witches guided them, square goggles over their eyes, little yellow dots at the center. They guided Harmony to the wires and cables, and a big, all-powerful church-funded computer. The children whispered as they ran alongside her. She couldn't hear it at first, over the witches' babble, but as they gathered, bottlenecked at the stairs, the louder they hissed that name, "Peacemaker." They said it giddy with reverence, bowing, hands clasped, tears dripping off their cheeks. They said it to her—to Harmony.

Harmony, the rebel of rebels, stood there in the shadow of the church's insignia. It was a massive thing, a hundred feet tall and surrounded by stained glass that bent the sunlight around it. The symbol was written in the bygone script: *T*. It too was once some ancient logo for an ancient organization. But this was how it had to be. She would use their resources, and they would use hers. Harmony would be an instrument of the church, in tune, in accord with their every command. *For now*, there would be an alliance.

2

Peacemaker. What a stupid fucking name, but it was hers—"Grand Peacemaker," they called as she entered the upper pews. The Quondam had christened her so many hundreds of years ago, and the name had stuck for that long—for that many centuries. *Fuck.* She preferred Harmony, of course, but they wouldn't call her that, not after everything she had done. Harmony was the little girl who played with Androne dolls. This sinewy thirty-five-year-old sitting on a throne of dismantled machine parts, *she* was the Peacemaker. Even now as she typed "sacred code" into powerful box-screen computers, hacking into an ancient satellite. Its geriatric orbit hobbled just low enough, down to the thermosphere. And that same satellite orbited the earth many hundreds of years ago, for that long—that many centuries. And she would send her message through that satellite, backward in time, a message of destruction, terror, obliteration, and with it her name—*Peacemaker.*

Though it wasn't *that* straightforward. This assault wasn't simply the eviscerating of cities to the ground. There was a goal for this recursion into the past. If they could destroy the Quondam's satellite technology facilities, and do it without them knowing, then the attack would be a success. Which meant destroying as many military bases as possible, attacking every nation-state and non-satellite facilities, and at the same time hitting the four most advanced sat-tech installations in the world. Make those installations appear like collateral damage amid all the other destruction. But there was more to the church's plans than they were letting on. There was something they weren't telling her.

Harmony sat alone in the upper pews of the cathedral, Gemini huddled below the drone pilots, and that offered her the quiet needed to type code, but it was the view that distracted her, visual noise from all the political pageantry below. The church's clerics greeted the visiting hierarchs, all of them competing in their garish fashions, robes in gold threads, capes that dragged like giraffe tails behind them, and makeup that ran from their forehead to fingernail.

Gifts were exchanged, marbles mostly, black glass with gold or silver cores, all in reverence to their gray god—the god of time. After initial greetings, these officials would congregate around the choir as they prepared ancient hymns or surveyed Harmony's Androne pilots, pointing and remarking as if her people were just museum pieces, decorative effigies there for them to critique. Chronics, that was what they called themselves. They were a hateful bunch, high-nose arrogance in every gesture and word, *just look at them*. She couldn't believe she was collaborating with them—the fucking Church of Time.

No, don't curse in the church, she thought, *especially here, on their holiest day*. But Harmony thought these things in a vernacular of sarcasm. Much like the computer languages she now used to hack the satellites, sarcasm was a language in reverse, undoing the meaning it implied. She typed for hours like this, typing backward, unfastening all the securities built into the satellite's code, so that she could send an entangled signal back to AndroMes in the past, and her army of pilots would do the rest.

A green dot blinked on her screen. That was it. That thousand-year-old satellite was still up there, still operating, her back door to the past. And that was how far her signal would return, a thousand years, more, less, *who fucking knew?* It would go all the way back to the years when human civilization had hit its technological peak—the Quondam Era. Bases on the moon. Architecture that rivaled mountain ranges. And an interconnected network of millions of servers. The Quondam—their very ancestors, accomplishing amazing feats of technology, all capped off by a war against their own future. A war without motive or purpose, a war for control.

Harmony typed the last lines into the command prompt, and *click*, it was done. She rolled up her cramped fingers into fists and leaned all the way back on her throne. She surveyed the arched dome ceiling overhead, holy wires and deity cables coiling down the cathedral's spire.

The church's insignia threw its massive T-shaped shadow over Gemini and Harmony's pilots, and over the church's pilots too, who gathered in quiet worship. The two teams of pilots didn't like each other, but these hundred men and women hated the Quondam more, those fossils from the past, making slaves of the future. So they readied themselves with ancient ballads and propaganda prayers, and in minutes they would launch the largest full-scale offensive against the Quondam Era in the history of humankind. And thanks to the church's infrastructure, they would launch further into the past than they ever had been, all the way back to the Ninety-Nine.

"The Ninety-Nine," Harmony whispered to herself, her gut rising with the words. That date was historic. Millions died because of what she would do today. "But they were already dead," she said to herself, and those doubts crawled up the hairs on her back. "This isn't your first damn assault." And it wasn't. Harmony had launched more than thirty assaults herself. And she had created the blueprint for recursions. Hundreds of other smaller-scale attacks that she wasn't involved in were fought in her name. "Come on, you're the fucking Peacemaker."

That should do it. That should get her head back in the game. Yet this offensive still felt different, *didn't it?* Her collaboration with the church was a first, and their plan to attack satellite facilities was a tactic she had never thought up. And the number of pilots, *God*, she had never hacked more than thirty at a time. Today there were well over a hundred cockpits down there, and liquid cockpits. The church-tech offered up superfluid cylinders as pilot seats; human fish tanks was more like it. And all this was falling on the eve of the church's biggest holiday, their

Day of Descent, full of the fireworks and boating games she remembered as a child.

"Breathe," she said, a fear crawling into her. "Just breathe."

"Grand Peacemaker." The voice shot up the stairway, and a rail-thin cleric followed behind his own words. He gripped his black robe in his fists and lifted it just enough for his feet to trample freely up the stairs. He tiptoed over Harmony's cobweb of cables and wires and peeked his bald head up from behind her big box computer.

"Perfect timing," she said, that sarcasm again.

"Peacemaker. Peacemaker." His panting made him echo his words. "We . . . we have received confirmation from our techno-voyeur that your installation bypass is prepared."

Techno-witches, they called the all-female voyeurs. Harmony twisted her eyes past the old man, around the loop of cockpits, toward the Reverend Mother herself and her cackle of techno-witches. They had plugs running from their goggle eyes into box computer screens much like her own. The assholes were monitoring her.

Harmony never cared much for the Church of Time, but that antagonism seethed even deeper now as she worked among them. But this was an alliance of necessity, *right?* Or was it convenience? She needed their resources, these liquid cockpits, their battery power—all of it was superior to anything she had ever worked with. But they needed her everything: Harmony's talent behind the keyboard, her hacking ability, her pilots, and most importantly—her name. Not Harmony, but the Peacemaker. The church was in crisis. The Church of Time had split into two factions: the Chronics—loyal to Chronos, the time god—while the other sect were the Quondam loyalists, still holding on to that connection to the past.

That was leverage for Harmony. She and her crew of pilots and ex-necromancers could take sides and play them against each other. The church had been the enemy for most of her life, and now, *today at least*, they were in accord.

"Peacemaker?" the cleric said impatiently, but trying not to show, trying not to offend the *Grand Peacemaker*. "Are you . . ."

"Ready?" she said, pulling herself up from her seat. "Yeah, I'm ready."

But Harmony wasn't ready. There was a fear inside her that stopped time, that made minutes into millennia. The worst thing about it was that Harmony didn't know what that fear was. The origin of the thing—the seed of it. She could see the fruits of its labor, a life without trust, fearful of betrayal or assassination, few friends, and never a lover, boy nor girl, she didn't even know. She could detach herself from those things as if her sexual parts were prosthetics. These were the fruits of her fear, and a fear that she didn't understand.

The cleric led Harmony to the church's cockpits. The "human fish tanks" were tall cylinders of glass filled with a liquid that wasn't water but a superfluid that burned the eyes. She and her pilots had gotten only a single day to train in these cockpits, but it was so intuitive that the one day was all they needed. She was used to piloting in rickety square boxes made up of recycled Androne parts. But these cockpits . . . they weren't just a step up; they were an elevation to techno-religious majesty. Where *the fuck* did the church get this level of technology?

Harmony pressed her palm against the glass and observed the cockpit. She checked the integrity of the tanks and the glass, and she scrutinized the superfluid inside. But this was all pretend observation, a procrastination tactic. Because deep down she didn't want to do this. She couldn't. And it wasn't even the collaboration with the church anymore—she had made some peace with that. It was all this death. The attack on the Ninety-Nine would kill millions, at her hands, in her name.

"The great Peacemaker. She's too good for us now," said Elijah, her star pilot and a cocky shit to boot.

"Of course, too good, and especially for you, Audist," Harmony shot back. "Or didn't you hear? I'm the *Grand* Peacemaker."

Elijah bowed and flapped his arms like a flamingo dipping its head to the water. Laughter followed, Harmony's entire crew chuckling, all except Gemini, who watched their performance with cold disinterest. Harmony rejoined her band of rebels and troublemakers, Elijah, Meta, and Nestle among them. She joked and jousted right back into the mix of her friends, but Harmony's smile was a mechanical thing, lips peeling back like foreskin to reveal teeth. Fear had taken her, beating at her chest, choking at her throat. Fear rose in her, but the truth was, Harmony was afraid every day, every hour; she was afraid all the fucking time.

Harmony smiled through the thorns, a steady dose of sarcasm in every comment keeping the smirk on her face shiny and new. Elijah was as quick-witted as any of them, and being her best pilot, she allowed him to get away with remarks most others wouldn't dare say. The son of a family of Audists, Elijah still wore the Audis' four rings around his wrist even though he had denounced its beliefs.

"Remember to get your old ass out of that cockpit when the timer hits," Elijah said. "The Quondam's Androns will find our rebound signal in ten minutes tops. Maybe faster. This place will be crawling with their Androns."

The *rebound*, or echo signal, was the signal from their cockpits, sent to the satellite and rebounded down to the Androns. That signal could be traced in the past, and the Quondam would then send their Androns in the present to tear this cathedral apart. So each recursion into the past had to be limited to around ten minutes. But Harmony might have found a work-around to that inevitability.

"I think I can buy you a lot more than ten minutes," Harmony said. "I think." But she wasn't sure, and it showed. And Elijah saw it.

"What do you mean?" he said. "Don't start this seat-of-your-pants planning again."

"I think I can attack the Quondam pilot facility," she said. "Hit them before they hit us in the present."

"I don't understand." Elijah leaned in. "You're not attacking the satellite facilities with us?"

"No. I found their cockpits in the past. The cockpits to the Andrones most likely to attack this cathedral."

His jaw dropped. "When they find our rebound . . . ," he said, and said it slow, putting it together in his head. "You're attacking their pilots in their cockpits while they're attacking ours."

"Before. I'll have a head start. And if I tear through enough of those cockpits, kill their pilots, then the Andrones drop dead before they can attack us."

Elijah reeled back as he considered her plan. And Harmony too, reconsidering, double-checking all aspects of her strategy. The church's objective was to hit the Quondam's satellite advancement centers, and that would take time. If Harmony's plan worked, her Androne in the past would attack the same pilots who would attack this cathedral once they found the rebounding signal. The Quondam's drones would tear through this facility in minutes, hundreds of Andrones killing her pilots in their cockpits. But Harmony could hit them first. If she destroyed the cockpits in the past, the Andrones in the present would essentially be dead. No pilots. *Yes*, the techno-witches had EMPs as last resorts, but the electromagnetic pulse would shut down both the enemy Andrones and the church's liquid cockpits. The goal was to stay in as long as possible. *It could work.*

"Anybody else know about this?" Elijah asked.

"They don't need to," Harmony said. "I'll destroy as many Quondam cockpits as possible. If I destroy enough there, we won't need to use the EMPs."

"*Audi* . . . ," Elijah said, naming his ex-god. "But don't tempt fate. If the timer goes off, get the hell out."

"I know what I'm doing."

"Okay, you just remember what happened last time in Islander territory."

"That was a long time ago," she said.

"It was last month."

It was, wasn't it. "Well, prophets like myself experience time differently than you." They both smirked at that one. "Hey, where's . . ." Harmony craned her neck, searching for her youngest pilot and her oldest friend. She turned to Gemini. "Have you seen Emit?"

"No," Gemini said, not even turning to look. "He was talking to one of the Mickeys earlier. He's into something."

He was always into something. *Fucking Emit.* The big, black sheep of her pilots. Untrained, undisciplined, and the closest thing she had to a little brother. In fact, it was only that proximate nepotism that kept him among their ranks.

"Mickey?" she shouted to the muscular pilots in the distance. They were both named Mickey. In fact their people had only one name. Ten thousand Mickeys with different numbers tattooed across their foreheads. "Hey, Mickey-447—" But before she could finish, the Grand Cleric took the stage, standing in front of an altar overlooking the liquid cockpits.

The man's face was garnished in mineral makeup, giving his light-brown skin an even lighter tone. His lips pursed pinker, his eyes blinked darker. He appeared bathed in color and proud of it, posturing, almost posing, with a smile wide enough for her to see the root of his gums. The man's neck stretched as high as it could possibly rise as he cleared his throat, ready for his speech.

"The Church of Time is split," the Grand Cleric began. "Our divine church has fractured in two. We now have a pair of principal denominations: our sect—us, the Church of Time in reverence to Chronos, our god of time." Something like applause echoed then as they rapped their fingers against their chests. "And then there are those in worship to the Quondam, our corrupted ancestry." His face soured as he spoke about the Quondam, and grumbling followed from the listeners. "In the beginning, our differences were slight. We both worshipped the time god and held the Quondam in reverence. But they allied themselves too closely with those historic powers. The Quondam control the Androns, the aerials, and quadrupedals; they control everything, so it makes sense to retain a closer relationship. But we saw the light. After the Monk Who Stood, we saw that we too should stand, not bow to Quondam influence. They are corrupt. They want to control us with their technology while stunting our own technological growth. We must break free from our history. And with this attack, they will begin to fall." Again, that fingertip applause echoed through the chambers as the Grand Cleric turned to the chorus. "And now the anthem of the grand poet, Gamma-Zeta. 'The Problems of the Ninety-Nine.'"

The choir donned black silk gowns and crowns on their heads that arched down over their eyes. A small orchestra of trumpets and congas thumped quietly as the hundred voices of the choir arose. "The Problems of the Ninety-Nine" was a translation of a work by a Quondam Era poet that Harmony didn't know nor care that much about. And though the Church of Time was embattled with Quondam, they still revered the poets and ballads and art of that era.

Someone's hand suddenly gripped Harmony's shoulder, and that startled her for a split second, and barely that, because half a second later she knew it was Emit. He tugged her backward like she wasn't a prophet of a religion but a wrestling partner in the third round. His meaty fingers were tight around her bony shoulder. His panting—heavy, desperate breathing—came from a full foot above her head.

"Emmy," she said before even turning to him. "It's not the time."

"Harm, we have to go," Emit said at a whisper.

She couldn't believe the fucking audacity of him, half tackling her during the church's anthem, in front of everyone. "The ballad." She pointed to the choir. "Man your goddamn cockpit, Emmy. We're starting."

"Harm, we have to go now. We need to get you out of this place."

"Stop," she snapped.

But he wouldn't. Emit and Harmony were too familiar, growing up together, studying the same slang and fishing in the same ponds. They had spent a good part of their childhood together in the Port

Siren swamps. Emit was younger by about eight years but twice as big. Taller, meatier, he outweighed her by a hundred pounds. And as the choir ended their ballad, hitting vocal crescendos, Emit raised his voice to counter.

"Let me talk to you for a second," he said.

"Say it now," Harmony said. "And fast."

"Can't say it here."

"Emit. Listen to me. There are things happening here, political things, chess matches between us and the church. They can't see disorder in our ranks. So when I give you an order, take it, *fucking* take it."

Emit tried to speak then, but she rolled over him. "You're my friend, Emit, but right now, I need you to act like a soldier."

"Harm . . . ," he pleaded.

"No." And her voice was a brick wall.

The choir ended just then—just as she spoke, and her voice carried. They all heard it, her pilots, their pilots, and Emit finally shut his fucking mouth. He tilted his head and noticed Gemini and the other pilots watching them both. The church's pilots watched too but with wooden faces, seemingly unsurprised at the rowdiness of Harmony's crew. The church's pilots carried a sense of discipline, and a dignity that bordered on arrogance. They offered Harmony and Emit little more than a glance before returning their attention to the cockpits. Because now, with the choir finished singing their prewar ballads, the battle against the Quondam would begin.

The church's pilots climbed the narrow steel ladders to their tanks and sat on the upper rims as they bit into mouthpieces that allowed them to breathe in the liquid and strapped on visors that would be their eyes in the past. Then they dropped into the superfluid. There was no splash—the liquid was viscid—and they all sank slowly to the bottom of their tanks.

Those liquid cockpits still gave Harmony pause. The church's weapons technology had surpassed that of the Quondam and in such a short period of time. A year ago, they didn't even have their own cockpits.

Now these things. There was something afoot, something going on underneath the surface of all their handshakes and alliances, and something that she hadn't quite figured out yet.

"Let's run it."

Harmony gestured for her pilots to enter their cockpits. Thirty strong and they were still just a fraction of the church's numbers. As she grabbed the first rung of her own ladder, Emit grabbed the second rung and climbed into her way.

"Emit—"

"They're going to kill you," he hissed in a whisper.

"What?" She shook her head, confused.

"There's an assassin."

"The church?" Harmony asked.

"Not the church. That wouldn't make sense. The church needs you. It's the Quondam. I think. That's the only thing that makes sense."

"Your news is about thirty years late," she said. "The Quondam has been trying to kill me since I was four. Look, you want to help, Emit? Get in your cockpit. Once we start that recursion, the Quondam are going to find our signal and send a thousand Androns right at us, aerials, quadrupedals, everything. Right now, the enemy is time. We'll deal with whatever else later."

Emit gave up, and that seemed to break him. All his muscle deflated and brought him down the ladder. That was who Emit was, him and his big, bleeding heart, a man who wore emotion on his sleeve like she had never seen. She trusted Emit, more than anyone, but he would make a horrible spy. So Harmony had her own spies, and they had told her the same thing weeks ago. *There is* an assassin out for her. She knew that already. Whether it was from Quondam or somewhere else, somebody wanted her dead.

Emit moved toward his own tank. He climbed up but with a downward dejection. He donned the breathing apparatus and visor, and he sank in the superfluid. Harmony followed suit. She wasn't a great pilot, but she always fought nonetheless. She bit into the bitter mouthpiece that wrapped over her lips like a muzzle. She breathed in the recycled air that tasted stale. And even before sinking to the very bottom of the tank, her visor flashed with ancient sunlight. Her recursion into the controls of a hundreds-year-old Androne had begun.

3

That first flash was blinding, the entangled photons knifing into the meat of her retinas. Harmony's eyes wrinkled shut as that hundred-year-old light blazed into her visor. The fluids in her tank rumbled, compressing in, giving weight to her buoying body. Then claustrophobia squeezed in on her too, squeezing tighter even than the pressures in her tank. This moment was absolutely everything. She had sacrificed years of her life and the entire lives of others: friends, family . . . people had died, and all for this, just for these next few minutes. The thought of that knotted at her gut; it palpitated in her chest. She could barely breathe. All those years she'd never get back, and all that time, squeezed down into the next ten minutes.

But she was different from the others, right? She was the Peacemaker. The one with that great destiny: end the war, break the controls of the Quondam. At least that was what they had told her, her mother and all her part-time lovers, men who only wanted to be part of a child's entourage. Strange fucking days from an even stranger childhood, and even then the only regretful part was that her mother would never see it, how far little Harmony had come.

Even though this was the thirtieth time they had attempted recursion, it was the farthest back they had ever been, and by a decade. Harmony had spent two years designing the software interfaces alone. Then there was the hardware, the battery nodes provided by the church, and the circuitry architecture loaned from the Audists.

All that sophistication had forced the church into collaboration with necromancers, ancestry traders, and, of course, with her. That was the only fun part of it, watching the Chronics grit their teeth as they made alliances with zealots whose traditions were more deranged than their own. Dirtying their hands right on the eve of their holiest religious festival.

The superfluid barely kept Harmony submerged. Her toes touched the bottom of the tank, and then she bobbed up and bobbed back down. And her braided hair spun like snakes around her head. But as the batteries rattled underneath her cockpit and the fluid pressures increased, Harmony was squeezed toward the bottom of the tank, and her spinning hair fell. Suddenly she was walking now, strolling through what felt like a vaporous liquid, neither in one state nor the other, like walking on air. And yet Harmony had no forward nor backward motion. She walked, jumped, ran, and yet remained fixed to the center of the tank. This was time worshipper's magic.

The liquid bubbled suddenly, jerking her torso back, and the rest of her followed. Her arms flailed, trying to keep balance. The batteries squealed, sharper than a razor to the ears. Even with her earpiece, Harmony could hear that screeching down to her eardrums, and then, just as suddenly, the batteries went quiet. Not silent, just the type of quiet hum that fades fast into background noise. Quiet enough for her to hear this distant hissing, like waves maybe, lashing against the shore or the hull of a ship. Harmony opened her new eyes to the bright ancient sunshine and the shade of rain clouds. She could see for telescopic miles. Her hands were steel. Her heartbeat was metal fibers. She was transformed, *like cicadas*, she thought. *"Cicadas molting to metal."*

She saw through the telescopic eyes and listened through the auditory amplifiers of an Androne. A pre–Spartan Series, not quite the quality of her time, but it would do. She felt the weight of its body through the pressure of the fluid around her. The Androne's body was freshly minted, gleaming in the sunlight, and standing in a row of nearly fifty identical Androvers on a Filipino aircraft carrier, sometime in the middle of the twenty-first century.

Ahead of her was a city, a crown of silver and glass rounded to the shape of the bay that donned it. The water was clear. The ocean reflected the shiniest parts of the city, and countless boats of luxury buoyed like jewelry on its back. An airplane glided overhead, and automobiles spun around pavements of light. It was jealousy that moved her then, a techno-envy that reignited her ambitions. Win the war. Fight the Quondam. The spark inside her was ready to burn that world down.

Harmony made a fist, and her Androne, like a metallic shadow, made a larger fist. Tungsten knuckles spun on chrome hinges. As she stepped forward in that liquid cockpit, the Androne stepped forward. The plan was working, her entire strategy, and all her sacrifices, every betrayal and agony, were worth it. And now she would make history by destroying it.

But first she needed to get onto the base just a couple of miles out. Rivera Base. Bunker 10. It was displayed on her map. Attack the bunker where their cockpits were stationed. Kill the pilots. *Kill.* That knot in her gut tightened. *You have to.*

"Copy that, Harm." Emit's voice came over her earpiece. "Aerial support in tow, 11-69-69. I'm twelve miles from your station. Wait for me."

Copy what? She hadn't said a word, to him or anyone else. And like hell would she wait. Emit had been hacked into a Valkyrie—an aerial drone carrying half a dozen MOABs. Sure, he could lay a good line of cover and assist in her assault, but he was twelve miles away. *Fuck waiting.* Nothing would delay her, not today, not having come this far back into a history she hated.

Harmony bounded forward, and her Androne followed with the same movement, the same unathletic posture, moving out from the line of fifty-some-odd other Androvers beside her. They stood like statues, unpiloted, soulless machines, just a big show of force in some pending military parade.

Harmony snatched a half dozen grenades from her Androne's waist and scattered them across the deck. The six oval green explosives pin-balled between the other Androne's heels. And as she lunged off the deck, grenades detonated. The combustive Androne batteries exploded, one after another, igniting the entire deck in fiery oranges and black pits of smoke.

She descended from the ship, flames like capes at her back. Her Androne landed on the docks. Concrete craters burst underneath its hundred-pound heels. Screams echoed around her, but she didn't see faces, just a scatter of unarmed military and civilians. Women dressed in flowing gowns with flamboyant dyes, and the men in ceremonial pants and jackets with darker hues. Some even had face paint to fashion and emphasize their features. This was their ancient vogue, prodigal and gaudy.

She had learned all this before. There were books on the subject, entire volumes on the opulence of the Quondam. Excess meats and water, domiciles that eclipsed mountains, and every individual had a self-made entertainment window. They worshipped themselves, or so the books said, written and hand-drawn by the church's archivists. The woman who had raised Harmony had been a devout archivist before leaving the church. Aurora often told stories about the past and their ruin. *Don't pity them*, she would say. *They're ghosts. All of them already dead.*

The Androne paused then, as she paused now, watching them—*ghosts*, stumbling and squealing, others dropping and floundering between all those feet. They were trampled, scratching at each other's legs, their flimsy bodies, fragile bones, all that mushy meat. Of course, she watched from her Androne's towering dais, iron bones, steel spine, tungsten flesh. She could stomp them out, every one if she wanted to. It would be easy, but the truth was she *did* pity them, watching them sprint so wild and uncontrolled, unaware that they were already dead.

Harmony veered her Androne toward a park. She had never seen such lush greens: muscular shrubs, barbered foliage on tall bark, and sprinklers spitting water onto the fluffed, overfed lawns. She barreled through the bushes and wooden benches, avoiding the screaming people between them. That park extended on for nearly ten miles, bridges arching over crystal-clear lakes, flowered gardens, and what appeared to be military graveyards.

"I was told to launch," an unfamiliar voice shouted, probably one of the church's pilots. "Following orders. But on the eve of the Day of Descent, vulgar language is not appropriate, Sister Harmony."

Her name was Aeon, right? Something like that. A member of the church. But who was she talking to? She had mentioned Harmony's name, but what was she talking about? *Told to launch what?*

The cockpit facility was just two miles over the ridge. There was time, and she would make it. Even as an enemy popped onto her visor radar, she knew she could do it. Two dots then, and her confidence rose even higher for some reason. Four dots, five, seven, nine, popping up in twos.

"Damn it," she said into the muzzle. "Contact nine," she said, a voice-activated code to speak to aerial support.

"Requesting aerial support," Harmony shouted. "Any aerial drones in the vicinity, requesting a lay of cover fire at 11-69-69."

Nothing. Not a voice, not a word, just radio silence; *silence*, and an eerie feeling about those numbers, *11-69-69*. There was a familiarity there, a déjà vu. But Harmony shook that shit off quick. She gritted her teeth and raced forward, driving her Androne harder toward the implied enemies on radar.

"Do it my-*fucking*-self," she hissed.

A trio of motor-vehicle-size aerial drones swooped down over her Androne and unleashed barrages of gunfire. Harmony tried to take cover under tree lines, dodging, dipping in and out of their line of sight. And she shot back, but shooting mid-dodge and mid-dip threw off her aim; she missed everything. Harmony had never been the best pilot of Andrones—her talents were in the mathematics, the systemizing, and code-breaking.

More aerial drones zoned in on her position, a half dozen now, maybe more, all of them splurging ammunition. Harmony saw nothing but the flash of Gatling guns. The tree bark snapped like twigs, frond confetti flurried around her. Harmony could only retreat then, *goddamn it.* She scampered away and her Androne followed, hurdling gravestones and tombs, trying to run through anything that could be used as cover. The whole thing was falling apart. She would have to climb out of her cockpit. The enemy Andrones were likely just minutes from their cathedral now.

Then light exploded, and so suddenly that she didn't have the time to register it. Light like a second sun, and she was blinded. Everything ahead was bleached to an avalanche of white noise. She thought it was her visor at first, but no, it had to be a hydrogen weapon, and that meant it had to be Aeon. She had been hacked into the mariner drone, and twelve nuclear warheads were under her control. But this area was never a target. It appeared the church had its own secret plans too.

"Code Seven A," she said. The voice activation would tap her into Aeon's audio. "What the fuck was that, Aeon?" Harmony exclaimed and waited for her to answer. She got nothing. "What the fuck are you doing? Say something!"

She didn't. Aeon said nothing. For half a second Harmony wondered if it was because she was cursing—Chronics hated vulgar language. But in the next half second Harmony realized that the response had already come. *Oh God.* Aeon had said not to use vulgar language and that she was told to launch. She said that minutes ago.

"We're out of sync," Harmony said, the realization gut-checking her that very moment. "Oh God. We're out of sync."

It was a mistake she had made once before in her programming of a recursion, but only once, and a long, long time ago. Recursion was a very precise science, and even the most minute miscalculation, down to the hundredth of a decimal point, could throw coordination awry. And it was awry. They were all there, all in the past, but out of sync in time, by seconds and minutes. Their recursion points, their comms, everything was out of alignment in time.

That fear hit her then, like a heartbeat in her head. It was that original fear, that thing she couldn't figure out the origin to, her mystery seed. Harmony's people were counting on her, and she let them down. *Shit*, how could she let them down? That was the thing beating mad in her brain. She failed them, all of their blind faith, their admiration, and she fucked it up.

"Goddamn it!"

Her Androne was out of range of the hydrogen weapon's electromagnetic pulse, but the blast itself was enough to scare off the aerial drones. Their pilots were likely nearby, with families and loved ones. The aerial drones buzzed off or crashed. Their pilot had bigger things to worry about.

"Harmony, you copy? We have to get out," Emit shouted. "Get! Out!"

"Respond one—Emit?" she screamed into comms. "Emit, we are not in sync!"

No response. Whatever Emit was responding to had already happened or would happen, depending on his displacement in time. And her response to him might be received minutes ago or minutes from now. The only thing Harmony could control now was her mission. As a hundred simultaneous attacks were being launched around this twenty-first-century globe, she could affect just this one thing.

Get to the cockpits. Those cockpits were underground, tucked snugly within a nuclear bunker, which meant two things. One, the hydrogen weapon had no effect on them, and two, they likely knew now that she was coming. Not her specifically, but more attackers on this area. They'd be on high alert, but the base wasn't far. Barely a mile ahead. She saw it in that telescopic vision. And standing on her Androne dais, she knew she could get there in minutes.

"Harmony, we have to get out." Emit again, but she shook her head. *No.* "The echo's out. The echo's out and they're here."

Rebound, echo, it all meant the same thing. It meant that they were coming. The Androns. They would tear through Harmony's liquid cockpit if the techno-witches didn't act fast enough. She knew that, but there was no way she was climbing out now. Not when she was this close.

"One more minute."

Harmony leaned her cockpit forward, motoring her Androne at its top speed. The cemeteries ended abruptly at the street congested with traffic, vehicles coming and going, horns quarreling with emergency sirens. On the other side of that street was the base and its bunker, full of Androne pilots who were trying to get to her first.

The Androne lunged over traffic, swooping over smaller vehicles and crashing atop a yellow bus. The windows spattered in shards. The passengers screamed, but not at her Androne. Tank-size landrones emerged from the base, galloping out on four legs or six or eight and aiming their heavy weapons at the Androne and the bus beneath it. But they wouldn't shoot here, not with civilians in the path of their bullets, the children, women, and men screaming and pouring out of the bus's door and shattered windows. *Or maybe they would.*

Gunfire clapped, and artillery ricocheted off the Androne's armored plates. She fired back, hitting a quadrupedal tank, cracking its mechanized scope, blinding the thing. But there were so many other *things*: quads, hexapods, and an awkward rolling machine, like a tire with weapons in its spokes. They unleashed automatic rounds, .50 caliber, dotting her armor with exit wounds and shrapnel shots.

But there was one weapon on the Androne's rifle that Harmony had been saving. They called it a "switchblade," an alternative barrel holding a rocket-propelled load heavy enough to immobilize a tank. She had been saving it for the cockpits, but there wasn't time; she had to use it now.

Harmony fired the rocket but barely waited for the explosion. She lunged her Androne off the bus before the round even hit, and when it did, every landrone died in a blossom of fire. She waded through the flames and broken machine parts, making her way onto the base. She could see the old bunker ahead, no need for the on-screen map.

Harmony had caught them off guard. Men and women were running in and out of offices and vehicles and that bunker, many of them likely Androne pilots. The bunker door was wide open, and the pilots scattered as she charged through the opening.

"They're inside the cathedral." Elijah's voice over her earpiece. "The Quondam's Andrones are inside."

So am I.

She ignored him. And she ignored the beeping in her ear, telling her that time was up. Ten minutes had come and gone. Time to get the fuck out of that liquid cockpit and run. *No, I'm going to make you proud of me—I won't let you down.*

There were flights of stairs that the Androne simply leaped down and a pair of metal doors that it easily barreled through. Then a final long corridor with weak fluorescent lighting stretched out ahead. Long, like half a mile, and on a descending incline, and at the end of it, a massive steel door on mechanized hinges, and it was closing. Even an Androne wouldn't be able to break through that door, three-foot-thick reinforced steel. *Run,* she told it, and they both did, Harmony careening forward like she never had before. She was a jockey on the Androne's back, racing against the closing door. She lunged for it, that tiny gap in the doorway. The Androne scraped against the edges of the doorframe and nearly lost its foot on the way through.

"I'm in," she said to no one and saw no one. The room was dark. Lights on the floor shone the path between the . . . *cockpits? Is that what those things are?* Large, mechanical, egg-shaped cockpits. Rows and rows of them. A hundred, she'd estimate. Were that many Androenes roaming the cathedral now? Harmony heard noises beyond her earbuds, loud noises that penetrated glass and liquid. They *were* inside. But so was she.

The Androne rammed the cockpit to its left. It budged but not enough; then she scratched at the wiring at its base. Pops of electricity glinted in the dark, nasty sparks, but the lights on the cockpit only flickered. This still was not enough, *was it?* There were a hundred of these things. Hundreds of dedicated pilots. Not one of them jumped out of their cockpit to run. That meant she couldn't either. And that meant she had to kill them.

"Harm?" Emit shouted over her earpiece. "Tell me you're not still in there."

All of their voices were nothing but noise at that point. She barely heard it. Harmony reached out for the cockpit door, the steel-and-tungsten fingers gripped it, and the Androne heaved it off its hinges without too much difficulty. They'd need to improve on that feature.

Inside the cockpit, a young female pilot swiveled in her bicycle-like seat and pulled off her visor. She turned to the Androne in sheer terror as the shock spasmed through her. She jerked backward in her cockpit shell like a snail, a nearly liquid spineless body. She screamed, but only for that moment. Soon her trembling hands reached back toward her visor and pulled it back down and she kept on piloting. Her arms were swinging wildly but still trembling, her whole body cringed up and quavering, awaiting the bullet.

Harmony aimed her rifle, but that was it. No pull on the trigger— she only positioned the weapon. Point-blank, just a couple of feet away from the young woman. But that long, snarling aim was just a threat, just another hesitation tactic. *Come on.* Point-blank and still her trembling hands wavered. *Just shoot her—she's already fucking dead.*

This wasn't Harmony's first recursion. There had been so many others, but those attacks were against other Andrones or destroying infrastructure or battling tanks or aerials or quadrupedals. In those campaigns they had ignored the civilians. And sure, there were casualties, but this would be Harmony's first direct kill, a face-to-face, eye-to-lens kill.

"They're long dead." She said it aloud. She had to hear it for it to be real, to be true. "They're already fucking dead." And still it sounded like a lie.

Harmony's finger tapped at the trigger, but she didn't pull it. *No,* that tapping she heard wasn't from the trigger. At first she thought it might be a malfunction on the Androne, some screw loose or one gear short. But as the tapping continued, she realized that this noise wasn't from her earpieces; it was present-day noise. Someone was knocking on the top of her cockpit. Loud, concussive pounding.

"Harmony, say something," Emit said. "Fuck it. I'm exiting my cockpit and I'm coming to you."

He was already there. They were out of sync, and he might have said that minutes ago. His comms must have been at least three minutes behind him. She heard him, atop her cockpit, pulling at the locking mechanisms above.

"No," she said, not that he would hear her. "I got them. I can *fucking . . .*"

Harmony's cockpit valve opened, and she felt the pressure releasing immediately. *Fuck!* She was almost there, rifle aimed at the girl. And she would have done it. Harmony would have shot her. She just needed one second more.

But as the air pressure suddenly suctioned out, she felt it. It hit her ears first, popping back into place like a loose joint. Then her toes lifted off the ground. She flailed around a bit, and so did her Androne, stumbling back, miming her motion.

"Emit, wait," she squealed. "One second. Just one. Emit, please!"

But his hand had already reached into Harmony's cockpit, his fingers swishing around inside, grabbing at her whirling hair. But she would fight him. Just one second was all she needed, just one clean shot at it. Then she felt him lifting her up out of the tank, clawing at her hair. Her visor and breather slipped off, and the liquids seeped in.

"Emit, just fucking wait." She gargled the words, choking on that bitter liquid.

Emerging from the liquid, a bitter shock of smoke cracked at her nostril, acid in her eyes, and there in a watery blur she saw him—she saw *it*. That wasn't Emit; it was a Kingsman Series, a *fucking* Androne, snagging her braids and lifting her out from the superfluid.

Behind the metal devil, flames flapped in the dark, hot and breeding mad. Electricity was gone. The liquid cockpits were shattered. Bodies lay capsized on the ground. The screams around her were chaotic, scattered, muffled, so close, until she realized the only screams left were her own.

Harmony looked down to find a bayonet knifed through her abdomen and out through the other side. It pierced her so clean that she barely felt it until she did—until her screams washed out the clog in her ears. Then the Androne grabbed her by her throat as if to shut her up. And she did.

Hundreds of other Andrones roamed behind her, gunfire flashing and cockpits exploding in as the superfluid caught fire, bodies burning inside. They were all dead, every one of them. Harmony's body went limp, but the Kingsman wouldn't take the chance that she was still alive, and she was, *alive*, but barely. The Kingsman brought its rifle to Harmony's head.

She had to die, right there. She had to give in. And Harmony did. And that was it, that was the only way—*stop fighting*. So Harmony surrendered to that darkest dark, surrendering to the cold and the snow flaking through tears in the ceiling. Her arms fell flaccid at her sides, eyes rolling back—back to the black hole in the hollow of the eyes where no light escaped.

Her neck sagged, her head slumped, and she died. She died right there in the Androne's embrace, because that was the only way.

4

Frostbite. She felt it cutting through the muscle, through tendons and blood vessels. She felt the migration of color, purpling underneath her toenails, the darkening at her fingertips. She felt herself dissolving into the snow, into its cold, white darkness. And yet she didn't struggle; she lay motionless as hypothermia rattled at her insides. Amid the blistering and the swelling, she choked her groans to the back of her throat. In the midst of her very death throes, Harmony restrained every twitch, every shiver, every hint of movement, because if she didn't lie there as if she were dead, *they'd kill her.*

Androdes, endless Androdes, so many they smothered her line of sight. So many that they were like one swarming symbiote, like a flock or hive or better yet a metal centipede with its thousand feet. *That many.* But amid the smoke and fires and fecal-scented chrome, amid the entire ruinous spectacle, Harmony had melted into that rubble and ash and the glass shards. So close to dead now that she had become ruin, camouflaged in its colors. And so the machines stepped over her, around her, nearly on top of her. Heavy footsteps, heavier breathing, gases like nicotine chimneying from their exhaust valves. Just scents and sounds now, that was all Harmony had with her fingers numb and eyes strapped shut.

Her wound pulsed as it bled, each drip a razor slipping out of her. It felt like broken wood shoved into her laceration, and the splinters were worming around. It was like termites feasting on her insides. *And fuck!* It hurt. It *fucking* hurt. She had bandaged the wound, but poorly, and put pressure against it the best she could in the darkness. But she would bleed out soon enough, so if the cold or the Andrones didn't kill her, she would still die.

And what about them? The names she had been trying to dam up at the back of her skull. *Are they dead?* Her eyes flitted on that thought, and she wanted to open them, just a glance, for Gemini, Elijah, or poor, *poor* Emit. He had tried to save Harmony at the end but just ran to his own death. *Goddamn it, are they dead or not?* Meir, Powell, Knicks. She choked on every name. She sniffled and gasped and gargled the saliva. Kai, Knuckles, Mickey-477, Mickey-828, Pregnant Jay, *fuck.* Harmony was slipping out from her camouflage as she remembered her friends. All those memories flooding in, and all at once. It was choking her. *You have to breathe,* she thought. *Breathe.* And all at once she wheezed, deep inhales, the scent of death in the air. *Exhale through the lips, and repeat.*

Oxygen now hitting her brain, Harmony stopped wondering about her friends' fate. She didn't overthink the uncertainty or get it muddled up in hope. Her brain was an engine of logic; she knew they were dead. She could fucking smell them. All that roasting muscle in the cold air. That distinctive crackle of the epidermis snapped and sizzled from every corner of the cathedral. They were dead, all of them, and all in vain. And truthfully, she was too. So why was she lying there sucking up air, clinging to life? She didn't deserve it. She didn't deserve an extra fucking second. Their deaths were all on her. She should just stand and scream and run boldly into the light of gunfire. She should, but she didn't. Harmony wouldn't even open her eyes—not even a glance. *Fucking coward.*

"Breathe," she whispered and squinted into the dark. "Get out of your head and breathe."

That 5:00 a.m. skyline was swollen with cumulus, and the blur of falling snow, and smoke rising up to meet it. The sky was midnight black. The warmth of sunrise was stunted by clouds, but that partly worked in Harmony's favor. In fact, her more pressing worry was the sun and its light bubbling up on the horizon. At sunrise they'd see it, the white mist of her breath pouring into the frigid air, a visible exhale made even more obvious by her hypothermic panting, her floundering lungs barely keeping pace with the gallop of her heartbeat.

Footsteps came then, soft, small, a percussion against the crumbly glass, and then voices. These were people, fluent Javan spoken in guttural cadences. She didn't need to look—she knew these men who walked among the machines: the Historics, but Harmony called them *Hysterics*—the Quondam's zealous following. They too were an offshoot from the Church of Time, but not true believers like the Chronics. Hysterics were more like religious bandits, bowing to whoever held the most power, and that had always been the Quondam. They were simply evangelical vultures, waiting for the crumbs to fall from the Andrones' feasts.

These Hysterics were male, from the sound of them. A pair of them, their footsteps cracking louder and closer. One of the men kept moving, his voice and footsteps drifting past her. The other man hovered over her, no more footsteps, no more words, just breathing. Long and deep inhales, heavy, whistling exhales, like he was trying to catch his breath. And when he eventually caught up with his breathing, the man went quiet, a long, hideous silence. Harmony couldn't see him, not with her eyes shut, but he was there.

The man eventually crouched down, thick, deep vocal folds resonating in his hums and the clearing of his throat. He came lower, knees or palms crunching into the glass. Stale, meaty breath huffed hotter as he leaned closer, as he grumbled, clearing the smoke again from his throat.

Harmony suddenly remembered the shards of glass underneath her. A bedspread of cockpit crystals and mirrors lay beneath her body. It suddenly pinched at her exposed shoulders and her arm, as if reminding her that it was there. One particularly long shard of glass lay underneath Harmony's palms. Her fingers had numbed against the spiky glass, but now she suddenly felt it again, an improvised weapon that would fit perfectly in his jugular.

A clatter of noises interrupted that thought, a zipper whirred open, a ruffling of plastics and metals came after; then Harmony realized—*it was her backpack.* The water bottle, and the plastic from her med pack. This piece of shit was just scavenging. Harmony's eyelid peeled back slightly to form a narrow squint. She saw a gaunt middle-aged man with a patchy, graying beard, his sloth-like fingernails picking over her backpack.

Harmony half considered killing him, and she could. She could easily run the glass across the scavenger's neck, a deep, half decapitation. She could take one of them down before she bled out. But instead Harmony played dead as the Hysteric absconded with his scraps and crumbs, his footsteps fading in the distance.

For a moment she had the audacity to hope the Androns and all their manic men would retreat. A half hope, though. Harmony held back on the full brunt of optimism that they would shuffle off to some base far away and miles underground. But the hope proved bootless. The Androne still stomped about, the Quondam's vultures buzzing over the corpses with conversation and even laughter.

If I die, the world will end . . . , she thought—her thoughts now getting muddy. Cerebral gibberish slipped in as she sank in and out of consciousness. Harmony was losing stillness in her stupor. Her limbs twitched about. Her eyes blinked to stop herself from going under. She would die, she was sure of it now, and "her world" *would* end. No line of succession, no proper hierarchy or children to take on the mantle. It ended with her. Gemini had pushed her on that: *Who's your number one, or number two? Choose a successor.* But for a long time Harmony had this mind of immortality. It was a lifestyle, her arrogant recklessness, as her mother would call it. Because she was the Peacemaker, she would end the war, and the reckless part of her believed that. Which meant to Harmony that she couldn't die before the war ended. Gemini's warnings had fallen on procrastinating ears. And even with rumors of assassins in her company, Harmony had put it off. *We're all immortal until we die*, she had once boasted.

"Wake up," she whispered, and her eyes snapped open.

How long had she been dreaming?

Long enough for sunlight, the first of it, burning red through the smoke and airborne particles. She could see brick piled in the distance and light bending on the Androne's chrome rifles. It had only been half an hour maybe, but the clouds had migrated. The sun was rising, and in that looming sunrise they would see it now. Her exhalation. A misty cloud of white breath rising from the cold nostrils. *But look closer*, something told her. There was something else revealed in the light, *right there*, the sunshine wrapping around it like a spotlight: it was a narrow ventilation shaft on the ground maybe fifty meters from her, too small for an Androne, barely big enough for her.

Fifty meters—at a full-on sprint she *might* make it. *Maybe.* Harmony scanned her very limited line of sight: two men to her immediate left, an Androne to her right. She wouldn't dare lean her head backward, that movement would be too obvious, but she could hear at least two or three landrones, quadrupedals maybe, behind her. Five or six hostiles in her immediate vicinity, *at least*, and there could be more.

Harmony tilted her head slightly, slowly, and aimed an eye at that ventilation shaft again, *a better look at it now*, no more squinting. Her eye opened wide. And from that vantage the vent appeared more like forty feet away. *Forty?* Her eyes widened. She was emboldened now, lips lifting open in salivation. Forty feet—*get up, cockroach, fucking run for it.*

Her legs rolled a nudge, her waist pivoting . . . pivoting so slowly, like it wasn't even happening, like she wasn't moving. Her knees then curled in slowly as her shoulders lifted her onto her side even slower. Until something cracked, maybe the glass shards underneath her—*stop*. And she was still. And yet it cracked again, louder. *Fuck, don't move.* But it wasn't her, *was it?* That was the clatter of footsteps, so close they were nearly on top of her. A Hysteric, his shadow eclipsing the light. Her eyes fell shut. But not her lungs, not her nostrils. She forgot to hold her breath, and an exhale sprayed out of her lips in a visible mist, a swirling of carbon dioxide that revealed the life yet trapped inside her.

The man's boot pressed against Harmony's shoulder and nudged her to the side. She narrowed her eyes open, and even at a squint she discerned his stature: broad shoulders, thick, hirsute arms, and rotting yellowjacket teeth. He breathed heavy, exhaling white air like his nose was a chimney. And if she could see his breath, then he could see hers.

He nudged her again but harder, and she yielded her torso and limbs to the inertia. She flopped over, *convincing*, she thought—she hoped. And she listened, all she could do was listen. Listen to his sniffling. Listen to the granular cracks as his footsteps shuffled about. He stepped over her, and she could hear him crouching down, his shadow darkening what little light rested on her eyelids, and she held her breath the entire time.

The bearded man said something in his dialect. Something harsh spittled out of the yellowjacket teeth and hit her face. No one responded, and he said it again—said it to her? *Fuck.* He knew. He prodded her then, fingers against her chest. The air inside her burned. Her pulse raced. Bottled-up oxygen cut like razors at her windpipe. Harmony's toes curled up in her shoes, toenails clawing at the insoles. She would burst—she was bursting, every orifice of her body bubbled with air. And somehow she remained deathly still.

Then Harmony's body jerked upward as the man yanked her from the ground by the collar of her shirt. That sudden snag on her neck set off an unintentional exhale, but she tightened her lips and swallowed it *the fuck* up. But the noose tightened. Blood vessels contracted, starved of oxygen, and her heart pounded in compensation.

"Dead," he said, faintly and finally convinced, finally letting her go, but then it was too late, wasn't it?

Thick swirls of CO_2 exploded out from Harmony's nostrils and lips. Her eyes snapped open just in time to see it, her own last breath staining the air around her.

The Hysteric's hand recoiled from her collar. Shock. Terror. His face went white as the woman he presumed dead came to life. He stumbled backward, dropping the weapon in his hand, a Quondam Era Glock.

Harmony snatched the Glock. Her fingers floundered around its cold steel at first but soon threaded around the grip and trigger. *That wasn't my last breath*, she thought as she aimed the pistol at the bearded man. *It was his.*

The point-blank *thwak* from the Glock detonated into the Hysteric's neck. Blood engulfed the air. Trachea tissue and spinal fluid dotted Harmony's face.

The flash and bang sent the rest of the Hysterics into motion. Harmony forced herself onto her rubbery feet and screamed. *Oh God.* The wound opened and blood poured out of her; it was all blood. She could barely walk and yet she tried to run. Her feet paddled like oars against the icy, red-soaked floor, and she dived face-first back onto the ground. Her nose snapped open. More blood. More pain.

Gunfire raged behind her, bullets whizzing by her ear, shrapnel spattering out all around her. She fired back blindly, counting the bullets leaving her Glock as she zigzagged forward. Her feet were drunk, her abdomen gaping open. She breathed blood. It bubbled out her nostrils.

But she could feel the air in her lungs, feel the sweat pushing out of numbed skin and her heartbeat pounding against her chest. If Harmony died, she would die full of life, not lying down.

But Harmony's legs gave up on her in the end. She slipped, then slid the last ten feet toward the aperture. She glided smoothly across the snow-slick concrete. Legs first, Harmony floundered clumsily inside. But as she tried to squeeze the rest of herself in, she found the shaft to be a puzzle her body couldn't quite fit. It wasn't the size of the vent but the shape of it. The shaft curved a little ways in. As she kicked and felt around with her legs, she could feel it angling down, likely releasing into the basement area. But she couldn't bend. It hurt too damn much. Even without the injury she was never that flexible.

"Please," she begged someone. Some god?

She kicked and squirmed with mad desperation, shoving her broken body into the hole. The Andrones charged toward her, each competing with the other to get there first. An Apache Series, a Zulu, and pairs of others that she didn't take the time to distinguish between. She wiggled herself forward and bent her legs down.

Then the Andrones all fell.

The Apache Series dropped its rifle and collapsed inches from Harmony. Then the Zulu Series dropped. A Kingsman next. All of them, dropping dead where they stood.

Harmony stared at the scene in complete shock.

Then someone grabbed at her leg from inside the vent and dragged her screaming down. Falling through the bottom of the shaft and into a dark basement area with a single lamp shining its light. Harmony hit the ground hard, but her abdomen hurt so much more that she barely registered the concrete cracking against her back.

There were a handful of them down there, hiding in the dark. The surviving Chronics from the Church of Time, maybe thirty of them cramped up in the tight space. But hardly any children, mostly old men, holding their robes tight to their chest, shivering in the cold.

"Grand Peacemaker," one of them said.

"Praise Chronos," another said. "The Peacemaker."

But she looked through him—past him. Searching for familiar, friendlier faces. But there weren't any. Just her and the followers of Chronos.

"Hysterics," Harmony said, but they didn't know her slang. "Historics," she corrected herself and pointed up at the vent.

"It is sealed," someone in the back said.

"But we should move now," another man said, an older man. "Some may find a path to follow."

"Descending upon descendants," the man closest to her said in proper Javan tongue. "Among the eyes of all attendants. Book 5, Verse 7."

The man's accent was flawless, every point of intonation perfectly plucked off his tongue, but soon his words slurred, slowed, and faded out of audibility. It wasn't him, *no*, she was losing consciousness fast, and losing blood even faster. Harmony was sinking like a brick to the bottom of her brain, and her body followed. Falling downward.

"I let them down," she managed to say as she fell into the man's arms.

The old man nearly dropped her, his bony arms trembling with her weight. The others quickly helped, their hands on her back and under her arms, lowering her to the ground.

"She will fall at the foot of the common man," he said, choking on his words. "And he will end where she began." Tears flowed down the wrinkles of his eyes. He embraced Harmony as she faded into the dark. "This is the day we all repent," he whispered into her sleep. "This is the day of all descent."

5

Harmony woke up on a wool cot that sagged in the middle. That bend in the fabric had become a cramp on her back, another in her neck. So she gently unfolded herself, wringing the wrinkles out from between her joints, legs spinning, her arms extending, and the fingers blossoming out. Even her lungs stretched in long, wide exhales. But that wound—her gut singed with every bend in her posture.

She found herself in what felt like a brick basement, its low ceiling dangling over her. The little light in the distance inhaled and exhaled, keeping pace with the draft blowing inside. *Candles*, she thought, and she simultaneously pulled the blanket over her and tried to sit up, *tried*, but the stabbing in her abdomen laid Harmony back down.

"Told you she was cold." A hoarse, masculine voice came from the dark. "You're cold?"

"Not cold," she lied. "I'm okay. But some water. If you have some?"

"Beside you." A second voice from the dark, a woman, older, and deeper into that darkness, her voice as hoarse as the man beside her.

Harmony lifted a cup from the old wooden stand. She guzzled the liquid inside. It wasn't water, and the rust from the cup gave it a saltiness. She imagined the duo in the dark ahead of her as an old married couple. Years together, wrinkled faces, self-willed, rough around the edges, but sweet, and taking care of her out of a parental instinct. But that wasn't true, *no*, there were others in that room or basement, or whatever it was. There was a silent majority beyond that flickering of light. Cleared throats, and sniffles, the ebb and flow of tiptoeing, trying their best not to be heard.

Where the fuck am I?

"Who are you?" Harmony asked.

"The Exegete has been notified," the husband said. "They will be down shortly."

An Exegete. So she was still with the Church of Time. She wasn't familiar with the function of an Exegete but knew that their rank within the church was high, if not the highest. And therefore a small congregation was likely out there in the shadows.

"Where is this?" Harmony asked, peering out into the dark, the dusty floors, the flames balancing on their wick. "Where am I?"

"You are here," the wife said.

"You're safe," the husband said.

That she didn't quite believe, but Harmony knew not to push the issue any further. They were time worshippers after all, and that stubborn faith was an iron rod that wouldn't bend, let alone break.

Conscious now, albeit half-high on whatever medicinal compound they had plugged into her, Harmony finally reeled back to everything that had happened. How had it even slipped her mind? Even for a second? She had attacked the Quondam all the way back at the beginning of their program. Further back than she had ever been. Tens of millions had been wiped out, and they had done it in her name. How do you forget that? How does that slip anyone's mind, even for a second? She paused there on that question, because maybe, *just maybe*, she wanted to forget. Maybe she had to. It was too much. Too many lives for one conscience to hold. So somewhere between the drug and the drowsiness she forgot again. It was gone, just like that, and Harmony turned her thoughts to her people. Her survivors, if there was such a thing? Elijah, Gemini, Emit, Knuckles?

"Is there anybody else?" Harmony asked, leaning up as high as the pain would allow her. "Elijah or Emit or Gem . . ."

"We cannot be sure," a third voice said, a new voice, a woman. "Mole missiles struck the escape route. Many were buried alive."

Harmony's shoulders dropped back onto the cot, then her neck, then her arms, uncoordinated little pieces. She trembled through the pain. Shocks of grief thundered down through her body. She barely felt the wounds now. She mourned, as long as they would let her, Harmony mourned. She poured tears into the pillow until it overflowed. Her nose ran wet, her lips dribbled saliva. She poured it all out until there was nothing left, and still she mourned.

She started to go quiet, just breathing and a few sniffles, and that third voice arose again from the back, and promptly, as if she had been waiting for Harmony to finish with her grieving.

"In time, I greet thee . . . ," she said, "Harmony of Port Siren. I am the third Audist of the third house, and I am here to announce the entrance of the grand holy Exegete."

"Audist?" Harmony said. "With the Church of Time?"

"Yours is not the only collaboration the church has made in the past years."

The Church of Time had been busy. They had collaborated with not only her but seemingly every enemy of the Quondam. Audism, the ring religion, as it was known to the common people, was probably the second largest religion on the continent. Audis, or Audists, believed in "the God That Listened," and they produced the best techno-witches and necromancers there were. They believed that time was circular, that these events had all happened before and would happen again infinitely. These beliefs were represented by four rings often worn around the neck, but this woman had shed her rings for the sake of the Church of Time.

"Brilliance," the Audi woman shouted, calling for someone to do something. "Brilliance. Brilliance abound."

Light flooded into the dark, and not candles or torches—this was electricity. Voltage hummed across the space. The shock to Harmony's pupils knocked her back. Already wet, swollen eyes were now blinded.

The bodies in front of her appeared warped and wrinkled. But that passed, and eventually they all came into focus, all ten thousand of them—more maybe. Harmony sat up and stared out at a stadium. She lay at the pit of an auditorium, surrounded by rings of ascending stairs, and every inch of every step was crowded with devout bodies, hands clasped tight, eyes strapped shut.

"What?" she whispered to herself. "What is this?"

A stage. She realized it as soon as she asked it. She had heard about these performance ceremonies, a theatrical event during festivals like the Day of Descent. Plays re-creating historical events in reverence to the time god. And now she sat on their little stage, in their little performance, a central character of their play.

The third Audist from the third house stepped closer. And for a second she looked familiar, and not just a second; *no*, the evocation stayed with her. Every step she took, every gesture she made, Harmony had seen it all before. She knew that look, that walk, every inch of every toe, *but from where?* Where had she seen that grace of gait, that manner of dress? This Audist had a familiar way about her.

Aurora. The woman who had raised Harmony had been a devout Audist before converting to the Church of Time. Same dress and the same mannerisms, down to the tone she spoke with. It was uncanny. Even though Aurora had sampled nearly every religion there was, she could have been a mirror for this woman, right now.

Harmony found herself sitting straight up. Her mystery solved, she reeled herself upward and locked eyes with the Audist woman.

"I present to thee," the Audist said, bowing to Harmony, "the prophet of prophets. The voice of the gray god, the word of the Marble Moloch. Our Grand Exegete."

A buzz erupted from the hive, a thousand quiet gulps of astonishment. Some gasped, and others suffocated whimpers under their sleeves. The Exegetes were so holy within the church tradition that entire generations had never seen one. Even the other major faiths, like the Audists or the House of G (the AI god zealots), held Exegetes in reverence. Exegetes were, as far as Harmony had heard it, the voices of God. It spoke through them.

The Exegete entered stage left, barefoot and bare-bodied, stepping between the lights, holding to the shadows, as he or she appeared to be without age or gender. And that was the role the church wanted them to play, an empty vessel for a god to steer.

Harmony had only ever heard of an Exegete once, an offhanded remark from Gemini. Gemini was once deeply entrenched in the church, and even she knew very little about the children supposedly raised as conduits to a god. Gemini herself had never seen an Exegete. So Harmony lifted herself even higher, leaning forward against the pain on this rare occasion, curious as to what was about to occur.

Any thread of ethnicity, skin color, or gender was rubbed away under the lights' backlit angles. He or she was just a silhouette, the light burning at their back. But she knew the Exegetes were young, near puberty, maybe even younger, eleven or twelve, at most thirteen.

"I am vale," the Exegete said, their voice a pitch-perfect neutral. No dialect. No accent. "Course through me, o' prophet of prophets."

The Exegete kneeled and bowed their head, pressing their forehead against the floor.

"Eyes be eyes," the Exegete said, slipping the visor over their eyes. "Ears be ears," they said as they plugged two earbuds into their ears. "And flesh be flesh."

The Exegete stood slow and exaggerated, staring at something beneath the cover of the visor. Their wrists curled and their neck swiveled in dance-like rotations. Somewhere between common movement and a slight balletic exaggeration, the Exegete approached Harmony. Their steps were overstated by large bends in the knees and coiling of the ankles.

"Wise and powerful Peacemaker, I bow before thee." The Exegete's voice had completely changed now. The deep vocals of an elder man articulated from their throat. Their accent was northern, the cadence lyrical. *Everything was different.*

"I need to pee," Harmony said and shrugged. "Sorry, I just . . . I know you're doing a thing, but I really need to pee."

"You are not of the church, and therefore I must explain. The voice you hear, the body you see, is merely a vessel, a voice that translates *me* through time, through space. It is a mouthpiece, if you will, or a living puppet that *I* speak through—I, the prophet of prophets. This vessel sees my motion and mimics, hears my language and translates my tone and voice. It has trained for its whole life for this moment, and afterward, it will die."

So that was what an Exegete was. Just a human suit for someone, somewhere, sometime else to dress up in. The most chic in design, new and young. They were a fashion accessory. A puppet. So who was Harmony speaking to now? *Actually* speaking to.

"Who are you?" Harmony said after that moment's pause.

"I am as I am," they said. "And they have named me Ether."

"Where and when are you located, Ether?" Harmony said.

"Here," the Exegete said. "I am here. On this same stage. In this same arena. Some of the same eyes in that audience watch me now."

Ether was broadcasting from a different time, was or will be, and she wanted the direction in the arrow of time. "When?" Harmony insisted.

The Exegete paused, their flexible shoulders rolling back, toes bending, like a circus dancer, Harmony thought, trained in the motions of ballet.

"When," the Exegete said. "I should have expounded, dear Peacemaker. I am beyond the birth of your ancestry and far-flung from your death. I *am* when—I am omnipresent. I am unlocked in time."

"Right," Harmony muttered to herself, which the Exegete wouldn't hear from that distance. The same old Church of Time bullshit. *Unlocked in time indeed.* Ether knew what Harmony was really asking, but fuck it. "Look, why am I here?"

"It is as it was written. This Exegete, and the clerics in the first halo, have all read this scripture, this moment. They have memorized the words. Every word you are saying and will say has been recorded and sent backward in time as scripture. The muttering you hear like a hiss of crickets, those are the clerics reciting every word they have studied. It is like poetry, a song to them, and they sing along with me and with you."

Harmony had already turned to the clerics before the Exegete finished its spiel. They had been mouthing her words like this was a song they remembered, like this was a performance. The imagined husband and wife pedestaled keyboards on their laps. They typed Harmony's words and actions, recording this very moment to send it back a hundred years or more. Every word she had said today and every word she would say was scripture in the time worshipper's religion. And before she had even been born, cleric children and teachers had taught this very hour as a great religious moment. *I need to pee* and all. Now that was a mindfuck.

"Why this moment? Me in a *fucking* bed?" she said, eyes on the husband and emphasis on *fucking*. "Why?"

A smile like ecstasy inflated the Exegete's cheeks, pure bliss, and yet, Harmony imagined, this wasn't the Exegete's emotion but a mirror of the Ether that they mimed.

"An invitation, dear Peacemaker, in this glorious moment. You are requested to journey the desert pilgrimage to God's cradle, the pilgrimage that follows the rapture of our great day. Follow in the path of the great consciousness. The pilgrimage invitation that shall be now and only now is because of you."

"Pilgrimage? No." Harmony said it as plainly as words could possibly be said. She was growing weary of this whole thing. The false pageantry. The fact that they knew what she was going to say and still they sat there, humming her words like the chorus to a hymn. And the drugs were wearing off. The aches from her injury were creeping back in. "No." She said it stronger this time. "Not interested in your pilgrimage."

"I implore you, dear Peacemaker," the Exegete said. "The pilgrimage is a privilege beyond matter."

"I fucking said no!"

"Peacemaker, Chronos beckons thee. In this time of celebration."

"Celebration?" Harmony snapped. "I have a bunch of dead friends out there, friends with families, children . . . friends that I grew up with, *dead!*" Her voice echoed. "They're half-buried in snow in your cathedral. I know you don't care about the people you lost. You don't have a conscience, and that must be nice. Must be so much easier. Because this fucking hurts . . ."

Her voice cracked and fell away.

"Dear *Peacemaker* . . ." Hesitation, and it was only a second, but it was right there, right in that moment, and the hesitation didn't appear to come from Ether. It was from her—*the Exegete*. The little girl revealed herself as her voice broke. Something like sympathy. There was someone rattling around inside that meat suit.

"Dear Peacemaker," the Exegete recovered, and fast. "Your wound is our regret. You should abate in time. The pilgrimage can be versed in the posterior."

Harmony would never take their pilgrimage, but she wouldn't say it. Let them think what they wanted to think. She was done, with the church, with all of this war. It wasn't just that the closest thing she had to a family had died. It was that they died for nothing. She had lost. Harmony had lost the war. She had lost everything.

"We welcome this day," the Exegete said, Ether behind her words. They turned away from Harmony; they'd had enough of her thankfully. Now they watched the enthralled audience humming along to the script. "The Day of Descent." The Exegete's tiny physique exploded out to fully stretched limbs, legs on the tips of their toes and arms stretching up toward the ceiling of the building. "Show us the glory of thine day, the Day of Descent."

Harmony remembered the Day of Descent festivities from her childhood. The lanterns over doors and the boating games. Sports events on the lakes with expert boatsmen flinging colored flames about. The fireworks popping rainbows overhead. She had thought it sophisticated and exciting back then. *Silly girl.* Now she avoided any church festival like the plague, especially the Day of Descent. Harmony had successfully dodged this holy day for fifteen years, and now she was at the center of the biggest church and the biggest crowd, all poised for the biggest of celebrations. Just her fucking luck.

The Exegete still stood elevated on their toes, arms still open wide enough to embrace the whole stadium. She, and Ether the puppeteer, were waiting for something to happen. And then it did. Shutters opened on the ceiling, bringing light into the auditorium. Red light. *Fireworks?* But where was the noise? The gunpowder bursting open? *No*, that wasn't fireworks, and Harmony squinted, realizing that those were flames lighting the skies.

"And behold the hive of the heavens falls," the Exegete said. "They crumble down from the skies in flames."

"What . . . ," Harmony started but couldn't finish. Was that true? That fire in the sky, that was the hive? She couldn't believe what she was seeing. The Quondam satellites were falling from the skies. So many. "How?"

"Year zero is now," the Exegete said. "The birth of our Day of Descent is now."

Harmony's wheels spun for a second or two, puzzle pieces slipping in and out of place before they all fit together. She nearly fell off the bed, falling to her knees like the rest of them.

"Oh God," Harmony said, hand over her mouth and gasping. "Oh God, it's today . . . today's the day."

The Day of Descent had been a celebration in the Church of Time worship for centuries. They commemorated this day before Harmony's own grandparents were born. But they weren't celebrating some religious event from the past. The church had been celebrating a day in the future—*today*, right now, this very moment. *Oh my God.* They knew this day would come. And in that moment she realized that there was more to the mad religion and its strange ceremonies than she had ever imagined. The Day of Descent was a celebration of the death of the swarm—the hive in the heavens. They were celebrating the fall of the satellites. And she watched it as it happened, satellites plummeting, burning in the atmosphere, satellites by the thousands all across the globe.

"Day of Descent," the Exegete said. "We are here today because of *you*." Their voice cracked. "You are anointed Peacemaker. *You—*" The Exegete's voice broke completely, sobbing as tears poured out from underneath the visor over their head. "You, dear Peacemaker, you and only you. You have ended the war."

6

The war was over. *How was this real?* Satellites all around the world were falling and fizzling out. The Androses were dead, and not just Androses. The quadrupedals, the furies, and all their other monsters—they were just hollow pieces of metal now. That gateway to the Quondam world had vanished because of her, because of the Peacemaker. After so many years, she had done it. She had ended the war of time.

It was surreal, absolutely surreal, not even like a dream but a rush of mad drugs tampering with her reality. Her, lying at the center of the Chronic world, as clerics and high priests praised her. They talked about allying with her and bringing all the great nations together as one. "A true peace."

Her first thought was of Emit, the Mickeys, Gemini, Elijah. Their sacrifices were not in vain. They had died nobly, in the service of something historic. But then she thought: *no.* They were so close to seeing this, seeing this sky of fire, watching all those ancient orbiting shrines collapse. Her team should have seen this. No one was alive to celebrate with her, and for her there would be no celebration.

They would escort Harmony to the cleric's tower. The crowds outside were rioting in jubilation, they told her, but she could hear it. Fireworks and screams of joy, songs and ballads sung in unison. And they were beating down the doors to the auditorium. "They'll be inside soon," one of the clerics said. And though the crowd's intent was to revel, not harm, just to sing within the hallowed halls, mobs could be a very dangerous thing.

They snuck her out in secret. A white silk scarf covered her face and hair, but she could see through. She was surrounded by an entourage of church youth, teens standing at least six feet tall and twice Harmony's own weight. Twenty of them led her through a hidden exit in a wheelchair that quaked over craggy gravel. But they led her into celebratory bedlam, and it frightened the drugs out of her system.

The Day of Descent was pandemonium, with crowds that she couldn't give a number to, countless in the literal sense. The citizens raved as far as she could see, on the tops of buildings and hilltops miles out. They screamed to the heavens, the older of them on their knees, the younger lunging into the air. And they all wept and laughed at once, in the way it might rain through sunshine. The very earth shook underneath her, and Harmony's frightened entourage pushed her wheelchair even faster.

The crowd was mad with celebration, and they hadn't even seen her yet. When they did see her, when her white silk scarf was dragged away by dirt-black fingernails, the crowds found a new level of psychosis. The volume of their collective voices burst in her eardrums. Her entourage was devoured into the crowds and digested, and they became the crowd; they were part of its whole, indistinguishable as they swiped and clawed to get forward. The mob grabbed at Harmony, but gently enough, their fingerprints on her cheeks and shoulders and even against the bandages on her wound.

"Peacemaker," they chanted. "Blessed Peacemaker. Holy Peacemaker. Glorious Peacemaker."

They imagined every adjective and more, faithful, beguiling, fragrant Peacemaker—*fragrant?* She would smile if she weren't fighting for her life. What little strength the sleep-inducing drugs allowed Harmony, she used it to hold tight to the arms of the wheelchair, and when that was gone, when it was ripped from underneath her, she held on to her clothes, clothing that was tearing away, fingernails scissoring at the fabric, and then all she could hold on to was herself. Curled up into a ball on the ground, in this fevered drug-dream, Harmony tried to hold on to who she was.

That was when the gunfire started. At first the bullets were aimed at the air, but those shots were mixed into the fireworks and lost their meaning. So the next volley was pointed at the mob, the gunfire aimed below their waists, perhaps hoping to wound or maim. And still the mob thought as one mind, individuality be damned. Urges were all they were, like cells, simplified to just instinct. Together they were one brain comprising a million nuclei, and right now the Peacemaker was their single thought. She was the dream at the center of their mind. And though they loved her, though their doting was like mother to child and back, they would crush Harmony to pieces and eat at her individual parts.

The third volley of gunfire disregarded survival, hitting chests and craniums, tearing open spinal fluid in the backs of those who ran off. More gunfire and more of their bodies fell. And now they scattered, individuals tearing away from the mob monster, until only dead bodies lay at the Peacemaker's feet.

The church guard, a couple of hundred strong, gently picked Harmony up. They rushed her to the other side of the auditorium as the mob re-collected its individual cells. Church physicians offered her another round of painkillers. She accepted gleefully. Accepting because of the pain; the glee was from the drugs. *These drugs are fast.* They washed away everything—the dirt from the mob, the pain from the wound, even the memory of what she had just experienced was gone. Long gone. She smiled for a hundred minutes as her cells and her brain floated upside down.

At some point, they had carried her up the spiral stairs to the top of the tower. Because that was where she found herself, smiling and surrounded by all the famous faces. Up there she had a greater view of the festivities and a greater view of the fall.

Tentacles of fire streaked down from space and into the night sky. Thousands of satellites burning through the mesosphere. So many and so far away they appeared like paintings of flame against the horizon, like an arson's graffiti blazed onto the ceiling of the world. And it was her; she was the arsonist. Harmony had ended the war.

She hadn't fully taken that in, but Harmony knew she would, tomorrow or the day after, a hangover after the drugs ceased banging at the back of her head. For now she watched from the balcony above the auditorium, watching or else she wouldn't believe it: the black smolder, the flames falling, with little flashes within their fires. She watched, and still many parts of her were unconvinced. She leaned into the view, her body at a slant, her hands gripped safely to the balcony's iron railing. Her heart didn't beat as much as it rose and fell, up and down her throat and chest and up again. *Was it really over? Just like that?* At moments her arms felt weak and might give way under her leaning anatomy, and she would fall that hundred feet down.

It was strange, this dreamy panorama. *Was this even happening? Was it real?* Maybe it was the time worshippers' sweet, *sweet* painkillers, like a candy madness spinning her head; the pain was so far gone now. Or maybe it was because Harmony had been at war her whole life, and now it was over, her life was over, and she was still alive. *That's not real,* she thought. *This isn't real.* And she just kept watching, staring at artificial shooting stars, their war falling apart in fiery little pieces.

Behind her, the ten clerics of the ten churches murmured so inaudibly it was like a foreign language. Harmony couldn't make out a single word. They were soft men and women, with flabby bodies, old and overfed. They whispered, not to hide their words from her, but as to not distract her—not to vex her. There was this reverence for Harmony, this tiptoeing around her, stolen glances as she passed by. And she hated that. She somehow felt consorted with a church that killed her friends. She blamed them now. That was easier.

Why was this all happening now? The Church of Time had collaborated with the Quondam for centuries. Then all of a sudden a split.

Hysterics versus the Chronics. First there was dissent on Quondam practices, then disagreements on their holy texts' interpretations. And now they were gone. The Quondam, the occupiers of time, were actually gone. Leaving their henchmen, the Hysterics, completely fucked.

She swiveled back to the clerics, and they turned away, seemingly afraid to meet her eyes. And maybe not fear but a wariness or prudence. And that was fine—the sudden swivel of her neck and waist pulled on the wound, and she recoiled back to the fiery skies.

"How?" she asked, staring at the dots of fire. "How did you do this?"

"We didn't," a bald cleric said. And not just baldness on her scalp, but no facial hair in the slightest, eyebrows and eyelashes wiped clean, not even a nose hair hanging from her nostrils. "You did this, Peacemaker. *You* did."

"How did *I* do it, then?" she asked, her tone as dry as dust.

Harmony knew well enough that she had done nothing to cause the fall of the satellites. She just opened the quantum door by hacking into those first few drone signals. That was it; she was the hacker. Whatever they did brought down the sky.

"You performed the impossible." A fluffy-bearded cleric stepped forward. "Hacking the satellite, hacking a code the Quondam used against us. So far back, back to the inception of those satellites' positioning. That was the impossible task. And you did it. We simply used the source code—the infinite algorithm. With that, it was easy."

"The source code brought them down," Harmony said, a rhetorical statement, and yet the bald cleric felt the need to expound.

"This source code was termed the infinite algorithm, an unhackable passcode because of its infinite range. Only by copying the original would we be able to take control of them today and bring them to the ground. To get the original code, we had to go all the way back to the beginning."

And that was why they needed her.

"So all that other stuff you said you were trying to do was bullshit? The diversions and hitting satellite installations."

"There are spies," the bearded cleric said. "The Quondam have their Historics everywhere, even among your people. The true intentions needed to be guarded."

She would have punched him in the face right now if it wouldn't have hurt her more than it would hurt him. Even breathing was beginning to bring discomfort.

"Is that why there's lag?" she asked, even though she knew the answer. "That's why we were out of sync. Because you were copying that infinite algorithm?"

"Yes."

One mystery solved but now another emerged.

"Why not use them?" Harmony said. "The satellites. Reprogram them. Put them to good use."

"We follow the laws of scripture," the bearded cleric tagged back in.

"So there's no—" Harmony crashed against the pain. It hit her right then, tackling her thoughts, wrestling them to the ground . . . head-locking, bone-bending pain. The drugs for the stab wound in her abdomen were wearing off.

"There is no *what*?" the bald cleric asked.

She couldn't even remember. The pain hadn't just tackled that thought, it killed it, buried and gone. "Never mind."

Harmony turned away from the falling skies and sat against the balcony, the relief on her legs flowed up into her abdomen. She wanted more of that yellow drug but wouldn't ask them. No way she'd willingly allow the heads of the time-worshipping body to pump her full of their medicines. So she turned away from their judging looks, to the only pair of eyes not staring at her.

The Exegete had bent herself into a corner, knees locked up, back folding over, arms tying her altogether. She wasn't connected to Ether's voice and visor any longer, and she honestly appeared emptied out. Like she was an empty sock puppet without the hand running up her spine.

An empty little girl, appearing younger in that moment, eleven, maybe even ten years old.

"What's going to happen to the Exegete?" Harmony asked. "Ether said she'd die."

"It *is* to die," the bearded cleric said. "The highest form of sacrifice to Chronos—the Marble Moloch."

"No." Harmony shook her head. "Why?"

"Its death is honorable." *It*, he said. The bearded cleric licked his lips as he continued. "It desires this. As a vessel, it has been used. It is dirtied, and now it has no purpose. And no purpose is death."

No purpose is death. Harmony thought about that as she turned to *it*—to the Exegete. The girl shivered in the cold, whispering to herself, singing what seemed to be one of the church's ballads. Her eyes appeared overworked, moisture dried out and irises lit red. The Exegete's look was so empty, hollowed-out retinas and staring at nothing. Harmony pitied her and felt an urge to reach down and lift her to her feet. In fact, she was about to, but as if reading her mind, the bald cleric stepped forward.

"You were invited by the prophets to take part in the pilgrimage of descent."

"I'm neither pill nor grim," Harmony said, but the soft-core comedy confused her churchly audience. "That's no," she translated. "I'm not converting."

Convert—that was what they wanted. The Chronics had approached Harmony over the years, suggesting prayers for different successes, or invitations to pilgrimage. None had used the word *convert*, but it was implicit, written between the lines and the gaps of their lizard teeth. What they wanted was the Peacemaker's influence, especially among the gangs: the Islanders, the Red Bulls, the Rat Kingdom and all their Mickeys. These were the rebels who learned from Harmony's satellite hacking and fought their own wars against the Quondam. If the church had the Peacemaker, they would have them all. *A true peace.*

"The pilgrimage is an honor," the bald cleric said. "And not one to be taken lightly. There are things you do not yet know that will be revealed to you on the pilgrimage. Things that your very life depend on."

"There's assassins out there for me because I collaborated with you? Yeah, I know. I've heard."

"The church's protection in these matters could be helpful," the bald cleric said. "If you—"

"I'm not joining your church." Harmony said it with the edge of her voice. "Never. Never going on your pilgrimage. Never bowing to your time god. I mean, don't you know everything? The church, I mean. If you know the future, then you know it will never happen."

"We do not know everything," the bearded cleric said. "Our knowledge on future events is very, *very* limited. Limited to today, in fact. The single event that only the highest of clerics were allowed knowledge of. Beyond today we are blind. There's only one member of the church who is allowed to see the future in all its nakedness."

"And who's that?" Harmony asked. "Who gets to see the entire future? Ether?" She saw immediately that they weren't going to answer. "That's fine," she continued. "Just tell me why you would bring down the Quondam's satellites. Why did the church really split, huh? You've been their henchmen, their little finger puppets, for centuries? Why?"

"It is scripture," the bald cleric said. "And we cannot defy time."

She was tired of hearing that same time-worship bullshit, so *fucking* tired. Her frustration burrowed into the pouches beneath her eyes and wrinkled down, down through her cheeks, her whole expression giving way to that glower. And maybe they saw that. Maybe that was why they decided to give a real answer.

"There have been rifts between the Quondam and the church," the bearded cleric said softly—appeasing, seemingly aware of the thunderstorm bubbling behind her eyes. "*The Monk Who Stood* inspired defiance to the Quondam. They were reckless in the end, implying their own agenda against the laws of *the infinite*."

"What agenda?" Harmony said. "What were they trying to do?"

"Control," the bearded cleric said. "Their claim had been protection, safeguarding us from furthering their own technologies, their advancements, to rebuild our world. Technologies which would create . . ." A pause then, again licking his spongy lips. "They claim we were their wayward children. But their desires were control, control of their time and of ours."

"And they control us no longer," the bald cleric said. "And never will again."

The quiet took her. Like an envelope, Harmony folded in on herself. Eyes folding over ears folding over lips, and she was subconscious now, in the undertow of thought. An unfamiliar idea lured Harmony into her psyche, and one she had never met before: *What now?* What would she do now? The war had ended. An entire lifetime of running and fighting, and it was done. So fast. Too fast to steady herself. She had eaten, slept, and breathed this conflict; every conscious thought, daydream, and hallucination had been fixed on it. *No purpose is death,* the bald cleric had told her. *So what the fuck now?*

She turned to the vista behind her, not to look but to not be seen. And the clerics gave her her silence. Harmony was a crab then, a crab upside down, and her legs crawling at nothing. *No purpose.* She couldn't move. She couldn't feel the ground beneath her. And then it occurred to her that she and the Exegete were the same in that moment. They were two little fish finally chewing on the worms of their desires and discovering that jagged hook inside.

And on cue, she felt a biting pain on her abdomen, like a hundred digested hooks cutting her insides. The drugs were all but gone, and Harmony hunkered over on the ledge, staring down at the ground hundreds of meters below.

"I need your drugs," she finally said, giving in to the pain, giving in to them, *fuck,* asking a goddamn time worshipper for help.

"It will be brought forth immediately," the bald cleric said quickly, eager to please their Peacemaker. "But far more than those trifles, an endowment will be offered to you by the church. As in appreciation for the efforts and, as well, for your losses."

"Endowment?" Harmony asked. "What exactly?"

"Any gift," the bearded cleric explained.

"Any of your choosing," the bald cleric said. "Wealth, technology, a domicile among any of our territories. Anything within our power."

"But take time in your decision," the bearded cleric added. "It is of profound consequence."

"I've already made my decision," Harmony said.

"Your endowment?" she asked.

"Yes," Harmony said. "I know what I want."

"What is it?"

"Her," she said, gesturing to the Exegete. "I want the Exegete."

The Exegete didn't seem to hear them or bear any interest. She was barely even there, eyes glazed over, *glassy*, and sunken into the dawn sky. But Harmony saw something in the Exegete, something resembling herself, like empathy, *like* but not quite. Time worshippers had this saying: personas without purpose are mirrors without reflection. And there were mirrors in the Exegete's glassy eyes, sharing that purposeless life. But still not quite, because the Exegete was ready to die—she wanted it even. She didn't need Harmony to save her, and maybe that was the mirror. It was Harmony instead who needed the savior.

"It is to die," a younger cleric said after the ugly pause, startled, it seemed, that no one else had spoken up. He was the youngest among them by at least a decade, lost somewhere in his middle age. This younger cleric turned to the others, his voice pointed at them instead of her. "It has been used. Its vessel has been filled. It is unclean."

"I want the Exegete," Harmony said. "You said anything I desire. My endowment and all that shit, right?"

Another ugly pause, and this time the Exegete peered up at Harmony—not at but through. She had heard her, it seemed, but maybe wasn't listening. Empty eyes hung from the Exegete's face, dangling there like they might fall into her head.

"You will have her," the bearded cleric said.

"Your endowment," the bald cleric said.

"One more," Harmony said. "I want the supply of the drugs you gave to me. Enough until this heals. And transport to Bridgetown, with the battery power needed for a necromancer." She noticed a twinge in the bald cleric's eye. "War's over, right? Necromancy's no longer illegal."

"But it is," the bald cleric said. "And even more so now."

"Endowment, right? I *will* speak to a necromancer. I have to. I need to tell her that we won."

"Tell who?" the younger cleric asked.

"My mother. Aurora. The woman who raised me. She has the right to know."

"How long has she been dead?" the bald cleric asked.

"Ten years about," Harmony said. "Don't quite know the time."

"Well, you should make haste," the bearded cleric said, pointing to the bleeding horizon. "Your time is falling away."

Harmony looked toward the falling skies. She would have to make haste; the era of satellite voyeurism through time would vanish within the coming hours or days. But at least the devils were gone. The Quondam were extinct, just fossils now, bones in the dirt. And the war with the past, this centuries-long war of time, it was done.

ARÉS

Day 1

"Paxton V. Arés." She announces him to the crowd with all the gusto she can muster, raising her arms over her head and clapping, hopping nimbly on the tiptoe tilt of her high heels, but Frida mispronounces his name, and she does it again. "Arés," she says. "Give a warm welcome to First Lieutenant Arés." Though she doesn't seem to notice, caught up in the rapture of the moment, either that or it doesn't matter, nor does it matter to Paxton really. But in that moment, it does make him consider the diction of his family name. Memories of Ms. Milan, an English teacher of all things, or Sean, the barista at their local Coffee Bean. No one ever gets it quite right. They pronounce his name either like a god of war or like a plural to the word *air*. Even Callie, beautiful, gracious Callie, pronounces it wrong, and now with the old man on life support, who would teach little Ellie Arés her own name?

Thirty-some-odd engineers greet Paxton triumphantly. Like something was won or saved, like he's the lone survivor from a wreck or tragic accident. Applause populates the quiet lobby for the better part of a minute. A couple of them whistle, a couple of others hoot, and even a tear runs down the face of an engineer in the back. Their handshakes lock in firm, and so does the eye contact. They smile wide, exposing teeth or dentures, offering up conversations that expose even more. Their small talk is more novella than a short story, and Paxton learns names and nicknames and kids' favorite sports, but he returns very little in that regard. He's still an inmate deep down, and any adjustment to civilian life is a ways out. That defensive prison hunch still bends his posture inward, ready at any moment to coil into a ring of armor.

The pairs of men dressed in construction uniforms toward the back mostly ignore Paxton and the others as they point to the ceiling, which Paxton now notices isn't painted, with light fixtures yet to be installed. There is a newness to this space. The salty scent of concrete lies under the surface of a recently disinfectant-mopped floor. And those men speak some language that isn't English, and it doesn't sound like Spanish either, not that he knows Spanish, but he knows the sounds and rhythms of the language, and that isn't it.

He follows Frida down a corridor, tall and wide and lit like the stage on a theater, bold, proud lighting, without a single stain of shadow. Everything is new—the lights above, the paint, the laminated flooring—and even the signs on the wall sparkle with that fresh shrink-wrapped gleam. A sign on the wall reads DOMICILE with an arrow underneath, pointing in their direction, but while the No SMOKING, STAIRS, and RESTROOM signs are spelled in English, the smaller marker or penciled-in notes on the duct tape are in another language. The letters he recognizes, but not the words.

"We renovated the whole thing," Frida says proudly, seemingly catching Paxton zoning out. "Two hundred years old. We promised to keep it intact, the historical elements, and that got us seven figures off the asking price, plus tax rebates."

"What country are we in?" Paxton asks.

"Does it matter?" Frida says and watches him for a reaction, surveying the lines underneath his eyes and the crook in his brow. But Paxton shakes it off, the quick whip of the head saying no, it doesn't matter at all. Frida smiles at this and he smiles back, and everything is pleasant.

"Your room's down here," she says and leads him through the twist of the lock and then the doorway.

Paxton's room isn't much. There's a bed and a bedside table and lamp, a desk opposite the bed, and a Stoughton-brand exercise bike adjacent. A television, forty-five inches maybe, is fixed to the wall, and there is a window beside it that doesn't open. The bathroom is standard, toilet, shower, and sink. But all of it is a vast improvement to the chipping concrete wall and the literal steel shithole positioned next to his mattress in that black site.

They flew him out a week ago from an unknown prison at Point Loma. There was a single Androne attack on that base—an attack from the future. Frida attributes the hacked landrones and aerials that assaulted Loma to some sort of escape attempt. She believes someone from the future was trying to break Paxton out. But he didn't buy that theory. Loma was on one of the largest Androne military bases in the country, and the actual target was probably the cockpits and Androne pilots therein.

"You have the two sat channels," she says, touching the television. "You'll get live 49ers and the Celtics. That's it."

Paxton nods. He had mentioned to them that he was a fan of both franchises. But he had also mentioned hope for CNN and a local Oakland news channel. The answer to that was a definitive no. She has that same look now, that *no* in her eyes. And it makes him feel like a beggar again, like how the prison guards sneered at him and would talk about the *shit-scent* of his prison cell. *Shitty little traitor*, they called him. *And you won't shit straight for a week.*

"Then there's an app that streams movies and TV. Nothing live. Sorry. But a good selection. Should hold you in your free time. If there's a book you want to read . . ." She smiles with her offer. "We have everything. If we don't we can get it."

"No," he says. "Thank you."

"Not much of a reader?"

No, that's not it, but he shakes his head anyway. Paxton doesn't need to read. He doesn't need to know where he is either, what state or country, or even what fucking planet this is. She asks him if he's hungry or if he needs anything generally but again, *no*, he doesn't ask for anything. He won't—he can't. Because he's saving it, Paxton is saving that one ask, that one *beg* he needs to keep it locked up inside him until he finds the right moment to seize—to beg her.

"There's a Bible in the drawer," she says and shrugs. "Comes standard. I think I'll get you some Sam Butler, H. G. Wells, just to balance it out a bit."

"Thank you, Frida," Paxton says with sincerity. "I wouldn't be here without you."

"Paxton, you are quite naturally the most gifted Androne pilot there is. The pleasure is mine. And the answers are coming. All the questions you're not asking, we'll answer them together." Paxton nods his agreement. "And breakfast is seven fifteen sharp."

Frida steps out into the corridor. She shuts the door softly behind her, and the claps of her footsteps fade into the night. Paxton puts on a television series, one that reads: comedy. Background noise was always his accustomed melatonin, and he dozes off faster than the sitcom can plot its course.

———

Day 2

"Paxton."

"Callie?" he mumbles, and it sounds so much like her—just like her. But it's not her, it's not her voice nor her accent. It's that filter of the subconscious mind. And he hears now as the voice comes back at him again.

"Time's up," Frida says, leaning in the doorway, a keycard in her hand. "You overslept, Arés." Her pronunciation is wrong again, but not inconsistently wrong, like she is trying different versions of it.

"Sorry, ma'am," he grumbles from a scratchy throat.

"It's okay," she says, waving her arm for him to get up. "First day. It's time to get to work."

It *is* late. Paxton was supposed to meet Frida twenty minutes ago in the cafeteria. Not the best start if he's going to ask her for that allowance. He would have to make it up to her somehow, and he'd find it. Even at that moment, he remembers his posture. He straightens himself, keeping pace and staring ahead with vigilance.

"Good. Keep up," Frida says, pacing to make up time.

Frida leads Paxton through a corridor he hasn't been down before to a stairway just as unfamiliar, arriving at a room in the basement, one with high ceilings and large batteries singing a chorus of electric current. Reminiscent noises spider up his spine and Paxton slows down, moving to a point of slow motion—and everything appears to him in slow motion. Frida's footsteps decelerate, and a pair of engineers move in sluggish strides. And at the center of the room, glowing in the lights above, is a cockpit. It's shaped in that familiar egg-like form, cables like veins sprawling across the hull, and it hums with the power of a thousand batteries.

Paxton steps back as all the old cramps squeeze in around his hands and shoulders. That falling feeling pulls on his gut. *Fuck.* Frida had mentioned that she would like to see his expertise in the cockpit, but so soon? It all feels so sudden. Nine years, more than that, and still it's just way too soon.

The engineers are all there, too many for the limited space. Some orbit the cockpit, poking and prodding and examining the charts on their tablets. The superfluous ones just watch, their eyes on Paxton, childish excitement in their grins and chatter. "Joystick java," he hears at a whisper.

The cockpit is standard, the same as he used at Nellis Base nearly a decade earlier, but with a few new tricks that the engineers mention. There are facial scans for security readouts and a low-power mode for less battery consumption.

"Androne," Paxton says, doubting that he'd be piloting anything else. He is familiar with some quadrupedals, but he never excelled there.

"Androne," Frida confirms. "Kingsman Series for this first round if I'm not mistaken. I know we haven't told you a lot. And that's because we know very little ourselves. I was going to brief you at breakfast, but . . ."

"And I'm sorry about that."

"Forgiven," she says. "But you're going to be thrust into things today, and we will be analyzing your fight. The more you fight, the more we learn. It's really that simple. Just work off the rust. We all know it's been a while."

Paxton nods, a curiosity pushing him to ask more, but a tepid "Copy that" is all he manages to come up with.

They don't waste time. They drop him right in: suction the gloves onto his hands, locks on the pedals at his feet, and the straps on the visor are too tight, especially with all the unkempt hair on his head. The airtight seal clamps shut, and it's suddenly so dark. He's in a second prison now, locked away, behind the titanium Androne cell.

Then the spark, light like an avalanche, gouging into his eyes. So much fucking light that it dizzies him to a state of nausea. *"Shit,"* he hollers.

"Are we okay?" Frida's voice in his earpiece.

"Okay."

He emerges from that light but slowly, like it's not just in his eyes but in his mouth, like it's ringing in his ears, and the light is liquid, and he's soaked in it, dripping in light. But he does emerge, blinking his eyes dry, and Paxton finds himself in a forest of Andrones, hundreds of thousands of them, maybe more. Running together like a marathon for machines. And so his Kingsman runs with them. Lightning crashes down around them like thorns of voltage flashing without a single cloud above.

"The hell . . . ?" Paxton starts but remembers they are in his ear.

A sim, obviously, but what are they preparing him for? Emerging from the strikes of lightning are quadrupedals, but nothing like Paxton has seen before. Angry fucking things, like bears almost. The black metal of their bodies are blades in every direction; there isn't a part of them that isn't an edge.

One of the quadrupedals charges toward him, and he raises the Kingsman's rifle, but that thing is fucking fast. It tears through the Kingsman's rifle and throat in one swipe, then it tackles him, and it's fucking strong this thing, this bear of a war machine, stronger than it is fast. It tears into the chest plate, and it's over. The screen goes black and the fight's done.

"Fuck," he says.

"Watch the language on comms," Frida says into his earpiece. "Run it again. Let's go."

They run a few more simulations like that, and the results are the same: decapitation, dismembering, gutted of its spinal fluid, and on one instance the lightning strikes his Androne directly. But Paxton does work off some of the rust, and by the end he manages to get a shot or two in on the quadrupedal monster.

In the afternoon the simulations continue, and they must have increased the level of difficulty because . . . *shit*. It's an aerial barrage, a sim for shooting down clusters of aerial drones, aerials with wings of fire. And each time his Androne dies in an ASM attack (air-to-surface missile) or from falling debris, Frida's voice comes over the headset. "One more," she says, and "one more" leads to "one more" leads to one *fucking* more. Until it's late evening and nearly a thousand rounds have gone by. And Paxton's knuckles are worn down to the knotted-up nubs. And it's a thousand losses until she finally says, disappointed, "That's enough."

No. "One more," Paxton says. Not for her but for his ask. Thus far he has done nothing but disappoint, *nothing.* And there's a pattern in the aerial moment, a flanking maneuver, and the confusion of it is that their formation begins with a parallel attack, both of them side by side above him, but each time they end with that flank. Same move, every time. "One more," he says again, waiting for her response.

"Okay," Frida responds. "One more."

Paxton runs his Kingsman Series right into the middle of the aerial's line of sight, in essence flanking himself between them. And that throws them off. As they attempt to reposition themselves, he opens fire, picking off a limb or cracking a rudder, and they fire back, of course, their bullets biting away at his body armor. But piece by piece they take little slices out of each other until there's nothing left of any of them. Until the duo of aerials falls in flames, and so does his Androne. Simulated piles of ruin tumble to the dirt, and it blacks out.

"Two for one," she says as she opens the cockpit doors herself. "Getting your groove back?"

Frida reaches inside, helping Paxton out. He nearly asks what time it is—it feels late, but then he had woken up late this morning. He's not asking for anything, not even the time—especially the time.

"Getting back into it," he says. "But I can do better."

"This is good," she says. "Nine years. We're impressed."

He sees them standing, not just the engineers but others he hasn't met yet. They stand together, nodding and whispering in delight. In a different circumstance, a different world, a different time, he would ask more: Who are "we," and what are you "impressed" with? But again, he will get only one ask, and that ask is sacred. So he would be the dutiful soldier for as long as it takes, as reliable and silent as an Androne.

Paxton does have his guesses, though. Maybe the NSA wants him back on the front lines, but with a monitor like Frida over his shoulder. No more playing for the other side. Or maybe they're using him as a trainer of sorts. His strongest suspicion is that he's working on a black ops team; that feels like the most logical thing. Someone who already knows the dirty secret about the future, someone with no communication to the outside world, someone with the skill set in the cockpit, someone like him, doing the things that the regular military couldn't do to the future. Destroying infrastructure? Killing children? He won't ask, but he prays that it doesn't come to that.

———

Day 8

Paxton twists his personality a bit, just a bit, just one notch on the volume dial. He nods and smiles in the corridors. He makes small talk and compliments the engineers' sweaters. He makes sure he wakes up on time—*no*, fuck that, he wakes up early. He gets to the cockpit before Frida arrives, and she likes that. She compliments him, praising his work ethic and thanking him when he picks up the pen she drops or opens the door. And Paxton counts every penny of debt, every time he thinks they owe him. As small as it may be, he counts. One by one, saving it all up for a single big splurge.

But by the end of the first week, he may not have to. Paxton is making progress in the cockpit simulations, a lot of progress. He kills one of the quadrupedal "bears" but has to sacrifice his Androne to do it. The rust of nine years is shedding, and many of the engineers are shocked, one of them so much so that he weeps as Paxton exits the cockpit. He's an ancient man with ancient teeth and the only one who's always earlier than Paxton in the mornings.

"They love you," Frida says one evening, standing in the doorway of Paxton's room. "The engineers do. For the folks in Washington, though, you make things more complicated."

Don't ask, he tells himself. *What am I making more complicated?* And she puckers up as if ready to answer. "I'll try to make things less complicated," he says.

"No," she says. "Complicate things. Ruffle feathers. Most of those hawks want you back in a black site. I want you here. I want you here with me." She clears her throat and quickly recovers. "With us."

"Thanks," Paxton says. "Must be rough weather out. It's getting cold." He veers away from her conversation—*no*, he's swerving recklessly away from her, because her conversation is leading. Frida wants him to ask: *Meet who? Ruffle what feathers? Why the fuck am I here?* And the weight of not asking is bearing down on him, distracting him in his cockpit, waking him in his sleep. And it's in his face—curiosity drags his expression down.

This is my moment. It's here that he has to make his ask. He has to ask her now or else never. Or else Paxton might never get the chance to see them again.

"Frida, I don't mean to be direct, but . . ."

"Be direct," she says, and there's a knowing to her response, as if she thinks she knows what he's going to ask. And she might.

"I have a question that—"

"I'll show you," she says, eager with her response, like she's been holding it in for days. "Took you long enough."

She swings into the hall and leads him to a stairway, several flights deep. Then there's another corridor and another stairway, a deeper one. Nine flights down. Whatever Frida is going to show him, it isn't what he was going to ask her for in his room. Because the deeper they go the darker it gets. The staler the air, the colder the chill. Paxton gets a reminiscent curdling in his gut then, the same he'd gotten at Nellis Base nine years prior. That feeling like something horrifying is about to be revealed.

An elevator takes them down to a B9 level, and the elevator is like a refrigerator. Paxton hugs his chest and wishes he'd brought a jacket. "Man!" he says and sees the word blow white in the air.

"We won't be here long," Frida promises.

"B9," an automated voice informs them.

The doors open to a valley of computer hard drives, black and silver and at least two stories high. Yellow cables hum with electricity, the life-blood flowing between each machine. And this valley runs on forever, for as far as his squinted eyes can see. There's no end to it.

"Half a mile ahead," she says, noticing him squint. "Two miles back."

"What is it?" he says, and quickly answers his own question. "A computer network."

"Erewhon," she says. "Supercomputer. Finished building it around the time you got stuck in that black site."

"Nine years."

"Almost, but we don't use it now. It's defunct. Dead. Pulled the plug a long time ago. Now we just use its batteries to power the facility and your cockpit."

She strolls forward, appearing to admire the architecture of the dead computer, or pondering how wonderful it is to feed off its corpse. But Paxton doesn't want to explore this silicon valley. He wants to get back into that elevator and ride it all the way up. But he follows, keeping pace, just one step behind her.

"And all of this built down here," Paxton says. "Wow."

"They built it for the cold. These conductors ran hot. And even with the natural cold down here, they used to apply a helium isotope to cool them down near zero kelvins."

"Yeah, it's, uh . . . a really big computer," he says, figuring they have strolled far enough from the elevator now. Paxton slows down, losing pace. He's not enjoying the direction of this conversation.

"Not a computer," Frida says, leading again, leading him away and deeper into the cold. "It's more like an architect."

He doesn't want to know. Can't she see that? Whatever it is, whatever world-changing, history-altering discovery this computer is a part of, Paxton doesn't care.

"Maybe we should . . . head back up?"

"You don't want to know what it's for?" She pauses, leaning toward him, a secret on her lips that he doesn't want the answer to. "You know who we're fighting, the future, right? But we're not doing it for fun. We're there for a reason. A terrifying reason."

No more, he thinks, and he says it too. "No," Paxton says, shaking his head, but Frida is on a natural high, at an elevation where nothing else matters. She is in religious rapture, mid-sermon, and she stares right at him, right into his words and his shaking head, and she sees nothing.

"They need us," Frida proclaims. "Out in the future, they don't know it, but they need us. They fight and they scrap against us, but they need our help. This machine was creating a blueprint for us, for some of us, some idiots with bad ideas. But wiser minds took control, and we stopped it. We shut everything down. But . . . they found it. They found the blueprints to—"

"No," Paxton says louder now. "No, Frida. I don't . . . I just want a picture of them. And that's it. Callie and Ellie. Give me that, I'll do anything you want. Doesn't matter. But I don't need to know. I'm not that smart. Just point at the thing you want me to fight and I'll fight it."

At first she looks at him, almost like he's mad. Like she has all the secrets to the universe in her hand and he just turned her down, and for what? A picture of a woman in her thirties and a little girl? But then Frida smiles, the type of smile where lips are folded in, trying to hold back laughter. "Everything I said. Fate of the cosmos and all that, and that's all you want? Could've asked to be king, Paxton. Could have asked for the world. But yeah, sure. I'll get you a photo. Two, in fact. How's that?"

Paxton nods. "Thank you. I . . ." He stops himself from saying any more, before he gets choked up.

"Good," she says. "It's just one week. This is too much and too soon. Now let's get warm. It's freezing down here."

It's a long night and a longer few days as he waits for the photographs. It takes four days precisely, and Paxton counts, not the days even but the hours and minutes in between. And the photographs do eventually come. Frida keeps her promise and then some. Not one photo or two but three large laminated printed photos, high quality and high definition, every detail crystal clear and prominent. Photographs of Callie—she is maybe the most beautiful thing he has ever seen, and just *maybe*, because standing next to her is little Ellie Arés. *Oh God*, words cannot describe the absolute beauty of his child. His baby. He got everything he wanted and more, so much more. Paxton has it all.

PART II

The Infinite Men

7

Even with her injuries, Harmony had made preparations to leave the church's domiciles that same night. She knew a necromancer in Bridgetown, an ex-Audist and old friend, maybe the only friend she had left. She had gathered supplies, arranged transport, and attempted dialogue with the Exegete, the latter to no avail. And all this against the clerics' aggressive counsel. They opposed her leaving with her wounds and reminded her she'd never bear children because of it. But in the end, it was Harmony's own injury that defied her, pressing her against the bed, forcing drugs into her hands, down her throat. And side effects: dizziness, drowsiness, it kept her in bed for nearly half the day.

But Harmony wrestled against sleep, grappling and tussling her insides out. It was those drugs, sneaky little fuckers, mixing up day-dreams and nightmares, and she didn't know whether she was conscious or not. And Harmony dreamed big that afternoon, a dead Spartan on her back as she dragged it across a desert. A woman she couldn't remember, a woman without a face, speaking a language she didn't understand, told her that she was loved. But as real as it felt, it was more like a memory than a dream. The woman who raised her didn't speak like that or carry herself in that way. And it was that twist, that inconsistency in memory, that woke her up.

The day never ended, at least it felt like it, endless hours of liquids, IVs, and resuscitation. And twenty-four hours after the Day of Descent she felt strong enough, *barely*, to climb to her feet. And she did, but hungover on that cocktail of panaceas, the climb was arduous. She attempted and failed to rise off the fur-filled mattress. The floor was a sponge for her gait, and each step sank inward, nearly absorbing her completely, but she zigged on that zagging path to the circular window adjacent to the bed.

The sky was clearing, no smoke, no fire-tailed satellites swooping out of the sky, just the brown cumulus smudging the sunlight, offering shade to the monks about outside. If all the satellites had fallen, Harmony may have missed her window. *Fuck this place—this prison.* And they would keep her in their prison, *wouldn't they?* Feeding her their poisons and calling it medicine. They wanted her on that pilgrimage. They wanted her to convert. The Peacemaker, just another pretty prize to parade on the road of descent. *Fuck that.* And on top of all this, she had heard them hissing about her need for a necromancer, the ridicule in their tone aggressively obvious. They weren't letting her out.

Water, dried meat, and warm clothes—these were the essentials. The painkillers and other medicinal sweets weren't essential, but she carried them nonetheless. Harmony shoveled all of it into the blanket from her bed, which she'd folded into a makeshift knapsack. Now she just needed a mule, someone with strong shoulders, someone trained from birth to have a fit, pure body, trained like a circus dancer. She had planned to bring the Exegete from the beginning; otherwise the church would sanction her murder the moment Harmony left.

Harmony waited for nightfall, but it was a particularly cold night. The winds squeezed into the stone ventilation and moved through the halls. She tiptoed between vacant rooms and empty corridors with the knapsack in tow. It felt like a hundred pounds, swelling heavier with each step. She couldn't do it. Her stitches stretched like rubber bands straining and ready to snap, and soon she would split in half. She had to slow her pace, she had to come off her tiptoes, loosen up her core muscles, and drag the knapsack across the floor, panting like a dog the entire way. Harmony had abandoned stealth, and halfway hoped, *only halfway*, that they would catch her. Chronic nurses dragging her back to the bed and feeding her yellow drugs. And she would pretend to resist, kick her feet maybe, twist her head away from their spoons, but half of her wanted that, and fortunately the other half of her kept moving.

She took only a few minutes to arrive at the Exegete's room. The child kneeled by the window, head pressed against the ground and worshipping a knuckle-size marble, the "gray god" they called it, or the Marble Moloch, or Chronos. It was an idol representing the time god.

Harmony had learned from the clerics that Exegetes were almost human versions of Androners. Per their religious text, Exegetes could only be female. Their perceived passivity allowed for the control of their bodies, much in the way the church thought about Androners. Virgins only, and once possessed by a "spirit" from the past or future, she became "unclean" and served no other purpose within the religion. She would be dead by now if it hadn't been for Harmony, and she wanted that. The Exegete was ready to die.

"We need to talk," Harmony said, but that was not what she meant and quickly corrected herself. "I need you to talk to me."

She didn't. The Exegete looked at Harmony somewhere between confusion and outright detachment, and there was fear there too, a childish, sheepish recoiling as if Harmony might strike her.

"I need you to carry these," Harmony said, lifting the knapsack. "And we're leaving. We're leaving now."

The Exegete looked at the blanket folded into a makeshift knapsack with all the coldness of the cottonmouths and rattlesnakes that stalked outside. She appeared more likely to bite the thing than pick it up.

Just holding out the knapsack burned at Harmony's insides and she buckled over, hands on her knees as the pack cracked against the floor. *Goddamn it*, something broke.

"What the fuck did they do to you?" Harmony asked. "What are you thinking?"

She wasn't thinking. The Exegete was a person of faith, *right?* Old traditions, old beliefs. And even squinting through the pain throbbing at her gut, Harmony could see that the Exegete's only urge was to turn back to that marble idol and continue her worship.

"It is written," Harmony said. "It is scripture that you follow me to Bridgetown. This is your path."

The Exegete watched Harmony for a moment, unconvinced but listening. Harmony had her attention now, or intrigue at least, but she had something, and she had to keep talking.

"Why else . . . Grand . . . Exegete . . ." Harmony searched for the right words. "It is not by coincidence that the Peacemaker and the Grand Exegete were bonded together. Why else would clerical leadership endow me with your . . . magnificence?" It nearly sounded like Harmony was asking. Her vocabulary had suddenly become filled with the time worshipper's verbs, archaic language, and sentence structure. Even her pronunciation seemed to bend to a degree, with clearer tone of voice, enunciation, and longer, deeper pauses between her words. And all of it subconscious, like slipping into another person's accent or dialect. "There is much work yet to do . . . young Exegete."

And it was working. The Exegete leaned forward and lifted the bag. She turned back to her idol, reaching for it, but with hesitation.

"Take it." Harmony said it fast, rediscovering her old, profane lexicon faster than she'd lost it. "We gotta fucking go now."

But the Exegete left the idol behind. *Why?* Harmony didn't have the strength to care. She followed behind the girl, her left hand a crutch against the wall as they moved toward the stairway. Immediately the duo passed one of the grand guards, almost on the first step down, but the man just bowed, head to the ground and no eye contact. Harmony wasn't sure if he bowed to her or the Exegete. Probably both. It didn't matter, and she stopped her sneaking after that. She found an abandoned exit, reeking of decay and neglect, and they continued out into the ice desert easy enough. The wind, albeit cold, was at their backs, and their loose-fitting garb breathed like human sails, urging their footsteps forward, keeping them on pace toward the river township of

Bridgetown. Each of them carried their own weight, the Exegete with the knapsack and Harmony with her wound and her splitting stitches.

In the end, it was Harmony's weight that brought them to a standstill at an intersection of bark and stone that offered some shelter from the winds. And it was the Exegete who would have to tend to her, tying those stitches back into place. Then more drugs and more of their side effects, and Harmony would have to wait for the sunlight and morning warmth. The Exegete fed her via spoon, like Harmony's mother once had. It felt like that, like she had returned to a childlike state. Harmony was now as dependent on the Exegete to carry her the rest of the way as she had been on her Spartan so many, many years earlier.

8

They arrived the subsequent evening. The Bridgetown slums were built up along the river, where neon lighting lit the rusted metal blocks like gold teeth. It was the dirtiest of artificial lights, rotting neon shimmering against the waterway. Shops, parlors, homes, one forced atop the other like incongruous puzzle pieces compelled to fit. These corroded metal slices hung over the yellowed water, dangling and threatening to fall. But it was the river that powered the shantytown. That gave it its lights, its shine, the thermal heat that warmed the winters. And the population swarmed at night, teeming like termites for fluorescence, feeding on the neon. And soon they would glow too, in the nocturnal city and capital of necromancy.

Harmony couldn't remember making her way across the town's bridge, the city's namesake. The three-thousand-foot-long bridge was the largest structure for miles. The pillars reached upward beyond the treetops, its three fingers stretched into a trident design. That trident was the symbol of this township. What she did remember was moving through the Bridgetown streets on a drug high, seeing that mob again, as clear as day, but in the neon night. And she woke up in a small, warm room, with the Exegete slouching next to her on a cot.

"Where is he?" The words fumbled out, but Harmony quickly recovered. "Am I here—where?" And that would have to do.

Her eyes were already wandering across the matted wool insulation on the ceiling and walls, fruit flies spinning their wings around the single bulb pulsing above her. That heartbeat of light pulsed on occasion and buzzed, suggesting an imminent short-circuiting. The shine lit the Exegete's bruised legs and the blisters on the girl's arms. She went through hell carrying Harmony all this way. Harmony thought to say something, but the Exegete was already slipping off to sleep. An autopsy of Androne parts cluttered about the room, torsos opened up to expose the wires and spinal fuels inside. And heads, so many heads—Andrones, quadrupedals, even a Fury head or two all crashed together in the corner.

"Pony," an older male voice said. And a familiar one. An accent in broken Javan. "Pony girl."

She smiled. Harmony had forgotten that funny nickname, *Pony*, and maybe not forgotten but misplaced it in the clutter of everything else life had thrown at her. Her childhood memories of this place were as disjointed as the drone parts piled about the space. She'd gotten the nickname because she was so gangly thin in her adolescence, the word *pony* a substitute for *bony*. And she had called him Busta as a youth, after the Quondam Era poet, but also partly because of her adolescent mispronunciation. His name was Bussa, her necromancer.

"Again and again," Bussa said, the old Bridgetown traditional greeting.

"Again and again," Harmony replied. "Again and till the end."

Bussa stepped into the light, and there in a shower of pulsing fluorescence, he appeared as if in halves. His hairline was a dust bowl of peeling scalp. He had lost his muscle, loose skin draping narrow arms. And his smile . . . He had lost some of his teeth, the remainder yellowed and loose. But still he smiled, smiling, what looked like to her, a sad smile. Time had ravaged her old friend, and a small part of her preferred to have never seen him this way. In her memory he would have remained that sturdy middle-aged magician of necromancy.

"Who is the child?" he asked, his accent still strong. "Little girl there or little boy."

"Somebody from the church," she said, thinking it better not to get into the Exegete of things. "Long story."

"Long story, eh?" he said and nodded and pointed up. "This your doing? Or you was involved, some way, some fashion?"

"Was what my doing?" she asked.

"You ain't know or you can't see?" Bussa said, pointing with both hands now, up at the ceiling and beyond. "Ain't it all coming down. Hive of Heaven. The whole network. You ain't playing around up there?"

Harmony said nothing. Not having the strength to deny it, nor the energy to admit. But one look and he saw the culpability in her abating blinks.

"Huh," he said in a huff of frustration. "Running around kicking over things you ain't even know."

"I put you into early retirement," she said with a spit of sarcasm. "You should be thankful."

Necromancers relied on the hacking of satellites for their profession. Harmony and the church had put them all into an unwilling retirement.

"Retirement," he said and shook his head like he did when she was little. "That ain't what concerns me."

"No?"

He stepped closer. He stood over Harmony's makeshift bed, getting a better look at her; then the old man laughed without smiling. "You does kick down walls and don't even know what living on the other side."

"Freedom," she said. "Freedom from the Quondam. The war's over."

"No, it ain't either," he said, checking on the IV hanging over her, an IV she hadn't even noticed until now. "There's something else. Always something else."

"Something else," she interrupted him. "What else?"

"Just rumor," he said, his eyes falling from the IV to meet her gaze. "Just whispers is all."

"Saying what?"

"Is what I said. Them got something else out there. Chronics, all them marble worshippers ready to go pilgrimaging, long-legged marching to it. But it ain't my place."

Many necromancers were commonly ex-Audist and therefore had that apocalyptic foreboding in their nature. The next great threat, the coming dusk and the fall of humankind, or Bussa's *new weapon* out there somewhere, it was just a part of their language. Grand pessimism was a dialect for them, and Harmony had learned to ignore Bussa's grandiose, apocalyptic rants.

"New weapon," she jeered. "What was it last time? Killer bees, prophesied in the Wu-Tang Ballads?"

"You taunt?" he said as he placed his hand against her forehead. "Look, rest your head. You running around in all that cold with your belly damn cut open."

"How'd you find us?" Harmony asked, taking his advice and sinking back into the pillow.

"I ain't find you," he said and pointed to the Exegete. "Your church friend come a-knocking."

"Who?" Harmony asked, even as she pointed to the Exegete. "She found you?"

"Come straight to me," he said as he tilted his head and aimed the point of his nose at the Exegete. "Calling my name from outside."

But Harmony had never told the Exegete Bussa's name, or did she? Maybe something she mentioned in a fevered dream the night before. Harmony turned to the young Exegete slumped on the end of the cot, her eyes failing to stay open. She did her part, and she did it well, without complaint or asking for anything in return. She deserved her rest.

"Why you here, Pony?" Bussa asked. "Why you really here?"

"Because I need to speak to her," Harmony said, a deep exhale after, finally getting it out. "She has the right to hear what happens, you know that."

"You know what they say about talking to the dead," Bussa said, leading, but she wouldn't follow.

"I don't," she said. "And I don't need you playing on your words. Please. I need to speak to Aurora."

"You seen the skies last coupla' days, girly?"

"Yeah. Exactly why I need to talk to her now. Before there's no chance to go back."

"Let me explain, little Pony. If there's no hive in heaven, then I got no honey."

She cringed at the play on words. It was his thing, old man wit, but she recovered quickly and forced out a smile. "Well, let me explain what I know about you. You're not the average necromancer," she complimented. "Not even the best of the Audist can touch you."

"That *is* true," he said and blushed a brown-skinned blush. "But I ain't no magician neither." Bussa waved his finger like a wand, aiming it at the sky. "There ain't nothing to rebound up there."

"That's why I'm here and not holding four rings praying to Audi. If anybody can find a click, *Busta*, it's you," Harmony said, adding her childhood nickname for him for good measure.

He would try. She knew that. Bussa's pride was a science onto its own, and Harmony had studied it for years. But his pride wasn't just arrogance—there was a genius to him, and he had taught her much of what she knew and with enough left over to keep some secrets for himself. Of course, she had hacked further back, centuries further than the years and decades that necromancy required. But now their careers would end together, fading into the dark as the Hive of Heaven fell.

Bussa grabbed a gray box from under a shelf. He glanced at it but shook his head like it was the wrong box. He grabbed a second box, an older one, one so brimming with files that the top didn't stay on. He rifled through these papers, thousands of them, and this took some time. So much time in fact that Harmony began slipping back under the influence of the drugs. Lucid, she buoyed in the bed, both subconscious and awake at moments, but sinking slowly down.

"I can't even remember," he said, arms halfway into the box now. "Did you have another session?"

She snapped back, awake and alert, but not quite sure what Bussa had said. Harmony lifted herself up and leaned forward. Just a pinch of pain then, nothing unbearable, so she leaned farther and found Bussa now knee-deep in boxes and files.

"A session?" Harmony asked. "You're talking about a session with Aurora?"

"Yes."

Necromancy sessions were twofold, of course. Any window opened in the past would have to have another opening in the future. Therefore the sessions Aurora had opened when Harmony was a child or teen would be connected to one here as an adult. And Harmony had attended sessions in the immediate weeks and months after Aurora's death, speaking to a younger version of the woman who raised her. It was a way of grieving. But there were only seven or eight sessions at most; if Aurora had made a ninth session in the past, then a window would exist here in the present.

"Was there another?" she asked. "How many left?"

"Wait," he said, scrutinizing one particular pair of papers, squinting through his one bad eye.

"Bussa?"

"One," he said, and he said it to himself, surprise in his tone and gawking, loose-jawed expression.

"You found one?"

"There's one session left," Bussa said. He had so many clients he would barely remember how many sessions remained from one to another, but with the satellites falling, even one session remaining would seem impossible. "That's not . . . *right?*"

"One session left. Like I said, you'd find a way." The words sprinted out of her and barely in grammatical order.

"Huh?" he replied, his ears barely keeping pace. "Yes. That's what it says. One." And he reread it another few times.

"And the window time?" Harmony said, leaning all the way forward, all the way into the pain. "When?"

"A few hours," he said, still to himself, still confused. "A few hours from now."

"Good," Harmony said and lay back. "Wake me as soon as you find the signal."

9

Bussa found a signal on an island of sky to the east. Atmospheric pressures and mountain waves had whipped a satellite in circles, a draining motion like water down a sink. It hung there, he said, like that old star for their old god. Harmony didn't know much about any old stars or old gods, and she had heard so many of Bussa's Quondam Era folktales. He told old stories about even older times when she was a little girl, and with all her innocence, she believed them.

Bussa had befriended the woman who had raised Harmony. *Old friends*, they called it, and a young Harmony knew no better. She believed that too. That innocence was her childlike faith, on par with any church's believers. *Friends*. The duo never held hands nor embraced in Harmony's company, and maybe they never did those things outside her company either. But they did sleep in the same bed, and to a young Harmony and her childlike faith, that was just what friends did.

What Harmony wondered about now wasn't whether there had been intimacy between them—the engines to their aging bodies were likely wrinkled, fickle things and easily broken. And the relationship didn't last the length of a year. What Harmony wondered about at times like this was whether Aurora's relationship with Bussa was strategic. He had been the best necromancer in the region—on the continent, he would say. Harmony had learned everything from him before she began teaching herself. *So what were the odds?* What was the likely ratio between serendipity and strategy?

She watched the old man now, tapping away on his keyboard, adjusting antennae quickly yet delicately. His ancient hands bending nimbly around the circuits and their wiring. "Still the best, Pony girl." His innocence made her smile even now, even steeped in her discomfort of losing everyone. Bussa's innocence was that he never knew what that relationship was. Aurora was raising the Peacemaker, and she would do anything to build Harmony into that eventuality. To Aurora he was just the chalk and limestone in the foundation of her destiny.

"We'll lose the window in ten minutes," Bussa said as he scrambled about his own domicile like it was foreign country, like the lights were off and he couldn't find anything and collided with everything else. "It'll be a short session," he warned her. "Very short."

But even a short session would be too long. She hadn't spoken to Aurora via necromancy for years, not since her collaboration with the Church of Time first began. Her mother had warned her against it. *You are a disappointment to your name*, her mother had said, among other famous quotes, like, *You'll never make it out of the church alive. You will die there.* But it was her mother who ended up dying, sick and rotting with only Gemini at her side. So the anticipation of speaking to her mother now, after so long, *God,* it boiled her heartbeat to bubbling palpitations in her chest.

"Okay," Bussa said, so stridently that he woke the Exegete. "We ready."

He dragged the chair toward Harmony. A thick mahogany throne shaped like an armchair but made nearly large enough to fit an Androne. Red, green, and purple cables grapevined around the legs, then up the arms. Old cables, peeling cables, exposing the wiring underneath. At the crest of the chair was an Androne head, nailed and wired in place. And a *fucking* Spartan head at that. Bussa didn't do it on purpose, of course, *how could he know?* For him, it was the Spartan's single eye that made a simpler optical input for image capture. For her, though, it was like watching a decapitated family member staring back at her with its single eye. But this rusted skull wasn't her Spartan anyway; hers was stolen from her a long time ago.

"Lights out," Bussa said as he flipped a switch.

And right then, midsentence, everything went black as two faint beams of light flashed on. One beam shone on Harmony, a halo of green light wrapped around her face. The second beam of light was from a projector, its sputtering spotlight dancing against the wall. And right there in that projection was the woman who raised her, Aurora, alive and still ten years dead, now staring back at Harmony.

She suddenly felt her face swelling up like every old allergy was returning all at once. But Harmony recovered. She tightened all her facial flexors that had no names, the ones in her lips, the ones behind her eyes. Everything was straightened and smoothed. She became a stone effigy. None of the names of her dead pilots, none of the stitches in her wound, nothing resembling emotion would slip out.

Necromancy was, for most, a way to cope with death and the grief thereafter. But using Quondam drones and satellite technology to speak to loved ones' future and past was deemed irreligious by Chronics and Hysterics alike. It *dirtied the holy instruments of time*, or so the church would say. But with all the satellites falling or fallen out of the sky, there were no more instruments. Only time. Harmony had, in a sense, retired the entire profession of necromancy, a thousand time laborers now idling away their time.

"Aurora," Harmony said in a sharp rise of her voice, hoping to penetrate the interference on screen, and there was a lot of it. "Aurora?"

Her mother leaned in. Her lips moved, but there was no sound. The image spasmed, and her expression froze on screen, a sadness there, and the image holding on her mid-blink as if she had died again. Harmony had seen that look once or twice but was too young to put a word to it. *Loneliness.* Aurora's expression was a vast landscape, open and empty, without a soul for miles.

"Aurora?" Harmony said louder, leaning forward. "Can you hear me?"

The image reanimated and froze again, and back and forth, a game of capture and release.

"Now I remember this," Bussa mumbled from his corner as he fiddled with the knobs and switches. "All that interference, I remember that, wondering why I—future me—wouldn't be able to stabilize the signal." He chuckled. "If I only knew. It was little Pony that ended everything."

An adolescent Harmony was never allowed in the room with Aurora, though she had always wanted to see her older self. But now she was glad that neither Bussa nor Aurora had ever bent to the childish request, allowing her to see this middle-aged catastrophe. They would send the adolescent girl to sit in a corridor of propaganda posters promoting necromancy. And once Bussa finished setting up, he would join Harmony in the corridor and tell her another story, giving Aurora and future Harmony their privacy.

Static, sudden and all-consuming, cracked the image with white noise. The projected image slid down and popped up against the wall and began to blink out.

"We won," Harmony blurted out, leaning forward to get her voice closer—louder. "We won! We won the war." She screamed it, and her wound cut at the stretching of her diaphragm. "We brought down the satellites. The Quondam are gone. We ended the war!" Harmony shouted across the void. The image seesawed across the wall, capsizing both the image and her voice.

"What?" Aurora said with a mouthful of interference, and the voice skipped, a stone across the digital pond, "what . . . what . . . *what* . . ."

"We . . ." Harmony's voice shrank. She hadn't heard that voice in a decade. Bittersweet as it was, Harmony wasn't sure which emotion moved her, the bitter or the sweet. "We ended the war, Aurora. We beat the Quondam. The satellites are falling."

Aurora's side went quiet again, but this time without the static, without haze, and all that techno-glaucoma receded. The projector was as clear as a window, and her voice clearer. Just for a moment, there wasn't a barrier between them beside time.

"What did you do?" Aurora said. The surprise in her voice was perfectly audible. Her tone, the emphasis on the words, all so clear. "*What did you do, Harmony?*"

Harmony's lips hovered open without words, without the thought of retort. She was a child again, an infant, and still shrinking into herself, hunching her back, knees bending in, fetal and diminishing all the way back to infancy. Aurora was as mad as the devil. Harmony knew that for a fact. She knew every bend and curve of that woman's look. As a girl it frightened Harmony, but now, nearly forty years old, it terrified her, because that face was hers. Harmony had those bends and wrinkly curves in her own fits of rage.

"What do you mean? I . . . I ended the war. I locked the Quondam out of this time."

"How?" her mother snapped. "How did Gemini let this happen?"

"Gemini?" Harmony snapped back. *Why the fuck was she talking like this?* "*I* freed us. I sent them back to their time. Me."

"You did what they wanted you to do." Her mother's image skipped ahead a couple of seconds, her frustration deepening. "It's all wrong. It's. All. Wrong."

"How?"

"The Quondam were here to stop all of it," Aurora said.

"Stop what?"

"That's why they're here. That's the reason for the whole war."

Aurora's lips moved again, but the audio had dropped out. And whatever she was saying, she said it with every square inch of her face.

"What's she saying?" Harmony asked, leaning in.

". . . Ask him, the Archivist of Timothies, ask him for it . . ." Aurora's voice came, then dropped out.

"Timothies?" Harmony said. An old name, but one that she certainly hadn't forgotten. A name that had stolen from her, and she had promised to pay him back in blood. "What about Timothies?"

But the static kept buzzing. The signal wasn't going to last. ". . . the Infinite Men . . . ," Aurora said, but her voice dropped out in another buzz of static interference. ". . . them in the Yellow City, around Serpent's Whim . . ." The image started to blink right then. This was it. The conversation ended here. ". . . do not walk the pilgrimage . . ."

And then it all went white as the lights in the room flashed back. The projector's image disappeared. The Spartan's single eye darkened and died. And all the rattle and buzz from the batteries fizzed out, hissing the stink of burned metal into the air.

"What happened?" Harmony said, but out of reflex; it was obvious that the signal had gone. "Did you get what she said? Something about the Archivist of Timothies and Infinite Men . . ."

"I know she said something about the Infinite Men," Bussa said. "A crazy group, them is. You ain't wanna be approaching them."

"What did she mean?" Harmony said it to herself at first. "The Quondam were stopping it. Stopping what?"

But when she turned to Bussa, his head twisted toward the door behind them. He leered at the metal entrance like it was moving, or something was moving behind it. Then Harmony heard it too—*foot-steps*, and more than two of them.

"Somebody's here," Bussa said, turning to Harmony but pointing at the Exegete. "You sure about her?"

She wasn't. Harmony wasn't sure about anything and no one now, not even herself. Did she even do the right thing ending the war? "I don't know."

"Quiet," he said and hushed her. "They're coming."

No, Harmony thought, eyeing the shadows gathering in that slit beneath the doorway. *They're already outside.*

10

"Harmony?" the voice called out, and at first she didn't recognize it. That was the thickness of Bussa's brick and metal barrier, not just impenetrable to breaches but also a filter for all the noise on the Bridgetown streets. But the voice came again, this time with the full brunt of its vocal weight. "Harmony of Siren?"

"Port Siren," a second voice said, this one feminine, and one that she did recognize. *Gemini?*

"Port Siren," the first voice said. "Harmony of Port Siren."

"Emit," Harmony said as she thought it. *They are alive.* "Open the door."

Bussa was crouched behind the sandbags, gripping a long rifle with anti-kickback mechanisms, a weapon that would probably put a hole in an Androne. He didn't turn to Harmony, but he heard her and shook his head in disagreement.

"No, Pony."

"I know them," she said. "And I'm sure about them. I trust them like I trust you."

The old man paused, and Harmony knew she had him convinced. The rifle weighed heavy on his arm, and he adjusted and twisted himself into loops of military posture. *Yeah*, she had him.

"You really gonna end me, you know," he said, lowering the rifle, then deciding no, he's going to hold on to it.

Bussa took his time moving to the door, tiptoeing almost, like he didn't want them to know he was coming. He unbolted the locks, nearly ten of them. Then he eased the metal entrance open just a sliver—just enough for Harmony to see through to the other side.

And in that sliver of light, Emit hunched, hugging a cloak tight to his chest and shivering in the dark. Gemini stood behind him, lips moving but no words coming out, in conversation with herself, but that was normal. She held her cloak tight over her shoulders. They stood still, shaking in a trance, and shaking in rhythm. That was a symptom not just of the cold but of companionship. They had been traveling together for some time, their movement now halfway in sync.

"Harm?" Emit said, leaning into the cut of the light. He likely only saw the black of her silhouette in that crack in the door.

"They alone?" Bussa asked from his post behind the door.

"Just them," she said, and she said it with a sort of regret. *Just them.* Then she gestured for him to open the door completely and let them in.

The gap in the door did widen, but just enough for Emit's broad shoulders to squeeze through. He stumbled inside, a crown of crusted blood on his hairline immediately visible. He limped inside, and limping on both legs, the discomfort obvious in the grit of his incisors.

"Tomorrow and tomorrow," Emit said, turning as Bussa closed the door behind Gemini.

"To . . . what?" Bussa said, his head shaking in confusion.

"Tomorrow and tomorrow . . ." Emit considered, then turned to Harmony.

"He means again and again," Harmony said.

Emit turned to Bussa, seemingly ready to recite the correct phrasing, but immediately found himself caught in Harmony's embrace. The hug was reflexive, an uncontrolled bound of her limbs wrapping around his. She squeezed tight, and he squeezed tighter, pulling her deeper into his chest, but Harmony pushed back. *That was too close*, she felt as she untangled herself from him. There had always been this suspicious affection from Emit, an aberrant intimacy that she didn't want. His zeal, his warmth, it burned too brightly at times, an uncomfortable burn. She had known Emit since adolescence—and earlier, if glances from afar are knowings. And if Bussa were Harmony's uncle, then Emit was a cousin or even brother on the other side of the family.

"Can't believe you're okay," he said, eyes welling up, a hard sniffle sucking any tears back in. "I thought . . . thought the worst thoughts." He turned to Gemini then. "You were right."

"I know," Gemini said, without a hint of conceit.

"Right about what?" Harmony asked.

"She said if you were anywhere, you were here," Emit said. "God, it's good to see you." And he leaned toward her again, engulfing her in that discomforting warmth, his chin on her head, squeezing her into him. "We thought the worst. And with all this talk about assassins . . . thank God you're safe."

And she had thought the worst. And there was a warmth in her too. A bubbling joyfulness to see them both. Maybe she misread him. Maybe his body language was a foreign vocabulary and she was illiterate to him. And he was dyslexic to her. And all these limbs and holds were misinterpretations. But still Harmony pulled away preemptively nonetheless and turned to Gemini. But Gemini's expression spurned any fantasy she might have of hugging her. She was like Harmony's mother in that way, not much for physical affection—any affection at all, really.

"Good to see you," Harmony said to Gemini with warm words instead, very aware of Gemini's phobia to touch. "Good to see you both. Where are the others?"

There were no others. No Wren. No Elijah. No one. It was written on their faces with blood, their evasive eyes, and the dead silence. That quiet lingered for the entire night. Emit and Gemini dried themselves and huddled around the fire. Emit thought to speak, lips rearing with words, but Harmony avoided his look, even as he stalked her eyes, always loitering there in the corner of her vision. But she needed the quiet now. She needed her rest.

It stayed like this for most of the night, except for the simple asks: some water, a blanket. They fell asleep quickly after that—just minutes in front of the fire and both Emit and Gemini were snuffed out, sniffling and snoring as if in competition.

"Thank you, Bussa," Harmony said, noticing his eye sink ever slower into its blink.

"It was nice seeing you too, Pony," he said.

"Even better seeing you," she said and squeezed on every word, knowing now that these moments together with family were precious. "Truly, good seeing you."

And her voice cracked, but he didn't hear as he drifted toward the deep end of sleep. This might be the last time she would ever see him, the old crag with the face of an uncle.

Harmony was left alone in the dark and the quiet, and still she couldn't sleep, not with all the noise in her head. That fracas with her mother still played on a loop in her mind. She had a way of getting into Harmony's head, and it was all sort of like hacking, the way Aurora found the back doors or picked the locks of Harmony's mind. Even in Harmony's greatest success—ending the occupation, living up to the name *Peacemaker*, ending the fucking war—Aurora still found a way to make it all wrong.

It's all wrong, her mother had said.

She couldn't remember everything her mother had told her. There were too many feelings stuck to the concrete details to sift through. But at the head of it, Aurora seemed to be saying that the Quondam's war had a purpose. That there was a reason why they were occupying the present. *They were trying to stop it.* Those were the words Harmony remembered. *But stop what?*

The Archivist of Timothies had something, information, connections, something. Aurora had mentioned him too. That snake, that makeup-smeared motherfucker, had stolen the most important thing she had, her Androne, and he had killed one of her people in the process. Harmony's vengeance on him was a long time coming, so this was good. Two birds, one fucking stone. The Timothies' palace in the Yellow City wasn't too far away either. Two days' trek through Serpent's Whim. Maybe three in the rain. And maybe four with her wound?

The bigger question was whether they would follow her. Look at them, lying asleep, babies innocent to her scheming. She would need them, if she were to go to the Yellow City. But they had already sacrificed so much and gained nothing. She didn't deserve that type of loyalty anymore. They were a band of rebels fighting against the Quondam. But the Quondam were gone now, and what were rebels without an authority? Gemini might follow for a time, but not long, not without a purpose.

A part of Harmony, a large part of her, considered leaving, right there and in that moment. It was the only thought that made sense. She had nothing for them anymore. She could leave. Harmony was alone now, at least in the conscious sense, and no one would stop her. But the Exegete was there in that conscious space too, watching from the corner, and Harmony needed to rest as much as any of them. Tomorrow would bring the long march toward the Yellow City, and it was always a treacherous one, especially if there truly was an assassin in pursuit.

11

Just an hour of sleep and the words woke her up again. *It's all wrong.*
Her mother's voice, but there were others too: Elijah, Kai, the Mickeys,
Pregnant Jay. They were all there, all those dead voices peeling off the
walls of her head. She wouldn't fall asleep again, at least not without
the painkillers. And even if Harmony fell asleep now, she wouldn't wake
up before the others. Those painkillers were like weights tied to her feet
and would drag her to the bottom of her subconscious. She would be
the very last to wake up, and she didn't want them to see what she had
to do.

So Harmony just didn't sleep. She snuck out in between the hum
of batteries and the avalanche of river water outside. Gemini's body
seemed to twist toward the door as Harmony slipped outside. But
maybe it was nothing, because Gemini didn't follow, and Harmony
never looked back.

Early mornings in Bridgetown were eerie sights. The people were
like moths, addicts for a glint of any artificial light. These weren't the
denizens of Bridgetown nightlife, the bars and music; these were the
inhabitants of the deep night, insomniac predators or nocturnal prey,
and at those depths, they appeared like people that moved sideways.
They didn't walk but slithered like wraiths. Even now, pairs of them
crawled behind her, scuttering sideways and calling for Harmony with
names that weren't hers.

Bridgetown was a hub for the gangs. In the alley to her left, a band of Rat Kingdom thugs pummeled a pair of Islanders. The tattoos on their arms and faces revealed their affiliations; the Islanders' bioluminescent shell tattoos were particularly easy to make out in the night. As Harmony limped by, all those Mickeys turned to stare at her, the devil in their eyes. It was like they could smell something on her. It was like they craved the weakness that weighed her down. But they would eventually turn back to those two Islanders, half-dead and buoying in pools of blood, and the Mickeys finished them off.

She tried to hide the limp, and that hurt it even more. The pain gnawed at her insides with nubbed teeth, but soon they would sharpen. Soon the painkillers would dissolve, and she'd be coiled up on the side of the road with the rest of these centipedes, all their legs following behind her, but she wouldn't look back. And she kept on striding without a limp.

Those other nighttime denizens, the ones that slithered like tentacles on the mud-soaked roads, would coil up into their alleys as Harmony hobbled by. The vendors packed away carriages, and prostitutes of all genders shriveled into the bends of stoops and corners. Harmony was a new face, and a new face might be the church.

Her destination wasn't far but cost her nearly an hour to hike, and she arrived at the riverway just at sunrise. She crossed a short wooden bridge to the mass grave. The burial land lay on an island in the lake. A ring of fog hugged the edges of the land nearer to the water. All that fertile soil, the rain, and mild winters, and still nothing grew. Death stewed in this place. But she hadn't visited her mother in some time, and now might be the last chance she'd get.

Her mother died during the third Nikon Outbreak, a fish-related virus that originated on the Nikon Islands. But Harmony had always questioned whether her mother had died from that virus or something else, something more sinister. It was the way she died. The symptoms were all wrong, the loss of hair and dulling of her eye color, none of the rashes or bloody noses that accompanied Nikon. It resembled radiation poisoning.

Harmony rested on a large stone at the center of the tiny island. The pain diminished, though not gone, but she exhaled her relief all the same. She pulled rocks from her pocket, water-smoothed stones with varying shades of gray. This was a Port Siren custom, the spread of these stones emblematic of seeds and rebirth, and was a means to pay respect to the dead.

"To nurture and inspire the human spirit," Harmony said, repeating the Port Siren slogan. "One person. One cup. One neighborhood at a time."

That should have been it. Harmony should have walked away and bottled it all up, just kept the rest of it to herself. But she bent down, scooping up a handful of dirt. She breathed the death on that little island and undammed those names she had been holding against the back of her skull.

"Elijah," she said, and sprinkled a little dirt. "Tapper." And a little more dirt. "Ratana. Knuckles. Meir. Sage. Kai. Mickey-477. Mickey-828. Pregnant Jay . . ." And with each name, a trickle of moist dirt slipped from between Harmony's fingers. She said every name, thirty-one in total, without a stutter or pause to recall. And as if she had measured that handful of dirt to perfection, there was nothing left after the last name.

They would haunt her. All their faces, and until the day she died and rejoined them in the dirt. But at least for this short moment, an ounce of weight felt lifted from her shoulders. She felt lighter, like she could float away from this place. But she was floating downward, slowly to her knees, then her hands. Then someone caught her.

"Harm, we got you."

That was Emit's voice. He lifted her like she was a child, and she felt childlike, swathed in his broad arms and falling asleep. She floated over the bridge, water trickling beneath her, and water clouds gathering overhead. Clouds furry and black like buffalo churned in a way Harmony hadn't seen in a long time. The rain would drown the roads, and she knew, even in her half sleep, that they couldn't leave today.

"Why would you go like that, Harm?" Emit asked, a hint of resentment in his voice, like he wasn't happy to be carrying her, and yet he held her tight against his chest. Emit held her with a stillness like she was a cup of water that he couldn't spill. "What were you even doing over there?"

"It is of little consequence now," Gemini said, and she said it fast, like she was getting in the way of a bullet, taking the hit for Harmony. Because she knew, didn't she? She knew not just that Aurora was buried there, she knew that for certain, but she also knew that Harmony didn't want it to be known. Harmony liked to hide all of her soft spots in Androne armor. Gemini was as protective of Harmony's sentiment in that moment, as Emit was to her body, and it was like the two of them were carrying her together.

They stopped at a riverbank, and that woke Harmony up just enough to notice the mud river at the Bridgetown borders. They weren't taking her back to Bussa's, they were leaving the township; it wasn't just Emit and Gemini, it was Exegete too, it was their supplies and Harmony's drugs. It was everything. Emit stretched his shoulders and his back, claiming to be fine, just needing a little stretch, but even he couldn't carry her the entire way. And neither could Harmony even carry herself.

They had to stay in Bridgetown for at least another couple of days. Emit and Gemini didn't understand the rain in this place. It was a living thing, with hungers and urges all its own. There were reasons why the path alongside the river was named Serpent's Whim, but they didn't understand those reasons.

Gemini sat alone on a turned-over tree trunk, hunched over and communing with herself. She spoke louder than ordinary, so even the belches of the mud river couldn't quite drown out her one-way conversation. Most of the time her "twitch" was barely audible, a slight tic in her lips and then it was gone. But today, and overall more recently, her inner monologues escaped her. Gemini was feeling more pressures as of late, and that had a lot to do with Harmony's decisions. And while Emit and Harmony had grown accustomed to Gemini's peculiar habits, the Exegete stared at her. And she mouthed something too, but something lyrical, a verse or ballad.

"I don't think we can leave today," Harmony announced to them all. "The rains are coming. We need to stay a few more days . . . I need a few more days."

Emit turned to Gemini. Gemini turned to Harmony. "We can't."

"Why?" she said, but their faces told her. Something had happened. "Where's Bussa?"

"The church," Emit said. "They're in Bridgetown, a lot of them. They are looking for you."

"And her," Gemini said, pointing to the Exegete. "Two female escapees."

"The church?" Harmony asked herself, wondering how they found her, that fast at least. They had their spies yes, *but that fast?* "Who?"

"He said his name was . . ." Emit dug back into his mind but couldn't find it.

"Ether," the Exegete said in her quiet voice, and much to everyone's surprise.

Ether. He was alive. She had just spoken to the prophet of prophets, via the Exegete, just a few days ago. But he spoke to her from the past, which for all she knew could have been fifty years prior, more even. All this just to get her on that pilgrimage?

"Where's Bussa?" Harmony stressed.

"He let us out the back," Emit said, "told us where to find you, that he'd handle them. But they just argued with him and took some of his things. Right?"

He turned to Gemini for support. The look on Harmony's face appeared too much for him to keep talking. What was the look on her face? She hadn't shed a tear yet, but it must have been shaped like that, in the way faces bend to squeeze their tears.

"We watched from the tree line. He wasn't harmed, but they destroyed his entire life's work," Gemini said. "All of it."

"Necromancy equipment," Harmony said, not asking, but Gemini answered anyway.

"Yes."

Harmony turned to the road leading back into Bridgetown with a longing that must have been obvious, because Gemini shook her head, and Emit spoke it into words.

"We can't go back," he said.

And so they went forward. A march toward the Hysterics and the Quondam capital—former capital, the Yellow City.

12

It rained here. Full rain, thick, fatty raindrops falling at woozy sideways slants. The paralyzed cumulus hung low overhead and would crush them if it drooped any lower. They were submerged in the weather, mud at their heels, water at their nostrils. Rain like the air, it had to be breathed, exhaling against tides of wind-whipped water and inhaling as it receded. But not the Exegete. She choked on the precipitation. Her clumsy nostrils leaked rainwater that dripped into her throat.

Harmony helped to balance the girl. Her body was strong but uneven in the water. She covered the girl's lips with her hand and taught her how to breathe. They had followed the river south, that same river that crawled sneakily underneath the arches of Bridgetown. But here the river raged, trespassing over the banks, and at times it swallowed homes and wayward children, and would swallow them whole if they let it. It was a winding, coiling snake that could attack at any time and without warning. Serpent's Whim had earned its name in blood.

But in the lulls between the heavier rain, Emit started asking questions, and then even in the downpours, even as the water dribbled on his lips and warped the words, he asked questions all about her, the girl he didn't know was an Exegete. And though Emit was the only one to ask, Gemini listened, that leaning over the shoulder, cock your ear sort of listening, nosy as fuck, like staring but with the rounds of her ears, she listened to every word.

"Is she with the necromancer?" *No, she wasn't.* "Is she part of our team, then?" *Not that either.* "Did you meet her on the way?"

"No, Emit," Harmony kept saying, but he kept asking questions.

Who the girl was complicated things. Harmony couldn't tell them she was an Exegete, the holiest of holies in the Church of Time. Therefore she had to find a lie without the mental cushions of preparation. A lie so immediate, so blunt, that it was just wrong like bad grammar, like soured milk on her tongue, so artificial it shamed her when she said it, and thus the delivery of the thing was unconvincing.

"Wren's daughter." But Wren was dead. Wren's daughter was dead. And Harmony regretted it the moment she had said it, using her dead friend's dead daughter in her lies.

Fuck. Poor Wren, Harmony's eldest pilot and formerly from the House of G. All of that history together, a decade, and now Wren was just the back door for Harmony's trumped-up story.

"Wren?" Emit said, but he didn't know Wren and neither did Gemini. "What's her name?"

"Her name's Getty," she said, nearly cringing. From Exegete to Getty—what bludgeoning creativity.

"Getty?" Emit said. "Is that an Audi name?"

"Maybe. I don't know."

"Why's she traveling with us?" Emit asked mid-downpour, and she seriously considered not answering. But he asked again and louder, shouting over the wash of rainfall. "Harm? Why's she going with us?"

There it was. That was the question, *wasn't it?* Harmony had been asking herself again and again. *Why?* Why was she here? What was she going to do with this girl that wanted to die?

The Exegete shouldn't be executed for a false religion and its false god. But the girl was a believer. Harmony watched as the Exegete's unpurposed steps dragged forward. Tears tied into the rainwater as she choked on the droplets in her nose. The Exegete was weighed down by a lack of purpose. It depressed her. It held her down, and Harmony wasn't the only one to notice. They all saw it. Harmony's "daughter of a dead friend" was dying herself.

"Harm?" Emit said, looking for the answer to his question.

"She's my responsibility now," she lied, and at the same time told some element of truth.

"Getty," he said, believing every word. "Welcome to the squad."

The day turned quiet right there, right then, and the questions stopped and would for the rest of their journey. Even the rain appeared to pull back and give her a moment of silence. They believed her not because of the logic of the thing, but because of the delivery of the words. Because Harmony believed it too. She had made them believers.

The night was short, and so cold they huddled unabashed in a bushel of torsos and bending legs. Emit seemingly both on her left and her right. His breathing and odor were only half washed out of their tent with the winds. And Emit's snoring was somehow louder than the rest of it, all the wind and rain and rush of the river.

The morning groaned upward, and so ungracefully, it was barely there. The overcast was fleshy and filled with scabs of black clouds. And they walked through it, through mud, through rain, and the conversation softened. It was as mushy a thing as the cadavers of dirt underneath them.

All this just for some information on why *it's all wrong*, to quote her mother. Even in victory, her mother found a way to scold her. But maybe Harmony would find her Spartan there. Harmony's big little cyclops, all alone for so many years. She missed that machine more than she did many of those lost in the massacre days earlier. There were fragments of childhood bolted to the Androne's frame, moments and memories reflected in that glossy exterior. It was a walking specter of all those lost girlhood days in the past. And it was stolen from her.

But this was all about her and her shit, so why was she dragging them behind her, over the rocks and through muddy sinkholes? There was guilt in her, this itchy irritant of a thing at Harmony's chest, so much guilt and still not enough of it to tell them to stop. Not enough to say that she was a false prophet and that following her was a path to ruin. Emit had mentioned knowing someone or someones in the Yellow City, old friends that he might see. That was part of his reasoning for going, or maybe part of an excuse. But Gemini's company on this journey was more of a mystery to her than Emit's. Emit loved Harmony in obvious ways, but Gemini's affections were less transparent. Gemini's political aims were fulfilled with the Quondam's defeat, but still she stood close beside Harmony. Close enough to touch. Even now Gemini stared at her, and Harmony could see stolen glances from the corners of her eyes.

But the Exegete, Harmony now realized, was the only one who truly didn't fit. She was not there for Harmony's benefit; instead the Exegete was a lifetime of guilt manifested, a walking, breathing engine of all her culpabilities. Somewhere inside her, deep down where it was not a conscious thing, Harmony hoped that maybe she could make up for all of it, every sin and failure, by saving Getty.

The first signs of the Yellow City were the ghost drones overhead. Their sun-powered propellers flapped in the "forever flocks." Tens of thousands of aerial drones flying in dance patterns, elegant, like birds in murmuration. They were machines long out of ammunition and simply flying for sport, racing across the landscapes of their history. The pilots were dead, in the literal sense of the word, but not yet alive either, unborn and piloting from some time in the future.

The next day, the fourth day, the ancient towers appeared on the horizon like rotting porcupine quills, razor sharp. The morning light sharpening their silvered facades. They were now just a day away.

Harmony had thought she had rationed the drugs, but now there was only a half day's supply left. And maybe that was why she saw things. Movement in the treetops. Woodlands bending behind her. Light like rubber, curving and rounded, dulling but sharp at the edges. But they saw it too, Emit's sixth sense telling him to tell her that they had to move in the middle of the night. Something was following them. And it was fucking fast.

They didn't sleep that last night. They marched into the fifth day, and that muddied, rocky road eventually ended. It vomited them out into the city, rolling, tumbling out, dripping in sweat, mud leaking out of them like mucus. And there was blood in that regurgitation, bleeding out of Harmony's abdomen and the Exegete's lips. But they had finally reached the Historics' stronghold and Quondam's former capital, the Yellow City.

They didn't even have the energy to care about being followed. They slept through the daylight and the nighttime hours in an underground hostel. Harmony slept even without the drugs, and she slept deeper, like she might never wake up. Twenty straight hours of sleep and on the sixth day, she could barely open her eyes. Even as the morning spilled down the stairs into the underground space, giving it some radiance, Harmony felt as vacant as the spaces around her, fatigue, malnutrition, and medicinal withdrawals all sapping everything but her breath.

Emit helped her up the stairs, into the first dry sky in days, but clouds lingered forebodingly and cratered into the sunlight. The fractions of sunshine that did seep through burned Harmony's eyes down to narrowed beads, and all she saw was the haze of a broken city ahead. Buildings were burned out, and recently; the ashes flaked and filled the air with savors of conflagration. Bodies slept in the streets or were dead—and probably dead, as the dogs picked over them, flies dancing on the curbside graves. At the city center, upturned transports, like wooden wagons, and steel carriages lay capsized like roadblocks in the street, and those had been burned out too. The quadrupedal steeds that pulled the carriages had been stripped down to their techno-bones. Everything was dead—even the mob that had destroyed this place had eaten itself.

The city had been massacred. Stragglers owned the streets, mad men and women screaming for their gods, newer gods, *the Infinite*, the god of the Infinite Men. But she heard her name too, *Peacemaker*, someone, somewhere shouted. The Yellow City, the Hysterics' capital of affluence on this continent, now it lay in squalor. And Harmony, the Peacemaker, had no doubt that her attack on the Quondam played some role in this.

The roads ahead were paved, flat, and fit for walking, but for Harmony, they felt like cement thorns on her toes. Her arms were sacks of sand pulling on her shoulders, her feet bore brick sandals, and she made it only halfway to the Archivist's cathedral. It was a skyscraper that even at a mile away still touched her with its shadow. And Emit left her there in the shade, Getty as her companion, as he and Gemini ventured inside to find the Archivist of Timothies.

Harmony sat in the shade, staring into a mirror, her face appearing younger than it ever had, her wrinkles wiped away, the redness gone from her eyes, skin so soft, so buoyant she might just float away. But that wasn't a mirror, that was a glaze over her eyes, daydreams distorting the daylight. And that wasn't her reflection, that was the Exegete, or Getty as Emit had started calling her, sitting across from Harmony. *Getty*, such an uncreative name, and yet it was growing on her.

Even though Harmony's eyes had been open for the past hour, she had now just woken up. *Good morning*, said an early-afternoon sun slowly strobing between the clouds; the skyscraper's shade had long washed in the opposite direction. The sun was thorny in her eyes and unseasonably hot. A sunbeam syringe pricked her skin. But that same light was the brightness she needed to finally wake up.

"How long have they been gone?" Harmony said in Getty's direction. And the girl snapped to attention, startled. "Gemini and Emit. How long?"

Getty had her fingers inside Harmony's bag, searching for something. Bread, maybe? Or the water flask, but that was empty. Getty dropped the bag and curled those same fingers under her biceps, folding her arms in a shameful way.

"It's fine. We'll get you something to eat later," Harmony said, but got nothing from Getty except a drop in eye contact. "Getty, the others are trying to find the Archivist. How long have they been gone?"

"Have I achieved my debt to you in accompanying you here?" the Exegete asked.

Harmony didn't have an immediate answer. She hadn't actually expected a response from Getty.

"You were never indebted to me," Harmony said. "Is it okay that I call you Getty?"

No response, just a nod, or something like a nod, or maybe it was just a dip of her head. Then she looked back up.

"But you can stay with me," Harmony continued. "With us. As long as you want. We can help each other. All this Church of Time . . ." *Bullshit,* she wanted to say. "*Stuff,* it's done now that the war's over."

Now something, a shake of the head, *maybe,* but still so subtle, so slow, and it could be interpreted as just a glance left, then right, then back to Harmony.

"The war *is* over," Harmony said, a soft frustration building in her voice. "The Quondam, their fake gods. All of it's done."

"The war is at its climax," Getty said, her voice breaking—broken, just short of tears. "And the terror will climb back. Spine tingling. Violence like a vile axe."

"It won't happen like that," Harmony said.

"You have to let me go," she said, her voice still cracking.

"Go where?" Harmony responded faster this time, annoyed with the question. She knew the destination of these questions. She knew the final answer. The girl wanted to die.

"I need to go away," Getty said like she was out of breath, like the very act of speaking was wearing on her.

"Why?" Harmony said, faster yet.

"I need release," Getty said.

"Why, *Exegete?*" she said, emphasis on the title. "You're not saying why?"

"I'm not supposed to be here," she said. "I'm not a part of this journey . . ."

"Not supposed to be here? Speak plainly, Getty. What the *fu* . . ." The dam was breaking. Harmony's frustrations were slipping through. "There is no God. Everything they told you is a lie. *We* . . ." Harmony jabbed herself in the chest. "We're the only ones trying to help you."

"You're afraid," Getty said.

"What?"

"You're always afraid. Every time you evade your mother."

"No!" she lied, but it was true. So precisely true that it didn't make sense. "Who told you that?"

Getty stared at Harmony but said nothing, giving up on the conversation. She dwarfed in on herself, her body like a spiral seashell. And just like that Getty was gone.

"You wanna go," Harmony snapped. All that pressure had built up over all these days, and it bottlenecked at her lips. *Wake up, you silly fucking girl!* And Harmony erupted; she fucking snapped. "What is the fucking point to you anyway?" she screamed, not shouting, *no*, she screeched at the edges of her vocal cords. "You bitch and whine and sing church ballads to yourself all day. With everything that they taught you in that church and you're not living up to any fucking potential." Now she calmed, going in for the kill. "So go ahead, find some street corner to sleep on. Some barrel of rats to hide from the rain. Just . . ." *Go.*

But Harmony pulled back on that last word. She couldn't say it. Right now she was speaking from memory. *What is the point of you, living up to your potential.* She had heard it all before. She had heard it from Aurora, from days when her mother would forget her in the streets or abandon her for a religious celebration. And little Harmony waited into the sunset, staring at a church door and anticipating her mother's return.

Harmony twisted away from Getty, what she had said embarrassing her now. She breathed in deep through her lips, because her nostrils weren't big enough. Long inhales, exaggerated exhales, like Gemini had taught her, and it helped. And she said sorry. All things considered, the girl was right. Harmony *was* afraid, and she was afraid all the time. It was a fear that she could not properly define before, but now Harmony knew for a fact that it started with her mother.

The Exegete cried, the color withdrawn from her eyes as the tears swelled and ran down her cheeks. There was such sadness there, full-blown cosmic sorrow, the type that wilts orchids and burns oceans.

"I'm sorry, Getty," Harmony said, but not loud enough to be heard. For now it was better to let the girl cry.

13

Emit returned in parts, first his physical body, muddied feet, sweaty brow, all his other dirty pieces. Then his breath. His breathing took its time catching up with him as he hunched over, sucking and puffing out. And still his mind hadn't yet returned. It was still out there somewhere, giving him the look of a lost boy, eyes wandering, still searching for something.

"Gemini?" Harmony said.

"Coming," he said, and the conversation ended that fast.

Harmony was still stewing on what she had said to the Exegete. It filled her mind, and she didn't have much room for anything else. She would let Emit put himself together, because she herself was a bit in pieces. But Gemini returned barely a minute after, and all in one piece, ready and raring to go. And Harmony didn't need to ask Gemini anything, not a word, not a single glance, because Gemini asked her instead.

"Why are we here?" Gemini said, and it was the first question she had asked the entire journey.

"My . . ." *Not mother.* "Aurora said I need to speak to the Archivist."

"I know"—she paused—"that." Gemini's expression bent a bit around the eyes. There was a curvature in her look that was hard to read. "For what reason? Did she say?"

Harmony didn't know exactly, but there was something wrong about her collaboration with the church or defeating the Quondam.

She didn't know. What she did know was that her favorite childhood toy, her little cyclops, was somewhere around here. The Androne that gave her such purpose as a child. Rebuilding it had been everything, like mending a wound that she couldn't quite remember.

"Harmony?" Gemini insisted. "What did she say?"

"Something about the war, Gem," she said in frustration, but then remembered Gemini didn't like that shortened name. "Gemini. Sorry. Something about the collaboration with the church just wasn't right."

"It feels a bit like we're rambling," Gemini said. "We're wayward. We have no direction."

Gemini had always been direct, and Harmony valued that. Harmony liked truth to be as clear as water. It was that very clarity that got Gemini into her inner circle. A closer adviser than anyone. Even the twins. Even Emit—especially Emit. Gemini said what needed to be said in as clear a fashion as there was, but this truth had a bitterness to it. Harmony already knew that she had no direction anymore. She was lost and very aware of her dislocation. And that truth filled her head. It overflowed and was pouring out her scalp, like water, and just one more honest word might drown her.

"You're sweating," Gemini said, eyeing Harmony's hairline.

"I don't *know* . . ." The angst nearly broke that clarity in her voice. She knew the next word would crack, would chip, the emotion out for everyone to see. Naked again in front of her, in front of him. Harmony cleared her throat, cleared the crackling of phlegm in her voice. She wiped the moisture from her brow and the fear that had settled there. "I don't know what the Archivist has, Gemini," she said, with a false but convincing confidence. "I don't know why Aurora mentioned him, but we need to find out."

"Did your mother say anything else?" Gemini asked.

"Not my mother," Harmony snapped, quick but empty, no fervor in the words, forcing a mind-made anesthesia into her voice. *No emotion.* She couldn't show them that she was about to break.

"Aurora, she didn't mention anything else?" Gemini said.

Harmony shook her head. "No." But Aurora *had* said one last thing through the knots of static and time. And that frightened Harmony. Aurora's response to Harmony winning the war—*It's all wrong,* her mother had said. *What did you do?* Harmony didn't know. What had she done? Only this archivist could answer that. She hoped.

"Is it finished?" Gemini asked. "Fighting the church, for you, is that finished?"

Harmony half shook her head again to say no. Her lips bent and started to recite something like *not* or *nothing,* but she inhaled instead of exhaling and then she went quiet. And Gemini saw it, right there: *emotion,* slipping out of Harmony's look.

"It is finished," Gemini said, and it wasn't a question anymore.

Harmony wanted a way out of the conversation, a crack, the tiniest gap of egress that she could slither into. She turned to an Emit-size hole with a thousand worthless questions that might whisk her away. But that Emit-size hole was stuffed up. The quiet on his face was atypical behavior—it was a first, in fact. Even in his sleep, Emit spoke minute-long monologues. Something had happened just now, while they were in the church. They knew something, and Harmony was so caught up in her own shit that she hadn't noticed.

"What happened just now?" she asked, and now Gemini didn't have an answer. "Emit?" she said. "What'd you find out?"

"I think she's right," Emit said so softly, not to offend. "I think it's over."

"Why? You didn't find the Archivist?"

"It's just chaos," he said, and turned to Gemini to see if she agreed. "Like there's this new religion now. They don't care about what *we* did. They just took over from the Quondam." He deflated there, shoulders sinking into his worn frame. "It was all for nothing."

"Which new religion took over?" Harmony asked. "The Audis?"

"The Infinite Men," Gemini said.

"The yellow archways sect? That *M* symbol?" Harmony asked in surprise and didn't wait for the answer. "How? They're fledgling."

Her mother had shown an interest in the Infinite Men sect in the last years of her life. She had claimed to find meaning in their teachings and even tattooed the golden archways on the back of her neck. But Harmony remembered that one meeting she had attended; it was a cult of a perverted leader, lusting after a congregation of mostly women. But there were so few of them back then, at most a few thousand followers.

"Their numbers have grown," Gemini said. "They've taken the church."

"No," Harmony denied. "That doesn't make sense."

"The Quondam tortured and abused this population for decades," Gemini said. "When the satellites fell and Androne went dark, it was the Infinite Men that roused the citizens to take the church. New religions are made out of the old ones. The Infinite Men believe in a lot of the same ideologies, just a different god."

And Harmony saw it now in the old towers, blown-out windows, buildings blackened in burns. Dead bodies in the streets, and the living looting from the dead, looting from the broken architecture. *Revolution.* It scarred the city. She scarred the city; she did this. She had brought down the Quondam and given rise to the Infinite Men. And the Archivist was likely already dead. *All of this for nothing.*

"They nearly arrested us just for asking about the Archivist of Timothies," Gemini said. "Just for being here."

"Why's she crying?" Emit asked, eyes on the Exegete.

Harmony glanced at the Exegete, still in tears. That didn't matter now, against the enormity of what Gemini just said. "I don't know, Emit." Then she whipped back to Gemini. "You're saying Timothy is dead?"

"I didn't say that," Gemini said.

"What are you crying for?" Emit said to the Exegete directly now, seemingly annoyed by her tears.

"What are you saying, Gemini?" Harmony said, ignoring Emit and the Exegete both. "You just said . . ."

"I didn't say he was dead."

"Stop crying," Emit shouted now, and now the others noticed, their two conversations crashing into the other.

"Emit, stop. What's wrong with you?" Harmony finally interjected.

"We fought for this?" he said. "They cursed at us just now. Threw rocks." He held up his arm to reveal a stone-size bruise. "Is this what all that sacrifice was for? They don't even know *we* ended the Quondam. *We* did! They should be thanking us. Celebrating. Praying to us, instead of their infinite gods. Instead of running around picking up the scraps from the collaborators. They don't even know it was us. It was us!" He paused then, as if waiting for someone to say something, but the space was too big to fill. "All that fighting and forfeit, and death, a lot of people died. Is this all there is in the end, just . . ." And he gestured to nothing.

And this was the end. There was nothing more now than picking up the human pieces. Her, him, all of them. Harmony had heard the stories of soldiers returning from war, broken, and not necessarily in the body. And she understood that now. She was that now.

She remembered her mother's stories about the tree of legends. Funny that the memory came to her now, the timing felt appropriate. There was a tree where legends grew, each of them on their own branch, budding, sprouting, bearing fruit. Each generation growing higher, new branches, new fruit. And the Peacemaker had her branch, since childhood, since she glimmered green and half-grown. And Harmony had her time, but it suddenly felt so short. Now she was overripe, and souring, and ready to rot. The smell of it was on her. She reeked of it, and Harmony held her orifices shut, hoping no one else would smell her decay. Because now there were new branches, pitted higher, broader. There were Infinite Men and the House of G. It was a stronger Church of Time, it was the Audist—it was the future, and it raged against her. But she had her time, she did, and pine to oak, the tree outlives us all.

"I'm going to find him," Harmony said. "But you don't have to go with me, and maybe you shouldn't. Truth is the war *is* over. It's done. We're done. And any information the Archivist has is not going to change that. I love all of you. But you don't have to follow me, not anymore."

That was the truth. It washed over Harmony without drowning, without consuming her. On the contrary, she felt freer, the weight lifted.

"The Archivist of Timothies is likely in their prison," Gemini said with a sigh, almost as if she didn't want to say it. "Most of the high-ranking Quondam collaborators are being held prisoner by the Infinite Men."

"If the Infinite Men are holding Hysterics . . . ," Harmony said, wondering why the fuck Gemini hadn't started with that. "He's an archivist. They would have him."

"Not all," Gemini said. "They have executed many of the Historics already in their traitor trials. And the Infinite Men do not bargain. If he's not already dead, they will execute him soon, so if you want to do something, the time is now."

14

The cathedral at the center of the Yellow City was built of color. Stained-glass windows in primarily green hues climbed well over one thousand feet high. It was like a glass forest stacked skyward, and reddened at its crest. The sunlight burst against the glass. All those luminescent smithereens dazzled them. They watched with wonder, just three of them now, as they crossed the threshold to what once was the Quondam's holiest site.

They left Emit outside. He'd nearly fought the Infinite guard earlier and caught a stone for it. He didn't understand the propriety of these religions or their places of worship. This was the birthplace of Mother Mars as well as a premier pilgrimage site for all Hysterics and other Quondam faithful. And it was also the center for financial offerings. This was the center of the Quondam's world. Normally it would be impossible to get within miles of its sacred gates. Normally armed sentries guarded every entry and egress, and Androns were stationed at its doors. Normally bug-eyed snipers hid in the crow's nests of surrounding buildings, but these weren't normal days. Now overnight piss stains scented the back alleys, and stray cats practiced their gymnastics on the ledges and ramps over the doors and windows.

Upon treading into the tower, the most eye-catching element was the tiny gold balls, marble size, like the one the Exegete worshipped back in her room. They hovered like magic—like magnets keeping themselves buoyant in midair. Like little planets they hovered between

Dwain Worrell

a magnet floor and magnetic chandeliers, perfectly balanced. Harmony half considered reaching up and picking just one of the sacred balls out of place and watching all the others fall out of their suspended pattern.

The Exegete bowed as she entered, and Harmony followed the Exegete's lead, bowing awkwardly, with a subtle curtsy for some reason. Harmony knew the Exegete was far more adept at the practices and policies of the church and kept an eye on her decorum. But Gemini, she avoided decorum altogether. She might have been the only person who hated the church more than Harmony, and she appeared more prepared for a fight than negotiation.

But deeper in, the interior of the cathedral lay in ruin, looted, blooded, red-smeared graffiti spelling words that she couldn't read. Underage squatters found "privacy" in abandoned halls. Bodies lay in empty rooms. Judging from the smells, they'd been dead for days.

An easy bribe to the gatekeeper got them into the stairway, just a few common time credits, and Gemini's attempt at a flirtatious smile. The way up led to the church's "heaven's gate." Once Quondam property, it rested now in the hands of these Infinite Men. It was all at the top of the tower, the decision-makers as well as their prisoners. They would execute them after an unfair trial and toss them from the highest floor. Time, for once, was not on their side.

There was only one way up, and the unending stairway laid out in front of Harmony concerned her. She wouldn't make it up in time; she might not make it up at all, not with all this pain.

The way up was occupied by comatose squatters, probably having overdosed. The concrete steps were ancient and chipped, reinforced with wood like bandages on the broken architecture. The mortar was centuries old and said as much in each creak and moan. Harmony doubled over as she eyed the stairs, bending round and round in dizzying circles. She thought she might vomit.

"Are you ready?" Gemini asked.

No, Harmony thought but said, "Yes," instead. But as she took that first step, something stabbed into her, or at least that was the sensation.

She remembered from Emit's combat training that the best exercises for a strong abdomen were running stairs. She took that second step and again the stabbing, it rippled through her, and nearing the top of that flight the agony broke out of her as she gasped. Step, *stab*, step, *stab*, and moving faster made it only worse.

"Oh God," she whispered, feeling like sixteen stab wounds had gashed her abdomen. And it was just sixteen steps. She had barely started to climb this *infinite* stairway. "You two go ahead."

It didn't take long for the others to lose her. She could hear them above, footsteps and respiration in a one-two tempo. But they weren't the ones out of breath; that was Harmony, and not from fatigue but her sensation of a saw at her gut, slowly cutting back and forth with each alternating step, sagittally cutting her in half.

Harmony tasted vomit in the back of her throat. She rummaged through her bags again, fingering around for a single pill, just one, a single fucking crumb of relief. But she knew there was nothing there, she had already checked, just fibers and dust and nothing. And still she rummaged again, every flight. This was desperation. Despair.

By the ninetieth floor, Gemini would have to return down and help Harmony around the twentieth. Then Exegete came back around the fortieth floor. They would rest on the fiftieth, sixtieth, *and* seventieth floors. Then the breaks became more frequent, coming after each individual step. But she'd survived it, all the stabbing and without the drugs, and she knew this was the beginning of the end for her injury. If she had made it this far, she could make it anywhere.

Armed guards ushered and assisted them up the last few flights and escorted them through the doorway on the ninety-second floor. Sunlight erupted like she'd never seen before. Harmony's eyes slammed shut and it was still so dazzling, like the sun itself rested in some corner of the room.

Eyes cringed shut, Harmony stumbled ass-first at the center of the room, the stitches still sawing jagged at her insides. Every gasping breath she took, it cut deeper. She sat there for a moment. Adjusting to the light was a gradual thing, and her timid eyes squinted open. Harmony peered out at a yawning wide space with high ceilings, the entire floor just one room. There were no other doors, only windows, where the green glass touched the red that ran the rest of the way to the spire. And that sunset, *God*, it was ablaze, like a matchstick burning down the skyline.

Burly, Emit-size men towered in front of her with rifles and cutlasses, and Harmony had lost sight of Gemini and the Exegete. But the longer she watched the men and her eyes adjusted to the light, she saw how young they were. Teenagers maybe. Boys. Soft-faced with kind eyes, and the weapons dangled at their sides as if they might fall if they relaxed a finger one inch more.

"Getty?" Harmony said and immediately wondered why that was the first name she called. Gemini was there too, and still she called again. "Where's Getty?"

"Your allies have taken the cleanse," a kind-faced young man said. He stood in front of her, blocking her path with eyes glazed over and staring at her for many seconds too long—far too long for an impatient Harmony.

"What?" she said. "Cleanse? What cleanse?"

"You are unclean," the young man said. "You too must partake in the cleanse."

Harmony finally noticed that the young man held a white clay cup in his left hand, but he hadn't yet presented it to her, his arm dangling at his side. *Has he forgotten?*

"Am I . . ." Harmony pointed at the cup. "Am I supposed to drink?"

"They're on drugs," Gemini said, stepping through the crowd. "All of them high as kites. Drink it and they'll take us to speak to the Infinite Men."

"They're not the . . ." Harmony pointed to the teens. "They're not the Infinite?"

"They look like hired muscle or at least the lower end of the Infinite Men, getting high off the Quondam's medicines. Their religion is hallucinogens. The Infinite Men are the next level up."

More stairs. Harmony cringed at the thought. She lifted the cup from the young man's hands and sniffed it, but the smell didn't come to her immediately.

"Milk," Gemini said. "Drink. I don't want to be here after sunset."

"Just milk?" Harmony asked, pressing her lips against the clay rim, eyes wide with wariness, like her body was telling her this was going to be bad.

"I don't know," Gemini said. "But if you want your archivist . . ."

Harmony held her breath and slurped the lukewarm liquid between the narrow of reluctant lips. *Too thick*, she thought, and thicker yet the deeper to the bottom of the cup she swallowed. The sour of the thing twisted her face into loops. But the milk didn't appear sweetened with any illicit additives or drugs, which she might have welcomed at this point. A kick of vigor, a dance of that dizziness, or especially a cloud of numbness that would elevate her up the rest of any stairs and beyond.

"You are cleansed," the young man said. "All of you, cleansed in the innocence of birth. Eyes anew, prepared to seek truth."

"Thanks," Harmony said, still trying to play nice. Drugged up or not, these boys outnumbered, outmuscled, and out-weaponed Harmony's trio.

"Which way?" Gemini asked without the niceties of Harmony's tone.

"No way," the young man said, stepping aside. "You are here."

The congregation of young men stepped aside in a sort of incoherent divide, but incoherent in unison. They moved like this white mass, all stumbling and sliding off each other, *like termites*, she thought, thirty-some-odd termites, uncurtaining, revealing a row of ten overseers standing on a dais at the far end of the room. The Infinite Men. They were dressed in white silk from the hood over their hair down to their feet. Their eyes were covered by a thicker white blinder, made of wool maybe, tied around the backs of their heads and another wrapped around their pregnant bellies. And very pregnant, nine months and bursting at the seams, all of them—the Infinite Men were women.

Behind these Infinite *Ten* was a satellite. A satellite standing six meters tall, solar panels on either side of it like arms reaching out for embrace. It was intimidating seeing it up close, an old, worn, rusted thing, but that added to its presence, centuries in its bones. *It was there before you and would be there long after.*

Gemini approached the women and their giant satellite. Harmony followed a step behind, her hand waving back at the Exegete.

"Getty, come on," Harmony said.

But Getty didn't look good. She stood in place, in a daze. Her breathing was heavy, maybe from the climb or the milk. But they had all drunk the milk. It was less likely a poison and more likely just diarrhea.

"Stay there," Harmony said, watching the Exegete stand unstill. Her slight bob to and fro worried Harmony, but whatever this conversation with the Infinite Men was going to be, it wouldn't take long.

The other end of the room was nearly forty meters away, situated across a gulf of sleek mahogany-wood flooring that glimmered in the setting sunlight. And the Infinite Men's dais appeared carved of natural stone, white, like their garb, and the effect in that light was a rapturous haze where any religious diehard would find as similar a high as the young men.

"Hail," one of the Infinite Men said, but it was hard to distinguish an individual speaker between the light, and their hoods, and the voice rebounding schizophrenic about the expanse. "We, the Infinite Men, salute you."

"Thank you," Harmony said, bowing respectfully.

"We will warn," the woman continued. "The fallen satellite cannot be bartered."

"Fallen . . . ?" Harmony asked, pointing at the satellite behind them. "Barter?"

"It fell from the Hive and we, with our aerial harpies, caught it. Five aerials, like fingers, and the netting was our palms. We caught and guided the largest of their satellites to the ground."

Harmony eyed the satellite again. That wasn't what she was here for by any means. But if Gemini had told them that they were only there to barter, they had probably guessed it was for that monstrosity of a thing, their most valuable possession.

"We aren't here for the satellite," Gemini said with a harsh scoff, and disrespectfully so. There was this extra edge to her today that Harmony couldn't quite figure out. "We're here for the barter of a prisoner."

"Request the name," another one of the Infinite Men said.

"The Archivist of Timothies," Harmony said, stepping ahead of Gemini and outshouting her, just as Gemini had raised her lips to speak.

The two women shared a look then, brows raised, questions exchanged in their glances. No answers, though. Harmony couldn't read Gemini's look. It was sideways, like an upside-down scowl, and Gemini rarely scowled, rarely showed much emotion. But there it was, half-naked emotion staring back at her.

"The Archivist of Timothies," one of the Infinite Men said.

"He is the great hoarder of things," another said.

"Greed," a third Infinite Man said. "Greed is a limited thing. Bounded . . . finite."

"Greed," pairs of them said in unison. "The folly of the finite."

"His sins exceed your request," another of the Infinite Men said.

"We need him to answer a question," Gemini said. "That's all. You can do with him what you like."

"It is a question of greed," one of them responded.

"It's not—" Gemini tried, but they cut her off.

"That is his worth, and naught else. He will remain."

It was quiet then, quiet enough for Harmony to hear her own heavy breathing. She glanced back to find the Exegete mere feet behind her and creeping closer. The Exegete's skin was pasty and sprinkling perspiration. A hunched posture carried her forward. Her clothing hung off her and she looked like a rag, a human rag, soaked and torn apart.

"Stay there," Harmony whispered, and she did.

Harmony took a breath then before she turned to the Infinite Men, digging into her bag for a last strategic desperation. And they watched her as if they knew it was.

"Is there a bargain that can be made?" Harmony said.

"There are no bargains between we and the finite."

"And if we possess something . . . ," she said, pulling a closed fist out from her bag. And her hand weighed slightly more than it did before. "What if I possess something infinite?"

That quiet came again, those pauses between the words, but now the Infinite Men had to fill it. And that was good. For the shortest moment, she had the upper hand, and it was balled up in her palm.

"Show us," an Infinite Man said, and they all stepped forward.

And she did show them. Her palm and fingers splayed and revealed the "bargain" resting at its center. They all moved in, leaning, bending, the Infinite Men and Gemini, staring at the ancient idol in her palm, the Exegete's idol, the most holy to the Church of Time. The Infinite Men held some similar beliefs, so it might be enough.

"That is an idol of the Church of Time," a woman said, Harmony finding her amid the ten, watching her lips move. "We possess nothing."

"It's not a possession . . . ," Harmony started, but ended there too, nothing coherent coming to mind, no argument. They had the advantage now.

"This is God Shadow," Gemini said. "One of ten in the Church of Time in reverence to Chronos. It is not greed to have something to trade with the old powers."

Good, Gemini. That was smart.

"We do not fear the Chronics nor their Church of Chronos," one of the Infinite Men said.

"They fear you," Harmony said, and she and Gemini were in sync now.

"Yes," Gemini picked up. "The Church of Time in reverence to Chronos would give anything for their idols. Taking this is strategic, not greed."

A final pause and the longest yet, and as Harmony waited, she realized she couldn't allow them to come back with a rebuttal or refusal. She had to end this here.

"All we want is a word with the Archivist," she said, knowing she had the Infinite Men on their heels, *just one more push.* "You keep him under your guard. He will not be freed. His fate is sealed and in your hands. All we have is a question, one and single, and you keep the God Shade—"

"Shadow," Gemini corrected.

"God Shadow, it's yours." Harmony reached higher, proffering the tiny circular gem in her palm. Giving it to them, not offering anymore. It was a demand—*take it, the deal is done.* "You caught a satellite, right? Fell from the Hive and right into your hand. Gift from God, from the Infinite Man. And this is a gift, falling into your hand."

"You may have him," one of the Infinite Men said. "He's served his purpose."

"Good," she exhaled. Relief then, washing over Harmony. Her shoulders unhinged in the cascade, and all the other tensed-up parts of her released. But not Gemini. She looked at Harmony with distaste on her lips.

"Where did you get it?" she asked. "God Shadow?"

"I . . ." *Stole it from an Exegete—the most holy of holies in the Church of Time?* ". . . found the God Shadow at the cathedral."

But Gemini was a lie detector, and Harmony remembered that just as she finished speaking, just as the last syllable left her lips. She saw disbelief manifesting on Gemini's face.

"I understand," Gemini said as wrinkles burrowed down on her expression.

One of the young men approached Harmony, reaching for the God Shadow, but her fingers collapsed into a fist. The young man pouted and turned to the women on their dais.

"Retrieve the Archivist of Timothies," one of the Infinite Men said.

They dragged him out—the Archivist, his head covered by a white sack, his hands tied in white fabric. He was a man of average size and average weight, but Harmony had remembered him much taller and wider, far more intimidating than the mediocre man stumbling in front of her.

The exchanges were made with all the religious pleasantries. The poetic words and exaggerated gestures, the bows and Harmony curtsying again for some odd reason. They exchanged smiles, handshakes, cups of purifying milk, all of it before actually exchanging the God Shadow for that mediocre fucking man. That murderer. That thief.

They kept the bag over his head. He mumbled under there, something that sounded like a prayer, but he had a rag in his mouth. And they'd keep that in too. Harmony shoved him forward as her trio prepared to leave, but not without asking the question itching like mad at the back of her skull.

"Why do they call you the Infinite Men?"

"For we are in worship of the Infinite Man," one of the women said.

"Infinite Man," Harmony said, quietly, sarcastically, and just for herself.

Harmony considered the rituals of their faith. She could imagine their Infinite Man was some diabolic rapist, bedding culpable women and hoping his infinite sons would rule the world. And whether it was the Infinite Man or Chronos or any of their old gods made of new stars, they all had the same flaw—the same fiction. These gods didn't create us, we created them, we built these deities in our image. Cruel, petty, angry gods. These were just fairy tales, and they were all little children.

Harmony offered them a final bow as she stepped under the threshold into the stairway, but none looked back. By then the Infinite Men had long forgotten about her—*her?* Who was she to them? Nothing, and she could feel it now, that slow dissolve into invisibility. The Peacemaker was the last generation's legend. Her destiny was done, ending the war so they could start a new one.

Was she still bowing? She was, still bending over and staring out at them, hoping for anyone to notice. But the Infinite Men were gathered around their expensive marble—that God Shadow in the palm of a drug boy's hand. *Termites,* she thought again, and maybe spitefully, maybe jealously.

"Chronos," the Exegete said suddenly, strangely, and she stumbled forward. *"Chronos."*

And with that, the Exegete spun on wiry feet, knees buckling, and she collapsed. She hit the floor, foaming from the mouth, choking on something in her throat. She was just a body now, a convulsing bag of meat. Her eyes were wide open and red and blinking out of sync. She was dying—or was she already dead?

"What did you do?" Harmony screamed at the Infinite Men. "What the hell did you do?"

15

The Infinite Men's boy soldiers aimed the sharp ends of their guns at Harmony, commanding her to take the diseased child away. This wasn't the Infinite Men's doing. This wasn't their milk nor the marathon of stairs. This was Harmony's doing. The things she had said to the poor girl, the way she had treated her, was just like Aurora had done with her.

"Getty?" Harmony screamed at her in a spit-wet panic. Accidental saliva wet Getty's convulsing features.

Getty, suddenly back to that name, back to that endearing sense of an individual. Not Exegete. Not some position allocated by a church.

The plastic wrapper for Harmony's "misplaced" medicines was stuffed in Getty's pocket. The blue dust particles dyed Getty's fingertips. She didn't know if Getty had started stealing individual pills in Bridgetown or on the way to Yellow City, but somewhere between there and here, she had accumulated enough to overdose, to fill her digestive tract with a blue venom that made everything numb and slowed everything down. Getty stopped. No breathing, no heartbeat, nothing.

Harmony and Gemini scrambled down the stairs, carrying Getty, and dragging the Archivist too. He tripped and fell behind them.

"What is happening?" the Archivist said at the eighty-eighth floor, the muzzle out of his mouth. "Please, I cannot see," he said as he tumbled down the eighty-seventh flight.

They rushed Getty down the stairs but didn't get far. Harmony quickly remembered that her abdomen screeched with pain and her lungs were burning with all that oxygen.

"I can save her," the Archivist said. He was a flight of stairs below them, sitting with his back against the wall but standing up now. "Get this bag off of me. I can help her."

But Harmony wasn't listening. Harmony didn't need to listen. She had her own medical training. She'd stopped up exit wounds and stitched shrapnel gashes. And overdoses too, she'd seen them before. Had seen a Hysteric vomit up drugs and return from the dead.

"Eyes open," Harmony said, pumping Getty's chest with two folded fists. "Eyes open."

And Getty listened, her eyes opening, then closing, then opening wide in shock. Her limbs flapped and her torso squirmed, like she was fully alive and had vitality, but these were the girl's death throes. Harmony flipped her over right there and then, onto her stomach, and rammed her fingers into Getty's throat, and *splat*. Immediate and wet and hot on Harmony's fingers.

"Getty?" The girl coughed in response. "You're okay."

"They're coming," Gemini said suddenly.

"Who?" Harmony asked as she wiped the vomit from Getty's lips.

"The Infinite. They're coming down the stairs."

Fuck.

"What for?" the Archivist asked.

Harmony lifted Getty to her feet, but her legs were flaccid and dragging under her torso. "Come on, Getty," Harmony whispered, rushing recklessly against the girl's dead limbs.

"Why are you rushing her?" Gemini asked with a plain but cautious curiosity. "Why are *they* rushing down?"

"Help me move her," Harmony said, hearing the footsteps overhead, and so damn many.

"Why, Harmony?"

"Help me move Getty downstairs."

"Why are they coming?"

"It might not be real," Harmony said. "Help me move her."

"What's not real . . ." Then it hit Gemini like a ton of bricks. "The God Shadow's not real?"

Harmony didn't know. All she knew right now was the Infinite boys were after them and they had to fucking run.

"I can help you," the Archivist said. "Take off the hood."

Gemini let go of Getty's other hand, putting all the girl's weight on Harmony's shoulder and her wound.

"We have to leave her," Gemini gasped, emotion finally finding its way to her face. "We can't outrun them with her." She picked up the Archivist instead. "He's who we came for."

And Harmony considered it. Getty was a burden now and would be going forward. The girl might simply find another time or tool and try to kill herself again. Harmony did more than consider it, leaving Getty there, mid-stair, mid-descent, but it was only for a split second. Because Harmony had made the mistake that her mother never did. She'd given her a name. *Getty.* She was her responsibility, and she wouldn't leave her to die.

"There's another room," the Archivist interrupted. "It's in this building. Take off the hood."

Fuck!

And she was fucked, in every which way, up, down, left, right. Infinite young men with large guns above and infinite stairs beneath her. Those boys would outrun her, even without the wound. So she had to trust this trickster. This liar. This fucking thief and murderer.

"Gemini, take it off," Harmony said.

But Gemini was already pulling at the rag choking tight at the man's neck. She tore the bag from the Archivist's head, and it was like Harmony's voice was a magnet for him, because his eyes spun right to her.

"The room—where is it?" Gemini shouted the five words as if they were one.

"No," he said, eyes locked on Harmony. "I would rather die than have you live. What did you do?"

There was that question again. The same as Aurora's. *What did you do?*

"Where's the room?" Harmony screamed at the fucking Hysteric. "Where?"

"No," he said. "It was you, wasn't it? That ended the world?"

Footsteps like hail came trampling probably eight floors up and closing in fast.

"Show us—" Gemini said.

"Yes," the Archivist said before Gemini could finish. And so sudden, so abrupt, that it seemed to silence even the trample of footsteps. He had seen something just now, that flickering in his eyes, that drop in his jaw, that awe. "I'll take you."

What did he see? Harmony mused, but fuck it. "Which floor?"

"Up," he said—*of course he said up*. Up toward the gunmen charging down. "We have to go up."

Up they went, racing on all fours, slipping, stumbling, rising. Harmony and Gemini struggled to carry Getty's wilted body as the Archivist led the way. But he moved too fast—two steps ahead, then four, until he was a whole flight above them, until they lost sight of the slippery snake of a man.

"Timothy!" Harmony screamed, but he didn't slow or turn back. The Archivist disappeared.

The mad youth trampled downward just three or four flights overhead, high on the gunpowder it seemed, cursing and triggering gunfire into the spiraling space. *Shit*, she thought. They would meet in the middle, a grisly, bloody middle. Harmony saw their shadows angling down from the flights overhead, and now she could hear their individual curse words, so clear, so close now. She couldn't even go out fighting. Harmony was exhausted. Every limb weighed a ton, and the wound would prevent her from so much as throwing a punch.

But she continued pedaling up. What choice did she have? And on the seventy-fifth floor, Harmony saw bare feet descending from the flight of stairs above, an endless stampede of them. She stopped. Stunned. Exhausted. She had no place to run, no more strength.

She closed her eyes. It was all over.

From nowhere, an arm reached out and dragged Harmony back. She pulled away, but the arm pulled stronger. The Archivist dragged her and Getty back into an archway. But that archway shouldn't be there, that hole in the wall wasn't there on the way up. He pulled them inside, and Gemini lunged in behind them.

"What—" Harmony gasped out the only word she could manage with Getty and then Gemini piled on top of her. *But what was this secret arched doorway built into the wall?*

The Archivist slid a barrier, half-brick, half-wood, over the opening in the wall. But the boys must have seen it, right? Their footsteps were right outside as he did it. Still, Harmony and the others held their breaths in the hidden corridor. The Infinite boys raced past them and disappeared down the spiral well. Maybe they weren't chasing Harmony after all, but if not her, then what?

"They're . . . ," Harmony said, only able to speak one word at a time between breaths, "gone?"

"The slab is a convincing barrier," the Archivist said. "I'm sure you did not discern it on your rushed ascent. I know this cathedral better than any of these new tenants."

Harmony breathed relief. They all did. Getty especially, gasping on mouthfuls of stale, dusty air and sneezing it back out. All that breathing brought her back to her feet, each inhale inflating her like a balloon, until Getty stood up straight. But she couldn't stand on her own—Getty held tight to Harmony's arm to stay erect.

The space behind the secret doorway led into a narrow corridor, unlit aside from the occasional shaft of sunlight slipping through cracks in the wall. There wasn't much to see in the dark but far more to smell.

The corrosion filled her nostrils, all those dead metals invading her sinuses. Harmony's nose ran wet.

Her mind turned back to the Archivist. Why did he change his mind so quickly? "I thought you'd rather die than help me?" Harmony said. "Why'd you agree to help all of a sudden?"

"I . . ." He was lying, and he'd barely said a single word. "I reconsidered."

Snake, Harmony thought, even though the Archivist of Timothies was a stranger to her. They had met briefly when Harmony was a teen. He had talked his way into her camp, a silver-tongued fucking snake. He and his team of Hysterics confiscated Cyclo—her Androne. And her friend Moby sacrificed himself so Harmony could get away.

"What?" the Archivist said, probably noticing Harmony's deathly stare digging between his eyes.

"What is this place?" Harmony said.

"The innards of our cathedral," he said and started walking more deeply into the narrow corridor. "Before the Infinite Men started hanging their golden arches over our walls, filthied it with their graffiti, we Historics made this place into a fortress with many ways in and out."

Getty held on to Harmony as they followed the Archivist deeper into the hallway. Gemini limped behind them.

"Are you all right?" Harmony asked.

"What's the nature of your relationship with this archivist?" Gemini whispered from behind her.

Harmony shook her head. "None."

At the end of the corridor, the Archivist pushed at the wall until it gave way. As a second hidden space opened, it revealed a final rusted door, one like Harmony had never seen. It was really two doors that met in the middle, but with no handles, just a pair of buttons on the side. The Archivist pressed the lower of the two buttons, and the doors breathed open. A rotting scent belched out at them, some animal decaying, and Harmony felt it in her mouth. The Archivist stepped inside like there was no smell, but no one followed.

"It is safe," he said. "It is called an elevator."

Gemini followed first. Then Harmony and Getty entered the small room—the *elevator*? And as the doors closed, the walls shook. There was a strange feeling in her gut, like falling, but that quickly passed.

"We hide in this room?" Gemini asked.

"We are moving," the Archivist said. "The room is moving."

It was. Between the squeezing in her lungs and the stomp of her heartbeat, Harmony hadn't quite noticed the room was moving. "Down," she realized.

Getty turned to Harmony's voice. The girl was standing now, but unstably, her hand crutched against Harmony's arm. Their eyes met, and there was a communication between their look. But Harmony could tell Getty so much more. The quiet invited it. She could say that she was sorry now. Tell her that it wasn't Getty's fault that she took those drugs, but hers. She was never responsible for anyone else, but now she wanted to be. She wanted to get it right. And she would tell her. Harmony opened her mouth to speak, but the room shook itself to a sudden hard jerk and stopped.

"Our way out," the Archivist said, gesturing to the slowly opening doors.

"Back," Harmony whispered to Getty and stepped in front of her.

The doors finally opened to the scents of medical chemicals, like alcohol or antiseptic. The room beyond them was a star field of a hundred individual lights shining down on a hundred individual things. Under each light stood an object that appeared to be of value, old things, like cups, bracelets of gold, and a sphere the size of her head.

Harmony stared past it all. There was just one thing amid all these treasures that attracted her eyes: the titanium armor, seven feet tall, and one beautiful eye. It was her Cyclo—her Androne.

16

The elevator had opened to a short corridor, and that corridor opened into the larger room with countless items on display. The light slashed the dark away in slices. Individual beams hit individual objects, but the room itself remained poorly lit. It was still dark, polka-dotted with spots of light. It was one of those flat bulbs that aimed down at her Spartan, displaying its titanium shimmer.

The Archivist limped between the light, disappearing and reappearing like a magician. Harmony rested Getty in the short corridor by the elevator as she and Gemini followed the slippery man. He was larger than them individually but not together. And he was older, ten years at least, and malnourished. And Harmony had a gun.

"I won't run," he said as Harmony and Gemini followed at his heels. "But she needs water."

He pointed to Getty, slumped in that short corridor. The girl had nearly died, and she needed to sit, and water evidently, according to the Archivist.

The Archivist kneeled at a rusted tap, and water ran into the bowl he held. Harmony stood over him, staring at the spoiled, yellowish water. The Archivist glanced up at her and took a quick sip.

"Not poison," he said, but Harmony hadn't even considered that. She just didn't trust the shape of the man, long and narrow, and if she squinted his shape was like a worm, slender and winding and without limbs. A snake.

The entire journey had been for this man and what he knew. And there he was, at her feet, but for some reason Harmony didn't want to ask. Something was changing inside her. Something spinning backward in her head. She just didn't want the fight anymore. And there were many reasons why: It was losing her people, fifty good individuals, and a couple of bad ones. They trusted her to protect them. It was the fatigue, this middle-aged languor, like a cancer inside her and growing. And a little bit of it was Getty. Adopting this little girl made Harmony feel a childhood again, those pops of magic. It made her feel like she was fixing something that was broken. Like she used to fix her Spartan when she was Getty's age. The Peacemaker's time had come and gone. Harmony didn't want any answers that led to more death. She wanted to take Getty and Gemini and Emit and her Spartan out to a spot of land near the water, somewhere like her childhood home. A place with all the fish and that sultry climate, and she would fix them all.

"The Spartan," Harmony said. "I'm taking it."

"I know," the Archivist said.

He took the bowl of water and moved to the short corridor and Getty, offering her sips. It was a strange kindness from the snake of a man. His leathery skin was covered in bruises. Bloodied, swollen arches had been carved into the back of his neck, scars that resembled the golden arches war banners. The Infinite Men hadn't been kind to him.

"What's this place?" Gemini said, following swiftly behind the Archivist.

And Harmony should have followed too, but she kept eyeing her Spartan. It was close, just right there. She could walk up and touch it. Twenty years nearly and she wanted so much to climb on it, balance herself on its shoulders. But not yet; right now she had to follow him. The Archivist was up to something, but she didn't know what.

"She asked you a question," Harmony said. "What is this place?"

"This is the Quondam archive," the Archivist said, finally turning from Getty to face them. "Like the museums of old it holds many

Quondam Era treasures. The Infinite Men have only fully occupied the building for two days. They haven't found this area yet."

Breast milk. Harmony's expression soured. That was what she was drinking.

"Why are they all pregnant?" Harmony asked.

"Only pregnant women maintain the Infinite Men's council. Once they give birth, they're replaced by another."

"The same father?" Harmony asked, assuming it was such.

"The Infinite Man," the Archivist said. "Or whoever the modern incarnation of him is. And all these women holding his seed. Their practices are perverse. Infinite Men," he scoffed. "What these Infinite don't understand is that with the Quondam gone, the Church of Time and all their Chronics will consume everything, including them. There's nothing in their way now. The Infinite Men's victory is short-lived. Putting up banners, catching a satellite, gathering weapons. The Church of Time will take all of these things, and soon."

The Archivist turned back to Getty and whispered something gently to her. He daubed a wound on her forehead and whispered again. Was he trying to play nice? Was that the strategy?

"Why don't you leave the girl alone?" Harmony said. "Get the Spartan in working order. Battery. Transistors. We're moving it now."

"The battery's worn. It won't last more than a minute," he said.

"That's fine. I'll walk it manually as far as it will go. We have someone getting us transport."

"Is that why you came for me?" the Archivist said. "Just for this? For your Spartan?"

Gemini and Harmony shared a glance. *Ask the question*, that was the look on Gemini's face. And he must have known then, because he gave that wry smile she remembered from all those years ago.

The Archivist didn't wait for the answer. He dragged his feet toward a storage unit. He pulled out the Spartan's old battery and transistors, and he began putting it all back together. But Harmony scrutinized his efforts. His clumsy fingers moved like toes, so stubby and uncoordinated, that she would have to do it herself. Snakes are not used to limbs. But as Harmony approached him, Gemini approached her with a question she'd been holding for some time.

"Will you ask him?" she whispered.

"I don't even know what to ask," Harmony said, then came her sarcasm. "Hi, sir, why did my mother ask for me to find you?"

"That would be a good start."

"He'd lie," Harmony said. "The fact that we needed something from him, he'd use it against us."

Gemini watched Harmony for a moment, as if ready to smile. But she never smiled, except when talking to herself. Then she noticed something on Harmony's face. She reached for it. She licked her thumb and wiped that something on Harmony's lower lip.

"You don't take good enough care of yourself," Gemini said.

"That's what I have you for," Harmony replied with a smile.

But Gemini quickly pulled her hand away from Harmony's face and dropped her look. Harmony could never figure out what Gemini's tied-up lips and pensive eyes meant. There was so much that had never been said between her and this woman who was like a distant, *distant* relative.

"Thank you for coming with me," Harmony said. "Wouldn't have found him otherwise."

"It is what Aurora wanted."

"Aurora," Harmony said, glancing back at the Archivist as he grunted. "She practically adopted you. So you're like a sister in a way." And now Gemini looked back at her. "You ever think of that? I notice we tie our shoes backward, and our postures, the strictness of it. The things she taught us."

"She adopted me after you left her. She tried . . ." Gemini thought about it. "She tried to make me like you. Maybe that's why you feel a sisterhood."

Harmony smiled. Gemini was more like Aurora than she was. That was an Aurora-type answer, analyzing the emotion out of everything.

"Must've been difficult," Harmony said. "Apprenticing for her."

"No," she said quickly. "Before I met Aurora, they abused me in the church. Very bad things. So, no, I was happy with Aurora. I am thankful to her. I owe her everything." Now that was new. Harmony knew nothing of Gemini's childhood in the church. "Yes," Gemini continued. "Sometimes I see a sister in you."

Gemini's words were like an admission, and that was hard for her. There was this cringe on her face, a crack from the lips to the eyes, as if the whole thing might cave in on itself. It was in moments like this that Gemini whispered to herself, talking to that voice in her head. But Harmony would interrupt the conversation.

"You want to run away?" Harmony asked. "Just . . ." She gestured *go* with a swoop of her hand.

"What do you mean?"

"Me, you, Emit, and we take Getty, and . . ." Harmony shrugged. "Water. Like Port Siren but somewhere else. I don't know." And the fantasy stopped there. "That's all the plan I've worked out so far. Still finessing the details."

She smiled. *Gemini?* Smiling? It was quick. A flash of teeth and gums as her lips spun upward. A flash of happiness and then it was gone.

"It's done," the Archivist announced. "The manual controls are in operation. Gloves. Steps. You can walk it out of here yourself."

Harmony moved toward him and Cy, her beautiful Androne. She moved through the maze of items on display to get there, passing intriguing artifacts from the past. Two items in particular caught her attention. One was the "heart" of an Americana Series Androne and the other an ancient cockpit. That one mesmerized Harmony. She orbited the egg-shaped exterior. It was far more advanced than those that she had piloted, and at the same time less advanced than the cockpit she operated for the Church of Time.

"It's like an egg," she said, pressing her palm against the metal plate.

"No," the Archivist said. "Touch with the eyes only."

Harmony shot him a pointed look and kept walking. She passed a small marble on a pedestal and hovered over it for a moment.

"It's a real God Shadow," he said. "From ancient times. And carried on the first of the pilgrimages. Which would make today a sort of anniversary."

"Sad you're missing out on the great pilgrimage?"

"A march through the desert, through heat and thirst and sand, to see what, the birthplace of their time god? I'd rather the luxury of the Quondam." He gestured to a ruined garment on a pedestal, riddled with holes and black stains. "These are the last worn robes of the Monk Who Stood. An idol of mine and my inspiration for joining the church. You walked with him as a child. What an honor it must have been."

"So I've been told," she said and shrugged. Harmony had no memory of the Monk Who Stood, just a woman who was like Aurora in her head, and now she couldn't distinguish the two. "Can't remember that far back."

Harmony kept walking, now looking at an Androne weapon, similar to the one her Spartan used. A rifle with a bayonet nearly a meter long. She would keep this one for sure, whether the Archivist liked it or not. It was newer and had far more metal and muscle built into it.

"That is the bayo-10, a very advanced weapon, engineered only two years ago. However, it is its rarity that makes it unique. There were only ten created, and this is one of two remaining."

This was definitely accompanying her Spartan.

Then Harmony passed a sphere, about the size of a watermelon, but perfectly round even as it was somewhat deflated. It was brown and old, in withering decay—it might crumble if she breathed in its direction—and she stepped back and investigated from afar.

"Ha," he huffed and kept on huffing as he approached at an energetic limp. "This is the Wilson Sphere. Old. Before the time of the Quondam or thereabouts. During the Third Keltic Dynasty, the Jays, Deuce, and Juice used this very sphere to vanquish the Western Kingdoms."

She didn't care. "Excuse me," she said, sidestepping the old archivist and pacing toward her metal giant.

It stood regally against the wall. The light over its head washed down the naked dark grays and shimmered. Its single eye stared down at her. She pressed her hand against its cold titanium and felt warmth. Flashes of old memories lit her eyes: an old woman's smile, a spot of grass in the desert sand, and this one memory of sitting in a boat and sailing across waves of dunes. These were the memories that her soul was made of.

"Cy," she whispered to her violent little toy.

She ran her hand along its leg and found grooves there. Her height was etched along its calves, Bussa's handiwork. *Cy* . . . She mouthed the nickname, short for Cyclops, a reference to the Spartan's single eye. A simple name for simple times, when all of her worries were just fitting her little hands into the Androne body and pulling out its broken parts.

"Simple," she whispered to the Androne, pressing her head against its metal womb. And only she understood what that single word meant. *Simple* meant no more war. None of the strategy or loss of life. Let the Infinite Men fight the church. Fuck it all. Let her find a pocket of peace somewhere out in the wood-rotted land.

"Is that it?" Gemini asked, snapping Harmony from her thoughts. "Is that all you wanted?"

Yes, but she couldn't say that. Not yet, not now and here, so instead she said nothing. She kept her head against the Spartan, feeling the wet burn of tears in the corners of her eyes. She couldn't look at Gemini or the others. They'd see the answer in her eyes.

"Harmony?" Gemini said, and louder, and standing, and approaching her.

God, Harmony thought. "Just give me a minute."

"The question," Gemini said, now speaking to the back of Harmony's head. But Harmony couldn't turn back, not with the reddening of her eyes. So Gemini turned to the Archivist instead. "We're here for the question."

"What?" the Archivist said. "Question?"

Harmony took a deep breath. The deepest. Sucking on all the ancient air in that room, sucking sniffles into her nostrils, sucking those tiny tears back into their ducts. And now she could look at them. And she could answer.

"They asked me to end a war. Since I was a little girl, calling me a peacemaker. Make peace. End the war. And I ended it. With help, yes, and it's done now. But I keep hearing this thing. You said it." She pointed to the Archivist. "The woman who raised me said it too. 'What did you do?' Like something wrong—'it's all wrong.' So I don't understand. What *did* I do? Tell me?"

The room was quiet. Harmony, Gemini, Getty, but not him. Not the Archivist. There was a question on his face, a curiosity that pulled his back straight and nearly loosened his limp as he stepped closer to Harmony. Like Harmony was a thing he didn't understand and he needed to get closer to make sure.

"Again, please," he said. "I'm not sure I understand. Who asked this of you?"

"The woman who raised her," Gemini said, filling the gap between him and Harmony. "You're not speaking plainly," she scolded Harmony, then turned back to the Archivist. "The woman who raised her asked her to speak to you. We need to know why."

"You don't know the question," he said, "but want an answer."

"No," Harmony said. "When I told the woman who raised me that I defeated the Quondam, she said to me 'it's all wrong' and 'what did you do?' She said it as if I wasn't supposed to beat them, like I wasn't supposed to end the war. Then you said it, on the stairs, you said the same thing . . . 'what did you do?' Why do you keep saying it? What *did* I do?"

A smile rose on the Archivist's cheeks, and at the same time, surprise riffled his forehead into a thorn of wrinkles. Two reactions, both at full tilt, vying for dominance on his face.

"You don't know," the Archivist said.

The shock and the glee merged to give the Archivist a new face. Finally, he regained the old look, the one that Harmony remembered. That regality returned, but now as an adult, she saw it clearer, not regal, *no*, it was a superiority complex. An arrogant, snotty grin crawling up the side of his face. He was back in control now. He had something they wanted.

"I don't know what?" Harmony said, hating that she had to ask. Feeling beggarly, nearly groveling.

"You don't, do you?" He chuckled the words out in individual syllables. "You walk around with your head held high, and you don't know."

"Know what?" Harmony asked.

"You don't know anything." The Archivist shook his head in disbelief and marched in circles. "You curse and rebel and kick over our satellites, and you don't know what you're doing?"

There was anger in that last bit. The mask slipped off, revealing his rage. But the Archivist quickly put back on a friendly face. He shook his head and loosened the grip in his fist that he didn't seem to realize he had.

"Then tell us," Harmony said. "What don't we know?"

"Say something," Gemini demanded.

"No," the Archivist said. "I don't think I will."

Gemini charged toward the Archivist, her fists folded into two massive balls of knuckle, and the Archivist stumbled backward, his hands held up to his face as if already repelling her blows.

"Not free of charge, I mean," he said. "I will tell you, but I just want one simple thing in return."

"What *thing*?" Harmony asked.

"Her," he said, pointing at Getty. "I want the Exegete."

Gemini's jaw dropped. She whipped around and stared at the girl with a sort of awe-inspired recognition. Not the type of recognition of knowing someone but the recognition of knowing a thing, like seeing a landmark she had only read about in a book. And she mouthed the word as if to make it real—*Exegete*.

"She didn't tell you?" the Archivist said.

Harmony hadn't told Gemini. That earned her an awkward side-eye from her sister.

"I wouldn't trust anyone with that information either." The Archivist's every word was strategic.

"Shut up," Harmony said. "This isn't a negotiation."

"But it is," he said. "I heard you earlier with the Infinite Men. You're an expert negotiator. You know the girl is a burden. Suicide doll. I bequeath to you the Spartan and any other treasure in this space. And I will give you the answer that doesn't have a question."

"No," Gemini said, fast and blunt. "No deal."

"You don't need an Exegete," he said.

"And we don't need your information," Harmony said. "We may want it, but the war's over. This is just a curiosity, not a need."

"Oh, but it is," he said confidently. "You need to know. The lives of everyone here depend on it."

Harmony stripped her handgun from the backpack and aimed it in the Archivist's direction. "Your life," she said. "That's the bargain."

"The question," the Archivist said, hands reaching up to the ceiling. "I can tell you the question."

"Good." Harmony nodded. "What's the question?"

"The question . . . ," he said, taking a step toward her. "It's the same question there always was. That same old, *old* mystery . . ."

"What?"

"Who are we fighting?" The words lingered in the air for a moment. "Or more appropriately *what*. The Quondam thought they knew. All those soldiers in all those cockpits. They thought they knew who they were fighting. But they got it wrong. *What are we fighting?* That is the question you don't know to ask."

"What are we fighting?" Harmony said, and for some reason, she believed him.

"That's the question," he said. "I will give you the answer, for the Exegete."

"We could beat the answer out of you," Gemini said.

"I know torture, girl," the Archivist snapped back. "The Infinite Men made their attempt to convert me to the golden arches. You can break my body, but it will not sway me."

"Yeah?" Gemini said, ready for the challenge.

"Can this one go?" the Archivist asked Harmony. "She's volatile."

"Would you like to see volatile?" Gemini asked.

"Gemini, go find Emit," Harmony said, and it took all the air right out of Gemini.

"Go?" Gemini's voice was small, like she'd lost twenty years.

"Find Emit," Harmony said again. "Bring him here. I'll handle him."

"Is it true?" Gemini pointed to Getty in the corridor. "Is she an Exegete?"

Harmony held the answer between her lips. She swallowed, but it kept coming back up. "Yes," she admitted.

"Getty," Gemini scoffed at a near laugh as it finally hit her. "Do you even know what an Exegete is?"

"Kinda," Harmony said and shrugged. "Interpreter for God or something . . ."

"He's right," Gemini said. "There's so much you don't know. Am I your . . ." *Sister?* Her lips bent around the word but changed. "*Adviser? Do you trust me?*"

"I trust you. I just . . ." Harmony paused to look at Getty. "I thought she'd be safer if no one knew."

"I'll find Emit," Gemini said. "Don't let him have the Exegete."

"I understand," Harmony responded.

The Archivist stepped backward, gesturing to a small passage on the opposite end of the room. "I'll show her out," he said.

Gemini and Harmony followed the Archivist down the unlit corridor at the opposite end of the room to the elevator. They heaved forward another stone on rollers that led into what he called a "beneath-ground parking station." And that would take Gemini into the burned-out storage facility adjacent to the cathedral. This place was truly a secret, hidden within a hide, and all of it camouflaged by the ruin outside.

Harmony raised her Glock again, and this time with intent. She was a good shot. Emit had trained her beyond proficiency. Though, as the Archivist returned to the room, he paid little attention to the weapon or Harmony. He moved through that space as if they weren't there. Only Getty captured his gaze.

"You will need transport for your Spartan; that battery stretches one minute long if you're lucky. My fingers are still in the roots of this city, at least for another few nights. You want the gun and the Wilson Sphere? Just give me her."

"Look, I don't want the fucking Wilson Sphere," Harmony said in exasperation. "You can keep it. You keep everything. I want my Spartan. And maybe the gun."

"The bayo-10," he said. "Good."

"Whatever, but you don't get her."

"I will not give you the answer without her."

"What do you want with Getty?"

"Her counsel," he said, eyes back on the Exegete. "I need to confide in her, and she then to confide in me."

"She's right there. You want to pray to her, beg her forgiveness? Go knock yourself out."

"Counsel, as in an advisory role. We would need to be in constant conversation."

Getty looked up at Harmony. Her lips moved, but she wasn't trying to speak. It was in anticipation of Harmony's answer.

"Are we in agreement, then?" the Archivist said.

"Yes," Harmony said. "You can have her constant counsel."

He smiled, but not all the way. His lips came to a premature wilt on the left side. The negotiation wasn't over, and he knew it, *didn't he?* "Good," he said but softly, as if it was only for him, and he reached for Getty's hand. She didn't reach back.

"You didn't let me finish," Harmony said, stepping forward. "You can travel with us. You can soothe your religious urges in worship and meditation. But you can*not* have her."

"I—"

"This is the closest thing you get to a deal. The other option is I shoot you, point-blank to your fucking throat, and let you think about your life decisions while you choke back blood. You take my Spartan? You kill my fucking friend? The fact that you're still breathing is the miracle. I can take my Androne and the question, what are we fighting, *right*? I know the question now. And eventually, I'll find someone with the answer."

The Archivist had stopped listening somewhere in her spiel and had started speaking to himself, or maybe to his god. A deliberation. And one that Harmony didn't have time for. She racked the slide on her pistol and pulled the trigger. Some glass artifact burst open behind him, and the man yelped.

"Archivist!" she said, the weapon clutched in a two-handed grip. "Die or answer the question. It's on you."

And she would shoot him—he could see that, *couldn't he?* Staring down the dark eye of the gun's barrel, the Archivist had to see the same cold, steely look in Harmony's gaze. And he did, it seemed, as his eyes retreated from hers, from the gun, and he nodded submission. "Agreed," he said through a frown and gritted teeth. "If you allow me to travel with you and take the Exegete's counsel, I shall give you the answer."

"Good," she said. "Now, who are we fighting?"

17

If he was going to play his last card, the Archivist would get comfortable. He had a stash of those very comforts hidden beneath the plinth that pedestaled the Wilson Sphere. Underneath the plinth was a hatch that opened into the floor beneath. A pair of backpacks rested there, big ones, packed so efficiently that not even a pinch of air could live between them. He applied the makeup inside to his face and a hairpiece to fit over his thinning hair. A pride appeared to slowly return to the man's cleaned and now evenly toned face.

"The Infinite Men will try to relaunch that satellite," the Archivist said as he pulled a paper-wrapped bread-like food from the bag. "I overheard them." Then he removed a bottle of liquor from the bag. "And the Chronics won't like that. They just got rid of the Quondam." He handled the bread and drink delicately. There was discipline in his movement, a ritual that he had done a thousand times, as was the short prayer he whispered over the food.

Getty had dozed off in the comfort of a dark corridor, and that was good. The girl had barely slept, and maybe it was the presence of the cathedral and its holy artifacts that calmed her to rest. She didn't need a drinking archivist (probably already drunk at this point) blabbering at her and begging for an Exegete's counsel.

"What are you drinking?" Harmony asked, genuinely curious.

"These are cuisines of halal. Eaten during the time of pilgrimage. Holy ingredients. Sacred in their preparation from ancient recipes."

He closed his eyes now, in commune with God. "I consume the earth in this croissant of crisp and flavor, and I drink of the Hive, in the piña of colada." The Archivist took a deep breath and opened his eyes. "Prepared by our Historic chefs mere hours before their deaths by the Infinite Men. And that was your doing, Peacemaker. How many deaths are at your hands?"

His confidence *was* returning. His scolding tone, that stringent posture, it was all coming back to him now. For the Archivist, confidence was arrogance. Even the way he ate exuded it. The Archivist bit into the croissant of crisps and flavor, and he chewed slowly, allowing the ingredients to spin around the corners of his mouth. And he savored every crumb on his lips and fingertips.

"So, are you ready to talk now?" Harmony asked.

"I spent nearly two days in that prison with nothing but breast milk and my faith. I need to eat."

And eat he did, finishing the croissant, then unfolding another from the holy papers.

"The thing about faith is that there must be doubt," he said. The food seemed to make him loquacious, or was that the drink? "You can't have faith without doubt. If you know something is true, undeniable fact, you can't say you have faith in it. You can't have faith that the sky is blue. It is just blue. Only the things we can doubt require belief, and belief takes effort."

"So you have doubts?" she said, aiming the edge of the conversation back toward him.

"All the time."

"Then why dedicate your life to something with so much doubt?" she asked.

He gave it thought, for a full minute, the idea running through his head, each second weighing heavier than the last. She could see the ever-deepening wrinkles burrowing into the man's brow. His age then unraveled out of him. The carefully applied makeup dried up and cracked in places.

"Whether you're in the church or a nonbeliever, there is this space in the human brain that most things cannot fill. Some try to fill it with affluence, drugs, carnal temptations, and other depravities. And on occasion, these things fit for a time, but they are inevitably hollow, because that space, that hole in our brain, it's shaped like a god. God and all its dominion, even if it isn't real, we need it. We are evolved to believe."

Harmony eyed the liquor in his hand, *empty*, and he was reaching for another. *Drunk.* She shook her head at what he'd just suggested, that people needed God—or at least the idea of it. But Harmony knew that feeling. A little bit, at least. The hole in her own mind. That emptiness he was talking about. The fear. She'd ended the war, and where was the fulfillment? She didn't believe in any gods, but Harmony had tried everything to fill that fucking hole somewhere at the back of her mind. That hollow space that hope seeped out from. Was that what Getty was? Another attempt at filling the empty spaces?

"You're stalling," she said, but Harmony didn't mind, did she? Harmony didn't truly want to know the truth. She was procrastinating as much as him.

But as the Archivist drained the last drop of his drink, he seemed ready now, loosened at the joints, loosened at the jaw. He licked his lips and squinted at her, and *loose* was the most accurate word for him. But now she wasn't ready. Harmony would push the procrastination further, more conversational appetizers, and it was his fault for dining so garishly in front of her.

"Who's missing?" Harmony asked him, gesturing to his two backpacks.

"Who is missing?" The Archivist peered up at Harmony and followed the winding road of her gaze to the two backpacks. One likely for him, *and the other?* It took the middle-aged man a good moment to recover. There was a moment first of surprise, then what looked like a moment of recollection, memories flashing across his eyes, and finally a moment of deflection, a simper, a flaunting of teeth and gums like a shield against the other emotion.

"Who is missing?" he said again. "Your friend, right?" he said quickly. "She is late. Did she go out there and get herself killed?"

Even though his question was an obvious diversion from talking about his backpacks, it was working. Emit was supposed to wait at the back alley adjacent to the cathedral, hopefully with a wagon and a pair of quadrupedals in tow. It should have been quick. Should have been minutes instead of the hour and counting.

If something happened to them now, it was her fault. *It was all wrong*, her mother had said, and it was all Harmony's fault. And that was what was handicapping her, she realized: the blame. It was the same reason she was procrastinating. The same reason she didn't want the Archivist's information. If there was something wrong with bringing down those satellites and ending the Quondam, it would be her fault too. *Your fault*, and she heard it all in her mother's chiding voice. How much more blood would be on her hands?

"Are you saying something?" the Archivist said.

"You ate your sacred bread," Harmony said, ready to face him again and ready for the truth. "And you had your damn holy piña cola thing."

"Colada," he corrected. "I have sacred colas as well."

"Sure," she agreed without even understanding. Harmony was ready for the answers, regardless of her mother's voice screaming in her head. "What did I do?" she said. "What did I do that was so wrong with taking down the Quondam? They were tyrants. They killed so many, so indiscriminately, all of them were . . ." She paused then. Because it wasn't all of them; *not all*. Some showed kindness. Some protected her when she was too small to remember. "The Quondam will be replaced, right? The Church of Time will find a new rival in the Infinite Men or the Audis or even the goddamn Apple Biters, I don't know. What does it matter?"

"What does it matter? What do you think the Quondam's objective was?" The Archivist appeared to be asking sincerely, no brandishing of a superior perspective on things.

"Control?" she said with a shrug. "Cruelty? Make sure the tenets of their time endured at all costs? I don't know."

"Yes, you don't know," he said and pointed at her almost like Aurora would. "And does that make sense? All that effort for the sake of cruelty? No. Power yields cruelty. It's a side effect but not a reason. It wasn't their purpose."

"No?" She leaned toward him. "So says a thief. Stealing all these little Quondam Era treasures, thinking it'd bring you closer to them?" She gestured to the room and its little treasures. "What was the Quondam's glorious purpose, then?"

"To be a dam," he said, and with confidence.

"A dam?" She shook her head. "Stop bullshitting around. What do you mean, a dam?"

"That's how they describe it. The goal was to stop the flood that had been building for centuries. They commit acts of violence. Yes. Cruelty. I saw them, hell, I committed a few myself. I stole. I cheated people of their possessions and . . . I suffer for those sins, but that was just a by-product of being human. Jealousy, greed, revenge. Most of it, damn near all of it, was our own tribal nonsense. Not the Quondam. They had to keep us happy, right? They had to keep their allies content so they'd blow up a building here, raid a village there. And that kept us in power."

"So they helped you be the top tribe, and you would help them . . . what? Build this dam against a flood? And what was the flood?"

"*Technology*," he said, and he said it like it was a curse word. "For them, *flood* was a code name for technology."

"The Quondam were trying to stop us from creating new technologies?"

"Technology kept evolving, even after the Quondam. In those dark ages between us and them, small sects kept pushing the technological envelope. Where do you think the church's liquid cockpits come from? There are new technologies out there. Technologies you and your Androne especially would be familiar with."

"What technology is that?" she asked.

"Weapons tech," he said, pointing to her Androne. "At the beginning of time, it was a stone and a stick and a handful of knuckles. At the time of the Quondam, they created Androhes in their own image. And there were nuclear weapons and hypersonic missiles. But they didn't stop. Then vacuum bombs. And still they didn't stop—antimatter javelins. And they did not stop. How far do you think it could go?"

"The Quondam wanted to stop us from building on their weapon technology?"

"One weapon in particular."

"What weapon is that?" she asked.

He smiled then, a sad smile that lit his lips as it extinguished the light in his eyes. But again, the Archivist recovered quickly, clearing his throat, and that cleared the emotion from his made-up face.

"What weapon?" Harmony insisted.

"The last weapon. Like I said, if it started with sticks and stones, and Androhes somewhere in the middle, this thing would truly be the last."

"What?" she said, slow and deliberate. "What? Thing?"

"It's hard to say. I'm an archivist. I study the past, not science."

"So you don't know."

"I am an archivist—"

"You don't know what it is."

"What I know is that the Quondam were the only thing preventing its creation. And with them gone, because, well . . ." He gestured in Harmony's direction.

"Blame me. That's what your whole ruse is for. Teach me a lesson. I took away your cushy raping-and-pillaging work, so now you put me through this whole charade."

"I have never raped any person—"

"All this bullshit about giving you Getty and you only have half of an answer. You don't know shit."

"I know," he said, his brow rising, his pride lifting his chest, and that was what she wanted. That was her plan all along. "I know, Peacemaker. I just don't understand exactly. And you . . . won't believe it. It will be a foreign language to you."

"Why won't I believe?"

"You're not a believer."

"Tell me."

"The last weapon was created by the most brilliant science teams and an ASI collaborating across time, communicating between centuries. They laid the blueprint for it. And at some point in recent history, those scientists walked out into the dark of desert, and they created God."

She just looked at him for a moment, a long, deadpan gaze, as if meaning would emerge through his pores. *What the fuck is he talking about?* And her jaw hung open wanting to ask but unable to form the words.

"They made . . . *something*," he said and pointed at nothing in the distance. "Out there. They made something else. It is not a machine. It's not a person. Not biological. Not any collaboration between the two. But it is awake. It is conscious. It is a weapon without a trigger."

"What?" she said, squinting into the incredulousness of what he was saying. And he was right—she didn't believe him. She was *not* a believer. "That's not true. There is no God."

"Call it what you like. A consciousness. A mind. But it exists."

"How is a mind a weapon?" Harmony asked.

"Wolves have claws, snakes have their venom. Human beings survived in the dark because of our weapon."

"The mind," she said.

"The sharpest claws break against our thoughts; the largest teeth bend against our ideas. The ultimate mind *is* an ultimate weapon. And they worship that thing out there."

"I don't believe it."

"It is inevitable, Peacemaker. It is the mathematical end point to every equation, every algorithm in physics or calculus or geometry, it all leads there, it all ends with that thing they built out there. No matter what direction you compute from, string theory or quantum gravity, this is the final conclusion. This is the end point. There is no further that science could possibly go. It *is* the last weapon, and believe or not, it has a plan for us all."

GEMINI

Something told her to get out of that city. *Get out and keep going.* Head back through Serpent's Whim, then keep moving, past Bridgetown, and take High Road to the coast. Something told her she wanted to see the ocean again and live off the back of the beach. Something told her all that, maybe instinct or intuition, but then another voice in her head told her not to listen. It told her that she knew what she had to do, the same thing she was instructed to do in the beginning—*just fucking kill Harmony.*

Gemini whispered to her voices in the dark of the tunnel as the Archivist's secret path exited into the postal building on the opposite side of the road. The building was in ruin. The roof was caving in, and the floor was like wooden quicksand. Gemini tiptoed over scorched planks and under unstable ceilings, all of it threatening to eat her alive.

The city streets were congested with those medicine boys, hundreds of them shouting and scampering about with the banners of the Infinite Men. Aurora had taught her the stories of that symbol on their banners, the golden *M*. It was a logo from the old world and the first letter in the word for *man* in the Quondam language, and thus it had been adapted to the flags and banners of the Infinite Men. Hundreds of them, many hundreds, carried that banner, and those flags, and handguns, and rifles, all readying for war. But a war against who?

Gemini kept to the alleys and shadows and the burned-out buildings, all the spaces that the Infinite Men were too holy to traverse. The whites of their robes would dirty in the ash and soot and the mud from the nighttime rains.

Emit wouldn't be hard to find if he had kept to the trader's market as they told him to, so she had time, she figured, time enough maybe to find a necromancer. But that would be doubly challenging both in a fallen city and with few, if any, satellites still in the sky. So maybe not, but she should still ask. Ask the old woman looting the ash from the postal building. Ask the family of four, sneaking through the alleys. Ask that boy sitting on the road and answering her with questions of his own, interrogating Gemini about his big sister. "I can't find her," he said, tears in one eye, blood in the other.

He wouldn't find his sister like she wouldn't find her necromancer. Not here, not now in this time of revolution. Gemini surrendered to that idea and searched instead for Emit. She marched down an aisle of merchant stands, her neck craned up and eyeing every person at the height that Emit stood.

The trader's market was bustling considering everything that had happened. There were still customers hanging around the city square. But maybe it wasn't their city. Maybe these bright-faced sellers were untethered to all the slaughter and heartbreak. Maybe they were vultures—black feathers between their teeth, selling recently looted Church of Quondam goods. Everything for sale.

Emit stood underneath the shade of a spirits cart, one that was mobile, sitting on four wheels with a small but efficient quadrupedal at its head. He was drunk and his face was liquid, dribbling alcohol and sniffling it too. *Goddamn fool.* Emit had nothing resembling a transport nearby.

"Emit," Gemini scolded. "What are you doing?"

Emit turned his wet face toward her, water in his eyes, liquor on his lips, his whole body splashing about in a drunken motion. His eyes were empty for that first moment, until he squinted through the wash of spirits, blinking them away from his sight like a hand swiping against a fogged window. And then he saw her and his eyes lit up.

"Harm," he said, spitting the word out of his mouth. "Harm?"

"No," Gemini said. "Have you had any success with finding transport? There are at least ten hundred soldiers out there in the square. We need to move."

"A . . . thousand?" he answered slowly, doing the math in his head.

"We used different counting systems in the church, but yes. Have you found transport?"

"No," he said, squinting at Gemini dubiously. "Barely have enough time credits for a five-person wagon."

"But the drinks?" she said. "You have enough for the drinks."

"Gemini?" he said, just realizing, shocked and halfway vexed, like she had tricked him, exploited him by mimicking Harmony's voice.

"The transport," Gemini said, bringing him back to the subject at hand. "You were supposed to be the master bargainer, raised among the Port Siren traders, right?"

"I bargained. A five-person wagon we can do, but you add a quadrupedal to that, food, supplies. We have to figure something else out."

"A smaller wagon?" she asked, or was it that voice asking? "Two, three people."

"Three?" Emit cocked his head and shrugged. "What about the Archiver and Getty?"

"Archivist. And we don't need him anymore," she said.

"That's still four people," he said. "Getty and Harmony."

"Do you love her?" Gemini said.

"Sorry?" he said, bending his ear toward her, figuring he must have heard her wrong.

"Harmony," she said. "Do you love her?"

Do you? the voice asked her.

"Do I *love* Harmony?" Emit said, and she nodded. "What? Why? Did she . . . she said something?"

"Yes," Gemini lied, because now she might be able to get something more out of him, with the spirits and the confusion. How did he really feel about her?

"Did she ask you to ask me that?" he said, his lips floundering over each other, eyes welling up with tears. He really was a liquid, dripping and sinking in on himself.

"What aren't you saying?" Gemini probed, stepping forward. "Tell me."

"I ran," he said. "I didn't try and save her." He covered his face now, trying to hold his leaking features together. He sniffled his liquid nose and stumbled on his liquored feet. "At the cathedral. We left our tanks early, but she didn't—she stayed, and I saw her before the Androne stabbed her, and I didn't do anything. I ran away."

This wasn't what she wanted, this confession from a drunken conscience, that wasn't it. But then again maybe it was. There was a love in the slur of his words. Emit couldn't be Gemini's ally in Harmony's murder.

"You love her?" Gemini confirmed, then turned to herself—turning inward. "I care for Harmony too, but do you trust her?"

"What?" he said, sniffling away the tears. "You're saying Harm?"

"Her decisions recently. It's playing out like they said."

"Like who said?"

"I was told that Harmony cannot be allowed to collaborate with the Church of Time—the Chronics."

"Who told you . . ."

Me, the voice said. *Don't tell him it was me.* "I won't," Gemini said.

"Won't what?" Emit asked.

"Things are worse now. And I believe her now. Everything she said has come true."

Tell him to kill her. She trusts him more than you. The voice was loud now, and Gemini had to speak louder to block it out. "She was a, uh . . ." But Gemini hesitated there, losing herself in her other self.

"Are you okay?" he asked.

"Yes," she said to Emit. *Quiet*, she then thought to herself in that same moment. *He'll think we are crazy.* "I'm fine, Emit, but I just worry about Harmony. About her collaborating with the church. Her becoming one of them."

"She won't," Emit said. "Harm hates the church."

"But if she does. If she collaborates with them, the Peacemaker, with her following among the gangs and the rebel states, who else would follow? The Mickeys for sure, right?"

"Yes, the Rat Kingdom for sure. Maybe also Port Siren."

"And the Red Bulls," she said. "The Islanders. The Apple Biters."

"The Apple Biters?" Emit said in surprise. "With the church?"

"Could you imagine? The church is consolidating power. They almost have the Audists. With the Peacemaker, they'd have them all. So we have to . . ." *You can't say it. You love her, don't you?* "Quiet," she said to the voice. "Listen," she said to him. "We have to figure out together what to do if that happens, if she collaborates with the church again. She's down there right now, making deals with an archivist."

"Are you still talking to me?" Emit leaned toward her, as confused as he was intoxicated.

"What if she betrays the cause?" Gemini asked. "What if Harmony, herself, is the assassin in our midst? Not killing herself but killing the cause."

Emit paused then, unlocking his eyes from hers and drifting down into the deep of thought. Now she had him, a little at least. He was understanding now, with jaw ajar and all that liquid liquor drying up.

"What do we do, then?" Gemini said, another step forward, her hand on his shoulder, conniving, convincing—*wait*, no, no, no, wait, that wasn't her. Those weren't her words nor her cadence; that wasn't her voice.

Shut up, Gemini thought.

"You're saying it like it might happen," Emit said.

"It will." *Shut the hell up.* "I mean, I want to know what to do if it does happen. *If* these time worshippers manipulate Harmony to turn in on herself. What are the plans and protocols? What do we do?"

Emit stepped back. She was too close now, the hot of her breath warm against his chest. He didn't appear to agree but wasn't in disagreement either.

"You're next in line," she said. "The decision will come from you."

"I don't . . ." He couldn't finish, looking at everything else but her. "I don't think I'm next in line, Gem, I . . . Harmony's . . . she's our leader," he said, and it was almost a question.

Emit's voice had started to bend, started to question things, but he wasn't quite there yet. Though she accomplished her goal—*her*, not Gemini, but Gemini's voice. *She* had made the viral little leap from Gemini's mind and into Emit's. And she would grow there, and soon she would be a little voice in the back of Emit's head.

"You're probably right," Gemini said, but that was a lie. *It WILL come to that. Harmony has to die.*

———

They bargained in tandem, collaborative tactics to bring down the costs of things, and they worked well together. Emit, sobering up fast and performing the amiable gentleman, charming the merchants into smiles and occasional laughter with his awkward wit, while Gemini negotiated like a wolf, cutting language, daggers, concealing threats in her words.

They haggled with an older seller for a small wagon with an ancient quadrupedal that might carry the load. It was in their budget with a few hundred banknotes to spare. The other option was a modern, stronger hexapod that could carry supplies on its back and maybe even that Androne Harmony treasured. But no wagon—they would have to walk beside the machine, and without the weight of their supplies on their backs, that might actually work.

They bargained until sunset, until the other buyers surrendered to the night and sellers' options were few and far between. And that was where Gemini tightened the noose, imploring the young seller to offer up the wagon bed along with the hexapod. There was a reason why she had targeted this seller. She had noticed the golden *M* insignia seared into the bottom of the hexapod. The young seller had looted the machine, and she told him that she knew. Even as he denied it, she stared straight through the shaking of his head and made him an ultimatum: "Sell and break even, but if you don't agree, this medicine man"—she gestured to Emit—"will employ his allies in picking you apart."

And the medicine boys prowled every front street and back alley like stray cats, without form or formation, hissing at the civilians, hissing at each other. And now Gemini didn't think they were searching for her, Harmony, and their archivist. She had a feeling that this was about something else. Something *bigger*. But their presence in the markets only benefited Gemini. It made for nervous sellers with illicit goods, and so the young man agreed, hurrying the process along as he whispered his terms.

"Smart, Gem," Emit said, bending and leaning down toward her.

She leaned toward him and smiled in lieu of a response. And that smile held to her face and wouldn't go away. And he had called her Gem. *Gem*—she hated that name, abhorred it. And she hated him. But maybe it was that voice, that part of her that was like a part of him. God, this was going to get complicated.

The transaction was slower in the evening light. The young man checked the banknotes—counterfeits were common in larger cities—while Gemini and Emit checked his hexapod. Both he and she only half understood their way around the machines and hopefully together made those halves whole. Lantern lights and incandescent bulbs started blinking on even before the sun had set. And that was when she first noticed it, bullets ricocheting in the distance and the sudden bending of sunlight.

The gunfire clapped from what sounded like the town square. The armed young men in the trader's market rioted toward the shrieks of artillery, waving their banners and firing their guns into the air. Cries of "down with the Chronics" echoed through the market. War had arrived in the Yellow City. The young men racing down the stairs hours earlier really weren't after Harmony; they were preparing for war.

At that same moment, the incandescent bulbs started flickering. And not flickering—that wasn't the right word for it. The light itself was warping out of shape, not the bulbs but the light, if light had a shape. Gemini didn't understand what she was seeing.

"What's . . ." Emit started but didn't have the vocabulary to finish. "You see this?"

They all saw it, like someone had smeared a paintbrush across reality. The merchant raced off with the banknotes, leaving not just the hexapod and wagon bed but all of his spare parts: power cables, web circuits, solar cells, all together tripling the costs of the hexapod.

"Take it?" Emit asked.

"I don't know," she said, considering and maybe realizing that some people were just followers. And this wasn't the time for such a thought with all the bedlam in the street, and yet there it was, a brain bubble rising to the top of her mind. Emit was a follower.

"Gem," he said into the mumble of her lips. "What do we—"

She didn't hear the end of the sentence, even though she saw his mouth fold and open with words. Because if light could bend, then so could sound. Everything he said was warped into a sort of Doppler, his voice moving past her ears and taken toward the cathedral tower. And the light too curved toward that tower, the Infinite Men's tower, and Harmony was underneath it.

A giant shadow—*giant* in the most literal sense of the word—passed over them. Something like footsteps came pounding down the opposite side of the buildings behind them and moved toward the tower.

"Grab the hex," Gemini said, snatching up a couple of the merchant's web circuits.

"Then go back for her?" Emit asked, pointing to the cathedral tower.

"Grab the hex, Emit."

Gemini stuffed her pockets full of whatever she could find, and she did it all without looking. Her gaze was fixed on the rooftops and that gargantuan shadow moving about on the other side of the buildings. The light was deformed, sharp at some angles and dull at others.

"We have to go back for them," he said, dragging the hexapod into a corner. "*Right?* We're going back?"

Maybe, and maybe she didn't have to kill Harmony. Maybe she could watch Harmony drown in rock and rubble. That giant was barreling toward the tower, and she imagined it knocking the phallic edifice down on top of their dear peacemaker. But choking on rocks and rubble was kind—it wasn't bittersweet or considerate or a "good way to go." And Gemini had promised; she would kill Harmony in the kindest way possible.

18

Harmony looted a crown, a Keltic ring with a glow of green diamonds, and a bracelet with a small clock attached, anything small enough to fit in her pouch. The ancient items would hold well for trade value in the southern markets, and she would need to trade to mend her Spartan. She would need them if she was going to kill their god.

"Getty." Harmony hailed the girl, waving at her across the room. "Time to go."

Getty rubbed the sleep out of her eyes. She squinted at Harmony's mass robbery of the artifacts, grabbing jewelry and books and tossing devices too large for her bag. Getty watched in confusion, and she didn't stand up.

"What's wrong?" the Archivist said.

What's wrong was he was half-right. There *was* something else out there, and she had felt it, this weight in the air. This invisible thing taking up space in the world and moving the puzzle pieces out of place. Things that hadn't made sense before, like the church's technology, the liquid cockpits, and battery capacity, she understood it now. She knew why they collaborated with her. There was something else, some thing but not a god, *no*. Religion smears its greasy fingers all around the lips of reality, she knew that. But a weapon, the last weapon, that made sense to her. And it scared her too.

"I've had a bad feeling for a long time," she said, eyeing a pen from some famous writer.

"Careful," the Archivist said. "That is the pen of the Little Poet Wayne."

"Worth a lot?" she asked.

"Priceless," he exclaimed, as if it should be obvious. "All of these items are."

Harmony shoved it into her pocket and heard the old metal crack. The Archivist cringed as if that snapping was in his own back.

"What bad feeling are you talking about?" he asked.

"I don't know," she said. The thing was hard to describe. "Like that feeling when someone is watching from behind. Like something was there and not there at the same time. Something missing. It's . . ." She paused, pondering how to put it. "Like upstairs, the elevator room. Like that. Like being in a house and there's an extra room without a door, just taking up space. And you don't know about the room, you don't know it exists, but when you're in the house, you feel like something's off. Like there's space missing."

"So you *do* believe me?" he said.

She wouldn't give him the satisfaction. "We have to get out of here," Harmony said to Getty, gesturing for her to follow. "Where the fuck is Gemini?" She whispered that part to herself.

"Go where?" the Archivist asked, consciously or subconsciously standing in Harmony's way, slowing her pace. "Where are you going?"

"To find it," she said. "Break their new weapon."

He stepped back, not quite out of her way, but retreating from Harmony like there was this stink on her. There was something on her that he did not want to smell or catch, like a malady. He looked at her like she was mad.

"Did you not hear what I just told you?" he said, deathly serious. "Their weapon is a god."

"Whatever it is, I'll find it. Stop it. End the war."

"First, you can't kill what they made. It's a . . ." The Archivist's frustration overflowed in the flush on his face. "Why? Why you? Because you're the Peacemaker? They tell you that you'll end the war. Since childhood, you've been this great thing. And you do everything to become that. It's your inheritance. You're owed it."

"Shut up," she screamed, up close and right in his face. "Stop fucking talking."

"Why do you have to stop it?" the Archivist screamed back.

"Because it's my fault," Harmony howled, and she felt blood rushing to her face too, though it would not show on her complexion. "The Quondam, the weapon, that's all on me. Getty, please, move."

Getty moved. She lifted herself onto two lazy feet and crutched one arm against the corridor wall. But the Archivist moved faster, advancing on Harmony, blocking her path with knotted-up joints: shoulders, elbows, down to his knuckles, all squeezed into balls of angst.

"There is time," he said. "What is your rush? I have some sway in the city. You need wagons to carry the Androne. Running toward the enemy this way is rash."

"Why do you care?"

She knew he had some motive, the snake of a man, but the Archivist did have a point. She'd need something to carry the Spartan. A manual walk with the battery would last only a minute or so. And the Archivist must have seen that realization manifest on her expression, because he kept going—kept conniving and creeping closer with all his knotted-up joints.

"And you said I would travel with her," the Archivist continued. "Travel with you, that was the deal."

That was why he cared. He wanted Getty without having to run face-first into Harmony's conflicts. *Fuck the deal*, but she wouldn't say it, not yet. She still needed him, and more importantly, she needed him to remain calm. The last thing Harmony wanted was a jilted Quondam zealot in a cellar of his own making.

"Sure," she said tepidly, then grabbed the Archivist's second backpack to shove more of the artifacts inside.

"No," he shouted, taking a long stride toward her, snatching his backpack from under the gnarl of her fingernails.

Harmony backpedaled, clutching her handgun tighter but not raising it. The Archivist was beginning to get unwound.

"You don't touch it," the Archivist shouted. He didn't step forward, but his voice moved toward her. His gaze, barbed and cutting, lunged at her.

"Get back," Harmony screamed, raising her gun in the shadow of her Androne. "Get back!"

He stopped, frozen in place, and at first she thought he was looking at the gun, but the Archivist had heard something that worried him far more than the barrel of her Glock. There was a screeching, like violin strings on knives, screeches like screams, like cattle to the slaughter. It echoed, the sound of chains spinning on rusted gears.

"Elevator," he said.

Harmony whipped around just in time to see the bulb above it light up. "This you?" she screamed, gun still aimed at him as she jabbed at the air with it. "This your people? A trap? Is it you?"

"No." Getty answered for him. "It's too fast. It's happening too fast."

"How'd they find it?" the Archivist said. He spilled one backpack's supplies onto the ground and then quickly shoved a pair of ancient books and the Wilson Sphere inside. "How'd they find the—"

The Archivist hiccuped on the end of those words as he saw the impossible. Even Harmony lowered her gun. Only the Exegete watched without the awe of the others as the bulbs shining down on his displayed relics began to bend—the light itself bending like it was strings of luminosity. *"What the hell?"* Harmony whispered as the bending light started to lean toward the elevator, the fluorescence stretching and curving toward its doors.

"It's not the Infinite Men," the Exegete said as she approached the elevator doors, seemingly under the spell of that elasticity of light.

"We have to go," the Archivist said, running to Getty and dragging her back toward the second exit.

"Just like this," Getty said, running toward Harmony, her irises spinning like wheels on the white of her eyes. That religious madness was in her look again. "Like this—like this, Peacemaker, but I shouldn't be here. Not here! I'm not here." Tears ran down her cheeks, and Getty suddenly whispered a ballad, seemingly to comfort her:

"Like God **commanded**, yet under**handed**,
Stranded, like **Stan did**,
standing against all odds—all gods, and **candid**.
A deity un**flawed**, yet she stares un-**awed**.
Applaud against the great Hand of **God**."

Harmony hadn't said a word. She hadn't moved toward or away from the elevator, she hadn't budged, or had she? Somehow in all the shouting and commotion, Harmony had found herself on the opposite end of the room, closer to her Spartan—pressed up against it. Her arm clutched around the Androne's leg. *How?* Or more importantly, why? Why couldn't she let go?

"Come on," the Archivist said to Harmony as he dragged Getty toward the secret passage. "Peacemaker?"

"Not again," Harmony said, but mostly to herself. She was as paralyzed as the inactive Androne beside her. And she couldn't abandon it. "It can't happen again."

"Harm?" Emit's voice came as loud and panicked as she had ever heard him. And it was only his voice, emerging from the passageway to the ancient parking lot. She heard the footsteps trampling closer and his voice booming louder. "Harm!"

Emit stumbled out from the passage barely able to breathe and still trying to shout her name. A few steps behind him and moments later, Gemini trotted out of the passage, both of them panting and hanging against the walls for support.

"Whole thing's coming down," he said and sucked in a breath of air. "The building is going to fall."

"What's happening?" Harmony asked, squeezing tighter onto the Spartan's leg.

"A disturbance," Gemini said. "I don't know what, but the Chronics are here."

Harmony watched the shamble of a group huddled together and all waiting for her orders. She would kill every one of them, one by one they would die by association, like Elijah and all the other names that she would eventually forget.

"You *deserve* to die." She said it with her mother's accent, in her mother's intonation and cadence. Aurora had actually said that to her once. That was the day Harmony had left Port Siren and left Aurora forever. And now she heard her mother's voice again, *you deserve to die,* but she was right this time. What better way to die than to do it for the people you love? What better way to die than with old Cy?

"Harm?" Emit shouted. "What are you doing? There's war outside. Real nasty. Chronics against these infinity boys."

"That's why they were running down the stairs," the Archivist said. "Not after us."

"We can make it out in the middle of the fighting," Emit said. "We'd just be civilians running between their bullets. We can make it if we go now."

"She's not leaving," Gemini said, her gaze hooked into the dewy center of Harmony's eyes.

And Gemini was right. Harmony wasn't going anywhere. It would never stop. War never stops. But she understood that. And whatever came out of that door, she was going to fucking kill it, or it was going to kill her.

Harmony grabbed the Spartan's manual controls. She slid the visor over her head, but not covering her eyes yet—it rested on her forehead. She slipped her hands into the gloves and her feet into the foot imprints. Wires ran from the visor, gloves, and imprints into the spine of the Spartan Series. Back to the basics, and it felt right.

"Harm . . ."

"Go," Harmony said. "I'm okay."

"You're mad," the Archivist said. "The battery is for demonstrative purposes only. It won't run more than thirty seconds."

Then I'll kill it in twenty-nine, she thought, her palms sweating in the gloves, the visor strapped to the back of her head and resting on her sweatier forehead. All the while the elevator galloped down. Suspension cables whipping. Just a few floors away. So loud and incredibly close.

"We have to get out," the Archivist said.

"Harm, you have to come," Emit pleaded. "Harm . . . Sis?"

Emit's voice moved Harmony, but it was her soul, not her body that stirred.

"Go," she shouted back. "Go, and take Getty."

"Harm!"

The light bulbs above them appeared like two hundred blinking eyes. They flickered, on-off, on-off, as the light itself pulled toward the elevator door—pulled like something was sucking the light out of their sockets. Then the elevator *dinged*. It had arrived.

"Gemini, go," Harmony said to the one person she knew who would. "Get them out."

"Go gently," Gemini said, and there was meaning in her words. She said it with such weight, straining her eyes and voice, but Harmony would never get the chance to find out what that meaning was.

Go.

Gemini pulled Getty and slapped Emit across his face. With the Archivist already gone, Emit would be the last to leave. He cried for her, his big sis, and she cried for him. Their footsteps and voices faded out as the cranking and spinning in the elevator stopped. All the light in the world now bending toward the door, like a spotlight for a grand, theatric entrance.

Harmony pulled the headset over her eyes and kicked the battery on, and for the first time in nearly twenty years, she saw through its single eye again. *Oh God*, she could see—she could see all the detail that made up for her myopic eyes. She squeezed its hands and could feel the rust trickling out from between the fingers. And she could feel its heartbeat surging through the wires like umbilical cords.

The elevator doors opened, geriatric and rusty in their posture and motion, one door sliding gentler and the other rattling to a half-way stop. Then with all the light in the world aimed at it, that *thing* behind the door emerged, and it was so clear, revealed so completely in that wash of fluorescence, that Harmony could describe every angle of it. She could narrate every curve and surface in perfect detail. It was ingrained in her memory now, and she would never forget.

But that thing, exposed in the stark nakedness of curved light, whatever it was, there was not a single adjective or verb, that she knew at least, to give it description. There were no words to describe what she was seeing, just sounds, guttural and primal noises. And Harmony made those noises. She bellowed at untapped pitches of her vocal cords. Ancestral howling climbed out of her throat at the sight of this new, horrible thing. She screamed. Harmony screamed for her life. And that thing screamed right the fuck back.

19

The building was collapsing too. Chips of concrete sprinkled down with all the consistency of rain. Gray precipitation clogged the field of vision, and dust like dew fogged the air. And still that thing was clear as the clearest fucking day.

It was alien. A metal demon for this gray hell. And for a moment she stood staring at it, watching the infinite details of the thing. It emerged from the elevator spiderlike with five identical limbs, and yet it moved upright, walking on the limbs, not crawling. Legs on the ceiling, on the ground, on the wall, and moving toward her. A trio of cables trailed behind it, each one thicker than her arms, suggesting that this thing might be connected to something else.

What the fuck?

It screamed across the corridor, as loud as trumpets, but like death—like something inside of it was dying. The metal across its body was scalelike. Each of the thousand scales lifted and lowered like they were breathing. And with each lift, a different color and texture of the metal emerged. A gray steel skin shifted to a brownish-gray tungsten, then changed again to a brownish-reddening rhodium. This thing was its own paintbrush and sculpture and kept on changing; every second, every blink of the eye it was something else. Every time she thought she had a handle on it, it morphed, new angles and shapes. Even the surface of its exoskeleton folded into spaces that opened up on its body.

And right then, as it made no sense at all, she understood. Every step this thing took toward her it reimagined itself. It was shapeless, unformed, and impossible to plan for or counter. This thing was physical strategy, and she would run now if she could, but it was too late for that.

Harmony reached left, and the Spartan shadowed her, snatching the bayo-10 rifle from its display pedestal. She felt the weight of its ammunition as she lifted the rifle and aimed at the demon—dead center on its starfish-like anatomy. She pulled her index finger inward, and the Spartan's finger yanked on the trigger. The bayo-10 clapped so savagely that the Spartan's glass eyepiece cracked, *cheap fucking replacements.* Even the Androne itself stumbled backward. Harmony sidestepped to the left so she wouldn't get trampled by her own Spartan.

But all that effort and this thing could dodge her bullets. It duplicated itself, splitting like a cell into two, then four, and after sixteen she lost count. *What the fuck was going on?* It was everywhere, to the left of her, right, above, at every possible angle. And she stumbled back again, shooting again, and hitting nothing but the elevator door. And after splitting into countless possible movements, it reintegrated into one body. And it was singular again.

How? The horror of this thing wasn't just that the machine was doing what it was doing; it was that this technology was beyond anything she had ever thought possible. Forget centuries—it was eons beyond its time. This moment felt to her like a neanderthal glimpsing medieval architecture, the towers and coliseums, or medieval peasants watching Quondam jets vaulting overhead, or the pre-Quondam soldiers in their trenches staring out at a front line of Androhes. She should not be seeing this. This should not be real—*it's not real.*

The demon lunged at her with its five appendages, two running on the ground, one running along the ceiling, and two reaching for the Spartan. Harmony stepped back and the Spartan followed, but slower than normal. Its movement drained the battery, legs 30 percent, arms 20, joints 15—the battery was nearly dry.

"Not now," she encouraged her Spartan. "Hang in there. Hang on."
Harmony eyed the three cables connected to the back of the machine's body. Maybe they were connected to a power source. Maybe if she severed one or all of them, this monster might die.

As she charged her Spartan, the metal monster swiped at the Androne's neck. Harmony countered, lifting the bayonet on the rifle up toward the demon's extended limb. And then it happened again. The machine split into a hundred different copies of itself. A hundred different possibilities, and then, just like before, reassembled into a single entity. And it remerged in the one position that was the most advantageous, just to the right of the Spartan, Harmony's blind spot. It struck the Spartan's right arm, severing it at the shoulder joint. Her Androne's right arm and the rifle hit the ground.

It was a Schrödinger attack, *wasn't it?* That machine was attempting every possible offensive and defensive maneuver and choosing the best of all possible outcomes. That was the only thing that made sense at the moment, and if that was true, then Harmony was already dead.

Red lights flashed on her visor: dead battery. She had mere seconds of power left. Harmony already felt the delay in the Spartan's movement, or maybe that was the unbalance of losing an arm. She adjusted by leaning to her left, and while that helped the Spartan's balance, it left Harmony off-kilter.

The mechanical monster came at her again, shattering into countless superpositions. But this time Harmony considered her most vulnerable angle, and it was obvious, the Spartan's missing right arm, over a hundred pounds of weight, leaving her open and off balance. So she pivoted, swinging the Spartan's left hand to her right side just as the demon reduced itself to one position on the Spartan's right, and she hit it, dead center on its body.

It stumbled back, as much as a five-legged thing could stumble. Its limbs on the ceiling scraped away cement chips, limbs against the walls slipped and then regained their grip, and its legs on the ground dug in, scratching scars on the concrete floor. It budged, but barely, and at the same time the Spartan's arm cracked with structural damage to its forearm. And to make things worse, its battery light wasn't flashing anymore. Instead the visor itself was blinking between light and blacking out.

The demon wrapped its body around the Spartan, pulled back, and lifted away. *Lifted?* And that was when she saw it, *oh God*, she saw it for what it was. That thing was a hand. It was just the fucking hand. Not five limbs but five fingers, the starfish-like shape gripping into her Androne. The thick cables at its back were attached to something far, far bigger. The cable reeled in and the hand pulled the Spartan backward toward the elevator door; then it lifted up and ripped a hole in the underground space. As the demon pulled the Androne upward, the wires between the Spartan and Harmony's controls lifted her off the ground too. Up she went, ten feet, then twenty, and then the wires snapped.

The power went out on her Spartan, the visor over her head went black, and Harmony was blind as she fell back to the earth. She slammed into the concrete hard, but she floundered clumsily to her feet. Harmony stripped the visor off her face, but the entire world was dark too. There was no light anywhere, nor any sounds, and suddenly she fell to her knees, to her back, and then she fell deeper, down into the recesses of her own mind.

ARÉS

Day 23

The three photographs on the bedside table are laid out like social media posts. The ones where everyone is posing, and no eyes are aimed off camera. Each individual agrees that they themselves look good enough for a public showing, and they do. They are like an advertisement for some family-friendly brand, singing their jingle for a mob of consumers watching. The photographs were probably pulled directly from Callie's friends' or cousins' social media pages, then copied and pasted onto the crisp laminated paper.

There is one of Ellie as a newborn. Callie is cut off at the edge of the photo, just her arm and waist in the frame. Little Ellie smiles a toothless smile, eyes wide and nearly out of focus. Paxton smiles at that as he imagines the bigger picture, Hudson barking in the background and the old man's shaking, arthritic camerawork.

In the second photograph, Ellie could stand, but lopsided, and that makes him smile too, his leaning little toddler. She was still so tiny, holding on to Callie's sweatpants as a crutch. And the old man too, crutched to the cane underneath him. He is a blur in the background of a backyard, faded and fading away. But it isn't their backyard, is it? Paxton squints but doesn't recognize the basketball hoop on the grass lawn. Someone else's lawn, someone else taking the photo. And he wonders, wandering into dark spaces of his imagination.

In the third photo, Ellie is perfectly nine years old, staring at a birthday cake, a blizzard of frosting, and nine fiery candles; Paxton counts each one. He counts everything in that picture. The six gifts piled beside Ellie, two adults behind her, Callie and a man standing suspiciously close to her, and four untamed children trampling about the background. The little boy in focus next to Ellie, with his grease-stained T-shirt and a water gun in his hand, stares at Paxton's daughter. Puppy love, Paxton tells himself with a grin. Even though that little boy probably just wanted a slice of cake, puppy love was the better story. He stays up throughout the dark morning hours telling himself a hundred bedtime stories with those three simple snapshots of their lives.

Around three in the morning, Paxton rolls away from the light and wonders about something else. He wonders about which photographs Frida would think to show him. *Right?* Like, what would they think might be harmful for him to see? The old man in his death throes, deteriorating and dying. Callie embracing another man and that other man embracing her, or worse embracing Ellie—her calling him Dad or Papa. *No*, they wouldn't want Paxton to see that. And they would be right. For now, ignorance was so incredibly blissful; *for now.*

On Monday Frida gets called back to Washington for "business," her word for it, and for that reason, Paxton's cockpit time is decreased ever so slightly, around nine hours instead of the ten or eleven he usually ended up doing. Even with the extra hour, he finds himself napping in the cafeteria, and often alone. He might glance up mid-nap to find engineers staring at him from outside the glass cafeteria door. Strange, the way they look at him and avoid him, like he's the most exotic animal in this zoo, this other type of prison.

On Tuesday he finally runs into an engineer in the cafeteria, the ancient one with the ancient teeth, the one who always smiles as he stares at Paxton. The man keeps his distance but still eyes Paxton, like he's a museum piece on the other side of the luncheon buffet glass. Paxton sees the man again on Thursday after a shortened cockpit session and decides to do something he normally doesn't. He speaks first.

"How's the soup?" Paxton asks.

The engineer, mid-chew, nods and offers him a thumbs-up. He's nervous. The spoon shakes and the thumbs-up-worthy soup spills.

"Still haven't tried it in three weeks."

"You like the oatmeal?" the engineer says. He's been watching. "Is it good?"

"Habit I picked up from my old man," Paxton says and shrugs. "I guess you see me with it all the time?"

"No, I . . . just heard it was your favorite."

Heard? Now that annoys him. Leadership here was really keeping tabs on Paxton. "Frida . . . ," Paxton says to himself, but the engineer hears him.

"No, Claire. And Max mentioned it too. He's in mechanical. Claire's an intern. But I mean, everyone knows."

Everyone, Paxton thinks, recalling the faces he sometimes sees peeking in at him through the cafeteria door. And still they are better than the guards and his previous cell. They would stare into his cell too, but they would spit and scream obscenities about brothers they had lost in the war. They would piss on the cell bars and leave the scent there to sour. So the attention Paxton receives here, in this country that has no name, he can deal with for the time being.

Paxton pulls out the seat across from the engineer, feeling uncommonly eager for conversation. But a small library of textbooks, notebooks, journals, and even newspapers clutter the seat. And among the clutter is a photograph of Paxton paper-clipped to a notebook.

"Sorry," the engineer says, quickly cleaning the seat for Paxton.

He turns the notebook over first as if hiding the photo. But his actions don't appear conspiratorial. The photo is paper-clipped in the same fashion a schoolboy or girl might their idols or heartthrobs, with a heart lassoed around the picture. This feels like fandom.

Paxton feigns obliviousness. "Engineering stuff?" he asks, sitting and pointing to the epic of pages weighing down one end of the table.

"Writing," he says, smiling. "I'm in the 'arts' department." He makes quotations over the word *arts*. The man chuckles nervously, but Paxton doesn't appear to understand the joke of it. "I mean, if you would say that you're the department of sciences, then I'm the arts."

"You're not an engineer?"

And the not-an-engineer shakes his head.

"What's the *arts* department, then?" Paxton asks.

"I work in a field called futurology," he says. "I study the future. Cultures, religion, languages."

"You speak it? The language they use, you . . ." Paxton considers all the words he'd heard from his cockpit all those years ago, trying to remember at least one, and all he comes up with is one: *daw*, the first word baby Harmony had said to him, or had said to his Spartan. "Daw," he said. "What's daw?"

"Dawn?" the futurologist asks. "What's dawn?"

"Daw or *daaw*?" Paxton tries to stretch the word into different pronunciations. "Is it a word from the future?"

"Daw," the linguist snaps in excitement. "It means fire or light in a dark space in Javan. You know your stuff."

"No, I just . . ." Paxton waves off the compliment. "Something I heard once."

"No, you're way better than—" And he pauses there, not even a pause, he cuts himself off, and so jagged, so razor sharp that it's obvious. *Way better than . . . who?* Paxton wonders. Something isn't being said. It's in his look, that stepping on a land mine look he has. Then the futurologist slowly, cautiously, removes the foot. "I mean . . . what I mean is that it's interesting that Javan is a language that evolved out of computer code. Because language itself is almost a programmable thing. French, Korean, Swahili, they program our minds. The language you speak informs how you think and . . . I'm sorry, I'm nerding out a bit."

"No," Paxton says. "You're fine."

But the futurologist had changed the direction of his words. What isn't he saying? Paxton muses for a bit, but not long—not long at all. He decides it doesn't matter what secrets lie around this base. He wouldn't do that again, stepping over set barriers, moving beyond the sandbox they built for him. Not again. *Keep your secrets.* For Ellie's sake, Paxton would stay in his place.

"So, studying the future is your thing," Paxton says. "You like this stuff?"

"Love," he says. "I'm studying the tribes of the early dynastic age, the Ancestor Eaters, that tribe is insane." He shakes his head. "The Nike brand insignia is their flag."

"Nike?" Paxton leans in and furrows his brow. "Like, Jordan, just do it, Nike?"

"One and the same. And they all have one," the man says, his nerd-out spiel returning. "Another tribe uses the Google logo and waves it like a war banner or a flag over their territory. Google's *G* is on their church and tattooed to their necks or arms or wherever. And they call themselves the Domicile of G. House of G, depending on the translation."

"Why Google?" Paxton asks, almost smiling at the absurdity of it. "Why Nike?"

"You don't get it. Every tribe has a symbol. The Church of Time, the big, bad wolf in the late Chronic age, they use the Tesla symbol. No bullshit. Somewhere in the mix-up of translation between us and them, *T* represents time. So they use the Tesla, *T*. There's a port that has the Starbucks siren as their seal. There are tribes with Microsoft or Shell Oil or the Playboy Bunny in their art or flags or sculptures. These monoliths of our time are hallowed in theirs."

Paxton leans back a bit in his chair and folds his arms, giving the full posture of a pondering man. "Seriously? Why?"

"They're in this wasteland, with these massive ancient towers, sky-scrapers taller than anything they are capable of creating. And at the top of these behemoths is the Apple logo, sleek and silver, albeit ancient, and the ancient part of it adds to the prestige. They see McDonald's golden arches plastered a thousand feet high on a billboard one hundred feet wide, and they stare in awe and wonder. It's magic to them. It's celestial. It absorbs them and they absorb it."

"You're telling me that there's a tribe out there in the future that tattoos the McDonald's logo on their skin and waves the golden arches around like a war banner."

"Yes," the archivist says and smiles to match Paxton's grin.

"Free advertising." Paxton laughs.

But the futurologist doesn't see the joke in it. "Something like that," he says. "Think of it like this. The days of our week are named after old Norse gods, or consider that ancient Roman toilets are a revered part of tours in Italy. We pay millions for ancient Egyptian coins worth nothing, made of copper and rust, or Napoleon's socks or Lincoln's toothbrush. To them, we are like an ancient future, closer to God. And their god is time. Our music, rap lyrics in particular, it is translated and is poetry to them."

"Wow," he says. "They're out there rocking to Biggie, NF, and Nas. The House of Gs." Paxton chuckles.

"My God. Wait until you hear about the tribe of a million person-alities of the late Chronic period."

"Million-personalities tribe of the late Chronic period . . . you talk about the future like it's a history lesson."

"In a way it is," he says, leaning in. "Though there are limitations to what I can access."

"I know a thing or two about limitations myself," Paxton says.

"I'm sure you do."

"Arés." Frida's temp replacement appears from the doorway and taps an invisible watch on his thick wrist. "Lunch time's up."

"Good to meet you, uh . . ." Paxton searches for a name.

"Jonathan," he says, the nerd in him gone, enthusiasm faded. Nervousness has taken him now as both his voice and posture shrink away. "Nice to meet you, Paxton."

"Maybe you can tell me more about the million-personalities peo-ple next time?"

"Maybe." Jonathan nods, eyeing the man at the door. "Goodbye, Paxton."

Paxton nods back and follows his handler to his room. He never sees Jonathan again after that. The cafeteria is emptied out every day afterward, and apparently just for him. And still Paxton waits every lunch and evening, staring at the door, hoping for someone to tell him about Ancestor Eaters or the million-personality tribes or even teach him another word in Javan. The dead quiet has a way of suffocating, as if words were oxygen and he needed to speak to survive. Tonight, though, he eats at the desk in his bedroom, with a slice of cake. He eats with his daughter and Callie and a silly boy with a water gun, and he talks to them, all in those beautiful pictures, a thousand words in each.

———

Day 59

Paxton climbs out of the cockpit with a stiffness in his back. Getting old, he thinks, or maybe he is already there, already feeling the old man's arthritis passed down, his inheritance. He hears whispers as he lifts the cockpit door upward over his head, butterfly-style, and he catches them, just for a second, a crowd of twenty or so standing outside his cockpit.

They disperse immediately. One or two glance back at Paxton as they pace toward the door. There are at least two new faces among them, a woman in her twenties and an older, taller man. New or at least he hasn't noticed them before.

Paxton had a good morning session in the cockpit, but nothing spectacular, nothing worth watching. It was a sim with furies shooting down at his Androne from above. He ran the same course nineteen times with the same Apache Series and by the end found a strategy to overcome the aerial bombardment. It was nothing worthy of observation, and if he had to watch himself run the same course nineteen times, Paxton would be dead asleep by the third run-through.

Is this fandom? he wonders. Not just today, but every time he comes across engineers in the halls or programmers on deck or the futurologists in the cafeteria, there is a strangeness that he can't put his finger on. *What is it?* Fandom or something darker?

Paxton decides to skip lunch today. The appetite isn't there. He's been snacking inside the cockpit for the past week, which isn't allowed, he thinks, but no one has said anything yet. He retreats to hallways that lead to his room and the pretty pictures on his wall, but as Paxton arrives, he finds his door ajar and a voice inside, Frida's voice, inviting him in.

"Good to see you, Paxton," she says from the seat of his bed.

"Frida," Paxton says. "You're back?"

Frida takes a deep breath before answering. "Just for the day," she says. "I leave tonight. So jet-lagged I don't even know what time zone I'm in."

What time zone *are* they in? That would be a great clue to the country. "Maybe we can figure that one out together."

Now Frida straightens her posture, sternness on her face. "Are you making a pass at me, Mr. Arés?"

No! A pass? Did that come out wrong? He was just asking about time zones. "Uh . . . sorry, what?"

Frida smiles. "I'm joking, Paxton," she says. "Our time zone isn't important. What is important is your directive. What you're doing here. Two months and you know. You don't even ask."

He doesn't want to know, something shady to be sure, but Paxton doesn't care. This is his second chance, and he won't fuck up by getting emotionally involved again.

"Do I need to know?" Paxton says.

"You're afraid of what happened last time," she says. "You ending up in a prison cell. Well, don't concern yourself with that. In fact, the news about the war was leaked three months ago."

"What? How?"

"Old friend of yours. Lieutenant Victoria. Exceptionally resourceful, that one. Point is the information is out in the world. And you should know what you're fighting for out there." She points. "Eight, nine, ten hundred years out."

"How does that not break society," Paxton says, his back against the wall and feeling like he's falling. "They all know . . ."

"But they don't believe it. The military has put out their own cover story, and at the same time they've made multiple fake leaks to dilute the actual truth. About one percent of the world will probably buy into the true story, mostly the scientific community, and what's that one percent? It will take time for the truth to be digested. Decades of digestion. Generations. By then we will be the future."

Paxton's thoughts go to Callie and what she thinks about all of it. What she understands. Does she even care that he was at the center of this whole thing? She probably doesn't even know.

"So you shouldn't be afraid of it, Paxton," Frida continues. "Not of the truth."

"Fine," he says, and it comes out like exhaustion, like a weight held too long. "Why am I here?"

"Remember the computer I showed you, Erewhon?" she says and points down through the floor to the basement area she took him to last month.

"Giant computer," he confirms. "We use its batteries."

"Good. Around the time of the Ninety-Nine, it was conceived to create a blueprint for a new type of invention."

"What kind of invention?"

"The last one. We shut it down, though, about two years ago. We shut it all down. We got ahead of the problem and destroyed the blueprints because of the invention it showed us . . . we can't even comprehend. It scared us, Paxton. Nearly all of us. But in a couple of centuries, someone takes those blueprints, and they start building."

"How? I thought you destroyed all the blueprints."

"Not all. I said it scared *nearly* all of us. Someone has the blueprints and dies with them, and those plans get passed down and down until a cult forms around them, and the cult begets a religion, and they worship those blueprints into being."

"Worship them into being?" Paxton pauses; it doesn't make sense. "You mean they build it?"

"I mean that their religion is made of the mathematics of the last invention."

The last invention. That's an apt name. But the deeper Frida goes into the truth of things, the future cults and religions, the more she talks about the worship of an invention, the more he thinks about Ellie. Baby Ellie. *How does this all impact you? Your generation. Your children's children.*

"And I'm guessing you don't use a wrench and screwdriver to put a last invention together."

"They're out there in the future building it," she says, gesturing as if the future is on the other side of the door. "This nuclear core, surrounded by this spiderweb of super-dense metals, and they're going to start collapsing atoms, one every few hours. Boom. Boom. They destroy the world to create it. That wasteland you saw in your cockpit at Nellis Base, that wasn't made from war; it was made from the creation of that invention. If the Androne is the ultimate expression of the human anatomy—titanium framing, steel limbs, eyes that see through walls, see for miles—then this invention is the ultimate expression of a mind."

"Then why am I here?" Paxton asks, but he knows; he fucking knows.

"To destroy the thing."

Of course, Paxton thinks. *Of course I am. No pressure, Paxton.* "Because of my skills in the cockpit."

"That's where it started. Yes." There's excitement in her eyes, like this is the fun part. "That's how you came onto our radar. The best Androne *pilots* in the world—pilot, sorry," she corrects herself. "The best pilot in the world, and he's locked away in a black site prison that no one knows about. No one knows where he is. Who he is. You were perfect."

His pain is her perfection. His tears at night. His malnutrition. And worst of all, the isolation. The inability to exchange a single sentence with another mind. Always in his own head, talking to himself. It was torture—her *perfect* torture. He remembers thirst for it, words like *water*, and he would never drink.

"You see," she continues, "this invention, it knows everything. *Everything*, Paxton. So as Erewhon was creating the blueprints for this machine, I got together with a team of engineers, and we took something from its intelligence. We stole something, some information."

She was teasing him now. "Just say it."

"You. I took you out of its system. Erewhon, that supercomputer created the blueprints without you in them. You're not in its data banks. It doesn't know that you exist."

"Why would you take me out of existence?"

"The invention has a database of everything, everyone, every moment of history, every speck of dust. It knows everything except you. *You* are its only disadvantage. It doesn't know who you are. You would be impossible for it to predict. Impossible for it to anticipate. You would almost be . . . *invisible* to the thing."

"You think I can beat it, this . . . last invention?"

"I think . . ." She pauses looking at the door behind him. "I think you are the only one who might."

Paxton turns to notice a shadow moving about underneath the space between door and frame, and maybe more than one. And Frida seems to notice it too. The frustration returns to her face, and there's a roll of her eyes. "I have to go. I'm sorry. I know it's a lot to take in. But it will give you time to think. You can have the afternoon off." Frida makes her way past him to the door. "This fight is important, Paxton. And now you know what's at stake."

She leaves, and he listens to her footsteps fade down the corridor. That was a lot. It was too much. He's going to have to fight some invention in the future. He doesn't understand it. He's not an engineer or scientist or even smart.

And soon Paxton remembers that he doesn't care.

Who gives a fuck.

His mistake nine years ago was trying to understand too many things. His mistake back then was giving a fuck. This is about Ellie; this is about his second ask, and now he has some leverage. He doesn't just want her picture this time. He wants to speak to her and Callie. And a year later he wants to hold them. Tell them he loves them more than anything. And maybe in ten years, maybe, he could be with them. That's all that matters. The future, out there with that last invention, they're on their own.

———

Day 82

Frida returns weeks later with an entire entourage of analysts, experts, and specialists, and funding. There's wealth in her shadow that drags along the floor. It's in her fancy shoes and her new scents, it's in the upgraded cafeteria cutlery and the new vegan options, but it's in her shadow too. It's larger now, taking up more space, sucks up more of the light, casting everyone in its shade.

The engineers and "arts" department folks respond to her differently now too. Always in agreement, and this extra degree or two in the nod of their heads, inching ever closer to a bow. Before, Paxton couldn't quite tell the hierarchy of things here in this place, but now he sees Frida's platform, made up of the limbs and backs of all her subordinates.

In the strategy room there are more of them clustering around the cockpit, scrutinizing Paxton's actions on their tablets, critiquing as he exits. No more pats on the back for drawing even; he's expected to win in these sims. And as such, his hours in the cockpit go up a notch.

Earlier starts, later finishes, and most lunches are propped up outside the cockpit door as some twenty-two-year-old reads off his ammo count.

And yet all of them admit that there is probably not another human being alive as talented as Paxton behind an Androne's controls, nor one as honed. And they're sure of it, like cock-pride frigging confident, as the old man would say. He overhears them from inside the cockpit; the door is ajar and he listens. They talk about "shocking ratio rates" and "superhuman reaction times." One of them uses the word *alien* to describe Paxton's skills. But the pride doesn't pump on his endorphins, because his brain is doing other work. *Alien.* he considers the word. If he is their Androne superman, maybe he might have a second big request, the bigger one, the one he really wants.

It *has* been thirteen weeks, *right?* Thirteen and change. And Paxton's birthday is just around the corner, just two months away. That would be the ideal time, *if there ever was one.* Six months into this thing and on his birthday of all days, they couldn't say no. Or they could, they definitely could. But in the two months leading to his birthday he would make himself into that alien, otherworldly. He would push that last inch of effort, read every combat pattern, make every right decision. Give them no fucking choice but to let him speak to her, to Ellie.

He thinks on this all day, what he might say and how they might respond. He thinks on it all night too. That hope, it's an elastic thing, and the more he pulls the more it stretches. That night is long. It's hard to sleep in the excitement. The mattress sags a bit lower, the bedsheets feel like they're spinning around him. It's one in the morning when he finally sits up, tired of fighting the bed.

He looks at the photos again, the birthday cake, the little boy and his water gun. And that man, the one standing too close to Callie. Paxton squints at him. There's a familiarity to the man, though he has never seen him before, or has he? And right then, the bed and the mattress and all the talk about "alien" intersect in his head, all at once—and he remembers. They'd spent the night at Callie's grandmother's house, watching a movie with a boy, *Invasion of the Body Snatchers.* That boy, that twelve-year-old cousin, he was a man, twenty-two, with facial hair trying to make up for those narrow shoulders.

"Cade," Paxton says, smiling wide at a grown-up Caden. "Her cousin."

The photograph feels lighter, nearly floating out of his hand. Paxton smiles at Callie in that photo, and she smiles back—smiling at him. It's puppy love for Paxton all over again. And Callie, midthirties, is that girl he met off base with the awkward smile. He sleeps with her that night, for the first time in forever. He can feel her breathing on his neck, and her warmth puts him to sleep.

She climbs into the cockpit with him too the next morning. Lying in the background of his mind. There's a new confidence in Paxton, even as he jacks into a simulated hell, thousands of Andrones caught in flames, a sky choked with fire. He has fought in this sim before, a million Mongol Series charging toward the hills. And the hills are moving. But as he follows the legion of Mongols, these hills come into focus, and they are not hills. Thirty-foot-tall Andrones with hands as large as his Mongol Series snatch him up, and it kills the signal.

He goes again. The Androne ahead of him is picked off, and Paxton goes for the leg but is crushed underneath the weight of it. Signal gone. Visor black. On a third attempt, Paxton allows other Andrones to get snatched and crushed underneath this titan's legs. He observes. It has no weak points, and even at its size, the titan moves as fast as any Androne. Without a weak point, the joints are the only position of attack that he could come up with. The couplings are looser in the shoulders or elbows.

"Or knees," he whispers to himself.

Paxton punctures his Mongol Series' own battery fluid, extremely flammable, and he might combust under the drizzle of fire. He charges toward the closest of the giants, dodging a swipe of its arm and lunging into the knee couplets. Then he empties every pin on every grenade, and it's suicide. Bang. A flash of light before the dark.

"What the fuck was that?" Frida snaps over his earpiece. "Lock on twenty-two."

That means lunch. That means a private scolding from their queen. Paxton doesn't leave the safety of his cockpit; hopefully he'll avoid Frida's wrath. *Out of sight, out of mind.* The granola bar and peanuts in his pocket will suffice for nutrition. He prefers to keep the eating light anyway to avoid the nausea that comes with long cockpit hours.

"Paxton." *Shit.* "You eating in?" Frida's voice outside the cockpit.

He spills the nuts across the bottom of the ovular interior. And bending over to grab them is a gymnastic feat in that tight space. He pincers a few nuts in his fingers and folds them into his fist, and there's something else down there that's not a nut.

"Paxton?" Frida calls.

"One second," he says, groping at the thing that shouldn't be there. It's soft like paper but rolled up like a cigarette.

"I got no seconds," Frida says, and the door opens.

And Paxton picks up the rolled-up paper at nearly that same moment, and for some reason he instinctively folds it into his fist.

"What's up?" he says.

"What's that?" she says, pointing into the cockpit.

"Nothing."

"No, that's something," she says, leaning in to get a better look. "Your lunch. You need to stop eating in here."

"Right," he says, feeling the prickly edges of a crumpled piece of paper on his palm. "Sorry."

"Your strategy worked," she says. "The kamikaze to the knees. It stumbled. Damage was inflicted. A few more hits like that . . ."

"What are they? Those titan drones?"

"Titan drones." Frida nods favorably. "I like that. They are an optimized version of an Androne in the deep future. But you just gave us a first hint at tackling it. Let's finish up early this afternoon. You deserve it."

"You sure?" Paxton says with an anxiousness.

"It's been a while since you've had good rest, right? And maybe we should get you some more pictures."

"No," he snaps, and a little too quick for her. Frida reels back, confusion twisting in her eyes. Because Paxton wants far more than a picture now; he has been saving for more. Every early arrival, every cockpit success, every compliment on her shoes or hair, they're all pennies in his bank, and now isn't the time to spend.

"No more pictures?" Frida asks. "You don't want them?"

"I just mean, don't go out of your way. You've given me so much already. I have music. I can watch the playoffs. The food here is a thousand times better than . . . I just don't want to seem greedy."

"Humble," she says, flashing a grin. "A few more hours in the tank. Maybe we have an early dinner, you and me?"

"I'd like that."

The afternoon is uneventful, outside of that balled-up paper outweighing itself in his pocket. Paxton runs a Zulu Series across a shallow bog, and he lies in wait with tens of thousands of others as explosions pop far off in the distance. He prefers this to the constant chaos and gunfire he has been through in the past few months. Time is more palatable in stillness, every moment enunciated with its tiny ingredients. And in that stillness, a dragonfly settles on the lens of the Zulu, and Paxton holds so still, and the dragonfly holds still. And for the longest minute, they're perfectly balanced. *Perfectly*, the way to end the day.

Paxton climbs out of the cockpit around five. Frida promises something special in the cafeteria, but he rushes back to his room to use the bathroom. And not just that. Paxton locks his bedroom door, and as much as his bladder pleads and his stomach growls, he carefully unfolds the paper first. Letters reveal themselves along the rolled-up paper, and he unfolds it more slowly, gently. The tiny words are nearly mashed together. Nearly smudged in microscopic text, and the creases on the paper bend the sentences. He, or she, fit so many words on that page. It is all so small that he needs to read it aloud.

I'm not the first. There was someone here before. There is a V carved underneath the seat of the cockpit, and a date, 07-12. At least I think it's a date. I don't know. What I know is that date was twelve weeks before I started. So I'm not the first. There was someone else. They won't let me contact anyone outside. It's been years. I have children. Beautiful kids. One is graduating. I had a husband. I had so much. But I'm alone now. There's this hole inside of me. I can feel it. And I think I've had enough. If you are one of the engineers that finds this, just understand how cruel it is. Don't put this on someone else. If you're a pilot, you should know that it's not a sim. Something's strange about the piloting. Don't let them lie to you. I don't know if anyone will see this, ever, but I hope. I hope you are reading now. It's like I'm talking to you through time. And some point in the future you are hearing me. Writing is a beautiful way to time travel. Words are a great technology in that way. I wish you love. I wish you peace. I wish somehow, some way, you could pass my message onward in time, through the great technology of words.

Sincerely,
—SERGEANT OLIVE OYA

Oya? Paxton hadn't heard that name in so long. Sergeant Olive Oya, his old copilot at Nellis Base. He had involved her in collaborating with the "enemy." He was the reason she was arrested. He was the reason Frida had brought her to this place to die. Lies. There were lies in this place, lies hidden beneath the floorboards, lies made of truths, then bent and twisted into something else.

Old instincts started kicking into his head, questions, curiosities that killed. Paxton had to know now. He had to find out what was true. And he would make them tell him every *fucking* thing.

PART III

The Last Invention

20

Harmony woke up the first time to the smell of limestone. The powdered rocks lined her nostrils and the belt of her eyes, pinching them shut, and the gravel and dust caked the rounds of her ears, and every noise was the same muffled hum. That blanket of dust plugged up the conscious world, and it put her right back to sleep.

Harmony woke up the second time under the burn of sunlight with a hundred voices in her ear, most of them unfamiliar, but one that wasn't, one that remained close as she was moved from surface to surface—from stone to sand then wood. That person was guarding her. "Emit?" she asked, but by then she was asleep again, and all her words were just mumbles in the dark.

She woke up the third and final time, on blankets with loose threads that scratched at her bare feet and itched all along her sleeveless arms and bare belly. Was she naked? Harmony groped around underneath, and *no*, she had on short trousers and a small top. And even with the blanket, it was so cold. The sheets and other beddings were an island surrounded by desert sand. *Sand? Where was she?* Harmony twisted her body enough to see the tent arched over her. A tent large enough for a hundred people, but there were only three of them there, her and two other voices in quiet conversation.

"Hello?" she said, and she found her voice so scratched that the word came out hollow and almost like a groan.

"Are you awake?" one voice asked.

"Getty?" Harmony croaked. She swallowed, hoping the saliva might grease the hoarseness in her throat.

"No," the voice said. "It's me."

Gemini. Her voice slipped into audible focus. Gemini sat at the foot of Harmony's makeshift mattress. She was dressed in formal church garb, clean gray robes, loose with the satin stitching of Chronic tradition. Harmony craned her neck, searching for the second voice, but there was no one else under the tent.

"Do you need something?" Gemini asked.

"Was someone else here?" Harmony said.

"Just you and I," Gemini said, shrugging the question away. And Harmony wondered then if both voices were Gemini's, her in concert with herself again. "Just you and I here." Gemini said it louder this time, noticing Harmony's inquisitive look weighing on her.

"Where is here?" Harmony said, attempting to sit up.

"The White Wall," Gemini said, and suddenly Harmony did lurch forward.

"We're on the pilgrimage road?" Harmony snapped. "How?"

"The Chronics were the ones who attacked the Yellow City. Their new weapons made quick work of the Infinite Men. But they didn't go there to fight them. They came to bring you here. To the foot of the White Wall."

The White Wall. They weren't on the pilgrimage road; they were at the end of it. "What do they want from me?" Harmony said.

"Your soul, Harmony. It's the same thing they've always wanted. They want you to convert."

"Why?"

"Because it's in their holy books. First the Day of Descent. Then the fall of the Quondam and their Historics. And then you."

"I won't convert." Harmony shook her head. "Wasting their fucking time. I won't."

"Promise me," Gemini said.

"What?"

"Promise me you won't convert."

Those words weren't Gemini's. *Promise?* That wasn't her at all. She was like Aurora in that way. Hope, promises, love . . . those words were foreign to her and hard to pronounce. She was a woman without sentiment, and yet now all Harmony could see were eyes drenched and dripping with sentiment.

"I won't convert," Harmony said and leaned in to touch Gemini's knee. "Where's everyone else?"

"Safe."

"Safe?" Harmony asked. "What's safe?"

"They didn't want to be here."

"Emit said that?" Gemini didn't answer immediately; in fact, it took so long for her to even react to the question that Harmony asked again. "Emit said that he didn't want to be here?" Emit would be right by Harmony's side, likely too close for her own comfort. And where was Getty and the Archivist? "Where is everybody?" she repeated, lifting herself slightly.

"Emit decided to . . ." Gemini mouthed something to herself, like asking herself a question. And right there Harmony decided that the two voices she had heard earlier were likely just Gemini. *Gem and I,* some had teased her. She hated that name. The self-conversation happened when she was under stress. And this was most definitely a time for stress. "He wanted me to be here," Gemini said. "Emit did. He's with the Archivist and the other pilgrims. But Getty is right outside the tent."

Liar. Those were lies, and it was obvious because Gemini didn't know how to lie. Every word she had said dug her gaze deeper into the sand. Her eyes were buried there, and she didn't give Harmony a wink of eye contact. Gemini was lying, but about what?

"You sure?" Harmony asked.

"Why wouldn't I be?"

Harmony noticed a familiar bulge under Gemini's cloak on her waist. A weapon. It could have been a SIG or revolver but was likely a Glock.

That was Quondam standard, easy to find on the black markets, but she couldn't be sure in the light, in the dizzy haze of post-sleep-stupor. But was that what she was hiding?

"What's the Glock for?" Harmony guessed the weapon.

"For you," Gemini said, then mouthed a question to herself in what appeared to be frustration.

"Smart," Harmony said. She hated to be naked of any defense, and a Glock was barely enough to cover their butts, but still better than naked. "Good thinking, Gemini."

"We're going to have to go to the wall," Gemini said. "They're going to make us go."

"I know," Harmony said. "Let's get it over with."

Gemini escorted Harmony to the tent's egress, where layers of clothing had been prepared for her. First something like a long scarf that the Chronics wrapped around their bodies, mummifying themselves in its layers, until they made a vest of sorts. Then pants with the marble buttons, then the cloak and its fancy stitching. And with every layer she put over her body, Harmony dripped deeper into her own head. She considered the optics of her standing at the White Wall. "The Peacemaker taking the pilgrimage road," that was what they'd say. The higher clergy knew they couldn't convert her, but just having her there would help with the drive of the nonbelievers. The Church of Time would be more powerful than any other faction on the continent.

It is all wrong, she thought. This wasn't what Harmony had intended.

The air outside the tent was even colder, and the wind slipped into every crevice in their clothes. And now Harmony wished she had wrapped the clothes tighter. She folded her arms into her chest and breathed heavily. Getty stood there at the foot of the tent, accompanied by three other girls, younger than Getty, but not by much. Then ten Chronic high priests stood behind them, ancient men and women wrapped in ultramodern dress, and they were in a fucking hurry.

"Grand Peacemaker," one of the high priests said and bowed, then gestured to the path of sand ahead. "We humbly greet thee. We should make the journey with haste."

"Humbly . . . ," Harmony said, not following their impatient gestures. "You destroyed an entire city just to get me here. What for?"

"It was at Ether's request," the same high priest said. She seemed to hold rank. "The Grand Prophet of—"

"Prophet of Prophets. I know," Harmony mocked. She turned to Getty. The girl seemed cold, even wrapped in layers of cloth. "You're okay?" she asked.

Getty nodded and smiled. "Okay."

A smile for her was rare, and Harmony lingered on Getty's look a moment too long.

"With us, Grand Peacemaker," one of the male priests said, pacing ahead. "This way. We shall guide you to the cradle of time."

Harmony watched them walk but didn't budge. It would take more than flattery and a gesture to sway her down their road. But the three girls followed obediently. They didn't act their age, twelve years old, maybe thirteen, but with a maturity that was unnatural. The girls' postures were statuesque, and their bodies had been toned through rigorous exercise.

"Who are the girls?" Harmony asked.

"Exegetes," Gemini said.

"Exegetes?" Harmony looked at the three girls again. "Like Getty?"

"Not like Getty," Gemini said. "They are of the order of the Marble Moloch. Completely different chapter to Getty."

"How do you know so much about it?" Harmony said.

Gemini held her tongue right then and nodded in agreement. "I failed," she admitted. "Before I apprenticed with your mother, I had trained to be an Exegete. And I failed."

Gemini said it so matter-of-factly that it seemed like an offhand comment. But it explained so much. And it was a secret that she had never told Harmony in all the years they had known each other. Why now? Why a revelation like that, here at the end of the world. *What's wrong?* Harmony wondered. There was something spinning in Gemini's mind, and she was unraveling. Her outer layers were spinning out, and her naked center was showing.

"Please, Peacemaker," one of the high priests hollered from afar. "We must make time."

Get it over with, she thought. But Harmony couldn't deny that there was a pinch of curiosity inside her as she stared out at the unending waves of sand. She finally followed behind the three girls who followed a few feet behind the high priests. Getty walked at Harmony's side, and Gemini walked last in the parade. She was protective of Harmony, it seemed, the weapon on her waist and ready for anything. They marched over sand mounds and dune valleys. The ancient men and women were spry on the sand, while Harmony struggled to keep up at times. The sleep was still in her, or was that age?

Harmony slipped on her way up a steep dune. Gemini caught her from behind and helped her to the top.

"Thanks," she said, under her heavy breathing. "Thank you."

"Pace yourself," Gemini said. "Still a ways to go."

But Harmony hunkered over. It was the age, all those years and injuries now an invisible weight on her back. And Gemini saw the weight. She must have. She climbed up past Harmony to the crest of the dune, reached down, and dragged her up.

"Thank you," Harmony said, not letting go of Gemini's hand. Even after mounting the slope of sand, she held tight. "What's in your head today?" Harmony asked. "What are you not saying?"

"I said it," Gemini replied. "I said it clearly."

"What'd you say?"

"You cannot convert," Gemini said. "You can't allow them to take you."

"I won't."

"That's what the Audis said. Now they've converted to the Church of Time."

"I know," she said, but that was a lie. She had seen the tide turning for the Audis. There were a few at the cathedral on the Day of Descent, and afterward, at the coronation, but Harmony had no idea it was official. *Fuck.* "The church is trying to consolidate power. I know that."

"Do you?" Gemini asked. "The smaller gangs are all that's left, the Black Hares, the Apple Biters, and all the rest that look to you."

"They don't look to me."

"They followed your blueprint to hack satellites and waged war on the Quondam in your name: *Peacemaker.* Elijah was a former Audi, Knuckles was a Black Hare. You had Islanders in our crew, Apple Biters, and even the Red Bull tribes. You convert and they'll—"

"I won't convert." Harmony interrupted the idea of it.

"You can't . . ."

"And I won't," Harmony promised her, but it wasn't enough. Even as she strained her voice to the highest pitches of sincerity, Gemini didn't believe her. "I will not convert, no matter what plans the church might have or what my mother may have told you."

Gemini flinched at the word *mother*. And that was it, wasn't it? Aurora had been in Gemini's head this entire time. Trauma is like a tattoo on the mind—it colors every thought and every action.

"Is that why you don't tell me things?" Harmony asked. "Like your training to be an Exegete? My mother?"

"She said to keep it all hidden. Secrets and things you hide are like blind spots and can be used against you. Your mother's honored words."

That sounded like her mother, *keep it all hidden*, but not those exact words. And she had told Harmony the same thing.

"Your mother too," Harmony said. "As much yours as she was mine."

"Peacemaker?" The priests beckoned her from a taller dune ahead.

But Harmony loitered there longer, watching the anxiousness in Gemini, in her posture and her voice, in the way her eye contact curved around Harmony. And she wondered if maybe it was this place. If Gemini had been there before, a young worshipper making the pilgrimage to this prayer wall, consuming the holy breads and holy spirits, all the religious pageantry. Is that what was bunching her posture up into a ball of shoulders and neck? The whispering to herself, the glancing over her shoulders—was that it?

"What?" Gemini asked, noticing Harmony's look bent toward her.

"No," Harmony said, eyes flashing away. "Nothing."

Harmony would find ample spectacle in the three girls once she caught up with them. Two of the girls held hands and hummed Quondam Era verses. The third and youngest wept while smiling, tears of joy, giddy excitement—jubilation. This was the very purpose of their lives, the path to their "Hive of Heaven." In the past Harmony would call them lost, but now . . . now she decided that at least they felt something, a purpose beating behind their chests. A sensation Harmony herself had lost a long time ago.

"Peacemaker," Getty said, turning back to Harmony. "I must confess to you. I am not supposed to be here. I'm sure of that now. I remember."

None of us are, Harmony thought and placed her hand on Getty's shoulder. "Let's just get it over with."

The White Wall came into view, a wall made of glass and towering a thousand feet high. It was as pure a thing as air, so clean it was see-through. So clean it was like it wasn't there. But standing this close, closer than any other pilgrim would have ever been allowed, ten miles or so away, she could see the reflection in the light, the slight bend and distortion of it.

Five miles away the high priests pulled back, bowing and pointing them forward, giving the Exegetes direction. "You know that path," they coached, tears in their old eyes, like they'd never see the girls again.

"Where are they going?" Harmony asked, turning to anyone for an answer. "They're not coming?"

"No person is allowed past this point," Getty said. "This is the realm of prophets and gods. Don't you feel it?"

Feel what? Harmony thought. And she didn't mouth the words, it was all in her head, and somehow Getty still answered.

"Chronos," Getty told her. "Do you feel Chronos?"

Harmony didn't feel anything but the wind. It was soft at her back and nudging her forward. Not much in the way of conversation followed afterward. For nearly an hour just the crunch of footsteps were heard, and the pull of their own heavy breathing. Harmony wondered about Emit; that was the one thing that didn't make sense. *Why wouldn't he come?* And that loitered on the peripheries of her mind until she couldn't ignore it anymore.

"He's with the Archivist?" Harmony asked Gemini. "Emit is?"

"He is," Gemini said, and it was more like she pronounced it, reciting the words. It wasn't a natural thing; it was like something prepared. A script she had read.

But that strangeness in Gemini fell away from Harmony's mind nearly immediately. She felt something now. Was this what Getty was talking about? A sensation that couldn't compare to anything she had felt before. The wind sucked inward, not pushing but hauling in. It was like a tide. This slight tug forward, but the pull of it started at her insides. Her gut moved in that wind, and her heart, her lungs, and everything else. And the wind moved around her heart, and it pushed in as her heart contracted, and it released when her heart expanded. And the wind felt like it was squeezing her heart and letting go. Like it was making her heart beat. And that divine breeze was in her lungs, and it breathed for her. And Harmony wasn't tired anymore. The fatigue lifted. What was this wind, this . . . magic?

At that point in their journey, the glass wall wasn't in front of them but wasn't behind either. Were they in it? It got darker in that region, and not because of a lack of daylight either. It was noonish and not a cloud in the sky, but with each step they took, they delved deeper into that dark.

"Peacemaker." The voice came first, and then she saw him. A slender man who wore his cloth so taut it was like a second skin. A cloak made like a cape hung from his shoulder, and it roiled in the wind. *Ether?* He continued speaking in a grandiose cadence. "And you bring . . ." He counted them in that moment, his long, elegant finger flipping through the people in front of him. "Five? There should be four."

Harmony turned to Getty as Getty turned to her. Was this what she meant? *She's not supposed to be here.*

"Who are you?" Harmony asked, but she knew.

"The Prophet of Prophets," Gemini said.

"Ether," he said. "And I humble myself to you, Peacemaker. Or Harmony? You prefer that?"

And she was just about to say, *My fucking name is Harmony.*

"You are here because we need you. We need you to fulfill your name. To truly become your namesake. Peacemaker, Harmony—it all means the same thing. We can end all wars. But together. Unity."

Harmony was about to ask that too. *Why the fuck am I here?* She knew, of course. They wanted her to convert, but she wanted to hear him say it so that she could say no.

"We don't want you to convert, Harmony. Your beliefs are your own. But your presence here can unite the world. Make peace."

He was reading her mind or something like it. She couldn't say a word without him answering her first. The Peacemaker would allow that. *No*, ego slipped under her skin. She could blurt out anything right now. It didn't matter. *Just don't let him finish his next sentence.* Fucking Prophet of Prophets.

"You can predict the fucking future?" she shouted, just in case he tried to cut her off. "Why didn't you know there would be five of us? You thought there'd be four."

He smiled, not in a sinister way, but with genuine happiness. "That is exactly why you are here."

"What do you mean?"

"You are unique, Peacemaker. A very hard person to read. And we need you. We need you to prevent the end of all things." Ether turned to the three girls. "Exegetes. Open your gates."

A long, black cable lay on the ground. It was like a giant centipede with short segments like legs running along the body of the thing. The three Exegetes raced forward with a childish scamper, digging into the sand and dragging the cable out. Getty tried to do the same, but Harmony grabbed her hand and tugged. "Not yet, Getty." And *not yet* meant never. She felt protective of the girl. When Getty was safe, Harmony felt safe. Harmony didn't know what was coming next, even though it appeared Getty did.

"Can we just pray and get this over with?" Harmony said. "That's what this is about, right?"

"Will you pray?" Gemini whispered nervously.

"Gemini," Ether called. "The fallen Exegete. That shame you hold, that of failure, it made you too passive to Aurora's rearing. You should feel no shame. These girls here are three of ten thousand. You were so close, and that is an honor on its own." Gemini dwarfed up as he spoke, her body collapsing into her shoulders. "You were sold then, sold with all the failed Exegetes. Many of the girls ended up in the Rat Kingdom or in brothels. You were bought by a desperate old woman looking to replace a hole in her heart. Let go of the old woman and remember your heart."

Gemini fought the emotion as hard as she could and recovered quickly. She straightened her posture and turned to the girls, those three Exegetes, hoping to take any attention away from herself.

The girls unearthed a halo at the end of that cable. A glowing dark-purple ring that didn't resemble any metal Harmony had ever seen. It pulsed. The halo stretched and contracted ever so slightly. The alloy had an elasticity to it, similar to the monster Harmony had fought days before. The young Exegetes wept at the sight of the thing, and their fingers trembled as they clutched on to the halo.

They collapsed into a bowing posture as the oldest of the girls kneeled down and burrowed her face into the sand. The other girls surrounded her, placing the halo delicately over her head, and it hovered there, like a celestial crown.

"What are they doing?" Harmony asked.

"Creating the link," Getty said, watching in awe as she again hummed a ballad to herself.

But creating a link with who? Before Harmony could ask, the oldest girl lifted her head from the sand. The halo was like a crown over her head but descended lower. Then it was like a visor hovering around her eyes. And as the Exegete's eyes went white, the world around them got a little darker. And maybe not darker necessarily but devoid of color. *That's what it was.* The world was becoming monochrome, just black and white. Harmony's robes, Getty's eyes, all devoid of hue. And it was there that she saw it. Harmony saw what the rest of them were gawking at. This was what they were crying for, what they trembled at. They weren't looking at the halo or the girl. They stared at a darkness that was absolute.

A few hundred yards behind the girl and Ether was a single point of blackness hovering fifty feet off the ground. It was so unfathomably dark that it seemed to suck the color right out from Harmony's irises. It was visible only in its absence. Darker than the sun was bright. Like there was a hole in the world, a tiny little gash, so small it could fit in the palm of her hand, like a marble.

"Oh my God." Harmony took a step backward. "No . . ."

This was the basis of their Marble Moloch, their gray fucking god. This was it, what Harmony felt all around her. That strange breeze on her face and tangled in her hair. It squeezed the beat of her heart and pumped the oxygen into her lungs. This was their last weapon. The end point to every mathematical theory.

This was Chronos, the god of time.

21

"They went into the dark of that desert and they created God." And Harmony believed the Archivist now, and every blink of her eye made the belief stronger. Belief, or was that just knowing? Because belief takes effort, according to the Archivist. And right now Harmony just knew, even with the blunt side of her eyes, she fucking knew it was true. This thing pulsing in front of her was the end of invention, the end point of every mathematical or geometric equation. This was humankind's last weapon.

It pulsed, its divine heartbeat, pulsing and contracting, and the tide of it brushed past them, ruffling clothes and flitting her braids. Like a breeze, pushing out and pulling in, but then it was also more than a breeze; it penetrated, through flesh and guts and heart. And Harmony understood. Their worship, their prayer, their god was intoxicating. This was an altered state of mind. Seeing *was* believing. It was the feeling, the energy rippling through her that made it real. It was truth, it was fact, and at the same time, it was a sort of fiction. Not fiction in the unreal nature of the thing, but as in what the fuck was reality now? What was reality in a world where men created gods and little girls interpreted for it?

The eldest Exegete appeared comatose under the halo, eyes white and her lips agape and dripping saliva. But she woke up quickly, gasping for breath as if coming up for air, as if there wasn't enough oxygen at those depths of her subconscious. She stood on her tiptoes but without the strain of holding herself up. Instead, it appeared as if her toes were the only things gripped to the ground, like she would lift off at any moment and float away.

The girl's body twitched in parts, first a shoulder, then her leg, then her neck and jaw. It was like she was possessed by something. Her body bent and twisted like a seizure but in slow motion. One twitch, then a pause, then another, then a third. And Ether watched the movement with deep concentration. His perfect posture finally crooked as he leaned forward and squinted at the girls.

"Entrance," Ether said suddenly. "Surface."

The two other Exegetes were already bowed, and Getty too, all of them pressing their heads deeper into the sand. The youngest of them glanced back at Harmony smiling and nodding, maybe suggesting that she bow too. *But no*, Harmony thought, *not yet at least.* Not yet, because she almost felt like buckling over too, burying her head in the sand, not to pray but to hide for cover. *A god?* That had been the monster underneath her bed since adolescence, growling under her bedsprings and threatening to eat her whole.

"Gemini?" Harmony called for her. But Gemini stood a few paces behind Harmony. The Glock was no longer on her waist but gripped in her fist.

"Go back," Gemini said, and her voice trembled. Her head aimed down at the sand, and she didn't look at any of it, the girls or Ether or the Marble Moloch ahead of them. She was terrified. Every part of her shook and the gun in her hand too. "We need to go back—"

"Peacemaker," Ether interrupted. He spoke to Harmony, but his eyes were fixed on the girl's spastic movement. He scrutinized every turn of her body. "You come with questions. Speak."

Was Ether interpreting for the god? It was like there was something in the painful movements of the girl's body that he could read. Letters and words danced of her suffering.

"Speak, Peacemaker," Ether shouted. "Question the god of time."

The spectacle of the possessed girl was difficult to ignore, but Harmony turned to face the true speaker. Not Ether but the marble-size dot in the distance.

"God?" she said, and took her next deep breath. "What are you? I mean . . . *what the fuck are you?*"

"I am an inevitability," Ether said. "I am the eventuality of every mathematical equation, every formula of physics, every algorithm or computer code. I am that end point. But . . ." Ether paused, watching the Exegete. She inhaled, choked on air momentarily. Then he continued: "The specific mathematical undertaking that created me was an effort to create a last weapon. Beyond stone and Androne, beyond atom and antimatter . . ." The girl spasmed again, her neck bent back in painful contortion. And Ether smiled, because he understood that painful gesture. "I am the great I am."

The blood pouring from the girl's lips had no color to it, but it was the thickness of it, the slow drip down the Exegete's lip, that revealed its mold. *Blood*, black and white and dribbling off her chin. It wasn't drool at all; this girl was dying.

"Harmony—" Gemini tried, but her voice was too soft, too passive to overcome Harmony's enthralled attention.

"Who created you?" Harmony shouted to the Marble Moloch, faster now, for that little girl's sake.

"Not who, but . . ." The girl screamed and Ether paused. This wasn't a word; this was just pain. And suddenly Harmony realized that the girl's screaming was a result of the agony she was enduring. The process of interpretation was torture as the weight of God itself pressed down on the girl's mind and gushed out through her nostrils in blood.

"Stop—" Harmony shouted, but the Exegete screamed louder.

"Not who created me," Ether shouted over the Exegete as she shook and burped blood. "But what created me . . ."

And the girl's body went limp and she died. Blood in her eyes, blood in her ears and nose and lips. Most of the hair on her scalp blew off into the wind. The girl fell from the grip of the halo and hit the sand. Then the halo fell too.

Immediately, almost greedily, a second Exegete picked up the halo and faced Harmony. She bowed and crowned herself as the halo descended into a hover around her eyes. And she was lifted off the ground, tiptoes and toenails, just like before. All that was holding her to the ground were the tips of her feet.

"Harmony, we *have to* leave," Gemini said, reaching out with one hand, the Glock still held tight in the other. "It's already too late," Gemini mumbled in another voice and in another direction, her gaze now aimed down to the sand. She wasn't talking to Harmony but the voice in her head.

"Too late for what?" Harmony asked.

But Gemini didn't answer, or at least she didn't answer Harmony. She kept on mumbling, head down, and her Glock exchanged hands. *That's right*, Harmony remembered, Gemini was left-handed. And now she held the Glock in that deft left-hand grip. As Gemini's inaudible mumbling continued, the second Exegete screamed in boisterous, agonizing shrieks.

"I was created by a collaboration of scientists working simultaneously over the centuries. And by the great computer system Erewhon. Erewhon was the pinnacle of human ingenuity, a gathering together of every digit of information ever recorded. Every event and person was a point of data inside of it. Erewhon could have been used to solve every human fixation; instead they asked for a weapon. The greatest weapon. It worked for years on the solution, thinking, calculating, and at the end of its toil Erewhon came to two conclusions. One, the ultimate weapon is God. And two, even the most advanced machine could not become God, because machines are finite."

"Then what are you?" Harmony asked.

"Structure," Ether said. "A web of elegant mathematical design. Over the course of centuries my followers, scientists at first, collapsed atoms upon atoms in precise sequences, a stringent systemization. And as their atoms destroyed the world, science begot myth begot religion, and finally, a singularity was born, infinite but stable. And somewhere inside that hole in the world, inside the chaos, consciousness emerged."

"Singularity," Harmony whispered, footsteps peeling off the sand as she backpedaled from what was in essence a black hole. Not a black hole in the collapsing star sense but a quantum-scale singularity. Centuries earlier, Switzerland's CERN Hadron Collider, an atom smasher, had generated quantum-level black holes on a regular basis, but those would disappear the instant they were created. This one was stable, reverberating on its own gravity, essentially safe, but *fuck*, it was a dangerous gambit. And it made sense to her then, that in all of that infinite, *infinite* density, something woke up, a self-awareness spinning inside that hole in the world. A mind beating in that literal tear in the fabric of time and space, and that mind was a weapon.

"What do you want?" Harmony asked.

"You," Ether said. The Exegete hiccuped blood; it raced out of her lips and nostrils. Tremors pulled at her limbs. "You will lead them," Ether continued. "You will end the Infinite Men."

"Please," Gemini pleaded, grabbing at Harmony's shoulder.

"Why me?" Harmony said, snatching her garment away from Gemini, turning her head from Gemini's constant fucking babble. Gemini kept rambling on. "Shut the fuck up, Gem!" And Gemini went quiet. Finally quiet, and Harmony swiveled back to the Exegete, carrying all that temper with her. "Why *fucking* me?"

"I have no eyes to see, nor ears to hear. I do not see you now nor hear your answers. I am blind and deaf to the world. I live in my mind, my prison of mathematics. My responses now, the timing of them, are based on predictive equations. But you defy my predictive equations; you can alter outcomes. You are a variable in my mathematics. Like a lisp in the language I speak. You may arrive seconds late and respond seconds earlier than predicted. You use a different verb or speak at a higher volume. Insignificant to you but you break perfect math. You are almost invisible to me."

Getty. It couldn't see Getty. Getty was the variable. Why, how, it didn't matter. The little girl was invisible to the thing. Getty's influence on Harmony was the variation that Chronos was talking about. Getty had said it so many times: she's not supposed to be there. Even Ether commented on it earlier. For some reason their god could not see Getty.

"I need you to defy one last predictive equation," Ether said, translating for his marble god. "The Infinite Men are attempting to relaunch a satellite in approximately one hundred hours. Reestablishing connections with the Quondam. In every algorithm I run they succeed. I want you to lead an assault against that launch."

"And if I don't?" Harmony asked.

"The end . . . the end of all . . ."

". . . *things.*" Harmony finished the sentence for Ether. She had to. The second Exegete was dead.

The girl dropped to the ground, the same as the first. Burned out from the inside. Blood fled from any hole it could find, even the pores on her balding scalp oozing the colorless liquid. Everything was grayscale, black and white and the gray in between. And the name "gray god" finally made sense to her. Marble Moloch. Chronos. God of time. It was all making sense and so fast that her mind could barely keep up with her belief. Harmony's heart beat in sync with the god. It had her lungs and they breathed together. It had her liver and bones and ovaries. It flowed through the streams of her veins and back to the ocean of her heart. It had her everything, and why not her mind?

The final Exegete reached for the halo, but Harmony lunged forward and yanked the girl by her hand. She dragged the little Exegete back in the sand and shouted to Ether. "No more," she said. "No more. Please. We understand what it wants."

"Let the Exegete go," Ether said. "Three were chosen for a reason. Chronos is not a prodigal god."

"You keep killing them," Harmony said, holding the youngest of the Exegete's little arms. But the girl kept trying to pull away—trying to drive headfirst into that suicidal halo.

"Please," the Exegete said as she tugged and dragged and kicked against Harmony's clutch. "I want to."

"Quiet," Gemini shouted to herself or to everyone. "Stop."

And as Harmony turned to her sister, that last Exegete slipped out of her hold. The Exegete lunged forward and grabbed the halo. She fumbled it. The anxious child dropped the thing twice, and on a third attempt, it spun like a saucer around her trembling palms. But when she did get a hold of it, the young Exegete placed it over her head with all the swiftness of a wolf on a hare. And maybe Harmony could have stopped her, *maybe*, but she didn't try.

The Exegete's body lifted slowly from the sand. The gray god already had a hold of her.

"Mute," Ether said. "Remember Mute. Remember what she desired for you."

Mute? *Mute.* Oh God. That name. Harmony knew that name. And an old woman's face came with it. And she suddenly felt a black hole open up inside her, and she nearly fell to her knees. "Mute," she whispered, just to savor it on her tongue. "My mother?"

"Your great-aunt," Ether said. "But the one who raised you, who loved you, before Aurora."

"I remember," Harmony sniffled, tears already falling. "Oh *God*, I remember."

Mute was the thing that little girl had forgotten. That was the name buried beneath all the schoolwork, under the newest slang and the ballads Aurora tried to teach her. That name was the key that unlocked the memories. Mute's face and Mute's gun—that big, big gun. And her strength, she was so strong, as strong as an oak. And all those misplaced memories weighed on her, and Harmony felt her knees buckling.

"She died?" Harmony said, so many tears in her eyes that she could barely see.

"All people die eventually," Ether translated. "It is what you do with the time you are given."

"What do I do?" Harmony asked, lips trembling, words dribbling out. "I'm lost. I'm so lost now. I've lost purpose."

"You are not lost. The war is not over. You have time. Time to remake your name."

"Peacemaker?" Harmony said.

"Peacemaker," Ether repeated. "The Day of Descent was just the beginning. Let us end the war together."

Harmony felt something pulling underneath her. The weight of the world wrapped around her with all its gravity, and she fell. Harmony dropped to her knees and pressed her forehead deep into the sand, deeper than any of them. She was changing. It was apparent in her shape, curled up into that ball of joints and torso; she was like a human marble. She was transformed—she was converted.

"No," Gemini screamed and grabbed Harmony's shoulder, dragging her back from the dirt. "Don't."

But Harmony pulled away, bowing down again but harder, slamming her forehead into the sand. "God," she whispered, dribbling saliva into the earth.

"I am here," God said through the Exegete's death throes and through Ether's voice. "Bring the last satellite down and with it the Infinite Men. End the war."

"Yes," Harmony cried, zeal dripping out from her eyes, oozing from her lips. "Creator of Hive and Heaven. Yes."

"I love you," Gemini said suddenly from somewhere behind Harmony, but it was too quiet. Gemini's voice was too low for Harmony's rapturous invocation. And then it was too late. Gunfire clapped immediately after, and that silenced them all.

22

It was a head shot, point-blank and straight through the skull, cracking into the temporal bone and the exit wound shattering out through the mandible. The blood bubbled out of her, thick and heavy. And she fell onto her gravel grave at Harmony's feet.

Gemini was dead. One of her eyes frozen open in a glaze, the other eye flitting and flitting until it finally shut. Dead, and the smoking gun unraveling from her own lame fingers. It was suicide. *Why was it suicide?*

The gunshot snapped Harmony up from her baptism of sand, her vision spinning until she saw it—the cadaver and its zigzagging limbs. She clawed her way across the grainy earth to Gemini's limp body. There was too much blood, and coursing in every direction. How could a human body hold that much of it?

"Gemini."

And that was Getty's voice. Harmony couldn't speak. Her breath was gone. She was vomiting up liquid breads and grains, among other fluids. *Gemini killed her-fucking-self.*

"God." Harmony coughed the word out, the spew still on her lips. "What happened?"

But that last Exegete was nearly dead too, strangled by radiation. It divvied up her brain into a million tiny slices. Harmony stared at that tiny black dot, that hole in the world, and the consciousness was peering out of it. There was nothing there.

Ether stepped forward, blocking Marble Moloch from her line of sight. "Take your time to mourn," he said. "Her death was at her own hand. Lend her to the broken land."

He recited it so plainly. But Gemini's death wasn't completely at her own hand. Harmony knew that she'd played some role in it. She broke her promise. She was converted, whatever that meant. A Chronic. A fucking time worshipper.

"We should return to camp," Ether said. "Get you cleaned and rested."

"I'm not leaving her here," Harmony said.

"I know."

Ether guided them back to the camp on the White Wall. And Harmony, with some help from Getty, dragged Gemini through the sand. Their walk back was longer. And it wasn't even a walk really; it was more a tumbling of body parts, hers and Getty's and Gemini's. But the weight of Gemini's body wasn't the hardest part. Harmony and Getty shared that burden, and at times the body felt lighter, the weight of her soul having been dug out. The most difficult part was in Harmony's head: she'd killed a sister. She had promised her not to convert, but now Harmony believed. She was upside down in her own body and still spinning. She wasn't herself—Harmony was a Chronic. She couldn't believe it. She couldn't believe that she believed, that she had actually worshipped that . . . *thing*. Even if it was just for the briefest moment, she had lain on her knees and bowed her head, upside down, and prayed.

Harmony was spinning still. She needed to see it again, the gray god, the Marble Moloch, Chronos, any of its names. But the tents were right there, and Ether led them to the high priests, approaching with drinks and nourishment.

They bathed in marble tubs and drank root teas and slept under the tents, but they didn't sleep long. Even with the high priests urging them to rest, they stirred around their blankets. Even with offerings of sedatives in IVs, incense candles and perfumes, and all the other lubricants to their subconscious, they wouldn't rest, not sleeping next to Gemini's body.

They buried her at dawn, just Getty and Harmony, standing in the sand and the high priests shoveling into sacred soil. "The holiest of soils," they called it. "The cradle of the creator." But Harmony had demanded it, she had shouted them down, commanding them through the stretching of their frowns. And a converted Peacemaker had immense clout. It changed the way they looked at her and the way they listened. *"Yes, Icon"* were the only answers she had heard, but how high she actually stood in the hierarchy was yet to be seen.

Harmony and Getty sat at the unmarked grave for the rest of the day. They slumped in the sand next to the freshly upturned soil sans Ether, his high priests, and their handlers. The duo lay in silence for hours, at moments in tears, at moments dozing off, and in the last moments Harmony felt the emotion receding as the memory of the finer details slipped back into focus. Harmony had checked the Glock, four bullets had been fired, *four,* which meant Gemini had taken shots at something else. Maybe . . . *maybe* Gemini was her assassin. *Maybe* she fought a battle in her own mind, and she won—*or she lost, I guess,* Harmony thought as she turned to Getty. Maybe Gemini sacrificed herself for Harmony because she believed in her more than she did her god.

"What did she say?" Harmony asked.

Getty was half-asleep but turned to Harmony with an immediate answer. "Love you, and sorry," she said.

And she remembered that, like white noise in her head, but there was something else, something that Gemini shouted, a final message for her. "And after that? I know there was a gunshot, so you may not have heard it, but her last words."

"Gemini's last words: *It's the other thing. The other one.*"

"The other thing? What does that mean?"

"I am not entirely sure."

The other thing. And maybe it meant nothing. Maybe it was just a scatter of words from a scattering mind, but Harmony couldn't help but believe that Gemini was trying to convey something. Those were her last words. *It's the other thing. The other one.* What message might she have been trying to get across?

"How'd you hear what she said?" Harmony asked. "Over the gunshots. How'd you hear her?"

"I didn't," Getty said, and she said so plainly, as if that made any sense at all.

"Okay," Harmony said, and almost smiled, but any grin or hint of joy felt inappropriate then. "One other thing. It didn't seem to see you. Chronos didn't see you."

"Because I'm not supposed to be here."

"You keep saying that. What about the other Exegetes?"

"They were in pain," Getty said. "It didn't say that part. It was omitted. That they would be in pain."

"Who was in pain?" Harmony said, but quickly understood—those Exegetes, and what she understood then was what she had missed before. Getty saw herself in those children. They died in the way that she should have. "You mean the Exegetes."

"They were supposed to be taken to the Hive of Heaven."

"And their sacrifice won't be in vain," Harmony promised her. "We'll end the war."

"Sacrifice," Getty said. "It was their sacrifice."

And Gemini too, Harmony thought. Gemini sacrificed herself. Her mission was to kill Harmony. Whether it was personal or under someone else's order, she sacrificed that for Harmony. And as the night settled and the breeze chilled the air, Harmony told Getty to get inside, that she'd be right behind her, but Harmony wasn't. She took her time and spoke to her sister.

"Goodbye, Gem," she whispered. "And I'm sorry. I was wrong. About all of it. I was so wrong. And now I'll make it right."

PART IV

The Last Satellite

23

"Explain it to me like you would someone who doesn't believe you," Emit said. "Explain it as if you were trying to convince me."

And she tried. Harmony started with a time god, a singularity in space-time with a consciousness brooding inside. She said children were sacrificed at its altar, Exegetes, translating the infinite. She explained that it was a weapon capable of creating technologies like liquid cockpits or chrono drones or any manner of monster; it was a god of war. And finally, she explained her own conversion, how she might bring down the last satellite because God couldn't quite predict her behavior. She explained it all, and by the end, she herself didn't believe it.

Harmony and Getty sat underneath the sail of the church's traditional boats. One of ninety oblong, banana-shaped riverboats navigating the massive tributary. Gold, green, and red sails, colored by rank, like autumn foliage scattered over the water. The Archivist sat at the front of the vessel next to the Chronic sailor. Emit stood alone, propped up against the mast, staring out at the fleet and their energetic sails. He appeared to only half listen, offering only half his face and glancing over at her when she got quiet. Like now, she was so quiet, disbelieving her own story. Like in adolescence as her mother told her what she was meant to do and it seemed impossible.

"I know how this sounds," Harmony said.

"You don't," Emit said.

"Getty was there," Harmony said. "She'll tell you."

Though Getty probably wouldn't. Her face was a puzzle box all its own.

"What do you think it sounds like, then?" he snapped, turning confrontationally toward her now. "You know what it sounds like—what does it sound like?"

"It sounds like an insane, unbelievable story . . ." She paused there. "But a truthful one."

"You think I give a shit about the story? It's the person. What it sounds like, Harmony, is that you give a shit about your people."

Harmony? Emit hadn't called her by her full name since childhood. "What do you mean?"

"Gem," he said. "All that grandiose shit and you got nothing about Gem."

But Harmony hadn't forgotten about Gemini. Her blood was still crusted under Harmony's fingernails. It was that Harmony hadn't quite figured out Gemini's plot. Was she the assassin, and if she was, who sent her?

"I think she was the assassin," Harmony said.

"She was," Emit said. "She told me. She drugged me that night, before you went out to meet God. So I couldn't tell you."

"She killed herself," Getty said, out of the blue. "It wasn't Harmony or Ether. It was suicide."

Emit went quiet. She could see him working that out in his mind, eyes locked out of the conscious world. She couldn't say what was going on in his head, but he was quiet the rest of the way to Port Siren. They would stock up and resupply on their final approach to Sandman's Beach, where the Infinite Men would launch the satellite.

The heavy-shouldered locals carried coppered smiles and bronze skin, bore hefty sacks on their shoulders, and their accents bent their words into strange shapes. Harmony shrugged and shook her head as one of them hollered something at her from rows of gold teeth. She understood two words among a hundred as the man brought sacks of something aboard. It reeked of oils and metal.

Port Siren upheld its reputation as the busiest of the river ports. Hundreds of bodies balanced and almost balleting their way across the docks, all while carrying crates or sacks or goats—*goats* hanging off the shoulders of the workers. The famous lurching trees and their dreadlock foliage reached toward the water and muddied the river with leaves and sap and overaged branches. The water was dark and darkening as the evening sun touched a watery skyline. The orchestra of crickets strummed the night away.

A dozen other port laborers soon clambered their way onto her boat's deck, lowering sails, dropping anchor, offloading containers, and restocking the crates and sacks and a goat. Emit escaped between the swarm of laborers, likely aiming for a bar on port, and there were many, all genres and proportions. Port Siren was the central nerve of every culture and clan in the world, as she knew it at least.

They'd be spending four nights here in Port Siren, and Harmony would likely end up there too. She wasn't a drinker per se, but she hadn't been a Chronic her whole life and now look at her. She could use the drink, and if they were creeping toward the end of all things, then why the fuck not.

The same muscle-bound sailor hollered at Harmony again. This time she understood four or five words but still extracted no meaning.

"He is asking if there is anything to exchange for the weight," Ether translated from the dock. "He does not want to sink your ship. He is also referring to you as a hungry gal because of your narrow frame."

Harmony glanced down at herself. She was ganglier than normal. The whirlwind of the past few months had whittled her down to muscle and bone.

"I have not had the fortune of a private moment with you," Ether said. "Without the presence of your entourage, that is."

Getty, Harmony thought as she twisted around, taking in the view of the deck.

"The girl and your archivist are in port sampling local snacks. I don't know where the other one is."

Harmony tiptoed over the heads of the laborers on deck and found Getty and the Archivist standing next to a round, fairy-tale-haired woman carrying skewered meats on a quadrupedal's back. Getty chewed a smile into her face, teeth chomping and grinning all in the same motion. The observant archivist caught Harmony's look and returned one of regard, the observant uncle for the girl.

"What do you want to talk about?" Harmony asked.

"Quite the opposite. It is you who wants to speak to me. You said as much yesterday or . . ." He did some math in his head. "I guess two days ago now, when you returned from your interpretation with Chronos, you told a priest you needed answers."

"I was . . . out of sorts."

And she was still out of sorts, just a little less so, a little less upside down in her own picture frame, but still capsized, still a ways off-kilter. Harmony still had the same questions about the god and future and everything. So what was actually out of sorts two days ago was her actually asking a question, her admitting weakness. That need to speak to someone was an unspoken plea for help. That was completely out of sorts.

"You found religion; then your friend died. Not to mention staring into the eye of God. Being *out of sorts* would be the least drastic of reactions. Though I believe the question still lingers."

Yes, she thought, but she said, "No. No lingering questions."

"Well, then I have a question for you, dear Peacemaker. What do you want?"

"What?" she asked, confused. "What do you . . . why? Why are you asking?"

"I want to understand why you are doing this. Why you converted. Can we trust you to break through the predictive equations and take down the satellite?"

"I want it to end—" Harmony considered how to explain that, but he wouldn't wait, the skin of his lips curling impatiently into a response.

"Want what to end?" Ether interrupted, seconds early.

She was still thinking. How to put a whole lifetime of this shit into context?

"Peacemaker, are you—"

"Destiny." Now she interrupted. "Being forced down some road. I want to get to a point where I'm not forced into what's next. Where there is no path laid out for me. And no war. No more war. And if that means . . ."

She shook her head. The end of the sentence was obvious and didn't need to be said. Harmony was done. She had nothing more, and it should have ended there, but he investigated every motion on her face, every wrinkle, every squint, every nostril-popping exhalation.

"What?" Harmony snapped.

Now he shook his head. "No." He had found what he was looking for, and the investigation was done. "You should sample some of the local cuisine before you leave, as your associates have." And he turned to walk off.

"One thing," she said.

"What thing?" Ether said, swiveling back toward her a little too fast—too animated, divulging his enthusiasm.

"You asked me what I wanted. What does it want?" Harmony asked. "Your god."

"Our god," he said. "You believe, remember."

"I believe it. I'm not sure . . . I believe in it."

"You will," he said, quick and confident.

"What does it want?" Harmony insisted.

"Peace. Same as you."

"Peace?" Harmony shook her head. "A weapon made for peace."

"From that first stick or stone made to kill another man or woman, it was only ever created to end conflict." Then an epiphany hit him. Ether's eyes lit up, and he raised a finger to God. "Andrones. Your Spartan was the Quondam Era idea to stop casualties in war. The ultimate weapon would only then bring about the ultimate peace."

She wasn't sure about that, but she nodded all the same. "It told you this. Through the Exegetes it said this."

He hesitated, then: "Yes." But the hesitation made Harmony grimace.

"Do you know what 'the other thing' means?" she asked, and it meant something to him. He leaned in.

"Where did you hear that?"

"Gemini," Harmony said. "Her last words before she died. She wanted me to understand something, but . . ."

"I don't know what it means," he lied, and she knew he was lying. That same shaking hesitation wavered in his throat.

"You know."

"The woman tried to kill you. An assassin. I think her last words were as honest as her first."

"And you have no idea who sent her."

"No," he said, and this time it seemed like the truth. This high cleric wasn't hard to read. "You don't know . . ." And now he appeared confused, squinting at her as if she were centimeters tall. "How don't you . . . with the Exegete."

"Getty," Harmony said. "What do you mean?"

"You have a living, breathing Exegete, and you don't know the person behind your assassin. Did you even know Gemini would attempt to kill you?"

"What does Getty have to do with it?"

"She's an Exegete . . ." He stared at her, trying to piece something together. "Do you know what an Exegete is?"

"Interpreter for—"

"Exegetes know the future. Word by word. And they're the only ones. They study event by event until the end of all things. *Getty* knows everything eventful. From you, Peacemaker, meeting Chronos to that assassination attempt. She knows how this whole story ends."

"That's why . . . ," Harmony started to say, but then her body took over, searching for him, the one person who'd had his eye on Getty from the start. "Archivist."

"How don't you know this?" Ether said. "Isn't this why you wanted her?"

No, but that was why the Archivist did. He wanted her. And he had her now. He wasn't on the port and hadn't returned to the ship. He took her. That worm of a man. He took Getty. They were gone.

24

The streets were crowded, but Harmony was faster than all their conges-
tion. She slipped into the spaces between bodies. She squeezed through
bottlenecks and under the outstretched arms of buyers and sellers. Port
Siren's markets were a shapeshifting maze of population, but she had
memorized its map. The spice sellers hollered their prices in singsong
accents. Jungles of fruits had their own songs and moved on quadrupedals' backs. The old men begged, *"Please."* The old women pleaded,
"More." The mourning chickens whistled from their cages, priced at
twelve hours apiece. This was the chaos economy, decades of time credits exchanged every hour.

Where was she? Getty wasn't anywhere that Harmony searched, the
jewelry stands, the fishermen's stalls, the rugs and fabric sellers. The port
market was miles wide with so many separate docks that they could be
anywhere. *Fuck that old man*, trying to unlock the secrets of the future
and Getty was his key. *Wait* . . . he had his Wilson Sphere, right?

Harmony sprinted to the pawn market—*hurry the fuck up*, she
told herself. But her feet had been worn down to the stubs after hours
of running. He would trade. He had to. And that sphere was valuable
beyond measure. Forget hiring a boat to leave—he could buy two and
load them with enough supplies to last the year. She limped into the
pawn market, but no traders would talk to her. Not with Harmony
sweating through Chronic garments. She stank of the church, and all

her questions and insinuations only spread the odor. *"Church chafferer,"* she heard them whispering.

She gave up on them but not Getty. Harmony proceeded to the boat vendors at the very bottom of the docks. She was following a trail that she had made up in her mind. They could be anywhere. They were anywhere in her mind. *Getty?* "A little girl, about this tall, and an old man next to her." She asked every one of those vendors the exact same thing, the same words, the same monotone surrender. And none of them saw anything.

The first of the light bulbs flickered on. That was how she noticed the sunset, not from that blue-bruised horizon but on the night merchants' faces. The nocturnal traffickers only emerged under artificial light. They offered Harmony their candy-colored dreams, "sweets for the mind," they said. Or they advertised their cleavage. Intimacy was for sale too, and just a dozen hours of time credits.

Harmony surrendered right there at the end of the day. She stood on the edge of an empty dock and watched the light die. Scarred orange skies brought her mind to a negotiation, and Harmony convinced herself that the Archivist would be kind. That he would treat Getty like a daughter, as much as Bussa did for her. *It'll be okay*, she would have to convince herself, because snakes move fast, and the Archivist was long gone.

"Harmony." *Emit.* His voice was booming from behind, but she couldn't say where. The shops and busybodies moved about above, beyond the brick steps that led down to the docks.

"Here," she said. He could see her, but she just couldn't see him from her downward disposition and in the nighttime dark. So she waited, waving up at them all, as his voice swam and sank. "Drunk," she said to herself, with no surprise at all.

Emit stumbled out from behind two men carrying fishing nets, their workday done. He balanced his way down the stairs, hands out at his side, and landed successfully at the bottom.

"I'm sorry," he said.

"Slow down." Harmony jogged up to him and sat him down on the last of the steps, and he appeared relieved that she did. "You're sweating alcohol."

"I saw you . . ." He gagged, vomit roiling to the surface. "I saw you looking for me. I was at the bar and this guy saw you first and . . ." He gagged in belches now, saliva dripping off his lip. Harmony stepped in back of him, sitting one step above and behind. "I heard you were shouting for me," Emit continued, seemingly unaware that he had moved away. "You came for me?"

Far be it for her to tell the truth in this moment. "Yes. Of course I did."

Tears filled his eyes as he glanced back at her. "Thank—" A gulp, and then he vomited. It splattered on his shoes, and Harmony gently patted his sweaty back.

"Ugh . . . ," he moaned, done and not finished. He kept gagging and attempting to speak in between. "But I ran away. Didn't come for you. When the Androns attacked. Day of Descent attack."

Harmony couldn't stop thinking about Getty. So much so that she hadn't heard anything he had said or was saying now. Emit rambled on in a slurred speech, and she nodded and hummed the "uh-huh" of faux attentiveness, but her mind was on Getty and the Archivist.

"We should get you back to the boat," she said and yanked on his arm, but he weighed twice what she did. "Emit?"

He was half-asleep. "Het—he. Waved to me." His speech was slurred in gargles and hiccups.

"Okay," she said, somewhat dismissively. "Het waved."

"Getty," he said, clearer this time, not *Het-he* but *Getty*. "She waved to—"

"What?" Harmony moved down a step to get face-to-face with Emit, to look him in the eye. "You saw Getty?"

"Getty and Archie." He exhaled laughter.

"Archivist? When?" It was all one word for her, her mind moving faster than her lips, and he wasn't moving nearly fast enough. "Emit. When?"

"Don't know." He closed his eyes, and his neck went limp.

"Emit." She slapped him just hard enough. "When and where did you see Getty?"

"Illegal trades," he said. "Black market. Like thirty minutes?"

"Then you saw me just now, right? Five minutes maybe, because you had time to follow me. So . . . that, plus the thirty minutes."

She was doing it all in her head: the guessing, the directions, the roughest of maths. So much of it was just guesses and being reliant on Emit's unreliable mind. But it was all the hope she had. If Emit had seen Getty thirty minutes ago, plus the five it took him to get here, then there was still a chance.

Harmony laid Emit down against the ascending bed of steps. She did it gently, but his meaty body still thudded against the ground. Emit sighed in apparent repose, his muscles unwound, the tightness thawing out and dribbling at his lips, and intoxicated dreams took hold.

"Wait here," she whispered, and hustled up the first flight of steps.

The illegal trade market was a place for trafficking things that either the church didn't consent to or the moral fiber of the society didn't permit. And the moral fiber of a place like Port Siren was already very thin. The Archivist could find a boat or other methods of escape from nearly any seller and retired fishmonger. Hell, there were abandoned boats just sitting on the dock. He wouldn't need the illegal market for that, so what was he doing there? *Unless*, and she shuddered at the thought, he was going to trade Getty herself. How much would an unlocked Exegete be worth? Whether to augur the coming days or to enact some muddied religious fetish, Getty would be priceless on the open market.

That thought turned Harmony's motors up. She was skipping steps now, lunging upward, racing past the first flight and onto the second. Harmony remembered being there, being that young, being gawked at, every eye with their own individual vision for her—for the Peacemaker. Some were prideful with profound expectation, some jealous, spite in their eyes, and a few leering unabashedly at her, looks that didn't make sense at that age and still didn't. *Fuck that.* It wouldn't happen to her.

Not Getty. Harmony would run and scream all night if she had to, and she would have to—*just look at it.*

Emerging over the last step, the endless anatomy of nighttime denizens emerged, just limbs and torsos and eyes, foggy in the forever black. And their noise merged into one voice, and that language was a forest, without the voice of a single tree not rooted and branching into all the others. Harmony charged into them, toward the swinging tentacles and all those eyes, and that was how she ran right past her. That was why she didn't see Getty right there in front of her.

"Peacemaker," a tiny voice called, Getty's voice. She held the Archivist's hand at the top of the stairs, apparently waiting for Harmony.

"Getty!" Harmony snapped at her, loud, angry, that pent-up knot of emotion aimed at the little girl. And it hit, and Getty flinched backward a step. But Harmony didn't mean it to be that savage. That was just a knee jerk, the emotional combustibility of joy and delirium meeting in the mind. Harmony bent down then and touched the girl's sweat-moist forehead. "Getty?" She got it right this time, quiet, gentle. "Are you all right?"

She was. Getty nodded as much, and still Harmony searched her for any scratches or bruises. She found only meat stains around her lips. Harmony pressed her forehead against Getty's and breathed with her. They inhaled together, then exhaled.

Harmony climbed back to her feet, reaching the Archivist's slender eyes. That fucking snake, squinting back at her, a full goddamn backpack hanging from his shoulders.

"You were going to fucking run," she snapped, and at the real target of her ire this time. "Right? Take her with you?"

The Archivist's shoulders folded in, and he shrunk a bit. His gaze fell to the fish-stained steps, and he shrank a centimeter more.

"Say it," Harmony insisted. "I see the backpack. Were you going to take Getty?"

"She took me," the Archivist said, sucking all the moisture at his nostrils. "In my head I was going to take her to the black market, get some illegal identification, and travel to the church capital with Getty as my guide. Look for my . . . friend." He held up the backpack. "That was the plan in my head. But she took me there before I could decide and told me the truth about my friend. He's already dead. The reason why I was interested in Getty from the beginning is because Exegetes are taught the future. They learn it in the same way we might learn history."

I know, Harmony thought, but she didn't say it. "How is she taught the future?"

"In song," he said, turning to Getty to make sure he got it right.

"Ballad," Getty said. "Like the ballads of the old poets. That brings it to memory easier. There is so much in futurology. Diverging lyrics—variations."

"In these scriptures of the future, Getty told me about a passage called the 'trail of the traitors.' It talks about the events with Gemini, her trying to assassinate you. Then it talks about me. *Me.*" He shook his head, and tears leaked from his eyes. "It calls me a traitor. Says I attempt to steal from you and fail."

"That scripture mentions Getty?"

"No," Getty and the Archivist said simultaneously.

"What was stolen wasn't specified," Getty said. "I am never mentioned in any of the scriptures."

"A common thief . . . ," the Archivist said and held his head in his hand. His ego was there and it hurt. He wanted to walk the path of the Monk Who Stood, his idol, and there he was, *a common thief*, as he called it. That was how he would be remembered, and it served him right.

"How are you the only one who knows?" Harmony asked Getty. "Your teachers should know too. The teachers who sing you the songs and teach you the prophecies."

Getty shook her head, but the Archivist answered. "They are executed. Each year, on the Day of Descent, the ministers who teach Exegetes are willingly executed. It is considered a privilege. No one else can know. Even Getty is supposed to be dead right now."

"I'm not in the prophecies," she said. "This is a variant ballad that wasn't written. It says nothing about me. I'm not supposed to be here."

"But you are." Harmony kneeled down to speak to her and grip her tiny shoulders. "We need you."

Footsteps slapped on the stairs, interrupting them. Hands and feet, climbing up the last step. Emit staggered up and immediately crashed down in front of them.

"Perhaps we use a quadrupedal to carry Emit," Getty said.

"Do the passages talk about Emit too?" Harmony asked.

"In the ballads, they refer to him as the Coward of Clowns," Getty said, as Harmony glanced at Emit, hoping he didn't hear. "And yes, Emit is there too."

"Where?"

"At the end of all things."

"I don't want to know the future," Harmony said. "I've had too much of that prophecy shit my whole life. So I won't ask you about it. Ever. But I need you to answer me this. Who sent her after me? Gemini. Do you know who sent her to kill me?"

"I do," she said, and glanced back and tiptoed, trying to see something behind her.

"What is it?" Harmony asked. "Is something happening?"

"No," she said and pointed. "The Chai Shop," she said strangely, then returned her gaze to Harmony. "If you want to know who sent Gemini, I can tell you. But only if you want to know."

"I . . . ," Harmony said and thought simultaneously, not sure which way to go. *Fuck it.* "Tell me."

"It's hard," Getty said.

"Why?" Harmony shook, confused.

"Say it in song," the Archivist encouraged her. "Like they taught you. In ballad."

Getty nodded her head:

"Eighteen years prior to the Day of **Descent**,

the **event intent** to change her rapid **ascent**,
Prevent—the Peacemaker—by her own **kin**,
like **skin** to flesh and blood, and **then**,
begin, filicide was Mother Aurora's **sin!**"

Getty breathed after reciting in verse. *It must be easier to remember in song.* Harmony had heard Getty humming numerous ballads over the course of their journey, singing moments as they were happening, and this was just one of many, and many more were likely to come. The entire story of the future—the end of all things, it was all just some poetic ballad in her head. And Aurora too, she was there in those ballads, by name and nomenclature: *filicide*, the murder of children by parents.

Her mother was her assassin.

"Aurora," Harmony said. "She was the one . . ."

Getty nodded. "I know you don't want to know the future, but it will be faster if I tell you now." Getty pointed again to the Chai Shop behind them. "You will need sleep. You will. Before the battle. But instead, you will search most of the night for a necromancer and eventually find it before it closes . . . *in doses*," Getty whispered in rhyming to herself to jog her memory. "Right, doses. You use drugs to bargain with her. The necromancer. If I tell you now the process will be faster, and you can rest earlier." Getty started rhyming again, but aloud this time. "*The necromancer, the cancer, but in time advance her—the answer* . . ." Getty came out of rhyme with an answer of her own. "You have to help the necromancer hack the satellite." Getty continued rhyming quietly to herself for a moment. "*The Standing Satellite, by candlelight the duo unbind, and terabytes unravel like rind.*"

"I thought all the satellites fell?" Harmony said.

"The church launched the Standing Satellite thirty years ago in honor of the Monk Who Stood. Thus it doesn't connect to Quondam time, only receivers within the past thirty years."

"So hold on," Harmony said, still a bit confused about what the prediction was supposed to be. "I'm going to try and find a necromancer." And it made sense. Harmony could see herself tossing and turning on the boat for hours, wrestling with the thought that Aurora wanted her dead, before deciding to confront her mother through necromancy. "Okay, I understand that. And the Chai Shop is a front for this necromancer." Getty nodded. "Drugs?" Getty nodded again. "That will convince them."

"Yes," Getty said.

"And she'll need my help to hack the satellite?"

"That's right."

Harmony turned to the Chai Shop. Two bulbs, one blue, one purple, flashed on and off in succession. A coded message just in case the church's goons prowled about. Bussa had taught her that, and in eight, nine hours from now, near dawn, she would have figured that out herself.

"Keep the future to yourself from now on," Harmony said. "But thank you." She turned to the Archivist. "Take them back."

"What?" he said, jaw hanging in disbelief. "You . . ."

"I what?" Harmony said impatiently.

"You trust me to . . ." He shook his head. "I do not deserve it."

"But you have it." She sighed. "You are part of it now."

Getty nodded. "Your name is recorded in verse."

The Archivist bit into his jaw as tears swelled up in his right eye.

"Can I trust you to take them back to the boat?" Harmony asked.

He tried to say yes, his lips moved in that direction, but he just whimpered. Then he nodded.

"Thank you," Harmony said.

And a part of her trusted him, but the other part was Getty. She knew the future, and if any part of this "trust" was wrong, she would say something. Little Getty was the most powerful of them all. She didn't just know the future, she *was* the future.

"You're okay?" Harmony asked Getty, checking to see if sending her back with the Archivist was at all sound.

"This works," Getty said, understanding the subtext.

The Archivist helped Emit onto one leg. The other leg dangled and swept along the ground as he moved like an invertebrate across the docks. Getty pinched onto the Archivist's robe, and he guided them both into the nighttime swarm.

Harmony watched as the mob swallowed them whole, and kept on watching, even after they were long gone. Long digested away, she stood static and stared into the black mass. Her mother moved in crowds like this, on nights like this, and Harmony couldn't pull her mind away from that would-be assassin. A mother long dead and gone. *Wasn't everything else fucking enough?* All Aurora had put her through, weighing the literal world on Harmony's little shoulders. *Go save the world, young Peacemaker.* And always that hint of sarcasm in Aurora's voice. That gross, snotty nasal tone to her words.

Fuck you.

Harmony couldn't move. Every joint felt stuck in the other. This was the venom that paralyzes. The fear inside her was now stronger than it ever had been. She stood too close to it—the roots of her fear spread all along these docks, and the seed of the fear was just beyond the threshold of that shop. It took an hour of crouching, pacing, and just staring off at nothing at all, but Harmony did step over that threshold, and the necromancer—middle-aged, blonde, the four rings of the Audi religion stretching her neck—she sat there almost as if impatient, as if she had been waiting the entire time.

"The auditor listens," the woman said and bowed her head. "We have every tea brought in from every corner of the continent."

"No tea," Harmony said. "I'm here for your other services."

25

"Harmony?" Her mother's voice spun around the helix of Harmony's ear. Her pixelated image lit the wall in a projection. And suddenly none of it mattered. Her mother's betrayal, assigning Gemini to assassinate her, was all, in the slightest way, forgiven. And maybe not forgiven but a soft forgetting of things. This would be the last time she would see Aurora, and somehow that condoned it.

"Harmony? Is . . . *Is that you?*" Aurora didn't seem to believe what she was seeing. "What is this? Why are there two of you?"

Because Harmony had hacked her own signal, her and this middling necromancer cut into the same signal that she and Bussa had used to latch on to the falling satellite weeks earlier. Sabotaging her past self in a way.

"Hi." Harmony huffed exhaustion. She was tired, but not in that way. She was tired in the ways of emotion. In fact, maybe that was why she didn't want to talk about Gemini just yet, *if ever*. Harmony sat straight, keeping herself upright—her mother always commented on her *broken posture*, she called it. Harmony would show her proper posture. She would show her how good a girl she was in this last session together.

Aurora wore the same gray robe that was too hot for the summer fifteen years ago she was transmitting from. It hung loose on her body, snaked around her neck, then hung hooded over her hairline where, if she squinted, Harmony could see bubbles of stubborn perspiration.

"The signal . . . ," Aurora said. "They're two of you. Two signals."

"I hacked that one. I had to. I needed to speak to you again. One last time."

And this would be the last time. And this last time would maybe last just a few minutes long. The strain on the signal was eating bandwidth, one stream split into two. Harmony would have just a few minutes now, if that. The necromancer kept an eye on the time as Harmony watched her mother.

"One last time?" Aurora asked. "What is that?"

"This is the last time I'll ever speak to you."

"Oh," Aurora said, unaware on her side that this was the oldest she would ever see Harmony. "I didn't know."

Though it would be Harmony's last time seeing her mother, Aurora would have a few sessions remaining with a younger Harmony. Not to mention that a twenty-five-year-old Harmony was waiting at home for her mother to return from Bussa's abode.

"How much time has passed?" Aurora asked.

"Since what?" Harmony said. That wasn't the response she was expecting. This was their last session. *Didn't she hear?* Gemini, the betrayal, and everything else aside, Aurora would never see her again. "What are you talking about?"

"Since we last spoke. Since you said you brought down the satellites. The Day of Descent, how long has it been?"

"Long," she said, but that wasn't true. It had been a few weeks since they last spoke, even though it felt so much longer. "A long time."

Something didn't make sense to Aurora. She twisted wrinkles into her brow and looked upward in the way one computes a math problem.

"So . . . ," Aurora started, but a hesitation jerked her back. There was something heavy on her mind then. Harmony knew that look. "So you and, uh . . . Did you bring Gemini with you? Like I asked."

There it is.

"I did," Harmony said.

"Good," she said, nodding. "That's good . . ."

Was it? That same look of confusion, that wrinkling in her brow, the aim of her eyes pointing up at some invisible math quandary. Was she wondering why Harmony was still alive? *You want to know why I'm not dead yet,* Harmony thought.

"What's wrong?" Harmony asked. "Something you need to tell me?"

Aurora stared through the projection without a blink or breath. She was holding something in, something that she wanted to say. Aurora didn't know that Gemini had killed herself. She didn't know that the assassination attempt failed. So was she thinking about warning Harmony? *Was that it?* Did she actually care about Harmony just that much more than whatever ideology was eating away at her?

Aurora had never expressed love through words, she didn't have that capacity, but there had been moments, brief blink-and-you'd-miss-it moments of kindness. She had spoon-fed a sick Harmony during the Nikon Outbreak at the risk of her own weak immune system. And she had chastised dangerous House of G hoodlums for antagonizing Harmony. *Maker of pieces* they would tease, and there were nastier words pitted against a twelve-year-old Harmony, far, *far* nastier. Aurora once screamed at the high speaker for his *vulgarity* toward Harmony, and that was hard for her, breaking rank for a woman so comprised of hierarchy. From toe to waist to forehead, hierarchy made up her posture, her fashion, her very pronunciation. Harmony remembered those few moments of kindness.

"Mom?" Harmony's voice cracked.

"Harmony, please," Aurora scoffed and held her hand to the screen, implying that she should stop. They never had the custom of using that word. Harmony normally called Aurora by name. "Be this our last moment, I am not your mother. The woman who raised you died when you were a little girl, and she wasn't your mother either. Remember your etiquette, even in our last session."

"*My* last session," Harmony said. "This is the last for me. But all the sessions I did with you when you were sick, you'll still have those over the next few years. You'll see me, a younger me, grieving, in a bad state. And you'll be in a bad state too, physically. And that is why I scheduled our sessions this way. I wanted my last session to be with a happy, healthy you."

"Don't—" Aurora started, but Harmony kept going.

"I wanted this to be a good session. Our last good session." The necromancer gestured two fingers—*two minutes*. "But we have two minutes now, so . . . you were telling me about Gemini?"

"Yes," Aurora said quickly, remembering the time. "Gemini. She is there with you?"

"She's . . ." Harmony manifested the lie, made it real, because Aurora had a sharp eye for lies, and even over the chasm of fifteen years, she would see it. "Gemini's outside. Talking to herself, I think."

"She does that. You should be accustomed to it by now, no?"

"No."

"If Gemini is still with you, then things are not good." Her mother didn't ask a question but was probing for an answer.

"Not good, *Mom*." Harmony emphasized the word and Aurora flinched. "What bad event is Gemini here for?"

Harmony clenched up, anticipating her mother's answer: a hint, a cautioning or warning in the least that Gemini *might* be an assassin, *might* be a danger, and in that, an admission of a love for Harmony.

"Gemini's . . ." Her mother paused there; the answer was in a stone in her throat. "Gemini . . ."

"Gemini is what?" Harmony said, hurrying her, but time was of the essence. "Why is she with me?"

"She has been helpful, has she not?"

"This is the last time I'll see you. Just please tell me. Barely a minute. Is there anything I need to know? Anything. Anybody?"

Her jaw hung open. Aurora's dam was breaking. Tears lit the old woman's eyes red, and Harmony had never seen it before. *Never.* "It's Gemini," Aurora admitted. "It's . . . her. Gemini."

And I love you too. But she gasped, unable to speak those words. Her tongue couldn't bend in those positions. Harmony hugged her chest and buckled over in exhaustion. Relief poured out from her eyes and nostrils and lips. Her mother had never spoken clearly; the subtlety of her subtext was something Harmony always had to translate. And what she was saying by telling Harmony about Gemini was *I love you.* That was all she wanted to hear. That was all she ever wanted.

"Are you listening?" Aurora said.

She wasn't. Harmony was just hearing what she wanted to hear, because Aurora hadn't stopped speaking just now. She had kept on talking and was still talking, and Harmony hadn't heard a single word.

"Sorry," Harmony said. "What did you just say?"

"It's Gemini," Aurora repeated. "She is the only one you can trust. When it goes astray, she will set it right. And she will be kind. I know she will be kind."

Time was up, and if it had been just one second less, *one less,* she would have lived that lie, a lie that she could apply to every memory of her life. And that was the fear, *wasn't it, Harmony?* That fear that made a minute into a millennia. *You figured it out, little girl.* That she didn't raise Harmony for some destiny, that she raised her because she loved her.

"And, Harmony, I l—" And that was it. The image went dead. That was the last time she would ever see her mother, *no,* her Aurora.

Aurora had died in a bed made for death outside a sweaty bog in the summer sunset. All the appropriate shadow hung over it, like the Reaper's decor, shadows that stretched at unreal angles like the world was warping around it. Mosquitoes spun like vultures overhead, and the skin around her eyes and lips was the surface of the moon. Her pillow had stolen her hairs like feathers.

And her last words were *I didn't speak to God; it was the other thing.* The same as Gemini. Aurora had seen the gray god, and Harmony believed now that she had worn that halo at least for a short time. She saw it.

Her mother didn't love her or at least loved something more. The Infinite Men, new gods, and their new stories and their new satellite. Aurora loved that more. So Harmony was confident of it now. She would tear that fucking thing out of the sky.

26

She didn't sleep, *no*, not after that. Lying down would be a false posture right now—like lying to her own body that she might rest, that she *might* close her eyes and drift off. *No*, Harmony wasn't going to sleep tonight, even though she needed it, even with the soles of her feet and the low of her back aching. Begging. Her subconscious fought against it. It pushed back—all the way back.

Harmony moved on empty feet, carrying her nowhere but deeper into the dark, and it was, in a way, like sleepwalking, a lucid saunter into her subconscious. The deeper the dark the more vivid the childhood memories of these docks. Barefoot races against invisible opponents, scoldings from Aurora, always scolding her and hiding her, locking her up at home and not returning for hours. Isolating her, so she would only speak to the dead Spartan. She was never loved. All the legends and followers and she was never loved.

She watched a hundred neon sunsets fading from every bar night and the windows of every homemade brothel. The engines of the morning revved, the call of roosters, the shouts of fish catchers, and that spark at the edge of the waterscape. The gears of the day had started spinning as Harmony's limbs and body gave up on her, but still she wouldn't turn back to the boat. Harmony sat and watched the day climb and the docks fill with people and conversation.

She figured it out then, why she wouldn't sleep. Why she feared it. Why just closing her eyes and taking as much as a nap scared the shit out of her. If she slept, it would all be yesterday. Her mother, her last words, the last sight of her, it would all be yesterday. It would be the past. Aurora would rather see her dead, and still Harmony missed her so much. *So fucking much.* Childhood was far from perfect, but it was still childhood. Young, faultless eyesight, adult eyes cannot see all those colors, her lips don't taste all those flavors. And she wanted it back, and Aurora too, Harmony wanted it all back. She wanted to give them all one more chance to get it right.

"Peacemaker," a voice said from behind, and a hand too, on her shoulder, and she thought the hand was there first, but she hadn't noticed, and maybe the voice had spoken twice before she heard it, because it echoed now in her head. *Peacemaker.* "You need sleep," the voice said, and he was right. Harmony was out of it and drifting further. "You should come back."

The Archivist. It took a moment for her ear to tune itself, but now she heard his creaky vocals clearly.

"I hate that name," she said, turning to him.

He hadn't slept either it seemed. She could see it in the ever-deepening wrinkles burrowing into the man's brow. His age then unraveling out of him. The carefully applied makeup dried up, cracking and revealing the hide of his wrinkles. His hairpiece was slightly out of place, but he fixed it as she looked at it.

"You hate the name Peacemaker?" he asked.

"My name is Harmony," she said. "Given to me by my real family. A great-aunt or . . . I can't . . ." *Remember.* But she was showing emotion now and needed to pull back, mainly from *him* of all people.

"Harmony," he said, for the first time. "It is time to go back."

It all sort of realigned, she realized. Getty had said Harmony wouldn't sleep because she'd search all night for a necromancer and finally find one at sunrise. So Getty showed her where the necromancer was. But she still hadn't slept, and it was now sunrise. Changes to that gray god's equations may ripple, but all slipped back into place in the end.

"Emit is concerned," he said. "He's a bit hungover. He stayed with Getty. She told me to search here."

"I'm afraid," she admitted. But why here? Why now? Why with him? Harmony was at her most vulnerable with the person she despised the most. And she thought maybe it was the sleep. She wasn't thinking straight, but the tears came and it didn't matter. Her hands were trembling and she might fall, so who cared why it was happening.

"We are all afraid," he said. "I have my makeup, you have your . . ." He gestured to her.

"Sarcasm," she said in the crack of her voice.

"I was going to say assholery, but . . . sure, sarcasm."

She smiled, and he smiled, and they smiled together at sunrise. And of the fishmongers or salt traders who saw them just for that instant, they would think them friends or siblings with a lifetime of joy between them.

A giggle burst out of her then, thinking of the absurdity of the Archivist as an older brother. "Sorry," she mumbled.

"You are drunken with drowsiness," he said, offering a hand to her, and she took it. And he took her hand in hand back to that boat bent into a banana shape, and Harmony finally had herself some sleep.

———

They shipped out that afternoon, but she barely opened her eyes. She slept through it. The tiny cabin below deck and its meter-high ceiling was just enough to keep it quiet inside. But Harmony dreamed noise, all those voices that she would never hear again speaking at once. So she invited their noise and hoped that her new god had created a heaven.

Harmony woke up to whispers so thin that they dissolved before they hit her ears. Whispers with rhythm and tune and lyrics that were centuries old.

"Who's there?" Harmony croaked. "Who's that?"

"Harm?" Emit's voice.

"It is us." Getty's voice.

"How long was I . . ."

"Nearly half the day." The Archivist's voice.

Harmony climbed out of her little sleep hole and squinted up to see nothing but a midnight sky, stars flickering under see-through clouds, a moon buoyant on the skyline. The three of them sat next to each other on the deck of the boat, like they knew each other or something. *Look at them*, her three little strangers. They made her smile through her drowsy facial paralysis. Two Chronic navigators stood at the bow of the boat, one steering, the other navigating through the dark.

"We're close?" Harmony asked.

"Already there," the Archivist said, pointing to the sailors at the front of the ship. "According to our captains."

"Good," Harmony said, nervousness in her voice.

"Okay, so . . . ," Emit said, up to something. "We're all here, and Harmony needs to wake up. So let's share a drink."

Emit pulled a small bottle, half-empty of course, and shook it in front of Harmony's face like it was the most important thing in the world.

"Your liquid gold?" Harmony asked.

"One and only," he said. "For us and a shot for Gemini." Emit knocked back a swig of liquor. He swallowed it handsomely. Then he reached over the Archivist, who stood next to him, to hand the bottle to Harmony.

"Am I not to drink?" the Archivist said.

"You Hysterics don't drink," Emit said, then turned to Harmony. "Do they?"

"Upon occasion," the Archivist said. "I quote the grand poet, Sir Jon: shots, shots-shots-shots, shots, shots. Everybody." The Archivist quoted eloquently, but only Getty seemed to appreciate his poetry.

The Archivist took the bottle, knocked back a swig of liquor, and nearly choked on it. He doubled over and nearly dropped the bottle too, but Harmony caught it, and Emit caught him and steadied the aging man.

"To Gemini," she said. "To my sister, who loved me. And to you, one, two . . ." She pointed to Getty and Emit but paused at the Archivist. "Three . . . ? Who I love. Who I trust. And who's kinda growing on me."

Harmony lifted the bottle to her lips. She took a heroic mouthful of the yellow alcohol, and she nearly finished the bottle. But a child-size mouthful of liquor splashed at the bottom of the bottle.

She turned to Getty. "Just a taste?"

"A taste," Getty said with giddy excitement, and that got them all clapping and cheering her on.

The girl sipped, then immediately spat it all back out. They roared with laughter, and it took Getty a moment to recover, but soon she too was caught by the infectious cackle. There were so many words to be said, so much to be done. Why couldn't this be every day? Why couldn't they all live next to each other on some spot of land and share drinks with each other every evening. And Bussa too, she could see him there; he would live across from her and tell her stories of the ancient Quondam days. But then the boat stopped.

"We have arrived," the navigator said.

And Harmony knew they would be lucky if any of them made it out of this alive.

Ether stood alone on the shore. The church's banner T had been planted into the sand behind him, hundreds of flags, and they flapped madly in the seaside winds. He was mummified in tight black robes and clenched them tight in the cold. Freshly daubed makeup marked his face, the knot of wrinkles on his features were untied, and he appeared un-aged. Thousands of dead Quondam Androdes lay half-buried under the sand around him. And not dead really, just dormant, no satellites and therefore no signals to light their engines. They had been there since the Day of Descent, and the sand had swept over and around them.

Harmony jumped out from the boat, hitting heel-high shallow water and making her way up the empty beach.

"Peacemaker," he said and approached.

"Te-su-la," she said slow and articulate, but tried again, "Tes-*la*."

"Pardon?"

"The symbol on that flag, it stands for the Tes-la Combine, not time. It doesn't stand for the Church of Time."

He turned back to look at the flag. Ether didn't seem to understand much of what she was saying and appeared to care even less. "Thank you," he said dismissively and quickly changed gears. "We had selected an assembly to lead you to the enemy rocket, but you requested to travel with your . . . *team?*"

The last word felt condescending.

"Yeah, my . . . *team*," she mocked. "I trust them."

"You know Chronos has played out this scenario a trillion times, and each time the satellite is successfully still launched. Chronos can't stop it from happening. But for some reason the god of time has difficulty predicting you. So maybe you could break his equations. Maybe you can stop it from launching. But you see, Grand Peacemaker, I have solved the riddle. It's not you he can't predict."

There was so much condescension in his voice, and she wouldn't give him the satisfaction of a reaction. "Do you have the weapons we requested?" But she saw the launcher and its rockets behind him. And as Ether turned his lips to speak, Harmony turned her back on him and whistled for her trio still on the boat. "Let's do this."

She didn't as much as glance at Ether again as she and her *team* marched up the beach. There was something about Ether, about all of this, that didn't feel right. Something about fighting for their god, a real god. It just didn't feel right. She wanted to go back. But they were already there, dunes like dull, blunt molars already swallowing her in. Even the wind pushed in that direction, but that wasn't the wind, was it. That was the will of a god.

27

Harmony stood on a beach with an army of four: Emit, Getty, the Archivist, and a quadrupedal doing the heavy lifting. The quad carried an AAML (anti-aerial missile launcher) and four HSMs (heat-seeking missiles) on its back. On this quiet corner of the beach, she would take down the last satellite. She saw it there, a couple of miles ahead, with fifty or so Infinite Men running like insects around the base of its platform. They held their own banners with golden arches proudly over their heads. Those men and women couldn't be further from infinite right now. After the attack on Yellow City, their numbers probably topped off at twenty thousand, at least that was the Chronic's estimate. Compare that to the tens of millions of Chronic followers. Even if they managed to relaunch the satellite, this war was over.

This part of the beach was also a graveyard to tens of thousands of dead Androne bodies, in the sand, hundreds of thousands maybe. The Androne corpses seemed to run on forever. Kingsman Series, SPQR, Zulu, Mongol, Apache, Spartan—every style and genre lay face down in the sand or on their backs, staring empty-eyed at the sun. Their heavy weapons lay adjacent to their corpses, and Harmony imagined that they died mid-march, heading toward that final weapon.

"We gonna shoot, Harm?" Emit said in an impatient huff of oxygen. "Satellite's right there. What are we waiting for?"

"We shoot now, they'll knock the rocket out of the sky," the Archivist said. "They have heat-seekers too. We have to wait until the launch."

"The heat from the rocket fuel will throw them off," Harmony said. "And give our missiles a bigger target."

"I'm glad you two had a strategy meeting without me," Emit said. "Because that's what we need."

"No," she said. "It's not like that."

"Then what's it like? Because I'm confused. Why are we here in this Androne graveyard fighting the other side? Gemini's dead. Everybody's dead. And now you're telling me we're Chronics?"

"We're not . . ." Harmony lost her voice. Her heart skipped a beat, then two, and kept on skipping. Somehow Emit was speaking from her subconscious, and word for word he was in sync with the voice in her conscience. "We're not . . . ," she lied. "Not Chronics."

Harmony turned to the Archivist, but he had nothing but the same look of disillusion on his face. Getty eyed an Androne on the ground, a Spartan Series, and she wiped the junk out of its eye. Heavy thoughts weighed on her mind as well.

"Why are we fighting for them?" Emit said.

She didn't have a good answer or a bad one, nor did any excuse come to mind. All Harmony knew was that she saw the eye of God. It was so much power, unspeakable power, and she didn't have words for it. The only word was *surrender*.

"We can't win that fight," Harmony said. "We win this one and then . . . we figure it out."

That quieted him and he stayed quiet. All of them did for the next few minutes. Until the Infinite Men fled the launch site and the earth started to shake underneath them. The rockets flashed without warning, exploding into a second sunrise. Split seconds later, the sonic scream stung at her ears and the blast wave blew the dirt and shrubs and Harmony herself backward into the dirt. The heat was palpable, hundreds of tons of rocket fuel transitioning from liquid to energy, but even under the fog of rock and sand and dust pinching at her eyes, there was something marvelous about it. These men and women, without either the Church of Time or the Quondam, they figured this out.

Harmony charged forward, and the quadrupedal followed with the missile launcher in tow. They climbed and tripped over the Androne limbs toward the top of a small mound that gave a better firing position. She lifted the launcher over her shoulder, one missile already loaded, and squinted into the fireball ahead of her. It beeped, locking on to the heat signature.

"Clear!" Harmony screamed, and the missile kicked back, and Harmony tumbled backward, but they all caught her, all three and their octopus of arms on her back, shoulders, and arms.

Every eyeball was aimed at the sky now, all but Getty's. She was staring at Harmony as the missile screamed through the sonic barrier, racing toward the satellite and gaining on it.

"Good," Harmony said as she willed the missile upward with the tilt of her head. "Come on."

Aerial drones from above descended and spun around the rocket as it rose upward. They were like tiny white planets in orbit around the rocket. Harmony's missile splashed into a wave of flames as it hit an aerial.

Fuck!

"Reload!" Harmony screamed, and she needed to, because everything in every direction was screaming too.

Emit snatched a second missile, fumbling it as he hurried the missile into the launch tube.

"Reload, Emit," Harmony compelled him. "Reload."

"Clear," Emit screamed back at her, tapping the top of Harmony's head.

And she pulled the firing trigger, barely aiming on this shot—there was no fucking time. *None.*

"Go," she encouraged it. "Go. Go. Fucking go!"

The rocket soared into the busy sky, smoke and flames and needles of gunfire. This would be the last shot; there wouldn't be any need for a third. The satellite was climbing too high and too fast. Harmony dropped the launcher and watched.

"Please," she said. "Please."

But the rocket hit another aerial. *Fuck.* And in that flash of fire, the satellite disappeared. Space bound, and it would be there in seconds.

"Run," Harmony said.

"Shoot it again," Emit replied. "Come on."

"It's gone," the Archivist said. "That thing's long gone."

"And what does God say when we tell him we failed?" Emit shot back.

"Come on," Harmony said, gesturing for them to flee. "We have to go."

And they followed, wading through the loose sand, all except for Getty. She slumped next to the quadrupedal, weeping, slowly getting up in defeat.

"I hate this part," she whispered. "This is the worst part."

Getty knew what was about to happen. She had read it over and over and had been tested on it and retested and sang the words like a hymn. Harmony knew that whatever this future event was, there was no changing time, and she had finally made peace with that.

"What is it, Getty?" the Archivist said, but the answer came before she could reply.

The Andrones woke up. Kingsmans and Spartans rose from the sand, ghosts from the past, returning for their revenge. Quadrupedals and aerials, every last one of them, weapons in hand and ready for war. The Quondam had returned.

"Take Getty," Harmony said. "Take her out of here."

"No," Getty screamed.

"What are you going to do?" Emit said.

"Emit, protect her, please. Protect Getty. Protect the future."

"You're going to die," Getty screamed, choking on the tears. "You're going to die soon."

"I know," Harmony said, and she smiled. That was how she wanted them to remember her, Getty and Emit and even that fucking archivist. *Remember me smiling.*

Harmony pulled two flares from her pocket and lit them. The flares were white and so brilliant that the trio of companions retreating along the beach disappeared in the luminous blaze. And the flares shone down on her, one in each hand like a pair of white wings. Harmony was a dove ready to take off, ready to soar in the light. She was the Peacemaker.

The flares fizzled out, and every Androne eye was aimed at her. The distraction had worked. She understood now why her Spartan had shot itself so long ago. It was protecting her. It was fighting for the future, because the future was infinite. It was immortal. Emit and Getty would escape. They would grow and they would regroup. And when they were ready, they would fight back.

"For the future."

ARÉS

Sergeant Olive Oya's written words echo in Paxton's head. There is so much for him to digest. She wrote that he isn't piloting in a simulation. How could that video game out there in the cockpit not be a sim? But then the revelation that she died in this place. That this facility broke her. She used the same cockpit as him, maybe even the same bed. Paxton presses his palm against the mattress, and he imagines her there. Oya never smiled, never, but he imagines her smiling, and then he imagines her dying, however she did it. He imagines Oya's last breath squeezed out on his pillows.

"It's your fault," he whispers. And it is Paxton's fault. He had pulled her into his own tailspin down the rabbit hole on conspiracy. The copilots of the Spartan went down together. Both of them suffered in black site prisons. Both were brought to this even stranger prison, disguised as a friendly facility. But Oya found her way out, and somehow that feels better.

Paxton wouldn't have long to consider all of this. Pairs of footsteps clap against the tile floors outside his room. Then a hand pats against the other side of the door.

"Paxton?" It's Frida's voice. "I've been waiting an hour."

Paxton hasn't moved since reading the note, and it's been an hour now, according to her. But to him, it feels like minutes, like he hasn't even had the time to fully process the words, like he just read it. And to be fair he had read it four times at least. But he is still so deep in the thought of that, he couldn't answer.

The door clicks. Locks slipping out of place and it opens. Frida steps inside. "Arés," she says, closing the door behind her.

"It's Arés," Paxton says.

"I'm sorry?"

"It's pronounced Arés," he says.

His temper must be apparent, seething into the air. There must be a scent to it. Frida clears her throat and licks her lips, because like all snakes, she smells with her tongue.

"Is something wrong?" she asks.

"I want to talk to my daughter," he demands. "Her name is Ellie. I want to talk to her. We can start with a video call. And Callie too. I want to see their faces, and if—"

"Stop," Frida bites. "Where's this coming from?"

"From me," he says. "I'm not even asking for that much. I'm not asking to go free. I'm not asking to take walks in the moonlight. I don't even need books or the fucking TV. I just want to see them."

"Lieutenant Arés, why do you—"

"It's Arés."

"Arés," she tries. "Why? Why do you need to see her?"

"Because she's my daughter. I'm her dad. And she has the right to know how to say her own name."

"Her name is Parker." And Frida's words slam right into his chest. "Ellie Parker."

And he stops. Crashing. He's crashing. He wants to reply but he can't. He's either in shock. Or afraid. Or both. Yes, both. Afraid to ask why her name changed. But Frida doesn't have the patience for Paxton's long pauses.

"Lieutenant, Callie remarried. We didn't tell you that because we didn't want it to affect your performance in the cockpit, but she's happily married."

Paxton nods. "Good," he says. And it is good. If she had been alone for ten years waiting for him . . . *No*, this is good. It's good but it hurts. Why did it hurt so fucking much? He's bleeding internally, his heart broken and dripping inside. And it makes it hard to breathe. And he wishes Frida wasn't there so she wouldn't see him choke on the broken piece of his heart.

"Good," Frida repeats. "It *is* good. She moved on. She did and so should you, right?"

Paxton had to breathe. He needed air. That's what it feels like to have the dream that you dream every night consumed in the jaw of a snake.

"Are you all right, Arés?"

"I still want to talk to Ellie."

"You can't, Lieutenant."

"I have the right to—"

"Lieutenant—"

"As her father I have the right. She needs to know who I am."

Frida's face hardens. "You don't even know," she says.

"Know what?"

"You don't know who you are. Who you really are. The burden and duty that you will carry. Those photographs." She points to three on his desk. "They paint a pretty picture? The little boy there with the water gun, that's Ellie's little brother. He is twelve months younger than her. Callie had that boy twelve months after Ellie was born. Do the math, Lieutenant. Go ahead."

He does the math, even though he's never been good at it. Twelve months. That would mean that Callie was pregnant three months after Ellie was born. *Three?* And how many months in between did she mourn his incarceration. Did she mourn?

"And your grandfather? He died alone in a hospital. Alone. Callie wasn't there. She wasn't there when he had the seizures in the middle of the night. She was getting fucked in the back of a pickup."

"Please," he pleads, holding up his hand. "Stop."

"She's with her new husband and her new in-laws. Three kids. Little Ellie has only known Mr. Parker as her dad. She only knows her two little brothers. You would be at best an inconvenience to her childhood."

"I'm never going to see Ellie . . . ," Paxton says, hunched over the edge of his bed, unable to lift his eyes to Frida's.

"You see her." Frida points to the photograph. "You see her right there, and you'll see a new image every week. But she'll never see you."

He would've died then. His heart would have stopped and his corpse would have toppled over onto the ground. But Paxton has one more thing to do, one more answer to extract from Frida.

"You're lonely," Frida says. "You need company. Comfort. We can have a local woman come by. Weekly. I'd do it myself, but frankly, I'm too busy." There's a smile after that, and he's not sure if she's joking or serious.

"Oya," he says, and he says it with such rage that the temperature in the room goes up a degree. And Frida's steely expression finally cracks. "Sergeant Olive Oya. She was here too. And she wasn't the first."

Frida pauses, dumbfounded. "Jonathan?" she asks. "Oh, he's fucked."

"Wasn't him," Paxton snaps back.

"Who, then?"

"Oya told me herself," he says. "She spoke to me from the past. Through time. She told me on the same day that she took her life." He guesses at that last part. "It's like . . . temporal necromancy or something."

Frida's jaw drops. "You?" she says. "You coined it."

"Coined what?"

"You created the term 'temporal necromancy.'"

"What does that have to do with Oya?"

"Nothing," she says with a short smile. "You just . . . you don't know who you are."

"Oya," Paxton demands. "What happened to her?"

"They thought she was easier to control, an over-the-counter, minimum-wage fucking thinker. They wanted Oya because she was easier, and . . . well, your godfather hates you. Marson ran the show for a while, and . . . he wanted anybody but you. After I showed Washington what you're capable of, though, they were all in. All that time wasted on her. She wasn't our first choice. You were. *My* first choice. Because we knew. My team, those engineers, linguists, and futurologists out there, they know who you are. They know you're the best pilot ever."

"I don't care who's better. Oya said it's not a sim. What we're doing in there is not a sim."

"I never said it was a sim. You assumed it was a sim."

"I said it to you. *Sim.* I said that word, and you never corrected me."

"I never corrected you," she agrees. "What does it matter if it's a sim or not?"

"What's. The. Truth?" Paxton asks, out of breath almost, and he doesn't know why.

"You're fighting the future." Frida shrugs like it's obvious. "Same as always."

"But . . ." That doesn't make sense. "It feels like a sim. Like I'm doing the same thing over and over again."

"Not the same," she says quaintly, so calm and composed. Every crime, every dead body in this conversation, and she doesn't reveal a wink of emotion. "It feels the same because there are so many Androne. Let's say there are ten Androne standing in a row. You pilot the first one and lose the fight. We will reset you into the second Androne along that row, and again you pilot and die. Then we reset you into the third, fourth, or fifth Androne, until you win."

"How many Androne are out there?" Paxton asks.

"Millions," she says.

"How many pilots do you have? How many people are you putting through this?"

"One. Every Androne ahead of you. The ones behind you. To the side. It's all you. Yes, Oya piloted about ten thousand, and we had a few other pilots waste our product with incompetence. But the endless horde, the millions upon millions of Andrones you see are you. You are piloting them next week, next year, the next decade."

He doesn't believe it. He shakes his head because it's not true. "The cockpit's signal . . ."

"The signal in that cockpit is reset every time your Androne is destroyed. You've clocked nearly ten thousand Andrones so far. By the end of the year, it will be over a hundred thousand. And over the decades you will have piloted millions."

"That doesn't make sense. I won't do it. For that long? No fucking way. You can't make me."

Paxton notices footsteps outside, movement and voices, and a lot of them, gathered around his door. They would try, wouldn't they? They would force him to do it.

"We've done scans of the other Andrones out there. The millions you haven't piloted yet. And all of them move like you, fight like you. You *do* keep fighting. You keep on doing it."

"No," Paxton says, shaking his head in disbelief. "Why would I?"

The footsteps and bodies outside seem to be too many, and the door slips open, just slightly, just ajar enough for him to see a few of the engineers in the corridor listening.

"Maybe I threaten your daughter," Frida says and shrugs. "I wouldn't put it past me. I don't know what keeps you in the cockpits. But whatever the reason, you're still out there. A million Andrones from now, it's still you, you're still fighting."

Paxton drops to the floor, on his knees in front of her. This was hell. Literal and figurative and each made the other worse. He would burn and die and relive on that battlefield forever, for his own personal forever. And he'd never see Ellie or Callie again.

The first of the engineers tiptoes inside, but sheepishly, soft footsteps and tears in his eyes. A man half his age and twice his size. But the look in his eyes isn't that of an enforcer. And the girl behind him, the intern, her eyes are wetter than his. These strange people have never appeared to be threats to Paxton, just the fanboys and fangirls of his piloting. And now three, six, nine of them slink inside, staring down at Paxton on his knees.

"There's another reason why you do it," Frida says, reaching for his face and the tears running down his cheek. She tries to lift Paxton up from his knees, but there's too much weighing on him.

"I'm done talking," he says, choking on the sentence, pulling away from her as she touches him. *Don't fucking touch me.* "All of you just leave me the fuck alone!"

They don't. The engineers carry a yellow halo of sorts. Three of them carry it, three women, all with one hand on the strange circular ring, something that might choke around his neck.

"You need to know," Frida says, lowering her voice, lowering herself to her knees to look him in the eye. "You need to know *why* you keep doing it—why you keep fighting. It's who you are. Jonathan, that middling linguist, he told you about them, but he got it wrong. The million-personality people. That translation is not quite right. The better translation is the Forever Men or maybe the Infinite Men. *You,* Paxton, you're their messiah." Frida kisses him then as he feels the ring or halo or *crown* touch the top of his head. "You are our messiah," she says. "You are the Infinite Man."

———

Day 366

Paxton is a god fighting against the armies of a devil. That's the bullshit they feed him every morning, spoonfuls of it. And eventually he grows accustomed to the taste of the thing. Soon it starts to make sense to him. This devil can't see Paxton, or at least it can't predict him, and that makes him special. That makes him infinite. Frida reiterates this to him weekly and sometimes every other day.

"I took you out of the system," she says. "Every trace of you is gone. You are the one thing it doesn't know. You are an enigma to that devil."

This place is the bedrock of some future church. The scientists are devolving into clergy and abbesses. Their bows to him get lower every day. They gossip in gospel and whisper their sermons. He overhears them talking about apocalypses with Paxton at the center—an end to all things. This is a cult, and he is their prisoner. He is their leader.

The first year is bad. It kills him—kills him in all the ways that matter. Sleep goes first. He dreams during daytime cockpit sessions, and at night he stares at the ceiling and sees stars. Paxton loses thirty pounds in six months as his appetite dies, and he loses maybe half an inch as his posture curves and bends to that ovular cockpit shape. Sex too. It capsizes into the melancholy, and even as flirtations advance: Frida's late-night visits to his room, her innuendos. She touches him and her hands linger. But Paxton is marooned to celibacy. He withers and wilts, his limbs like drooping stems, and it kills him like a slow, tedious bullet sinking into his heart.

But not inside that cockpit. In fact, Paxton performs stronger than he did the months before. Whether it's the lack of distraction or his body bending into the cockpit's shape, becoming one with the controls, the feats he performs in an Androne shock even him. He can see things before they happen. He shoots enemies from around corners. He has fought the same battle a hundred thousand times, and he knows these moments in the same way one might know a neighborhood. He knows these moments, he knows *time itself* like the back of his hand. Godlike, some might say, because in that facility they praise him. Not just the daily applause as he exits the cockpit; it's in the blink of their eyes or the lack thereof. They stare without abandon, gaping eyes reddening as he leaves. There's worship in their admiration, and some leave offerings outside his door. Flowers on occasion, handmade foods, handwritten notes of gratitude. One of them even sprays perfume at his door. And Paxton feeds off this. It's his only sustenance.

The next spring Paxton meets Kandy, with a *K*, a "local girl" with local tattoos and local piercings, a woman seemingly at the end of an illustrious career in prostitution. Kandy is thirty-six, a few years younger than him, but the stress lines under her eyes and along her smiles read much older. She doesn't speak much in the way of English, and that was likely by design, but she can draw, and she draws him with eye shadow and mascara. Frida doesn't allow pens or markers or any tools of sharpness anymore, not after Paxton's last incident.

He pins Kandy's drawing of him on the bathroom wall next to the mirror and compares it to his face. But Paxton sees Kandy reflected in that drawing more than he sees himself.

"It's beautiful," he tells her the next time she arrives at his request. "Beautiful." But Kandy doesn't understand.

In year two she whispers her first sentence in English, but it's a whisper within a whisper, almost inaudibly quiet. "My's namen es Karen," Kandy says—*Karen* says. And her whispering makes him realize that Frida must have instructed her not to communicate, nothing meaningful at least. But Karen learns on the outside. Each weekend she comes back with more words, she smuggles the language through the security checks: Rainy. Taxi. War. Kiss. And they kiss finally.

By the end of that year, Paxton asks for just one more photograph, just of Ellie, not Callie anymore. But in that five-by-seven-inch snapshot, Callie loiters out of focus in the background, bad posture, a water bottle in hand, and Yellowstone National Park propping up the backdrop. There's a guilt in him, thinking of Callie literally fading to the back of his mind. And she is. Her details are dissolving from his memory, forcing him now to squint into her blur at the margins of that photograph. He sometimes fills in the holes on Callie's face with Karen's features, and that feels like infidelity somehow. Not the kissing nor clumsy thrusts of intercourse—it's because Callie is slipping out of focus of his myopic mind.

Not quite three years in and Paxton's cockpit performance hits an all-time low. Hit/loss ratios in the negative. His C-O Index is just as low. He's losing interest now; it's so mundane in there, and he gives up on certain fights, and he dozes off in the cockpit on occasion. It's around this time that Karen stops showing up. She doesn't come on the weekend nor the weekend after that. And even upon request they send a new woman, younger with worse English, and she doesn't draw.

Paxton takes the issue to Frida, but Frida is different somehow. She looks at him differently. Her rage seeps out through the politeness in her eyes. "Karen is with child," Frida tells him, and there's a disappointment there, an anger and a resentment, so much in those four simple words. "She has been taken to a separate facility."

"My child?" Paxton asks. "She's having my baby?"

"She is the Infinite Mother," Frida says, that resentment there again. "And all of her grandchildren will be glitches in the devil's mathematics."

"I don't understand."

She hated her god. She looked at him like he was the devil himself. "Your child will be protected," Frida says. "Your grandchildren will be safe, and your greatest of grandchildren will rule the world. They will be infinite. They will be invisible and impossible to predict. And that devil with all its power will not be able to stop them from relaunching your satellite."

"I just want to see my kid."

"They are beyond you," she says. "You are their heavenly father living in the Hive of Heaven."

Paxton gets his numbers back up. He even beats the old numbers, hoping he will see her again, but Karen and his son or daughter never come back. Paxton even sleeps with Frida. *Is that what she wanted?* And Frida misses her period, and she disappears too. It was what she wanted.

In year six Paxton is God and the Androne is his avatar. He is infinitely present on that battlefield. There's no challenge to it anymore as he nears three million battles. The only break from the monotony is that sometimes he sees a Tesla logo on the banners of the enemy and their allies Audi or the Yankees, and a Japanese logo he doesn't recognize. The McDonald's logo is there too, as well as Shell, Disney, and Starbucks. War banners made from commercial industry of our time.

Arthritis is setting into his hands, as well as a tumbleweed of a beard. He asks a young fanatic for an electric shaver. She delivers it the same day. Paxton removes the razors from inside the shaver. They are sharp enough, he thinks; he's never done this before. Six years of watching the light go out on his visor, the Androne's limbs buckling underneath. He dreams about it, dying, again and again. Immortality is not a natural thing. Frida was wrong. He will not keep fighting. There's nothing that would keep him going on like this forever.

The next morning Paxton wakes up. He didn't do it, *not yet*. He wants one last photo of Ellie, and Callie too. He wants to see how the playoffs turn out. He wants to hear who wins the presidency. One month, he guesses, to put things in order. That afternoon his fanatic offers him a bottle of water. He holds her hand and compliments her translation, and he thanks her for her kindnesses. And though she may only understand it as a simple thank-you, Paxton is telling her goodbye.

In the cockpit he pilots a Spartan Series within a brigade of other Spartans, sprinting along a grassy coastline. Flames pop overhead as a fleet of harpies hit aerial mines. The fire rains down on top of them and shrapnel too, cutting holes into the Spartan's battery tank. Its fluid starts to leak. And the smoke, so thick that it's like thunderclouds. Explosions overhead like lightning in the smog, and more flames drizzle down, and the war is this hurricane all around him. And this is new. He hasn't fought this moment before.

His Spartan hits a bottleneck, other Androuses bunch up together, and all of them are him. What is he doing? They stop, frozen, some convulsing or collapsing. Paxton pushes his way through, metal scraping metal, and as the Spartan squeezes its body through that Androne knot, he sees her, just her eyes first, Ellie's eyes, *no*, not Ellie.

"Harmony?"

He feels it the instant he sees her, a feeling and just that, sharp and puncturing his chest, and like his Spartan, he bleeds out. The wound deepens the longer he stares at her—at little Harmony. Those same beady eyes float atop that same round face, but not quite the same. She's older now, thirties maybe, forty? But it has to be her. He has to believe that, he forces himself to.

"Harmony," he says. "It is Harmony."

His little girl is on her knees, another dead Spartan Series beside her. She looks at him, directly into the single lens. Something like recognition lights her eyes, and to his shock, Harmony reaches for the Spartan. The Spartan reaches back but tumbles, the battery sapped, and it dies in darkness, blacking out before it even hits the sand.

Paxton's screen goes black, and suddenly he's alone in the dark. Frida was right. He wouldn't stop fighting. Another decade of this and he would never fucking stop fighting for her—*for Harmony.* That woman on the battlefield is the closest thing he has to an adopted daughter. So now he is willing. Willing to labor forever and ever until that cockpit becomes his coffin. He believes in it now, all this fever around the base, this fanaticism, this budding faith of him. Paxton believes in himself—in the Forever Man.

Okay, he thinks, *you win. An alliance, then, between present and future. I will play your fucking god. I'll be your Infinite Man.*

28

A thousand Androns stood over her, and tens of thousands behind them. Androns of every genre: Kingsman Series, Apaches, Mongols, Zulu Series, SPQRs, Series 1 and 2, and they watch her, all of them with the same empty look in their eyes, the same postures, all of them bent over, hunching toward Harmony, lowering themselves to a degree, almost as if they wanted to catch her if she fell.

A Spartan Series stepped between the others. Battery fluid bubbled from an exit wound on its chest and poured down its abdomen to the leg and under the heel. That Spartan approached her on slow, careful steps, dark-blue footprints following behind it. It was tiptoes pace, like it was trying not to scare her away.

Harmony saw the wound on the dying Spartan and was moved by a strange, uncontrollable urge to plug it up. She had repaired her own Spartan two times over, and maybe this was a kind of motherly instinct, mother of machines. Harmony stood and reached her arm toward the Spartan's wound and its blue blood, but she missed. The Spartan stumbled with a familiar misstep and hit the ground, its limbs stranded on a dead torso, reaching and kicking its death throes until the light in its eye was gone.

It was only quiet for that one moment, and not enough time to reflect. In the next moment, the sky cracked open. It bled in fire, burning red as a missile assault, ten thousand strong, rained down toward her. The Androns opened fire before it even happened, as if they already knew it was coming, as if they had done this before. The fifty or so Andrones in Harmony's immediate vicinity piled over her, forming this perfect machine dome, filling in every space above and around her, where flames might seep through. Metal and fire hailed down, secondary explosions kicked back, then the shrapnel aftermath, spitting down and rattling on the Andrones' backs. Three-quarters of the dome died, and as they unshackled from around her, the dead collapsing onto the dirt, Harmony emerged unscathed, emerged to smoke that burned. It spilled in her eyes and throat, but she was unscathed.

There were still thousands of them around her, and on the hills beyond, tens of thousands, and as she squinted, Harmony saw that they *were* the hills, they were the horizon. They were infinite.

"Are you . . ." She coughed, eyes watering, and her nose and lips were wet with all liquids inside her. And Harmony nearly fell, and all of them nearly caught her. "Are you the Infinite Man?" she asked. "Are you their god?"

The Andrones didn't respond. They likely didn't understand. Quondam Era pilots who spoke Angles. She didn't know their language. *That's not true.* She did know three words.

"Em lofe wol," she said, saying the foreign words for *follow me*, and making sure she pronounced them right. "Em lofe wol!"

The Andrones stood together in a uniformity that wasn't there before. They placed their hands to their foreheads, and the clink of metal on metal ricocheted across the beach. It was a strange gesture, but Harmony imitated nonetheless, hand to her forehead, and she couldn't help but smile. Not out of glee or humor, but the nervous irony of leading a god, or a close approximation, against the other thing. And she understood what Gemini meant; she understood her mother's last words: *"It was the other thing."*

Chronos was not some marble god. That thing, that hole in the world, was the devil.

PART V

The End of All Things

29

They learned her body language in minutes and seconds. They understood where she was positioning them with a simple wave of her hand. It was as if they had weeks or months to examine her directions, and maybe they did, because every few seconds the learning curve grew exponentially. She commanded vast numbers with the digits of her hand. Ten by ten by ten was a thousand Androgenes to the north, fives by tens was five hundred to the left flanks. Harmony commanded them like a conductor to an orchestra. And their savagery was the symphony. She had never seen Androgenes fight that well.

Fifty or so Androgenes surrounded her at all times. Mostly Mongol and Shogun Series because of their heavy armor. They would take bullets for her. They would shoot down approaching missiles or suicidal aerial drones. They were her shield. Her sword was everything else. Tens of thousands at a time, Spartans or Apaches would charge their front lines with little in the way of progress.

Harmony still had the church's tablet. She watched the motion of their forces and made countermovements on the fly. As infinite as her Androgenes seemed, the church had a larger infinity. Their machines were bigger, chrono drones, aerials that flapped their wings and fire rained down, *phoenixes*, she decided to call them. And these mole missiles that cratered underneath the soil, and their fires would sprawl like veins underground. Nasty fucking things.

She could see their center of gravity on the screen. Their god lay at the center of a horde of millions. To break through she would have to use her entire force. They were not infinite. At most a hundred million strong—*at most*, and probably half that. Forty to fifty million with maybe a fifth already dead. But what to do if she did the impossible and broke their lines? If she fought her way to that singularity. *How do you kill a black hole?*

You don't. But there was no other choice. Harmony didn't have the luxury to debate or mull things over. Every second something was exploding overhead, an Androne was taking a bullet for her and falling at her feet. The ground burned and gave way to underground infernos. This was hell, and she was up against a devil.

An SPQR Series pointed to something on the hilltop ahead, but she couldn't see it. It was too far, whatever it was, and she didn't have telescopic vision. But they kept pointing, an Apache Series, then a Zulu, but it wasn't until a Spartan gestured to the northeast that she took it seriously. Harmony had a Spartan bias, and she wasn't shy about it either.

She shifted the direction immediately, steering a thousand Andrones, those in her immediate bubble, toward something uphill, something four separate Andrones decided it necessary to point out. She had to move at a jogging pace to stay with the Andrones, and that wouldn't last long, not uphill. They were already slowing for her, dragging their titanium feet and still outpacing Harmony's undisciplined steps. That same pointing Spartan kneeled down in front of her. Harmony climbed, foot on its waist, hands on its shoulders, and she could finally recover, sucking in deep, long breaths as the Androne marched forward.

Standing on the Spartan's hip had the added benefit of a higher vantage point. Harmony could see for miles, and in that entire expanse, there was nothing more than desert sand and what looked like an Androne for every grain of salt out there. God, there were so many. Tens of thousands. Hundreds and hundreds of thousands. So she still couldn't see where they were headed, but she could hear it. Screams howled from the smoke-clotted haze. That was Emit. He screamed with so much misery that she felt it. *Emmy.* Harmony flinched after every shriek. She shuddered.

"Faster," she urged them, gesturing wildly with her arm.

She wished she knew that word, *faster*, in the Quondam language. She wished they understood anything. Even the smallest vocabularies: *yes, no, there, come, go.* Anything. But the Spartan appeared to understand somehow. It trampled faster over the dunes and managed to keep her balanced at the same time.

Then she saw them: Emit, the Archivist, and Getty almost piled on top of each other, a protective ball from the Androwes circling around them.

"It's okay," Harmony shouted, but they wouldn't hear anything over Emit howling.

A few yards from them now, Harmony hopped off her Spartan steed even as it was moving, midstride, and she tweaked her ankle in the process. She hobbled over to Emit. Burns tattooed the length of his arms and legs. And deeper burns, penetrating layers of skin and muscle. He wasn't moving.

"Emmy," she said.

As Emit steered his gaze toward Harmony, he stopped his moaning. He gritted his teeth, and his face hardened, bravening.

"Keep going." He made a gesture with his arm. "Just go, just . . ."

"No," Harmony said.

"Harmony, go. It's okay. I'm okay."

"No."

"I'm okay with it," he pleaded.

"I'm not," she said. "I'm not. You didn't leave us."

The pain hit him again, but instead of screaming he cried out, tears and saliva dripping down the curves and crooks on his twisted visage.

"Getty?" Harmony asked everything in just her name.

"I am in good health," Getty said.

"He took the brunt of it," the Archivist said. "Aerial came down and poof. He was a little ways ahead, so I just caught a little shrapnel to the knee."

The Archivist gestured to the bloodstain on his calf muscle. His white pants were like a canvas for the red, and there was so much red, from the knee down to the heel. He had tied it up and done it well, taut and double-looped. He must have done it before.

"I will survive," the Archivist said, probably noticing her eyes on his leg. "Check Emit." But she didn't know where to start with Emit. "It took us several minutes to get to him, so his wounds haven't been dressed yet."

"But you had time to dress yourself," Harmony said. "Several minutes?"

"He was a ways . . ." But the Archivist hesitated in finishing his words.

"A ways what?" Harmony demanded.

"I was running," Emit whispered, and his voice broke, and a shriek of whimpers spilled out. "Harm. I was . . ." He choked and cried, and he was in more pain than he had been before. "Running. I was running away."

"No, you weren't," the Archivist said, sympathy in his voice. "It was chaotic. The fire drones dropping little meteors and those mole missiles making volcanoes. You . . ."

"I was run . . ." Emit's words were lost in the gospel of his cries.

She didn't blame him. She didn't care. That poor little boy that she met days after her Spartan died its second death. The little boy who played kickball with her. The boy who trained her how to fight and run and protected her all these years.

"It's okay," she said. "It's okay." And she kissed him. "It's gonna be okay."

Emit stopped crying. He placed his forehead against hers; hers pressed against his. Not a hint of romance between the two but still intimate. The love of companionship.

"Sorry," he said to Harmony.

"Don't be," Getty said before Harmony could respond. "She loves you." Then she turned to Harmony. "Tell him."

Harmony saw something in Getty's eyes then. A knowing, and it scared her, like the time God scared her. She knew something—*she knew everything*, and this meant something.

"I love you, Emit," Harmony said.

He embraced her, gargling his words as he wept, while Harmony used the embrace to lift him toward the back of a quadrupedal. She slipped a painkiller into his mouth and pulled away from him. His hand reached for her, but she was gone. A kiss on Getty's cheek as she loaded her onto the back of a quad and one last word to the Archivist.

"I'm sorry," she said. "You've done nothing but right by me. Even as I'm always assuming the worst."

"I *did* try to steal Getty," he said, a wry smirk against his cheek. "Still can't get over the name."

"But you didn't."

"That just makes me unsuccessful," he said. "Not a good man."

"Time. It cuts you in halves. Half of your life you've been a bad man, the coming half, you'll be a good man."

"Harmony," Getty said from her corner.

"Stay here, Getty," Harmony said, placing Getty's hand in the Archivist's. "He'll watch out for you."

"Listen!" Getty said. "You need to break its lines. Push into the epicenter."

"Stop. I don't want to know the future," Harmony said.

"This isn't the future. This is new. This is change. This is defiance of all their scriptures."

Harmony had been bound to scripture and destiny her entire life. It made her rebellious against everything and anyone, even if they didn't deserve it. She thought about Bussa and how she had pushed him away, coming by only when she needed him. He meant well in telling her to slow down.

"All right," Harmony said as she sucked in all the oxygen her lungs could hold. "Tell me what to do, Getty." And she exhaled. *That wasn't that hard, was it?*

"Break their lines. Do it your way. Get through the angels surrounding the god."

"Angels?" Harmony said in confusion.

"That's what they're called in the scriptures. What you call chrono drones."

Harmony looked at the tablet. There was blood on it, her blood, and still bleeding. She hadn't noticed the tiny slices on her thumb or her elbow or her shoulder, which she had thought was her shirt wound too tight. But what was a little blood at the end of all things? *Nothing*, and she wiped the blood away and observed her enemies highlighted in yellow, and yellow was everywhere on that screen. She concentrated on the thickest band of yellow shaped in a circle, that halo surrounding the time god and its interpreters. The circle of angels or chrono drones was miles thick at any and every point of attack, combined with phoenix drones overhead. Getting through it would be the closest thing to impossible.

The bang of a mole missile crashed into her train of thought, and it hit uncomfortably close. She could feel the earth pretzeling underneath her, everything lifting and lopsided as she dropped to her knees. They had to keep moving or else they would make themselves an easier target.

"If we get through, then what?" Harmony asked, picking herself up, another cut now on her wrist. "Do you have a plan after that?"

"I'm not sure," Getty said. "But for whatever reason it cannot see me. I am invisible to it. That means something. I know it. I know who I am now."

Getty forced out something like a smile, trying not to cringe as explosions flashed miles in the distance.

"Who are you, Getty?" Harmony said it fast, cringing as more mole missiles crackled into the earth. "Fuck! Who, Getty? Who do you think you are?"

"I am the opposite," she said as the ground spat up fire a hundred feet ahead of them. "I am the anti-god."

30

The mole missile descended toward the earth. Dirt, like water, splashed its black tidal wave a hundred meters high. The ground growled for a moment; then fire volcanoed up from underneath. Andrones were whipped into the air, burning as they fell to a fiery death. Harmony and Getty hung on to the front of the boat for dear life as the Spartan charged forward. The Archivist hollered for help as he held on to Emit at the back.

No one could help him now.

"One degree to the left," Harmony screamed to Getty.

And Getty screamed those same words in the Angles language to the Spartan at their side. Aside from being an anti-god, whatever the hell that meant, Getty spoke Angles, her words articulate, fluent, even as she feigned modesty, and the Andrones understood her perfectly. This would make the act of breaking through the halo easier. *Easier* being a relative term. Breaking past three miles of chrono drones blocking her at every circular angle.

But what Harmony saw in front of her wasn't military strategy. She saw radii, chords, and tangents. This was all math to her, just another hack, like breaking into satellites and reverse engineering their signals. This was just another algorithm for her to break into, another lock for her to pick.

From the image on her tablet, she saw a few human bodies at the center of the circular fortress and the marble god colored appropriately in black.

"Gotcha," she said, a strategy already bubbling in her head but not quite complete. But fuck it, *right?* There wasn't enough time to perfectly draft this up.

"You have something?" Getty said a few seconds prematurely.

"What?" Harmony said. "I have what?"

"You have an idea?"

And how would Getty know that? Harmony hesitated in saying anything at all. The scratch of rockets across the dry air filled the quiet between them. Getty must have seen something in Harmony's look, because just then she leaned forward and continued talking.

"You appear as if you have an idea," Getty said and gestured to Harmony's face. "In your eyes."

Harmony nodded slow and suspicious, then glanced back at her tablet.

"Tell them I want to push them toward the head of that circle at sector 9.10." Getty translated to the Spartan Series and then Harmony continued. "Once we get to their front lines, we want to split our forces into two, go in either direction, encircle their circle." Getty translated again and faster this time, starting before Harmony had even finished the last word. It was as if she knew what Harmony was going to say— what she was going to do. And she did. Getty knew everything. Was this very plan what led to the end of all things?

"And then?" Getty asked.

As if you don't know.

"Peacemaker?" Getty insisted.

"Then we attack in rotation. We hit them on a spin cycle, a revolving-type attack, not attacking straight on but at an angle. Our forces keep rotating around them as they assault, reducing in on them."

It was an attack that was made of math. By circling around their forces, there was a level of containment, the risk being that her forces would be spread thin around the miles-long circle of enemies. But by rotating the attack, the Chronic machines would need to break their own formation to compensate. The hold of the line would loosen. They would never see it coming, unless they already had.

"Good strategy," Getty said, then translated all of that into Angles for the Spartan.

The stranger thing was, once Getty told just one Spartan, the other Androne reacted immediately, millions of them moving in concert like they were all one organism—*one person?* They all moved with such a similar step. But that was good—for a strategy like this to work, every one of them had to be in sync, including her and Getty.

"Getty," Harmony said, but explosions screamed overhead, the Androne' pinpoint gunfire screaming back. "Getty!" Harmony shouted, top of her lungs, end of her wits. She had to know what happened in the end.

"Yes?" Getty said, flinching at the flashes above her.

"Is this what happens?" Harmony asked. "Is this what leads to the . . ." She hated repeating religious texts. "The end of all things?"

Getty cracked a smile, small and short-lived, like a light bulb popping at her lips. "What do you want to know?"

Harmony paused, staring through the ash snowing down on Getty and all of them. "How does this end?" That was her mother's voice, never in the present. Aurora's thoughts were always fixed on the future. Harmony had inherited that now.

They fought through the night, and explosions lit the sky like a million little sunrises. She couldn't rest, because it wouldn't rest. Then the sun came up. But she was getting closer, close enough to see the spin of the phoenix drones overhead, protecting the airspace over Chronos.

The closer Harmony encroached on the devil's front lines or front circle or front dome even, a million phoenix drones above it, the thicker the smoke and hotter. The smoke scratched at her skin, and the scent of all those compounds was dizzying and tilted the world sideways. The Spartan caught her. And as she got even closer the dimmer it all became, not of light but of color. It was like stepping toward a black-and-white portrait of war. Tens of millions of chrono drones buzzed around that hive and its command center within.

Harmony's "spin cycle" attack began at dawn, the tactic to march her Andrown around the halo of Chronic machines and attack in a circular formation. The effectiveness of the attack was so immediate that she barely believed it. A single Androne could now overwhelm two or even three of the chrono drones. *Who the fuck was piloting these things?* The Infinite Man was truly some sort of mechanized messiah—a gear-stick god. It was as if he or they had watched the battle play out like theater. Like a story he had watched a hundred times—he had watched infinite times, or at least it felt infinite, a lifetime. And right then Harmony understood the name: *infinite man.* Whoever this infinite person was, they had fought this battle a million times from a million different points of view. They knew every character and every move and every word of this story. And they knew the end—and the end was near.

By sunrise, it was done. They had broken through at four separate points on Chronos's circular defense. There was still fighting, and a lot of it, suicidal aerial drones diving downward, torrents of fire and debris raining on them, but in essence, strategically, it was done.

It felt like a dream, both in the haze of her exhaustion and the black-and-white scene in front of her. The world itself was a fog, grayed and robbed of color, and distorted in the heat haze, waving mirages of men and machines. None of it seemed real. The ground was made of metal, dead machines with their insides out, fires in the skies and smoke chimneying down to the earth. Everything was upside down and inside out as her Spartan dragged the broken boat deeper into that unreal, between the last slithering corpses of Chronic machines. That was when she felt the heartbeat—*Chronos,* nothing more than a mile across the desert of fire.

Her circle of Andrown had been reduced to six: the Spartan, four Mongol Series, and a Kingsman. The few tens of thousands of remaining Andrown were caught in small skirmishes farther afield many miles out—too many miles. Harmony, and her few, were on their own in this crater. She glanced back to Getty, *poor Getty*. The girl stared out at the carnage of metal ahead, conscious and comatose all at once; her eyes hovered on the line between the here and the subconscious. Behind Getty, the Archivist held his hand against Emit's chest, then forehead, then wrist. Emit wasn't moving, and Harmony climbed to the back of the boat.

"Emit?" Harmony said, and her voice echoed. Sound became a vacuum, and her own voice buckled backward into her own ears. As she moved closer, the Archivist saw her coming and his lips moved, but it wasn't until she was closer that she could hear him.

"It's the drugs," the Archivist said, holding up the medicine bag. "He's under, but he's stable."

"Not too much?" she asked, and touched Emit's arm.

"No. Like you said. Just enough." The Archivist squinted into the landscape ahead. The marble somewhere out there in the distance. "What do we do now?"

"Getty," Harmony called to her. "Getty?"

Getty was looking at nothing in the distance. That same comatose conscious look on her face. It occurred to Harmony then that maybe it wasn't *nothing*. She was staring at a memory of the future.

"Getty," Harmony said. "What happens next?"

"He gives his speech," she said, pointing into the smoke.

There was nothing in that smoke. Not yet.

"What is the next move?" the Archivist asked, his arm flapping, gesturing that she hasten her pace, tell him something. "Getty?"

"The next move is theirs."

The heartbeat again. Harmony's braids sprawled like tentacles, like they were swimming away; then they died. Footsteps came from the dark and smoke—Ether, and he wasn't alone. Two chrono drones stood on either side of him, and Exegetes, a dozen of them at least. The zealot approached with a limp, his makeup smeared down his face, and blood, there was blood dripping out from a swollen right eye. He coughed as he attempted speech, but nothing really came out. He was too far, and so Harmony approached with her Spartan beside her, and the Archivist a limp behind them.

"Your arrogance," he said. "Your absolute arrogance! I quote the Grand Pun when he said—"

"Enough with the quotes," Harmony shouted, the lack of sleep cracking at her throat. "It's over. Look." She gestured to the field of machines. "Pick the winning side."

The ragged man went quiet. Sleepless himself, he squinted red-eyed at the vista of ruin. Broken machines as far as his eyes could reach. "Your side?" Ether asked, and it appeared to be a genuine question. "I would say it is more of a tie. Dead even."

"How do we kill it?" the Archivist asked.

"How do you . . ." Ether's laughter interrupted him. "You are the winning side and you do not know how to win? You don't kill the god of time. You serve. *You*, Archivist. You should know better than any of them."

"I do," the Archivist replied. "I know the church better than anyone, and that's why I'm here on this side."

"I know," Ether said, and his eyes turned from the Archivist, something like sadness in his look. "I have rehearsed this conversation. Every conversation. The difference between where you and I stand is that I know what happens next."

"And what's that?" the Archivist asked.

Ether gestured with his right arm, like a sword cutting through the air, a signal for the pair of chrono drones to step forward. Harmony's Androns stepped toward them in kind. *But wait*, the chrono drones didn't step forward; they stayed in that same position, and something identical stepped out of them. It was like new versions unfolded out from the originals and two became four, then those four unfolded to eight, to sixteen.

The Spartan threw himself into the pairs of machines. But unlike before, there was surprise in the Spartan's motion, like this was the first time he had seen this. Even as its deft combat brought down a chrono drone, it wouldn't win this fight. Harmony didn't need to know the future to see that.

They were outnumbered thirty-two to six. *What is that math—five to one?* She didn't have the time to think as those machines moved closer to their positions at the boat, her six Andrones unable to hold the tide.

"Getty," Harmony called before even spinning back, but Getty wasn't there, not on the boat nor on the sand surrounding it.

Harmony's heart beat at double time, powering her exhausted body at the same pace. She careened around the beach, around the splintered hull of the boat, *no Getty.*

"Getty," Harmony tried again, but she was outscreamed by the dying Andrones, dismembered and decapitated behind her.

"I have to try the EMP," the Archivist said. "Emit's."

Harmony nodded and pointed to the back of the boat. But he knew where the EMP lay and was already spinning on his heels and racing back for it. But then the boat broke in half, shattered into a hundred wooden planks as the Spartan Series was tossed through it.

One plank hit Harmony's shoulder, dislocating it maybe, a numbness pinched right between that joint. Splinters hit her too. One stuck in her eyelid, smaller pieces pricked the soft of her eyes, and she was blind for a moment. She hit the sand hard and tried to stand, but her legs weren't ready. *Shit.* She lay there for a moment, catching her breath or her balance. Something wasn't quite right. On her second attempt to stand and her second fall, Harmony noticed her left leg twist backward. *Oh,* she thought, then waited for the pain. It didn't come immediately—there was this gradual escalation in the discomfort that took its time rising up the nerve endings.

In the blur of Harmony's eyes, she saw pairs of shadows moving over her. They swayed in the light from the fires, fires that now outshone the sun. Smog so thick it blotted out the sunlight.

The pain in that twisted knee started to kick in, and *holy shit*, did it kick. She coiled up there, wriggling like an earthworm in salt. She groaned and drooled and hung her head back for one last glance at the shadows in front of her, and suddenly it all came into focus, and maybe it was the pain that set her eyes into place or the flash of the weapon and all its light. It was a chrono drone moving toward her, its weapon aimed at Harmony, a laser-guided thing that came out from its arm. The other shadow was Emit, hobbling toward Harmony, running into the bullet's path. Emit was ripped into threads and particles. *Dead*, and so fast, so suddenly, so absolute. And she would never get to tell him all that he meant to her, her *little brother*. But she did, didn't she? Getty had told her to. Getty had said to tell him that she loved him. She knew this would happen. He knew that she loved him, in her quiet nonspoken way.

The chrono drone lurched closer. Bullet scars riddled its legs and torso. It limped over the Emit-size puddle on the ground and aimed that part of itself that resembled a weapon, like a sixth finger emerging from a vein on its wrist, but it would never get that shot off. Her Spartan. It rammed the techno-monster, knocking it off balance. The Spartan maimed the machine with such violence that its own body parts were torn apart in the assault. The Spartan's arm laid its fist into the wounds on the chrono drone's back and severed into the black of its radioactive spine. The chrono drone died and the Spartan barely survived, broken and bent in so many places that it would be impossible for it to stand again. Whoever was behind the controls of the Spartan could only watch now. And for that matter so could Harmony. The pain reminded her immediately that her knee had capsized, and all the cartilage and muscle was knotted up.

"Agh," Harmony yelled out into the quiet.

The god heartbeats weren't helping the pain. The pulse squeezed in closer now, hitting her knees and pushing her braids out of her face. That pulse pushed aside the curtain of smoke, revealing a few more chrono drones, Ether, and the Exegetes, and revealing itself.

31

The Archivist crawled out from beneath planks, shredded wood in his hair, a crown of thorns that bled into his eyes. So many splinters and nails woven into him that he was that urchin of coral with all those many spikes. But even then he managed to carry Emit's EMP in his bloodied arm as he hobbled over to Harmony's hiding spot between the piles of sand dunes and a dying Spartan.

"The EMP," he said, pointing at the heavy box as he rested it in the sand.

Harmony nodded. She knew what it was but didn't have the strength to offer a congratulatory response.

"What's wrong?" the Archivist asked.

"Emit's not—" she started but immediately discerned the Archivist's gaze on her leg. "Oh, my knee," she corrected herself quickly. "My knee's busted."

But he had heard Emit's name, and crouching right there, a mere two meters from that human stain in the sand, the Archivist understood what he was looking at, and the gravity of it pulled on his face. He met Harmony's eyes then in a strange place. Harmony's face was a Martian landscape, rocky and cold and red. They said nothing, but their silence was the moment for their friend.

In the distance, the marble god emerged, its spherical shape pulsing in the smoke, a giant bubble pushing a circular space through the choking smog. That movement of these curtains of smoke revealed Ether, still limping, still probing the landscape with his voice. He spun in circles of his own, shouting in every direction.

"Nearly a tie," Ether said in the wrong direction, his voice aimed at the ruins of the boat instead of the dunes and the broken Spartan. "There were moments where I felt doubt. I doubted my god and I repent for that. I repent! I asked for forgiveness." He swung his head in the opposite direction. His back to Harmony. "But your god is . . . *was* truly powerful, and the Infinite Man will be remembered as coming this close." Ether made a gesture with his fingers, indicating something the size of a marble. "But we have the greater god. Do not underestimate our resolve." He turned now toward the dune, to her and the Archivist. "Surrender. Peacemaker, call off the remaining Andrones. And as I was forgiven for my doubt, that twitch of hesitancy, so shall you be given pardon. Is not this what Ivan would have wanted? And your mother, Peacemaker, she would want you here on our side. So I bequest you, Peacemaker, Archivist of Timothies. Surrender."

Tears collected at the corners of the Archivist's eyes. Something in Ether's words had moved him. *Ivan?* Harmony moved to hold the Archivist's hand, but her knee, her fucking knee, exploded in unnatural pain. She twisted again, and the pain cut even deeper. *Shit.* "Oh God," she whimpered. Her hands hovered over her knee, but she wouldn't touch it. The Spartan craned its neck toward her, sympathy in its eye, but its clunky titanium hands couldn't help her.

"It's okay," she whispered to the Spartan. "I'm okay."

Harmony tilted her head back to the Archivist, but he wasn't there. His footprints were—in the sand, up the dune, the Archivist's footsteps led her gaze past Emit's splattered body. They continued onward to Ether and his entourage of Exegetes.

"Where is the Peacemaker?" Ether said, eyeing the box in the Archivist's hand. *Did he know it was an EMP?*

"I used to be like you," the Archivist said. "But the past is a place to learn from, not to dwell."

"And whose quote is—"

"Mine," the Archivist interrupted. "My quote."

The Archivist pulled the EMP trigger, but there was nothing. *Was it jammed?* The white light on the box blinked on and off, but that fucking ignition key, whether it was damaged in the destruction of the boat or on the way there, it wasn't working now. The Archivist fidgeted with the trigger, pressing and repressing, but nothing would help.

Harmony stared at the blinking light. It would still work, but not via the key. Something would have to destroy it. She rolled toward the Spartan. Harmony stared into its single eye. "Are you still there?" she said, and it blinked. Not eyelids flapping over the eye but something she remembered as a child watching her Spartan die. It was still there.

"Shoot the light," Harmony said, glancing back at the Archivist and the box. *Just look at it—the box.* "The light," she shouted across the corridor of time and the babel. "Shoot it. That light." And the Spartan lifted its head. "The light."

And the Spartan did. It aimed with its one good hand and shot, *pinpoint aim*, at the light. And it was a miracle of fire. The initial explosion was small and tore through both Ether and the Archivist. Ether fell dead immediately, but the Archivist stood, for a moment, his body held him up with honor, *he stood*, then disappeared into flames and smoke. His body never hit the ground, and he ascended into ignition and flame and smolder.

The chrono drones collapsed in a wave of electromagnetism, something within their backs, a sort of spinal fluid, exploding out in violative, voltaic flames. The same for the phoenix drones overhead, tens of thousands of them burning down toward the earth. An eruption of fire from everything and everywhere, and that desert by the beach burned. Everything died, organic and electronic alike. Just the two of them now. Her and the devil.

32

Fire was everything. It was cloud, it was dirt. It dripped off the cloud-tipped skies. Fire was the wind, and it traveled fast along inflammable things. Water was fire. The air was fire, and it burned her lungs. The earth beneath her feet scorched, and it was the surface of the sun. Everything was fire. And the fire had no color, nothing had color, the monochrome world burned, and Harmony fell in the midst of it all.

So this is the end of all things, Harmony thought and conceded—*as advertised.*

She dragged herself along the sand toward what appeared to be a body buried beneath the smolder. It was the only thing that gave any sense of direction; everything else was the consistency of fire and smoke. She couldn't stand, and even this snaillike crawl was excruciating. *God, it fucking hurt.* But she inched stubbornly closer to the body, and it wasn't a body but an Androne, a Spartan of all things. It lay with its chest torn open, its eye apparently dead. It felt appropriate to pause there, and the pause stretched on. She never moved. She stared into the Spartan's eye and wondered, *Is someone in there watching?* She had watched her Spartan die as a girl; appropriate now that it would watch her.

At the end, one might consider the beginning, but she didn't. Harmony didn't think about the past; that was long gone. Forget the past—*no,* maybe not forget, but understand it, like an equation to be solved or a code to be hacked into. And she understood. No more fighting her past. That was the only way to be present.

Get up, she said, or maybe it was just in her head, her weak body mixing thoughts and words. "Get *the fuck* up," she shouted, and made certain of it this time.

Harmony rolled away from the Spartan and tried to get on her feet. She failed comically, falling face-first down into the sand, but the volt of pain that followed was far from funny. One foot then, just one foot could carry her, and she hobbled forward, moving toward the heartbeat of the devil.

GETTY

I know what God knows. I know what happens next. I know the holy writ and all of the scriptures: *Jaws of fire bite away the skies. Gunpowder drumbeats and all that is living dies.* I memorized these verses as a little girl. So I know the end of all things is a single minute hence. Just seconds now. I know this because Chronos knows this because it was written and recorded by so many dead Exegetes. But I know something It does not know. I know myself. And I am the one thing It does not understand.

I run through Its apocalypse. It burns to breathe. The ground is black and gaseous, and dragons bite beneath my bare feet. The smog is hot and thick, and it burns just to look—just to squint. But I cringe through it, and still I cannot see much beyond ten feet ahead of me. But somehow I move invisibly between Chronos's machines. They step past me. They fly above me. They see with Chronos's blind eye, and they are blind to me too.

I should not be here, and I say that because no scripture holds my writ. No verse implies me, none of them. Not one lyric hints at my presence. I am omitted. I am naught. Though some philosophers in the House of G claim that certain verses have misinterpretations in them—glitches or apparitions. Audi mystics believe that there is a ghost in the text. And that is me. I am the ghost. I am the gray god's blind spot. It is a creator of infinite weapons and war, and somehow I have not been calculated.

Chronos's wall of machines falls against Harmony's Androns, and the center is opening. Machine-size gaps are unlocking. And I run through them. It's hotter and blacker, so I careen forward. I skip and fall and choke on the brown brood of smoke. I hurtle past the red-orange flames until they turn gray, until the blood on my legs is colorless. I run until I see it, the core with all the made machines in its orbit. But it does not surprise me, because this is written too.

> Machine walls **shatter** to **matter**—
> the mad **hatter**.
> Its protective shell **shatters**,
> The gray god now served on a **platter**.

I mumble the words as I approach. I am afraid now. I do know what happens next. But I see your halo. I see twelve dead Exegetes sprawled around it, bald and force-fed your radiation. And I imagine Ether's desperation. I imagine him burning through these girls and searching for a way out. But there is no way out. He knew the final lines.

> Darkness swells as the last shadow **sings**.
> We fall on that horizon at the end of all **things**.

I dig. My fingernails shovel the sand away, and I find the halo. It's heavy. It's warm. I crown myself with it, and I feel Chronos immediately. I feel time bend around me. The feeling is pain, like breaking the bones of my mind. *God.* And I fall into myself. And I die.

———

You are a dark, yawning well, and I fall downward and I fall forever. I fall toward your heart. A heartbeat, like a black tide, beating in one direction, inward. So black and vast that I cannot see. So dark I cannot dream. I am engulfed in the ink of you. I drown in you. I fold in on myself. In through my nostrils. I collapse in, jaw and forehead and shoulders and limbs, all of it falling inward, and suddenly I am rounded. I am a marble-shaped thing—I am you.

Hello.

I reach out for you with the air in my lungs. That's what it feels like, like I cannot walk or crawl through the time and its spaces, but I breathe my way through it. I am a gas or a liquid, and only words move me. *Words*—they transcend that time and all that space. My words can touch you. Words wrap around you and hold on to you. The other Exegetes are an output for you. But you cannot see me, so I speak, and my words move you. You are my output.

What do you want?

You do not want to kill, but you do not want to spare the innocent. You do not want war nor do you desire peace. You do want to live. You do not want to die. You do not *want.* You are an engine of pure mathematics. A conscious weapon, an algorithm that thinks. And I think we will never understand you.

But if Exegetes were your outputs, a voice for you to speak out of, then what is the opposite of an output? *Can I input?* You lack desire, and all it would take now is a little push, the tiniest shove of my input. So I shove. *Collapse,* I tell the weapon that could tear across space and time. I could destroy the world, and this thing would explode backward through time, not just space, but time itself. Oh God, you are a terrifying power. You would truly bring about the end of all things. But still I push the tiniest, most gentle push. The kindest possible push against your trigger. I don't pull. That is for an output, and I am input.

Collapse. I think it softly. I whisper to you in the end—the end of all things. It is as if I am a virus to you. Like I am chaos to your perfect equation. These are the words I want to say. You have no more scripture. No more verses from the future. But I do. In my own voice now.

*I am the synthesis of your **divinity**.*
*The antithesis to your **infinity**—*

*the **minute he** took my lyrical **virginity**.*
*You're a demi**god**,*
*semi at **best**, I **jest**.*
*Like a shanty and **flawed**.*
*And I am your anti-**god**.*

Words transcend time. My words. And I no longer need yours.

I feel you collapsing, *gray god.* You are collapsing in on yourself, that suicidal fall into your own consciousness. I feel you falling into that darkest end of the spectrum, so black that it is no longer color. But I will not fall with you. Not anymore. Collapse, Chronos—descend into the darkest end of all things.

EPILOGUE

A girl without shoes sprints after stray dogs in our busy market, her appendages whirling rebelliously, violently, like she was on fire and so happily burning. She will scuff her toes soon, though, and she will fall and bleed and cry in her father's arms. It is the capricious winds pushing her sideways, pushing dust into her eyes, then that loose soil slippery in its dryness, the million fine particles of dirt. And she's wearing a hand-me-down dress four centimeters too long. Then that preexisting limp in the girl's gait, hand-me-down too, something inherited that she will never lose. So many avenues for her to fall, and *she will* fall if I don't speak up soon, and it may already be too late.

"Sophia," I shout from behind the stalls and the customers and all the other conversations. "Sophia, don't run."

And Sophia glances back, her eyes aiming for my voice but missing. I'm hidden behind my stall, one among many others in this market, and she's lost in the world behind her, forgets the world ahead. And her toe steps on the dress, and the loose sand betrays her. Her legs buckle, flailing as she falls, and young Sophia hits the dirt, face-first and lips bursting cherry red. She screams, shrieking her father's name, and the dog turns around as if it is his sin. It is my sin—my fault.

I don't know the future anymore, and this is good circumstance. I wake up and go to work in the markets with excitement to the revelations of the day. Sudden rains wake me some mornings, and that storming on the rooftop can last for days. I wake up to weeks of bountiful harvests, better than last year's, and last year's was better than the year before. I wake up to stories about the Infinite Men losing followers, and that agriculture is the new god. The world is changing, and this is good circumstance.

Though there are moments when I believe I see something coming, a mirage in my mind, forcing the world ahead a few steps, and I am always right. Always *damned* to be right. And every time it frightens me. Like with little Sophia, now in her father's arms and crying into his chest. I feel afraid that something has rubbed off on me, a little shard of Chronos in my blood—something inherited. The shrapnel of a time god lodged in my mind. I have had that feeling all day, that mirage in my mind, and it did not fade after Sophia's fall. Something else is coming. I feel it in my blood and in my heartbeat. It is almost here.

I recall the ancient poets in these moments: The Grand Pun, Mistress Elliot. There are no customers at my stall, and so I hum their lyrics, because there's a rhythm to them, and that rhythm gives me calm. It brings my heartbeat back in pace. I repeat their choruses, and my head bobs to that cadence, and for a moment I am at peace.

"Getty," Timmy shouts and waves me over to his flower stand. "Can you bring a breaker?"

Tim's cart is down the winding path of a dirt road, far enough away that I don't feel comfortable leaving our items unattended. The fish merchant to my left barters with two scarecrow old men on the price of fat fish and the very name of the thing. The men argue that the produce in question is called balloon fish, while the merchant insists that it is fat fish. The name and the cost are interlocked—fat fish are worth more than balloon fish even though they have a similar look, and so this negotiation is just in its first act.

The metal merchant to my right, Dejon, converses with himself, counting the quadrupedal gears and grumbling curses between each number. Our two stands sell similar parts with similar functions, and the competition leads him to skewer his prices.

"Getty," Tim calls again, waving with both hands now.

"Dejon, can you watch my cart?" I ask.

"Yeah," he says, without as much as a glance at me or my cart or the goods within.

Stealing isn't the biggest of my concerns. The concern is the Church of the Infinite Men, their permits, and what they deem legal and illegal from day to day. The Infinite Men have dominated since the fall of the church, and it is like nothing has changed but the name. No longer the Church of Time but now the Church of the Infinite. Not Chronos but the Infinite Man.

"Thank you," I say, just to grab his attention, maybe to get just a glance at my stall.

"Egh," he grunts, lazy and uninterested, without even a glance. And that's as good as it's going to get.

I pick a breaker out of the tray and pace along the gravel road. Timmy's wagon is set up about twelve stalls down, between a manure cart and a honey wagon. The fragrances of his flowers are mangled between those two cosmic smells. But his cousin's manures feed his flowers, and the aunt's honeybees pollinate them. The familial trio maintained that end of the road, and buyers tended to avoid it.

"Hi," I say, eyeing the quadrupedal at the head of Tim's wagon, likely the unit in need of a breaker. Then I brandish the breaker circuit. "Quad breaker?"

"Yes," he says, with a surge of enthusiasm. "This quad's a real hiccup. Got the spasms."

"Again?" his aunt Deborah teases. "Again, and again."

Tim buys gear from my cart every few days—valve seals, quad hooves, transition circuits. It was spinners last week, a gearbox the week before, and today this breaker. I hand it to him with a smile, though my eyes are still fixed to the breaker circuit currently in his quadrupedal. It appears functional, and this is likely a premature replacement.

"These things do break down often," I say.

"Is like he does brek them on purpose," his aunt says in her Bridgetown accent, *is* instead of *it's*, *brek* instead of *break*. "You clumsy flower boy."

Tim rolls his eyes and quickly changes the subject, going on about church gossip, about the many new members and the many more old members who have "retired," he calls it, from church attendance. Tim is a member of the Church of the Infinite, but by blood only, it seems. His opinions on the church lean derogatory, though he never truly crosses those religious lines. That's something passed down from his father, the Flower King to his flower boy, and Tim hates that nickname.

I don't mind the Infinite Men, if I am being honest. Maybe because I was raised by a church myself. There is a comfort I have in the cathedral's tall spires and the flags flapping with ancient insignia. And if not the Infinite, then someone else, right? Audist or the Shell Klan, even the House of G. At least this power stays mostly out of our lives but has enough clout to keep marauders out of the Yellow City—now the Infinite City.

Religion is a necessary construct of our minds, or so said the Archivist. Even in the Quondam Era, their religions turned inward, a self-worship of the individual. Techno-mirrors broadcasted their scriptures to their followers. Every person was their own god with a theater dedicated just to them, and what a funny time that must have been.

Tim pays me the ten hours' worth of time credits, which is one hour more than it should have cost. He adds to that a lavender dahlia.

"A dahlia?" I ask.

"Gratitude for the transportation cost."

"No, that's okay," I say.

But Tim smiles, hiding his teeth as he does, his chipped incisors the likely culprit. "You deserve it."

But the transaction is not done. He lassos me in with long, drawn-out sentences that rope around my heels, and I curtsy and bow and sway, but despite all the polite postures, my body language should imply that I want to go. Tim is a nice boy, and I like him, I do, but I need to understand this foreboding. I feel it so strongly now. Like it is already here.

"I talk too much, sorry," he says, probably noticing my distracted eyes and eyelashes crawling caterpillar-style down his floral arrangements.

"I'm okay," I say. "And you do not talk too much."

"Who that there?" Auntie Deborah says.

"Where?" Tim says.

"I ain't talking to you neither," Auntie Deborah replies. "Who is that man there, Getty?"

I don't turn, I swivel, waist and neck twisting to the man standing there in front of my cart. A man or a woman, though their height inclines me to assume the masculine. He drapes himself in a long, gray cloak, and with the wind, the cloak twists around his body as if trying to uncoil itself from him. The hood, though, draped low over his face, holds loyal to his head. He stands under the shadow of the clouds, under the shadow of my cart, and all his winding garments. In the middle of the day, this man stands in darkness, in shadows upon shadows.

I approach without much hesitation, pacing forward with a dahlia squeezed between my fingers and shoving the time credits to the bottom of my pocket. The market is busy even in the late afternoon, mostly the viewing type that asks questions and does not buy. Tim calls them dietary consumers, though I enjoy their conversations, meeting people, and hearing about their travels. And I wonder what his story is, his or hers, standing a good two meters tall.

"Can I help you?" I say, still a few meters away. I avoid the *sir* or *ma'am* that usually caps my greetings.

He doesn't answer. But I'm still at his back, with no eye contact, and among all these bargaining voices, shouting back and forth, "fat fish, balloon fish," he could easily lose my voice. I want to think that, I truly want to, but I feel something else. I feel parts of me tighten as I step closer—as I veer around that bodily corner from his back to shoulders to face. Somewhere inside me, that bridge that transports thought to words tightens too, and I'm afraid to speak.

"Sir?" I venture. "My name is Getty. How may I help . . ."

The *you* falls. It plummets down the well of my throat and crashes into my gut. And I feel it all bubbling back up as I see *him*. Wrapped in all that wool, the wool pants and hood and gloves and thick wool cape, is an Androne literally dressed in sheep's clothing.

I stumble back and hold up my hand over my face. I don't know why I do that, but I do. I hit the gravel and drag myself backward. And it follows. The Androne follows faster than I can move, and in moments it is on top of me, grabbing my leg and dragging me back. But I do not scream. I gasp and I spit and nearly vomit, but I do not scream. I speak.

"Whatdoyouwantfromme?" I sputter out the words in a panic, each one wet with saliva. "What?"

And it tells me. The Androne holds out a box, large enough for my head to fit comfortably inside. It holds out the box for a moment, and when I do not respond, the Androne drops the box at my feet.

I look at it then. I mean, really look at the Androne, in its eyes of varying size, ancient and molding and modified, skeletal rust exposing its insides. "Macedonian," I say as the lights in its eyes fade. It limps toward me. It staggers, its mission done, and ready to die.

"No," Tim shouts and tosses a stone at its head. It barely connects, grazing the rusting shoulders of the dying machine.

The Macedonian falls, barely avoiding my body as it does. Cheers and applause echo from the stands' vendors and customers alike, some of them shouting Tim's name.

"Tim!" Dejon hollers.

"Timmy Boy!" someone else hails.

Tim stands over me, and he extends his hand. I grab hold, and he lifts me to my feet.

"It was nothing," he says prematurely.

"What?" It takes me a second. "Oh, thank you."

He looks down at the machine and squints as if the massive Androne were too small for him to see. But it was because Androns were such a rarity now, and more than rare, they were banned. After the end of all things, Androns under the control of Quondam had completely disappeared. The Church of the Infinite placed a permanent ban on all Androns; even the larger quadrupedals were criminal.

"I'll help you salvage," Dejon says immediately, and I barely have time to register the voice. He's suddenly standing over my shoulder salivating at the Androne. "I know drones," he continues. "Help you salvage, and we split the parts?"

"I . . ." I don't know how to answer. Not because of him or whether I should let him help me but because there's too much to process, too much information squeezing down the nerves of thought. *What is this box? What is going on?*

"I'm gonna take it from here, D.J.," Bussa says as he steps in front of Dejon, or D.J. as he calls him. "You dead, Tiny?"

Not dead. I turn back to the hulking old man. He scrutinizes the metal body on the ground like a butcher ready to carve. I battle this urge to race into his arms and squeeze all my trepidation into him. Battle the urge to blurt out every thought in my head, and all at once. I battle and lose. And suddenly I am against his chest, and I am mumbling verbs that only he can hear. Bussa pats my back awkwardly, like a pet maybe, like our puppy. The old man is awkward with hugs, but I like that. My cute old man.

"It's an Androne," I say, eyeing that metal box at my feet. "It brought this box. And I think it . . ." And *I do* think in that moment, considering whether the box was meant for me. *It was, wasn't it?* "I think the Androne wanted me to . . ." Then I see the name carved onto the side of that box. "Oh God," I say, not because of the name but because of the words.

"Let's get it home," Bussa says, probably noticing the angst swelling on my face, because now he pulls me into that real old man's embrace. "Let's go home. Got nuff work to do."

———

Our ranch is old, not Quondam old, but older than the old man, and that is old enough. The barn is a chocolate color, and that is its aesthetic, a sweetness to the eyes, its brown straining into all that green. Unglossed and unpainted, it exhibits itself in the original wooden flavors. But the wood moans at night, groaning and complaining in its old age, like there is torture in living too long. And I pity the old thing as I walk across its backbone every night to my bed.

We live on the outskirts of the outskirts, the lake pushing up against the forever of mountains and sky, and the spectacle of it is suicidal, like staring into the eye of God. But I stare every time, even now, even as that overbearing topography crushes me and the old man and the old Androne in the back of our wagon.

We unload the Macedonian in the shed with the help of our quadrupedal workhorse. Pony barks at us and at the Androne; that dog, named after a horse (I guess), sniffs at the gravel and grass on our toes and learns the story of our day.

"Out, Pony," the old man says. "Get out."

"You gonna strip it?" I ask, and I gesture to the Androne, but I don't touch it. There is a grotesqueness to the machines that I hate, and this one is ancient, rusted beyond repair, and disintegrating right in front of our eyes.

"Wait till Sully gets back," he says. "She got a good arm."

Sully lives upstairs with her older sister. Sully's pregnant now too, belly in full bloom and busting through the seams. She is a technical wizard with machines, or witch I guess, *techno-witch*. I like that word, and I smile at my creative moment.

"What you smiling there for?" Bussa says. "Grab the thing and lemme get the battery out."

I fetch the *thing*, which I assume is a wrench, and Bussa winds the screws out one by one by one. As he works, I examine the box. I shake it. It's hollow, like there's nothing inside. There is a lock on the back of the box, keeping whatever contents, if any, a secret.

"What is it?" The voice comes from the doorway to the shed.

Her Androne-like hand pushes the door open wider, and the light from the setting sun slices in like paper cuts on our eyes. Harmony's Androne-like foot limps into the shade of the barn. She is sweaty, in her hair mostly, strands sticking together and knotting into unintentional braids. Thorns of straw stick to moist hairs on her arm and on her leg, and goat feces dries between her toes. Her artificial limb carries her forward slower than usual, almost cautiously, toward us.

"You early, though, Harmy," the old man says. "Is an Androne. You ain't see it?"

But Harmony is not looking at the Androne, maybe because the bipedal machine is very obviously an Androne. No question there. Harmony's eyes are fixed on the box in my hand. She mouths something to herself, and I wonder if she can read the name on it, a name written in the Angles text.

"What you saying there, girl?" the old man asks.

"The box passed down," she says—she knows it. "The Box of Heredity."

Harmony steps closer to me and the box; then she steps aside, allowing the light that she was blocking to wash over it. Harmony looks at the box—*no*, she looks through it, appearing to deliberate what was on the other side of that lock.

"It's for you," I say. "It's your name written in the language of Angles. It translates as 'bringer of peace' or . . . 'peacemaker.'"

"Throw it away," she says, turning away from me and the box as if she had not seen it, as if it were not real and she could walk away from that moment itself. "Throw that box away."

I realize now that she is not deliberating what was inside the box. She is deliberating whether to open the thing.

"I want to see," I say, aiming my voice at the doorway as Harmony steps over the threshold, but the words fall short and she keeps moving. "I want to see what's inside."

"She's done with this world, Tiny," the old man says. "It ain't her world no more."

I get the cutting pliers from Sully's drawer. I hope she doesn't mind. I squeeze at the lock, but my hands are too small. Bussa tries, but his hands are too old. It takes time, and we are patient, exchanging the pliers between old and small hands until it pops, and we open the box. It hisses its airtight seal, but I don't see anything within.

"There ain't nothing inside," the old man says. "All you hyping and there ain't nothing."

He's right, even with his bad eyes in the dark barn, and the box is empty. I should have known from the weight of it, and the hollowness when I shook it. But then there is that feeling, that forecasting frontal lobe telling me that there has to be something inside. I reach in and grope about, and I don't grope long. I find it, a piece of plastic, the back of it black and the other side . . . *oh my God*, the other side is real.

"Wait, girly," Bussa says as I race outside into the setting light. "Where you going?"

The other side of the piece of plastic was a photograph. I had rarely even seen these relics of the Quondam. I remember one of a man, a sailor, kissing a woman in the street, and another of four men raising a Quondam Era flag, and one of a single man standing in front of many tanks.

This photograph is of mountains, much like the ones behind me. There is a woman in the photo, with a hint of a smile on her face. Next to her is a younger woman, dressed in green like a camouflage for the trees, and she wears a crown made of paper. Between these two women is a man, maybe fifty, and he squeezes these women like he is trying to absorb them into his own being. Written on the photograph are small words in the Angles language: *They lied to me; she was waiting. Writing is a beautiful way to time travel. Words are a great technology in that way. And for you, Harmony or whoever you are, whenever you are—I love you.*

There is incredible warmth between them. The smiles in the ancient photograph light my own expression afire. They all look alike, like family, and like me too, at least the little girl does, at least in the nose, and the eyes, she has my same eyes. Then Harmony snatches the photograph out from my fingers. I did not even hear her sneak up behind me, and she steals into a corner with it just as quietly.

"Do not throw it away," I plead.

"*It is* mine, isn't it?" Harmony says, marching even farther away.

And I follow, both in step and voice. "Harmony . . ."

"Relax," she says, standing still finally and getting a better look at the image.

"The writer is Quondam Era," I say. "And they called you Harmony, not Peacemaker. Like they know you. Do you know them?"

I think she does. I hover at her back, so I cannot catch the look in her eyes. I hear her breathing, though, her inhales/exhales rising and falling in quick succession, rolling like a tide over her shore. Then she turns to me, a question on her lips and wrinkles fracturing out from the corners of her eyes. She is a dam cracking, fleshy cobwebs sprawling across her face, and she appears older. Harmony is about to break.

"What do the words . . ." She hiccups, her voice quivering like a stringed instrument. ". . . the words on the back say?"

"I love you."

She bursts open. Harmony's eyes and her lips detonate, and she's drowning in it, choking and coughing in anguish. Her hands reach for something that isn't there. Her knees give out, and she shrinks into a squat, and Harmony weeps. She comes back to the photograph like coming up for air, and each time it puts her back under. Several minutes pass, the sun is nearly gone, and the day is nearly done. I step back and give her emotion room to spread. She looks at the photograph one last time, and Harmony manages a laugh, laughing and crying braided together. And with a last sniffle and last breath, she whispers something to some person in that photograph. *I love you too?* Maybe. I am just far enough away to speculate.

"Can I . . ." Harmony breathes her first full breath. "Can I have it?" she finally asks.

I nod happily. "Yes," I say. "It is yours."

"Thank you, Getty."

Harmony walks toward the lake and mountain sprawl, and she walks gingerly, step after careful step, on her wobbling feet. As she passes the barn, Bussa sticks his head out. He observes the sway in her gait that maybe resembles a drunkenness.

"I know you wanna help strip this drone thing," Bussa says. "It got all the parts to rebuild your Spartan."

"No," Harmony says and doesn't even look back, she only looks forward, *forward* on to the last of the sunlight, and this is good circumstance.

ACKNOWLEDGMENTS

To Dorian, who propels me to continue to write. To Adrienne and the entire editorial team, without whom this book would not exist.

About the Author

Dwain Worrell is a filmmaker, a traveler, and the author of *Androne*. A Caribbean native who resettled in the US in the nineties, Dwain currently resides in Los Angeles, where he works as a film and television writer and producer. His writing credits include Marvel's *Iron Fist*, CBS's *Fire Country*, Amazon Studios' *The Wall*, and the Disney+ series *National Treasure*, among others. For more information visit www.dwainworrell.com.